GW00865351

AND GOD CREATED BEDBUGS TOO

Hermann Kauders

ISBN 978-1-326-18654-8
Published by Lulu.com. UK bookshops £9.99. Amazon.co.uk.
Cover images: Front cover: Wiener Riesenrad (Ferris Wheel). Back cover: The author.

i

AUTHOR'S NOTE

It has taken me the best part of a generation to see this to completion. How things have changed since I started writing this! I'd like to acknowledge my thanks to my family and friends who have supported me, also to express my appreciation to the Rayleigh Writing Group and others, especially Clive, who have assisted with the editing and have helped me along this long road and got me over the finishing line.

FOREWORD

The countryside of Austria and the city of Vienna were places of contrast between the Two World Wars. The rural districts were mostly peopled by peasants: conservative, Roman Catholic and traditional in outlook. Vienna was more developed, a melting pot of people and cultures from across Eastern Europe and the Middle East. The City had become one of the largest settlements in the Jewish Diaspora.

In Vienna the Social Democrats were in overall control and strove to make the City an example of socialist politics. In the mid nineteen twenties the *Gemeindebau* (Municipal Housing Block) project was developed, consisting of the construction of monolithic blocks, often housing more than 60,000 people. Most of the buildings, which are still standing today, incorporated large courtyards. Construction costs were raised from so called "*Breitner Taxes*" – a tax on luxuries. The rents were subsidized, making them affordable to workers.

From 1925 to 1939 Vienna was a city at the forefront of development and innovation in music, science, philosophy and the arts. Arnold Schoenberg was writing compositions using the twelve-tone system and establishing the Second Viennese School with students Alban Berg and Anton Webern. Sigmund Freud was developing his controversial theories and ideas in psychology. Although not a member, Oscar Kokoschka was probably the most influential artist on the German Expressionism movement.

Contrasting this, the Viennese people tended to take refuge in easy-going sentimentality between the two World Wars, often typified by the Blue Danube Waltz, café houses, kitsch and cream cakes. Austria, like the rest of Europe, was unable to foresee what was to come.

The Social Democrat Party and the Conservative Christian Social Party incorporated paramilitary units: the Social Democrat *Schutzbund,* and the Christian Social *Heimwehr.* Skirmishes between the two opposing factions and the dissolution of parliament by Chancellor Dollfuss lead to Civil War in March 1934. Members of the *Schutzbund* barricaded themselves into the Municipal Housing Blocks including the showpieces Karl Marx and Engels Hof. Chancellor Dollfuss ordered shelling of the buildings. Nazis exploited the conflict. They assassinated Dollfuss in the summer of 1934.

Many Social Democrats turned to Hitler and joined the banned Nazi Party. They were known as *Illegaler.* Into this world came Alexander Anzendrech, little Xandi, son of Brigitte and her tram conductor husband Rudolf.

The novel, drawing on the author's own experiences, explores the innocence of childhood set against the sophistication and intrigues of the adult world; people whose lives were affected and changed by the tumultuous events occurring in Vienna and Europe at the time.

Robert Kauders

Vienna 1925

Zwischenbrücken

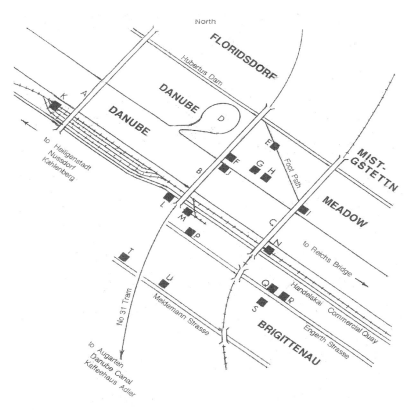

North

FLORIDSDORF

Hubertus Dam

DANUBE

DANUBE

to Heiligenstadt
Nussdorf
Kahlenberg

K A

D

MIST-
GSTETTN

Foot Path

E

F G H

B

J

MEADOW

I

C

L

M

to Reichs Bridge

N

P

T

Handelskai Commercial Quay

U

No 31 Tram

Meldemann Strasse

Q

S

R

Engerth Strasse

BRIGITTENAU

to Augarten
Danube Canal
Kaffeehaus Adler

PRATER

V

A	Northwest Railway Bridge	L	Children's Lido
B	Floridsdorf Bridge	M	Boiler Tube Cemetery
C	North Railway Bridge	N	Danube Coke Company
D	Zinkerbacherl	P	Police Station
E	Site of Tombola	Q	Milk Block
F	Covered Staircase	R	Cocoa Block
G	The Families' Very own Wee Place	S	Allerheiligenkirche
H	Refreshment Hut	T	Alexander's Birth Place
I	Stairway	U	Men's Hostel (Hitler's Earstwhile Abode)
J	Sewer	V	Riesenrad (Giant Wheel)
K	Marshalling Yards		

NO BALL GAMES ON THE DANUBE MEADOW

1925-1935

CHAPTER ONE (1925)

With a Twinkle in his Eye

People living in the Meldemannstrasse did not know, and wouldn't have cared much had they known, that a man called Adolf Hitler had dwelt in their street fifteen years earlier.

Now, the burning question was how to extract heat from empty stoves.

Brigitte Anzendrech, lying in labour, flung her arms over her head, her palms desperate to clutch at something. With an effort she turned her eyes on Gusti Spagola, her neighbour, as she came bouncing into the room. An impish naïvety, which Brigitte found endearing and men provocative, sprang from Gusti's freckled cheeks and large, widely spaced eyes.

"Holy Jesus, it's popping out!" she shouted.

Brigitte forced a cramped smile, but she managed to ask, "Are the children all right?"

"Sure. Stuffing themselves they are, your two and my two."

Brigitte's fingers curved around the iron bar of the bedstead. The droplets of perspiration on her knuckles glistened. The neighbour's voice hit her ears: "I'll run for the midwife."

Brigitte rolled her head from side to side. "Not yet. Not yet."

Gusti Spagola pulled at the bedclothes to straighten them out, chattering away as she did so. "I had a whole four-and-twenty hours of it with my Poldi," she said. "The Samaritan Hospital had never known such a birth. She wouldn't come proper, not my Poldi, it had to be the other way round with her, not with the cheeks on her face first."

Brigitte's attempt at another smile faltered as her lips stiffened into a narrow slit. She saw Gusti unfasten an apron to wipe her burning forehead, and heard her saying, "How you sweat, and you know I'm freezing. I thought I'd stoke the stove in the kitchen to get an extra morsel of warmth from it."

Throttled words grated through Brigitte's gritted teeth: "The price of coke."

1

"The price of coke, the price of bread, the price of everything! Except the price of sweat. That's for free. Herr Anzendrech still at work?"

Brigitte's fists relaxed. Relief. "Rudolf's been gone since the middle of the night."

"Spagola's starting on the buildings come Monday."

"The new housing blocks near the Danube?"

Gusti Spagola nodded. "The dwellings there have two rooms and a kitchen and some have a balcony thrown in, and your own water tap, and your own lavatory." She shook her head and a mop of flaxen hair unfurled and plunged over her neck and shoulders. "What I wouldn't give to have my own lavatory."

Brigitte watched a brown speck meander across the ceiling, then come to a standstill. She knew from past observations that such arrests in the progress of bedbugs frequently preceded their loss of grip.

"Like our little madam from the floor above," the neighbour went on, "that half-Gypsy fortune teller, Vikki Huber. Barely out of her nappies, she is. Did you know she carries a key to the lavatory in the basement that's private to the landlord? Her prim behind gets the preferential treatment! And I have seen her with men from the hostel!"

"I wouldn't mind if it's a girl," said Brigitte, deliberately changing the subject.

Gusti considered the point. "Boy or girl. Neither gives you a minute's peace."

Endorsing this forlorn outlook, a fearful shrieking burst upon them. Clumsy footsteps. Tearful, tubby, seven year old Poldi filled the doorway.

"I told you to stay indoors," scolded Gusti.

Poldi held in one hand a grease-bespattered news sheet upon which pink lines had been drawn, in the other the soft, broken-off corner of a flaking brick. She laboriously transferred the masonry drawing implement to the fingers hugging the paper, thereby freeing one hand to wipe the yellow mixture drooling from her nose, across her cheeks.

"You daft goose pimple, don't just stand there," Gusti berated the unhappy girl.

"Berti throwed his *Schmalzbrot* on my pi'ture." Poldi underlined the gravity of the calamity Berti's bread slice had caused, by sniffing up her mucus.

"Come here." The apron that had comforted Brigitte's brow now mopped up the child's face. "She won't say boo to a goose," Gusti explained. "She'll put up with any prank from any brat without a murmur except when it's her half-brother."

She led her distraught daughter back into her own kitchen where three little boys sat on the floor awaiting with charged curiosity the outcome of Poldi's tell-tales. The spread of rendered, grey fat on the bread slices of Brigitte's boys gleamed smoothly, but Berti's displayed ripples like miniature Danube wavelets, evidence of recent contact face-on with a foreign substance. Gusti strode up to her son and scolded him: "Naughty boy."

Berti howled and pointing at Brigitte's eldest, cried, "Rudi made me do it."

Four-year-old Rudi in turn directed his finger at the red cheeks of his younger brother Pauli. "She drew a Krampus on his face."

"It wasn't a Krampus. It was the Angel Gabriel," Poldi protested.

Now Pauli looked like bursting into tears. Gusti took him into her arms. "Poldi wouldn't draw a Krampus on your face. Would you, Poldi?"

"No, Mum."

Peace restored, Gusti put Pauli down, scurried into her bedroom and picked up a twenty-centimetre-long crucifix to neutralise any demonic forces conjured up by reference to the Krampus. They all knew the devilish creature in Vienna's December 7th tradition: while Saint Nicholas stuffs nuts into the boots of good children, his horned companion, the Krampus, beats bad children with a witch's broom.

Brigitte wished for a baby girl because they didn't make soldiers of girls. People had shouted "No more war" in 1918, but already, seven years later, some clamoured for another. She'd baptise her Alexandra after her own mother.

She hobbled to the window.

The thin morning snow cover on roofs, on chimney pots and windowsills transformed the rundown area into a Christmas postcard scene. She mused that nature reaffirmed, on this day of all days, original innocence, which must have come before original sin.

She dragged herself back to bed. Her chestnut brown eyes scanned the furniture as if seeing it for the first time: the homemade cot with knitted shawl and blanket awaiting the new arrival; the two short iron bedsteads for her sons Rudi and Pauli, another large one partly obscured behind a screen for her husband Rudolf, who had taken to sleeping by himself because of his irregular work hours and in preparation for avoiding the risk of a fourth. She winced at the narrow wardrobe, which had forever threatened to topple forward when opening its doors, until Rudolf had gathered hammer and nails and nailed it to the picture rail. Four chairs, the cream paint worn away in their centres, crowded round the family table. Another smaller, narrow, oblong table, featuring an inlaid chessboard, had been a wedding present from her sister Aunt Anna Jarabek's family. But it had never been used for its intended purpose, because Uncle Hans Jarabek, a clever craftsman but not an advanced chess player, had chiselled the white corner square in a position that required serious contenders to sit with the long edge separating them, and the physical effort when making a move was not in keeping with the game. It had become her sewing table instead.

A selection of flowerpots, and handle-less coffee mugs serving as flowerpots, occupied the space between the outer and inner windows. Next month a canopy of green would bring nature close. Brigitte believed in nature. Her faith sprang not from upbringing, and neither had she read about it in books. Nature was there for everyone to see. If others chose not to see it, they did so, she declared, because of the perversion of human nature.

Gusti Spagola returned and sat down on the bed.

Brigitte's head faced the ceiling. The brown speck clung on still, then fell. It brushed against Gusti's hair, and Gusti touched the spot to probe the disturbance.

"When Spagola makes good," she said, "he'll get us a little house on the edge of the woods with a little garden and a little dog for the children."

Brigitte's dream too. But she couldn't allow herself the luxury of dreaming or articulating it. She had to distract her neighbour from noticing the creature, now lying on its back on the white sheet, its wiry legs pedalling air.

She said, "Frau Spagola, if you'd be so kind. I could do with a sip of water."

Gusti hurried into the kitchen. Brigitte struggled to reach the insect. Her efforts moved the bedclothes. The bug disappeared into a fold. She drew her knees up to create a hill in the hope the intruder would roll off the bed.

"Maria-'nd-Joseph!" Gusti came rushing in with the glass. "Is it coming?"

"No, no. I'm sitting up for the water."

Gusti handed over the glass, picked up the crucifix and resumed the interrupted topic. "He's all right, is Spagola. When the wenches leave him be." She caressed the rigid wood with symbolic love. "He's got nimble fingers. He carved it for me. It keeps the devils at bay. There's always devils about to tempt us, Frau Anzendrech."

Brigitte, her perception heightened by impending childbirth, detected anguish in her neighbour's voice. Men, she thought, the instigators of misery. But it was nature's way.

"He's good to me, and he's good to the children, both of them, although only Berti's his," said Gusti, "and he's starting work on the council block in the Engerthstrasse come Monday."

"Rudolf's put us on the list for a council flat," said Brigitte.

"Ah, your man's with the tramways. Tramways is council property. If your man's working on the tramways..."

"What do you mean, Frau Spagola?"

"What I mean to say is the council dwellings that Spagola's going to build aren't meant for folk the likes of us. I tell you, the council men, they can make use of Spagola for tipping the sand from the barrows, or for carrying the cement up the ladders. But when it comes to allocating new flats with your own water tap in the kitchen, and maybe a balcony thrown in, and your own lavatory, they have no use for such as me and Spagola."

"Whatever makes you say that? Herr Dufft told us all families with two or more children will get council flats. Make sure you're on the list."

"Yes, but you see," said Gusti, her big eyes gazing fixedly into Brigitte's, "me and Spagola, you know, we're not ... It's a long story.

5

What with him and Richard Dufft. And Poldi without a real father. I'll tell you one day, but not now."

"Looking after children, giving them love and care, is more important than possessing a scrap of paper," said Brigitte emphatically.

Brigitte saw Gusti's forefinger run down the slender carving and pass within a hair's breadth from the oval shape of the bedbug. Brigitte fell back on her pillow. What did it mean? Was this a sign? God created bedbugs too.

She felt the sheets dropping away. Gusti tugged at them, pulled up the thin nightdress, and placed the crucifix on the swollen abdomen.

"Whatever are you doing?" asked the bewildered mother-to-be.

"Let's pray for a baby girl. You want a baby girl, don't you?" Gusti pressed the carving into the taught skin, and holding it there, recited rapid words of catechism, intermingled with pleas for a female birth.

Brigitte, bemused, did not protest. *God,* she pondered, *I have stopped belonging to the Roman Church, and Rudolf has had two religions; what a hotchpotch of ideas my children will be growing up with.* She wondered what God thought of it, but she had the inkling that if God was watching, crucifix and bedbug and all, it would be with a twinkle in His eye.

"I can hear somebody," exclaimed Gusti.

"It's Frau Dufft. She offered to cook supper for the children."

"I could have done that," Gusti's tone suggested resentment.

"I think … I think I'm ready," muttered Brigitte, steeling herself for another contraction, and vaguely wondering if Rudolf would be back in time for the birth.

Gusti hurried off to fetch the midwife.

Spagola's Gift for Rhymes

Gusti's habit of calling her common-law husband by his surname stemmed from the aftermath of World War 1, when Karl Spagola moved in as lodger, which in time resulted in the appearance of Berti coupled to the disappearance of Spagola. After a year and a half Karl resurfaced, acknowledged his parenthood, but could not bestow legitimacy on his son on account of having been enticed, in the meantime, to the altar by a frail but pretty hussy, who shortly afterwards contracted tuberculosis, and according to Karl's words, ran off with all his worldly chattels. Gusti did not need to invoke her belief in Christian charity to realise that forgiving was what she must do. In return Karl promised to bring up Poldi as well as his own son Berti, and possessing a way with crayons and a gift for composing rhymes, he drew for her a heart pierced by an arrow accompanied by the following, freely translated lines:

> To my own heart, dearest Gusti,
> Our love is true and trusty,
> Never shall it go false or rusty.
> You must remember this, my Gusti.

She determined to stitch him a pullover and sew in a big red heart, which, symbolic of her own, would lie near his. However the project remained dormant for some years until Poldi and Berti became less demanding. Officially retaining her maiden name Schattzburger, she made no protest when uninformed people began to call her Frau Spagola, and to simplify matters she pushed a ring over her finger. Seeking reassurance in a curious form of logic, she equated abstaining from using his Christian name with lessening the severity of living in mortal sin.

Three Umbrellas

By noon the snow had disappeared.

A drizzle set in, which saturated every bit of clothing exposed to it. Rudolf Anzendrech, wrapped in black oilskin, hurried home along the footway of the Northrailway Bridge, which spanned the Danube and the Danube Meadow.

Like his wife, he also believed in nature; but his attitude towards it meant breathing fresh air, drinking clean water, thinking clear thoughts, doing honest work, exercising his stalwart limbs. That's why he went by foot to and from the Floridsdorf tram depot in all weather, day or night, whatever the circumstances.

He recognised the back of a figure ahead. The man, of athletic build, wore neither overcoat nor hat, but held his shoulders hunched up to keep the rain from trickling down his back. He carried a bundle of three twisted umbrellas under one arm. His hands were thrust deep into his trouser pockets. He looked over as Rudolf caught up with him and cried out, "Hey, Herr Anzendrech. Good day."

Rudolf greeted his chess companion: "Hello there, hello."

"Whatever are you doing out in this *Scheisswetter*?"

"Me?" Rudolf strode on at a fair pace and drew his friend along with him. "Walking."

"I can see you're walking, or rather running. You get free travel on trams?"

"I'm quicker walking. And I do it for reasons of health."

"He does it for reasons of health! You want to catch pneumonia?"

"You know who are the healthiest people, Herr Dufft?" asked Rudolf in reply.

"Tell me."

"Sailors. At one moment they breathe in the foul tobacco smoke in their cabins, next they're up on deck in the middle of the ocean surrounded by pure oxygen."

"You say shifting from one extreme to the other is a healthy thing?"

"I'm like a seaman in a way. I'm inside the dirty tram car, crammed with people coming from the hospitals, coughing and spitting, and then I stand on the open platform as we go over the Floridsdorf Bridge, and I feel the fresh wind from the Kahlenberg blowing in my face."

"Ach, you're crazy," said Richard Dufft, shifting his own crazy umbrellas from one arm to the other. "Wind from the Kahlenberg. I don't sniff any such wind. All my winds come straight from the Floridsdorf sewer down there on the meadow."

Both men looked through the girders of the bridge to where, half hidden in the mist, the black, pungent effluent mingled with the clear water of the river.

"Anything wrong?" Rudolf queried.

"You mean in my professional capacity, or in my insane aspiration to emancipate the working classes?"

"Why are *you* out here?"

"I am also walking. In the rain. But not for reasons of health. You see my honourable press barons concluded that my inventive mind at supplying the weekly funny story for their illustrious rag is no longer a profitable investment."

"You lost your job?"

"So I apply my creative drive into the novel idea of turning over the bedbug-ridden mattresses on the rubbish dump, the *Mistgstettn,* of our beloved Vienna. I have heard tales of colossal finds of pearl necklaces and diamond rings embedded in the morass, and I thought I'd find myself one of these gems so I could retire from the thankless task of illuminating the gloom of the toiling masses, and build myself a palace and smoke fat cigars. Like my fat ex-bosses."

"So they did fire you?"

"I'm in a rotten mood because I've been groping in the filth on a day when the regular scavengers have the sense to seek out dryer places like their sleeping quarters underneath this very bridge. And what's the gross yield? Three lunatic umbrella relics of yesteryear."

He opened one. The ribs pointing in all directions, held together precariously by random pieces of cloth; it was indeed a lunatic sight. "Please Your Lordship, allow me to shield Your Lordship from the preposterous phenomenon, of which it is said it falls on rich and poor alike."

He held the umbrella wreck over the tram conductor's head and broke into a forced laugh.

Rudolf's habit of looking for a silver lining, even when the sky loomed grey all over, had taught him the art of manufacturing one: "I take the view," he said, "we all get our share of misfortune, and we all get our share of good luck."

"Who claims the credit of this very gratifying piece of philosophy? Rothschild?"

"No, I thought it up myself," Rudolf answered naïvely, "and I go further in saying that when a bad thing happens you never know what good may come of it later."

"Like my three umbrellas?"

"Like my learning the bakery trade."

"Perhaps if we rub them," said Dufft, miming the action, "a philanthropic genie will materialise from the rain drops, heralding better tidings?"

"Listen. I was an orphan and when the time came to learn a trade, I wanted to be apprenticed as a mechanic. But there was no vacancy for a mechanic, so they shoved me in with a baker."

Dufft nodded. "Like the sons of our press barons who get shoved in with bakers? Papa Dufft had the garment business and I didn't get shoved in with any bakers."

"I learnt to be a baker. I never liked it because I wanted to become a mechanic, and I never got used to the night work. My constitution needs sleep at regular hours, but I've never accomplished it, not even now as tram conductor. Back in 1914, they lined us up, us new recruits, and corporal shouts, 'All of you who are bakers: one step forward.' So I take one step forward, and they put me into the military cookhouse, and I bake bread for four years whilst the mechanics get shot to bits at the front."

"Eating May-beetles, raw, my men were," said Dufft. The rain had found a way down his spine, and he pulled his collar tighter over his neck. He now held the open umbrella frame over his own head. "They had a sweetish taste. And the soldiers on the other side lapped up the same diet. Come spring, I can see myself feeding Mama on cockchafers. But we'll have them roasted. That's progress, after seven years of peace."

"Times were better in Kaiser Franz Joseph's days."

"Any times are better than the present variety. But if you want my opinion, when we lived in the empire of nations over which the sun never set, any excess sunshine fell on the wider Hapsburg family, not so much on a national family."

"We never went hungry."

"One thing our Austrian Kaiser did do: he went out of his way to stop people bugging Jews. Over in Germany they're stoking the flames for another pogrom. Even Jews are becoming anti-Semitic! Queuing up for baptism in droves."

"Many Jews swapped religions years ago," said Rudolf.

"I'm no different from any other citizen of this our fatherland. But my birth certificate says I am a Jew. Fine. And our press barons, who have been Jewish for generations, don't give a damn for their brethren. You see, I am now venting my own version of Jewish anti-Semitism."

The roar of an approaching goods train rent the air. The bridge began to shake.

"People can't get on with one another," Rudolf said, raising his voice to drown the din.

"Why?" Dufft shouted back. "Why do we ram bayonets into the bellies of our fellow men? Because we love the feel of it? Why do we get shoved about, forced to become bakers for instance? From choice, or because someone's doing the shoving? Every day our office echoes with news of killings, of bombs, of gun shipments. There are people and people, Herr Anzendrech."

"Pardon?"

"There are people and people," Richard Dufft yelled. "Karl Marx said ...." But the controversial philosopher's utterance lost itself in the thunder of the passing train. Dufft, still shouting, was heard again when the last truck gained distance. "....that's why I've become a Socialist."

"What did you say?" Rudolf hollered.

"I said that's why I've become a Socialist."

"Before that."

"I said ...." Dufft shrieked, but cut his words short as he watched Rudolf inhale buckets of air and yield to convulsions of laughter.

"What's got into you?"

It took a while for Rudolf to regain his composure. "I've just seen the joke of the situation. There's you and me in the middle of nowhere in the rain, you with your umbrellas specially made for ducks, screaming at each other."

"Well, I'm supposed to have the eye for jest, and tickle me with a stick of salami, but I can't see the funny side here."

Rudolf, in a rare moment of quick repartee, replied: "I can't tickle you with a salami, but you could lend me one of your umbrellas."

"You're crazy." Dufft collapsed his umbrella with hurt dignity. "I'm a tolerably good journalist, you know. Wheedling out something to smile at these days is a miracle in itself. Those in the higher echelons of the editorial, quaking with fear of anything political, didn't like my jokes. For example: What's the difference between Hitler's putsch in the Bierkeller and an uprising in a lunatic asylum?"

The tram conductor thought, then said: "I don't know. What is the difference?"

"I don't know either," replied Dufft, "in fact nobody knows." After a few paces he said, "The editor's name is Herr Carry-on-Knocking, Herr *Weiterklopfen.*"

"And many a door is opened unto him?" asked Rudolf still in high spirits.

"A couple of weeks ago I did some research for a sarcastic article about the origin of certain Jewish names, like *Grünspan, Morgenthau, Sauerkraut, Halbkrank.* I pick up this story: when our forefathers came over from the east to settle in Vienna, the immigration officials couldn't cope with the Polish names, so they dished out new ones, anything that came into their heads. Those with an anti-Semitic bent weren't particularly choosy. If they faced a fellow with running blisters from the hazards of travel, they'd name him Pusdrop, Herr *Eitertropfen.* A generation or two later, the Jewish fellow's heirs were smart enough to swap one or two letters, so *Eitertropfen* became Weiterklopfen."

"Writing that cost you your job?"

"I made a joke of it. I didn't spare my own name, which originally was Violet-fragrance, *Veilchenduft.* Perhaps my great-great-great-great-grandfather had a partiality for garlic and was quizzed by a clerk with a sense of humour. My subsequent ancestors let the *Veilchen* wilt into a drooping f. Hence the double 'f' in Dufft. Funny, isn't it? The English got it right, when they say 'A rose,' or if you like, a violet, 'by any other name, smells just as sweet.'"

Rudolf said nothing but remembered that the bullies in the orphanage called him *Wanzendreck*, Bedbug-mess, instead of Anzendrech.

"So here I am, stirring the rubbish amongst hungry crows and starving dogs to bring home this junk." Dufft flourished the umbrellas in front of the tram conductor's face and continued, "When I get home I shall bend the bent ribs straight, and ask Mama to sew the black cloth together, so we finish up with one working umbrella from the lot. Then I wait for another rainy day and promenade the Ringstrasse in the hope a fat newspaper boss, Jewish no doubt, forgets his umbrella, so I offer him mine for a few groschen, and I buy coffee and a *Kipferl*, a croissant, for Mama. You see, I'm in luck; I haven't got wife and children. I don't know how you cope with your two kids."

"Three," said Rudolf.

"Holy wall of Jerusalem, so it's happened? Yes, Mama said she'll see to your dinners. Gusti's there no doubt. Congratulations." He grasped both of Rudolf's hands, and in doing so, the umbrellas fell from under his arm. "Boy or girl?"

"Don't know yet."

"Hope Gusti and Mama won't get into each other's hair."

He left his spoils lying on the water-sodden asphalt and Rudolf asked, "Don't you want them?"

"You know, Gusti and I played together when we were kids." Dufft bent down to gather up his umbrellas. The wet shirt and trousers stuck to his skin. "Damn!" he said as he pulled out the clinging cloth from the cleft of his seat. "This calls for a glass of Mama's *Ribisl*, red currant, wine! I'll put a jar aside. And listen, now you've got three, you're top priority for a council flat."

"I've put our name down on the list."

"He's put his name down on the list!" Dufft mocked. "God of Abraham. He thinks that he can sit on his posterior and wait until they come with the red carpet and clarion fanfare. You've got to be persistent with the housing committee, like a fly over a cow's arse. You're not Jewish?"

"I tell you something: I believe a man's religion should not be questioned."

"Agreed. How a man prays and how he shits are his private affairs. There's a reason why I asked: not all on the housing bureau take kindly to a Jew." Dufft laid the umbrellas on the top of the railings.

"Don't throw them in!" cried Rudolf, alarmed.

"The ritual of sacrifice intrigues me." Dufft raised the umbrella ends to test how high he could go before they would slide into the watery oblivion. "I suppose it started when the apes clambered down from the trees and began to understand what makes things tick, or rather to misunderstand it. Or if you want the other version, when Lady Eve enticed Adam to sink his teeth into the apple from the tree of knowledge. And I do believe the crafty serpent was having a bit of extra fun at double-crossing: perhaps it wasn't the tree of knowledge at all, but the tree of mis-knowledge, making us think we know when we know bugger all. Excuse the language."

They had come to a halt, and Rudolf, eager to reach home before the birth of his baby, said, "I can't stop."

Dufft, without moving, continued, "Ever since that time, folks have been obsessed with the singular notion that to please the powers in charge of the universe, someone must be put to death to pave the way for happier times. There's Abraham holding down his son's head on the chopping block, but he got reprieved. And there's your Christ nailed to the cross. He didn't get reprieved; perhaps if he had, his doctrines would have died instead. And Lenin nearly succumbed to an assassin's bullet, and his dogma is catching on. You see, I'm not a good Jew: too diverse in my views to fit any one creed. I'd choose another religion, only the religion to convert to hasn't been invented yet. I mean the one that poses questions instead of giving ready answers."

The air had become clearer. The Giant Wheel, the *Riesenrad,* lifting people high into the sky over the Prater Amusement Park, could be seen to the right of the distant Reichsbridge. Dufft fixed his eyes on it as he said, "And since we're discussing sacrifice, the question arises whether God in Heaven could be moved to alleviate our plight through an offering of lesser worth than a human life."

"A bedbug? "

"Do you know I harbour the feeling He would be tickled pink at the proposition. Or better still, at excluding all living creatures. So here we have three spent umbrellas, utterly useless, plucked from their place of rest during a futile search. And to underline their positive uselessness I don't think the scheme for their rejuvenation contained the germs of success. Do you?"

Rudolf liked Dufft for his eccentricity, and admired him for the absence of self-pity in the wake of the inflation that had robbed his family of an unspecified, but according to rumour, huge fortune.

"The handles could be made into hooks to hang my tramway satchel on. But I must go," urged Rudolf.

"A hook supporting a tramway satchel can also support a man's neck. No, we won't give the devils a chance to tempt us for a quick way out in adversity. Let the umbrellas be an offering on behalf of the new generation: Jews or Gentiles, Caucasians or Chinamen, or if that's too greedy, just Herr Anzendrech's two boys plus brand new issue. Umbrellas, symbols of protection, sink to your wet grave, and in doing so, ensure that Herr Anzendrech's offspring awaits a better world, for by all that's holy, the present one's a shit heap."

He tossed the umbrellas over the railing, and both men watched as the swirling, brown Danube swallowed them up. Rudolf looked at his drenched friend: "Come back with me. Brigitte can spare some bread and potatoes. But hurry."

"Don't disillusion me from my disillusionment." Now walking briskly by the tram conductor's side, Dufft carried on, "I'll catalogue your offer under the heading of last resorts, when we are reduced to eating roasted May-beetles. My colleague Razzenfuss, who runs the feature section on the *Danube Press*, pulled a few strings and got me to do some freelance work for his paper. To tell you the truth, the real reason for my rummaging around the Mistgstettn was to collect material for an amusing article on that august locality and the Gypsy folk residing there. The umbrellas were just a perk that went with the job."

"Cheer up," said Rudolf, who had heard enough of his friend's gloomy sarcasm.

"Actually I homed in on the umbrellas in an attempt to illustrate how an enterprising Gypsy can make an honest living restoring them."

They skipped down the stairs connecting the footway of the bridge with the riverbank. From there a gravel road led past the entrance gates to the coal yards and coke mountains of the Danube Coke Company, then across the dock railway line to the Commercial Quay Street, the *Handelskai*. Coal barges lay tied to the quay. A crane feverishly dipped its mechanical bucket into the river, hoisted it high above two peaks of steaming coke hills, and spilled the water over them. Rudolf saw in the huge coke cones the full breasts of a giant black woman, and in the jaws of the bucket a watery mouth caressing them. He felt in need of a woman. He inwardly cursed his luck and that of mankind. If hard times or your fellow men were not hounding you, the drive for sexual gratification was.

Dufft said, "They're building council blocks all over the place. But that's no reason to be sitting on your lackadaisical Viennese backside. As I've said, you go along to the housing bureau and pester the living daylights out of them until they turn green with bellyache at the sight of you."

"Yes," replied Rudolf. His mind had journeyed into dreamland, and conjured up the curves of Vikki Huber, the fortune-telling girl, underneath the white frocks she wore in summer.

"If you're not of Hebrew faith you should be spared the fun and games created for our benefit. There's a maniac who's forever petitioning the housing committee to keep Jewish people, and mixed race couples, out. He and his cronies say Jews are aliens not eligible for municipal housing. Aliens! Did you know percentage-wise Jewish soldiers won more medals in the war than all the rest combined?"

Rudolf shook his head.

"He runs the municipal laundry in the block next to ours. The building there isn't finished, but the laundry's already working. Anzendrech, when washday comes, on top of the normal upheaval, I'm spending half the morning calming Mama down. I'm telling her we have the same rights as the Gentiles. I'm telling her I'm a member of the Council. I'm telling her if the lout makes trouble, I'll send him off to hear the angels sing with an entrance ticket to ... no, not to his Saint Peter up in the clouds, because he wouldn't be journeying in an upward direction!"

An Old Romany Saying

Rudolf traversed the Meldemannstrasse in zigzag fashion to avoid the many puddles and entered through an open doorway into a narrow passage. There, shrouded in shadow, Karl Spagola crouched over a bicycle, the mudguards and wheels of which had been taken off.

"Herr Anzendrech, at last," Karl said, straightening up and placing his hands on his hips to ease the movement. "There's big news waiting for you. And you're big news. Yeah, even the government got the jitters. They're afraid that the inflation bug, having finished operations in the financial world, is staging a come-back to upset the population stability. Triplets. Two white nippers and the third as black as coal."

Rudolf's eyes adjusted to the sombre interior. He pushed the mudguards to one side and noticed another person leaning against the corner from which a staircase led to the floors above.

"Leave off, Karli," remonstrated a female voice, but the tone betrayed a degree of amusement. An attractive, dark-haired girl stepped forward, adopted a new leaning position against the wall of the staircase leading to the basement, and facing Rudolf, said, "Herr Anzendrech, you've got a baby boy."

Karl Spagola raised his shoulders and turned his palms towards Rudolf in a gesture of acquiescence. "Just a joke, Herr Anzendrech, just a joke. Fact is my Gusti spends most of the day with your missus, and most of the night with the Holy Virgin. She fussed over the little bundle as if she'd dropped it herself, and not a little bit of fuss to spare for anyone else. The door has been shut in my face so to speak, and I'm given no option but to seek solace outside my own abode."

A half-suppressed chuckle escaped the girl's throat and a tickle of jealousy mixed with annoyance stirred in Rudolf's chest.

"Which," continued Karl, "happened along in the shape of Fräulein Vikki Huber's bicycle. Punctures in both tyres. Front and rear. Wait a moment, Herr Anzendrech, I'll clear the road for you."

He grabbed at a wheel. The end of a broken spoke pierced his middle finger and drew blood.

"You've let it dribble to the ground!" Vikki Huber feigned apprehension.

"So I'll die of drowning?" Karl laughed and wrapping his handkerchief round the injured finger, said to Rudolf, "That's an old Romany saying. You needn't worry though, I'm a good swimmer. Vikki's read my fortune: she says I'll live to a hundred."

"You won't live another day if I see you seeking solace from her!" Gusti's voice rang out. She had come down unobserved. "Didn't you hear me call, Spagola? Your grub's on the table." And addressing Rudolf amicably: "Congratulations, Herr Anzendrech, mother and baby Alexander are fine. Frau Dufft's still with them."

Vikki went back to her original position and watched Gusti disappear up the staircase.

Karl Spagola resumed meddling with the wheels, blocking the gangway. "Ah, but it's a great event, and you're a lucky man, and I'm really only kidding, because none of us minds putting up with the disturbance on such a happy occasion, and the wine that goes with it, and the cigars make up for the inconvenience."

"That'll do, Karl Spagola," rebuked Vikki. "Herr Anzendrech's in a hurry. And the wine and cigars are for the millionaires, not for people living in our tenements."

"Herr Anzendrech's different. A bit of a dark horse as you might say. He's apt to spring surprises on unsuspecting folk. And on such a day, what's more natural?"

Karl Spagola regarded nature simply as a means for enjoyment. This uncomplicated philosophy was the key to his popularity with women as well as men. Gusti's religious preoccupation provided forever a target for his sense of fun, yet he would not hesitate to please her, if pleasing her was the order of the day, with a present of a pious nature. He treated her children fairly. After he had crafted a toy boat for his son, he visited the Mistgstettn and brought back a yellow cloth doll without arms for Poldi. He cared little for social conventions, but he endorsed the traditions of soaking sorrow with alcohol at the end of a life, and of teasing the father at the beginning of one. "What d'you think Herr Anzendrech carries home in his pouch," he went on, "can't you hear it jingle?"

"If you must know," Rudolf retorted, "the satchel's full of ticket blocks. Can I come by?"

"Jingle, jingle, jingle." Karl lifted the satchel. "Great Kalafati, the weight of it. Now no fairy tales, don't have us believe that anyone carrying such a cargo can resist the temptation of a drop of grog to stimulate the circulation."

"There's no money in it. All the takings are handed in at the end of work. I want to pass please."

"Tram conductors!" Karl winked at Vikki. "The yarns they spin. You know people say they're the sailors of the street. The tramcars toss about just like ships on the waves, and like seamen in every port, tramway men have a sweetheart at every stop. And at the terminus, I am too bashful to mention it!"

"Herr Anzendrech wants to see his son," said Vikki.

"Of course he does. And I am the last person to delay him. Triplets! I really had you worried. Considering the money you'll be saving having only one extra mouth to feed instead of three, and considering I'm in need of a little cash right now, I wonder, Herr Anzendrech, if you could arrange a small loan until pay day."

"You've got work?" Rudolf asked.

18

Karl nodded. "Five shillings in lieu of wine and cigars."

Rudolf escaped further embarrassment by Gusti's voice cascading down from above: "Are you coming, Spagola?"

Rudolf clambered over the clutter. Vikki made no effort to move out of his way, so that squeezing past her, his hand brushed against her lower body sending a tingle up his arm, neck and face. From the corner of his eyes he saw her looking at him fixedly. He noticed her dark pupils and the smooth forehead below the gentle waves of black hair.

Hot, flustered and vexed, he attacked the stairs two steps at a time.

The Watering Can

Brigitte took from her linen store a small blanket and laid baby Alexander naked on it, and shifted him along the floor following the moving patch of sunlight. The first time Uncle Hans saw this, he said, "Jesus, you'll be coming round with a watering can next."

Aunt Anna laughed all day, but Brigitte stood her ground. She knew what she was doing. Did not all nature's creation thrive on sunshine?

Alexander, Xandi for short, enjoyed digging his little fingernails into the soft filler between the curved-up floorboards. Then one day the corrugated planks gave way to a flat, shiny surface with a bitter taste of polish. Along with this new floor came new objects, new sounds, new smells. The Anzendrech family had moved into the light-grey building of two adjacent council blocks, of which the other had been finished in brown. Because of their colours, the light one became known as the Milk Block, and the dark one the Cocoa Block.

The new flat consisted of two bedrooms, one on either side of a kitchen-living room containing water tap and basin, with large windows looking down onto the tree-lined Engerthstrasse; a small entrance lobby, and leading off it, a lavatory. Aunt Anna was so enthralled with the dwelling's airiness that she likened it to the loftier world to which she had hopeful aspirations, albeit after passing from the present one.

The Engerthstrasse runs parallel with the southwest bank of the Danube from the Floridsdorf Bridge, past the Northrailway Bridge, to the Reichsbridge and beyond. Nearly all traffic, however, flowed over the bridges to the heart of the city, and the Engerthstrasse echoed only intermittently to the rattle of a refuse lorry; or the furious ringing of a bicycle bell prior to its owner swearing at a child whilst swerving to avoid hitting it; or to the clanking of the number 11 tram, which at quarter-hour intervals jolted over the points and ground to a halt, there to wait on the dual tracks until the oncoming tram on the single track rattled past.

People strolled leisurely across the street in long diagonals.

CHAPTER TWO (1928)

Naked after Fire Engines

Brigitte continued with the sunshine treatment until Xandi's cooperation to stay on the blanket frittered away. Convinced that the next best thing was to expose a growing body to the embrace of air, she let her three boys run around without clothes whenever weather and circumstances permitted. Eventually Rudi and Pauli became aware of themselves and took to wearing swim trunks, but Xandi remained happy to romp about as nature had made him.

The Wagnerian trumpet blasts of the Vienna fire brigade cut through the idyllic peace: tra-raa, tra-raa; the raa one fourth higher than the tra. Two, three, five fire engines, and more to come! And in the direction of their travel, past the Cocoa Block, thick billows of black smoke! Every doorway ejected men, women and children; each side street became a tributary to the main current. A happy few roared by on motorbikes, the rest came panting, sweating, intermingled with bicycles and dogs. Brigitte's boys flew like whirlwinds down the staircase.

"Keep an eye on Xandi!" she called after them.

They ran wildly with the stampede. The fire engines had raced out of sight, but their tra-raas cracked the air as before.

Xandi could not keep up with his bigger brothers. Rudi remembered his mother's words. He stopped and waited.

"Xandi, go home."

The three-year-old had no such thought.

"Go home, you're naked."

Xandi looked at his belly. Then he raised his eyes and saw the multitude: every man, woman, boy, girl, wore trousers or dresses or shorts or skirts or swimming trunks. Only he, he alone, was naked.

"Go home." Rudi turned to look at the clouds of smoke. Once more he told his little brother to go back, and he disappeared amongst the running people, like a drop of water in the Danube.

Xandi quaked with shame as he began the lonely trek back against this oncoming throng, which knew no end. He did not look at anyone, hoping that not seeing them, they would not see him. He reached the cool passage that led into the courtyard of the Milk Block. Even here, people surged the opposite way. Only Frau Czarnikow, the Slovak caretaker from the Anzendrech's staircase, whose thick, varicose veins constrained her from following the crowd, stood motionless in the entrance. She shook a long finger at him.

He had yet to reach Staircase 13 in the courtyard. A group of toddlers from the kindergarten and a big, heavy girl, unaware of the fire engines, sang, holding hands, walking round in a circle. Xandi crept along close to the wall, seeking cover, and ran his head against an open cellar widow. The impact reverberated in his ears and he screeched in pain; the children's eyes turned upon him. The fat girl detached herself from the infants and came over.

"D'you want a suck of Gugi?" She held a yellow, arm-less cloth doll to her mouth before offering it to the screaming boy. "He hasn't got no knickers on neither."

She took his hand and together they walked back to his home.

When Brigitte opened the door, Xandi gave vent to a fresh torrent of tears: "Mummy, Mummy. I'm naked."

"He banged his head on the window in the yard. Hard," said the girl.

Brigitte cuddled her son. "Hush, Xandi, hush." She turned to his escort: "What are you doing here, Poldi?"

"I'm playing ring-a-ring-a-roses with the children."

"Do you live here then?"

"Yes, I do."

Herr Rosenfinger from next door rushed in: "The paper factory's alight. They're crying sabotage; they're saying the Schutzbund did it. The Socialists always get the blame. They're saying Burgomaster Seitz is sitting on a fire engine, to stop another riot. Remember what happened when the Justice Ministry burnt."

Grosser Gott! Oh my God!" Rudi and Pauli stuck in the middle of the fray!

Herr Rosenfinger saw the fright his words had engendered. "It's nothing. It's a rumour. The National Socialists are stirring it up again. That's all."

Gusti's New Apartment

Washday came. Xandi and Pauli carried soap and scrubbing brush as far as the laundry's doors; there they flung them into Mummy's basket and ran off. Little treasures, an expression the laundry supervisor, Herr Brunner, used when referring to his clients' offspring, were not allowed into the steam-filled chamber and he enforced strict observance. Even Manni Czarnikow, whose flouting of grown-up bidding had elevated him to the status of king in the juvenile court yards, bowed to the laundryman's ruling.

The municipal wash-house occupied the width of the Milk Block, and as Brigitte turned the corner from the Engerthstrasse, she saw Frau Spagola, a tin bath of clothing wedged in her hip, walk up to the entrance from the opposite direction.

"Jesus-Maria-'nd-Joseph!" exclaimed Poldi's mother setting down her burden followed by clasping her temples in sheer pleasure. "Frau Anzendrech! This is a coincidence. This can't happen twice in a lifetime. How are you?"

"I had a word with your Poldi the other day, and I said to myself I said, the Spagolas can't be far away, they must be living in the Milkblock."

"Week gone yesterday we said goodbye to the Meldemannstrasse. Not many 's left there now. The fortune telling Gypsy madam's still there in her fine frocks, and she can hold the landlord's hand all day, reading his palm, I dare say!"

"Where's your new flat?" asked Brigitte, placing her load beside Frau Spagola's tin bath, anticipating a chat of some length.

"Oh, it's beautiful. The Holy Virgin heard my prayers. And my Poldi, she loves it. They let her into the kindergarten because of her being so good with the little ones, you know. And Berti sits all the while by the window counting ships."

"You look out on the river?"

"On the fourth floor we are, and we see the Danube, and the Danube Meadow, and Floridsdorf, and we see from Bisamberg Hill right down to the Lobau Woods. Where are your windows facing, Frau Anzendrech?"

"We look down on the Engerthstrasse. Xandi sits by the window watching out for trams."

"We see the whole of Brettldorf and the Mistgstettn."

"Brettldorf and the Mistgstettn?" Brigitte pulled the ends of her lips down in dismissal of these two localities from the array of beauty spots. A few thorns in her old neighbour's rosy vista lessened the touch of envy, for she would have preferred a view of nature's grass and water rather than man-made bricks and mortar. Brettl is a Viennese expression for plank of wood, and Brettldorf was little more than a Gypsy community, a shanty town erected from bits of timber and scraps of corrugated metal, on the edge of the city's rubbish dump.

"And we can see people on the Danube Meadow, and if we had binoculars we'd be able see all sorts of things, I can tell you."

"What sorts of things?"

"Things people get up to on the Danube Meadow, young and old alike, what do you think? Come and see for yourself, afterwards, when we've finished slaving. But I tell you, I never thought I'd live the day. Washing my hair I was, and I hear a knock on the door, and when I look through the peephole, who d'you think I see?"

"If I knew that," said Brigitte, still smarting at her friend's luck in securing a flat facing the river, "I wouldn't be scrubbing Rudolf's underpants, I'd be earning good money fortune telling."

"No other than Richard Dufft. Member of the City Council, Herr Richard Dufft. Sitting on the housing committee, he is, you know. All la-di-da like, official visit. So I says to him, could he come back another time, because Spagola's out."

"He wanted to see you about new housing?"

"It was a bit awkward. You see, my mum managed the Duffts' household, we lived in with the Duffts, when I was a girl." She brushed her hands down her skirt as if to flatten out folds. "We grew up together, him being only a year older." She looked straight into Brigitte's eyes, held her gaze for a moment. "But his family had his cousin Violetta lined up for him. He went in as a soldier in the war, and he came home because he had a bullet gone through his thigh."

"His thigh? I heard it went through his ... "

"His thigh or his what's-it, he cut a dashing figure in his uniform. His friend Antonius from the same regiment was on sick leave too. They held a party."

She paused. Events leading up that fateful night, so long ago, had put down roots in her mind, so that hardly a week passed without her reliving them: the officers' gala in Heiligenstadt; Richard escorting Violetta; Leutnant Antonius Freiherr booking his fiancée Fanni to entertain the party with singing. But the two betrothed quarrelled and Fanni stayed away, upset.

"Antonius knew I could sing a bit, so he asked me to do the honours. You see I won a prize in school for singing *Am Brunnen vor dem Tore*," explained Gusti.

"*Da steht ein Lindenbaum*," augmented Brigitte, speaking Schubert's song 'The Linden Tree' on pitch.

In Gusti's brain the reminiscences continued: Antonius pouring liquor from a little brown bottle into drinks and sending people wild; Violetta walking off with a colonel. And Richard and Antonius holding her, Gusti, up as all three staggered along the streets to continue revelling at home.

Gusti went on, "Richard shot off to university after the war. To Heidelberg on the River Rhein he went, where he had grandparents living. I see nothing of him for five years, then he shows up with a bunch of red roses, tells me his family's lost all their money and Violetta married the colonel. Says he wants to forgive me for Poldi. I put him wise to my situation, what with Berti hopping around." She stopped for a moment. "Maybe it's just as well the way things turned out, for without Spagola ..."

Brigitte waited, expecting to hear more.

"... I might have become Frau Dufft."

"Married Herr Dufft? With his injury?"

Gusti shrugged her shoulders. "I've heard he was cured in that department. Anyhow, I put Richard out of my mind, saw him only now and then when he visited you and Herr Anzendrech, and here he was again, with my hair all dripping wet, asking to be shown in. So I says to him, could he come back another time because Spagola 's out. 'Gusti,' he says, 'I'd like to exchange a few words with you,' he says. So I put the towel over my shoulders, and he starts off asking questions. This here and that there, questions about the children and Spagola, and all the time my hair dripping wet."

"It was about housing?" interrupted Brigitte.

"He wants to know birth dates and asks about the income and about the certificate, have I been to the altar with Spagola, and I says nothing, but he knows anyway. And mind you, I shall be wed one day."

"I'll bake a special Apfelstrudel for the occasion," joked Brigitte.

Fanciful but scary thoughts ran through Gusti's mind: *What if Richard pops the question again? I'm free to marry anybody. Love, real love, that would be nice...*

She resumed, "So Richard says he'll see what he can do in the circumstances." Gusti's large eyes grew larger. "And then Spagola walks in, and throws him out."

"No!"

"Took him by his arm and marched him out."

"Whatever did he do that for?"

"Showed Richard Dufft the door. On account of the compromising situation. Me and him alone in the room, if you get my meaning."

"I get your meaning, but didn't you say?"

"Of course I did. Anyway, he could see I'd been washing my hair. The hot water bucket on the floor and the saucepan on the table. And I said Herr Dufft never touched me nowhere, but it made no difference, out he went."

"Herr Dufft protested?"

"Did I let fly at Spagola! The names I called him don't bear repeating in respectful company. 'You silly pisspot,' I said, 'you've done it now. Herr Dufft was going to move us into municipality housing. The only time the council men will move us from this hole is when they'll put us into another in the ground.'"

Women flocked towards the laundry entrance, carrying their washing baskets, or wheeling them on trolleys their husbands had knocked together from redundant wooden boxes and cast-iron wheels, and which bounced over the cobblestones creating an ear-splitting rattle.

Gusti remarked, "This is my first washday."

"It's best to be early," said Brigitte. "We've got our regular tubs, but new women must see the supervisor."

The mothers bent down. They touched the rims of tin bath and basket, but Gusti began to speak again and like performing a folk ritual, they straightened up and both receptacles remained firmly parked on the pavement.

"'Herr Dufft's a gentleman,' I said, and Spagola shouts, 'Dufft's a lecherous Jew.' So I says to him, 'The pot's calling the kettle black.' 'Meaning what?' he says. And I says, 'Meaning the Gypsy witch, that Vikki Huber.' Spagola flies into a rage and shouts, 'What about Dufft's red roses?' He says Berti isn't his but Richard's."

Brigitte felt relieved that no man, not even Rudolf, ever gave her red roses.

"He smashes the oil lamp and walks out. A whole week we're sitting in the dark before I can afford a new glass for it. Now it wouldn't make no difference, as we've got th' electricity. Spagola stays away the best part of a week, then he comes crawling back. They always come crawling back, don't they?"

"My Rudolf's not like that."

"Ah! All men want the same thing. He comes back and I have to swear that he's the true father of Berti by blood. Then I have to promise to be faithful to him, see Richard Dufft no more, and I says to him will he be seeing Vikki Huber no more, and he makes a solemn pledge to lay off women. Yes, that's how we get by in our household. I don't mind telling you, Frau Anzendrech, because you are a body I can depend on."

Brigitte offered a silent prayer of gratitude that her own family escaped such trials, and she forgave Gusti for securing a flat overlooking the river.

"Time runs on," Gusti resumed. "I've pushed the incident from my mind and the postman brings this letter. Couldn't believe my eyes when I read we've been allocated new council housing."

"Did Herr Spagola eat his words?" asked Brigitte, and seeing a blank look on Gusti's face, she elucidated, "He called Herr Dufft ... names."

"Ach, that was said in the heat of jealousy. There's good and bad Jews as there's good and bad Christians. Sometimes I think two different religions joining in holy matrimony wouldn't be fair on the children, as they'd be neither the one nor the other, and in consequence easy prey for devils."

"I became a Protestant when I married Rudolf," muttered Brigitte.

"Xandi and your other two, they'll benefit, I'm sure." And Gusti pondered whether she would have adopted Richard's Jewish faith had she wed him, or he hers.

They lifted their washing containers waist high, and walking through the entrance, Brigitte asked, "How does Herr Spagola like the flat with the river view?"

"He hasn't been in it much. He's with Danube Coke. He works on the ships now, he does. Goes on the coal ships and passenger steamers to Budapest regularly." Frau Spagola inclined her head backwards in a posture of one-upmanship, for everyone understood the transport hierarchy: horse-drawn vehicles occupied the bottom, then came trams, then the railways, then motor vehicles, and at the very top, excluding a handful of aircraft, steamed the Danube ships.

The Chivalry of the Woman-eating Panther

"There's Herr Brunner," Brigitte said pointing at the supervisor in a khaki boiler suit. Gusti walked towards him, but he chose to busy himself turning on and off water taps over empty troughs.

Herr Brunner's attitude to nature implied that it must be bent to his will. He habitually strutted up and down the gangway in the manner of an eastern sheikh in his harem, master over his women, imagining all waiting to be plucked like grapes from vine for his pleasure. That nearly all were married added security to his designs as any consequences of his pursuits could be placed into the arms of cuckolded husbands. Wives, whether responding to his advances or not, though eager to gossip amongst themselves, rarely discussed laundry goings-on with their men. That's why the incident with Fräulein Lutschi Fritzer, being single, escaped into the wider world.

At other times Brunner pictured himself as a Roman taskmaster cracking his whip at his galley slaves of female gender. The troughs were arranged in rows of four, two on either side of a central gangway, and the women stood in front of their troughs, rocking their torsos backwards and forwards. But they did not pull at gigantic oars, they scrubbed shirts and sheets and long johns against rumpled scrubbing boards, and steam rose from their tubs, and sweat rose from their brows.

Herr Brunner habitually favoured women of his choice, giving them the best position for light, attending to their requests first, and allowing them to jump the queues for the wringers and dryers. He ignored complaints from those who refused to respond to his insinuating remarks, or had incurred his displeasure through emotive irritation like buckteeth, and they frequently had to battle with leaking plugs. He showed downright malice towards Jewish women.

In Brigitte's eyes, he represented the epitome of a cheap bully. The acrimony was born at her first visit to the laundry, when, unaware of the no-children rule, she had brought Xandi along. The boy had scarcely shown his face inside before he received a wet rag on it, aimed with precision by the man in the khaki boiler suit. Yet in spite of Brigitte's distaste, the laundry man had taken it upon himself to single her out, for the moment, as recipient of his sultry solicitations.

Frau Spagola waited patiently, and Brigitte joined her to see that fair play prevailed. Brunner continued to perform with the taps, and then very abruptly turned round and said to Frau Spagola, "You are fresh?"

Gusti, taken aback, shot a quick glance at her friend. But as Brigitte could offer no guidance, she replied, "As fresh as new baked bread straight from the oven."

The laundry supervisor grinned and said, "I haven't seen you in here before. I never forget a pretty face, like ..." he switched his gaze to Brigitte's eyes, and then running his own down to the region between her thighs, he let them linger there, "... like Frau Anzendrech's, for example."

"I haven't got time to stand here all day listening to idle prattle," said Brigitte, anger rising, "Frau Spagola needs to be allocated a wash tub."

"No offence meant, Frau Anzendrech." The supervisor did not relax his grin nor retract his eyes. "Just a polite pleasantry to keep the hours whiling by. I'm sure the fresh one won't object to me saying I won't forget her face in a million years."

Women all around plunged their arms deep into vaporous water; hands, wrists and elbows adopted a uniform tomato colour, and coupled to their shiny, red cheeks they assumed a homogeneous, ageless look; all of which resembled, as Brigitte was apt to put it, a human pickling plant.

"I'm sure the fresh one won't take it amiss," Brunner continued, "if I comment on the delicacy of her hands, into whose care I would entrust any of my nether garments. I mean for the purpose of washing."

He paused to see the effect of this witticism. Brigitte had heard it before. The discharge of hissing steam and shouting at the far end brought the parley to an abrupt close. He hurried off.

"He's a bit of a woman-eating panther, isn't he?" remarked Gusti.

"Like a snake," said Brigitte. "Lots of women are scared of him. My Xandi has nightmares because the ruffian lashed out at him. Even now, when its washday time, Xandi remembers and I have to cook milk rice with chocolate bars to calm him down."

"Perhaps he'd like to come over to have a bite to eat with us?" Gusti anticipated Xandi lapping up her *Reisfleisch*, a paella-like dish with red paprika, pork and rice, and Xandi telling his mum how good it was. She would enjoy showing off her cooking skill, which had been denied her at the boy's birth when it had been allotted to Richard Dufft's mother.

Before Brunner reached the white steam cloud, it vanished with the speed of its eruption. Wearing an air of grave importance, he struck a pipe with his wrench, listened to create the impression that the pitch of the clangs conveyed to his ears the cause of the disorder and cursed the boiler plant. He slouched back.

"Take number sixty-seven. You are behind Frau Anzendrech."

He led the way. After a few strides down the gangway he turned, let Brigitte pass him, and took the tin bath from Gusti, making certain that his fingertips brushed against her breasts. He completed the journey to tub number sixty-seven carrying Gusti's dirty washing, followed by a wave of commotion at this unprecedented act of chivalry. The women thrust their fists into their hips, or smirked, or just gaped.

Lutschi Fritzer on tub sixty-nine muttered to herself, "If I was in her shoes, I'd be strapping on a chastity belt."

The story of Lutschi's escapade was still alive in Milk and Cocoa Block gossip. Lutschi, barely out of her teens, flaunting heavy rings on her fingers and gilded chains over her neck, which, it was rumoured, were presents from Jewish Morgenthau, owner of the cheap jewellery-cum-toy-cum-sweet shop where she worked, had been surprised in the boiler room with her attire in disarray and her chains on the floor. She had asserted that her disconcerted state arose purely from a hurried quest for the supervisor because hot water had refused to cease pouring into her trough of smalls. When investigation failed to reveal neither flood nor even a trickle from the erring tap, the women likened her story to the fairy-tales she enjoyed telling children of Xandi's age when they flocked to the shop buying a groschen worth of sugar fish.

The Wild Party

Spagola's vests and Berti's socks and Poldi's bloomers tumbled into tub number sixty-seven. In no time Gusti's rhythmic body movements merged into the mass motion of the washhouse. She briefly questioned the wisdom of having revealed her private affairs to Xandi's mother but her neighbour of the Meldemannstrasse had always played the role of confidante. The repetitious labour brought on mental drowsiness. The tale told to Frau Anzendrech reverberated in her mind and the past opened out in front of her daydreaming eyes.

Here am I, at the Heiligenstadt Party, the last note of my song fades away. Antonius weaves his way to the table I stand on. He pulls me down, catches me in his arms, kisses me with open mouth. Two hot hands separate us. Richard's words pitched at Antonius: "You're stoned. Fanni is your fiancée!"

After the party, at Richard's house, the two officers' place bets on who would out-drink the other. By midnight Richard splutters that Antonius is in no state to leave the house and must stay the night. I garble too, until table and chairs and walls blur into a shapeless mass.

In the morning I lie in bed, Mother stands at the door.

"I feel sick," I murmur from my crumpled pillow.

"A fine mess you left last night."

"I don't remember."

"That's what Herr Richard's saying. He remembers nothing. Only the empty bottles tell the tale. When you getting up?"

A few days later Richard's father announces that Leutnant Antonius Freiherr has fallen at the front. Frau Dufft moves about wiping her eyes, but I know she is glad that the bullet spared her son. And so am I.

Six weeks later I'm pregnant.

"Who's the father?" asks mother.

"I don't know."

"You don't know. You don't know? How many men...."

"No one. I have never. Honestly I have never."

"How do you think the sap got into you? By a dart shot into your arse?" Mother turns to Frau Dufft: "It happened at that party."

"No." I am emphatic.

"Then where and when and who?"

In confusion and hopelessness I shrug my shoulders.

"It couldn't have been my son," Frau Dufft proclaims, "his lacerations, you know. But I passed Leutnant Freiherr's room during the night he stayed with us. May God have mercy on his soul. The door stood wide open. His bed was empty."

"I remember nothing of that night," I whimper.

Mother gives me a withering look. Later in the day the kitchen maid recalls having heard a noise in the early hours of that morning, and when investigating, she says, she came across Leutnant Freiherr on the stairs.

After ten months Frau Dufft insists that baby Poldi, myself and mother move into the Meldemannstrasse tenement block, to ease Richard's homecoming. But my childhood companion doesn't stay long before packing his bags for Heidelberg.

"There should be a law banning attractive ladies from menial toil," the man in khaki overalls said softly into her ears. "A mouthful of Nussdorfer wine restores vitality to all parts of the body. I have a bottle in the boiler room."

Brunner received no reply. This did not trouble him. Many washdays lay ahead.

CHAPTER THREE (1929)

The Aryan Purity Of White-robed Damsels

Heinrich Hildebrandt, a German Nazi, felt his pounding heart drive hot blood into the gash across his left cheek, so that it coloured purple-pink and looked newly inflicted.

But the skin had been torn open some years earlier, not by an adversary's sword, as neither his fencing skill nor his courage had ever attained duelling standards, but by the spike of a barbed wire fence when fleeing from pursuing dogs in a Rhineland country estate to which he had aspired to deliver political literature. He held his disfigurement in high esteem and permitted his *Kameraden,* his buddies, to interpret it as originating from honourable combat; such scars on German faces symbolised virility, valour and all things elite, and they were afforded the same respect that men of subtler nations delegated to their old school ties.

His vigorous heartbeat lengthened and shortened the shadow cast by the leather strap over his brown-shirted chest. Young men sat close together, their elbows touching. The pressure against their muscles fluctuated with the rhythm of their monosyllabic chants.

"Sieg heil! Sieg heil! Sieg heil! Sieg heil! Sieg heil! Sieg heil! Sieg heil!"

The speaker raised his hand, and the racket subsided. "The desecration of race is the original sin," he bellowed, striking the pulpit in time with his utterances. "The Jew is like a bedbug. You can't appeal to its better nature not to suck our blood. The only way is to crush the bedbug. Destiny is on our side. The future belongs to the National Socialist Movement. We model ourselves on Alexander the Great who conquered the world. Versailles must be annulled. German Austria must return to the Great German mother country."

"Sieg heil! Sieg heil! Sieg heil! Sieg heil! Sieg heil! Sieg heil! Sieg heil!"

Heinrich Hildebrandt threw back his head. He saw an hallucination of hazy white edifices, peopled with erect, blond, female forms in flowing white robes, all of which symbolised Aryan purity; and he saw himself, like Alexander the Great, leading columns of stern men in brown shirts marching in a straight line towards the vision, and nothing man-made or God-made left standing in their advance.

The Valhalla Hero

Heinrich Hildebrandt sat opposite his thickset, balding mentor in the garden of a *Gasthof,* an inn, near Düsseldorf. The blemished face bore the sun in its eyes, which blinked continuously; the older head savoured reassuring warmth on its hairless patch. Two half-empty beer jugs shimmered golden. They shifted their gaze along the quiet street, which meandered towards the River Rhein. A sensation of expectancy engulfed them.

"I was looking through a Vienna newspaper this morning," said the balding man, "picking out examples of political decadence, when my eyes fell on an ordinary news item. It said a gang of boys in a field got caught in a thunderstorm. They revelled in the downpour, but the youngest, a four-year old, who'd brought his train set along and didn't want it to get wet, ran into an empty hut. He stayed in it for a while, playing with his railway, before re-joining the others, and a fraction of a second after he had stepped outside, a lightning bolt struck the hut and turned it into an inferno."

"An act of providence," commented the younger man.

"What struck *me* was the boy's name: Alexander Anzendrech. Often a name and providence coalesce, like a conductor and an orchestra. Alexander, leader and defender of men. Alexander the Great. Alexander Anzendrech, born under a protecting star, smacks of a Valhalla hero of alabaster skin pliant to the touch, destined to elude disasters." The older man paused to wallow in his thoughts of gargantuan depth. "Take your name: Hildebrandt. *Ur-deutsch,* arch-German. Trace it back to your forefathers, will you not find men shining like beacons building the Reich. Am I right?"

Hildebrandt savoured the flattering words. "There is," he replied, "at least no question of my Aryan descent."

The older man acknowledged the jest with a short laugh. "The name Hildebrandt suggests to me a trail stacked with dedication, single-mindedness, achievement, leading to high office and privilege. You're a lucky man."

He leant back and inclined his head in the manner of a guru

suffering his disciple to glimpse the splendour of his own stature. He was *Gruppenführer* Smaliz, a high-ranking officer in the SA stormtroopers, the Nazi paramilitary organisation. He was also an elevated functionary in the NSDAP, the Nazi Party. He had left his uniform hanging in the wardrobe.

Hildebrandt, on the other hand, had raised the farewell tête-à-tête to an occasion demanding a clean and meticulously ironed brown shirt with highly polished accoutrements. He absorbed the analysis of his character and future career with the attitude of one chosen by a Higher Order to perform ordained works. He lifted his saucepan-shaped cap so that unfettered air could ventilate his brain. His scar twitched. He divined his destiny to be shaping deeds for the Great Cause, culminating, as his vision proclaimed, in leading stern men in brown-shirted uniforms marching in a straight line towards the blond, white-robed damsels of his oft-seen hallucination in remote, white, misty edifices, and nothing man-made or God-made left standing in their advance.

That he might be worshipping false gods did not occur to him.

The high-ranking Party official resumed his theme. "Take the name Hitler. Here is simplicity incarnate. Yet within this simplicity resides power, sanctity, vision, understanding, knowledge, leadership, heroism, statesmanship."

The aspiring younger man felt uneasy lest some vital attribute had been omitted from the omnipotence of the Führer. He relaxed as his mentor pontificated further: "Hitler embodies everything. One cannot improve on it."

"*Sieg heil,*" said Hildebrandt.

"Your departure to Vienna is part of our scheme to build a powerful Third Reich, to which the world will pay homage. Austria belongs in the Reich. The *Anschluss,* the annexation, is only a question of time. I have lived in Vienna, and so has the Führer. The saddest part of his life was spent there. His formative years, one might say. Perhaps that experience, like going through fire, is necessary for the development of a majestic personality."

"*Sieg Heil.*"

"Yes, I know Vienna," Smaliz went on. "The city was chronically diseased before 1914, and neither the war, nor the years since the demise of the Austrian Empire have seen a cure. You will find the modish streets crammed with Hebrew commerce. The whole of Vienna is rotten, like a huge rotting plum tree generating rotten, over-ripe plums. Slavs, Czechs, Serbs, Poles, Bolsheviks, socialists, clerics, liberals, communists, Jews, and always Jews parade there openly and vie with each other for attention. Public and civic administrations, newspapers, the schools, the theatres, the *Kaffeehäuser* teem with them. Even the parks and the wooded hills offer no escape."

"Preposterous," murmured Hildebrandt.

"The city needs a thorough cleansing, and providence is placing you in this dung heap so you may play a leading role in its purification. Wherever you can hit a Jew, go to it. If he has money, take it off him. Use your own initiative. Our boys here in Düsseldorf tipped lorry loads of slag and other dross, looks like coal but has the calorific value of black ice, into a Jewish coal merchant's yard. That coal merchant is no longer in business. But the path of destiny is not always straightforward. The signposts need bending into the right direction."

"Into the Führer's direction."

"Correct. As he writes in his book *Mein Kampf:* 'We believe in strength, power and force. Like a woman, who does not respond emotionally to abstract reasoning but prefers to bow to one strong arm rather than herself to dominate weaklings, so the mass of the people are drawn to a decisive leader and to a doctrine tolerating no other beside itself, rather than to a petitioner granting liberalistic freedoms.'"

"Heil Hitler."

"Put it this way: the Führer sets the goals; we the leaders, serving Hitler, lay the tracks. The populace travel on trains towards the goals. In place of windows we provide screens onto which we project the real truths of their glorious journey. But we the leaders are privileged to see the terrain. We look around; we find something we fancy. You understand?"

Hildebrandt felt that he understood as befitted a man in the throes of destiny to become a leader. *"Ein Volk, ein Reich, ein Führer,* One People, One Nation, One Leader."

"And one Party. And one Party line. A disciplined *Volk* is a victorious *Volk*. Let's say our Valhalla Hero Alexander Anzendrech plays with his railway set. He loves to see his train following twists and turns. He delights in the discipline of the line. He joins the Hitler Youth when Vienna is ours. He appreciates the discipline of the Movement, vows obedience to the Führer. He becomes a man, a soldier, marches through hell for the glory of the victorious Reich."

"Even unto death."

"Even unto death. But our Valhalla hero enjoys the protection of destiny. He will learn to turn every victory and every setback to our advantage. That is the meaning of destiny. Klug und Krapf are situated on the Franz-Josef-Kai?"

Hildebrandt removed papers from his leather satchel, and read out, "Commencement of duties: first July nineteen hundred and twenty-nine. Klug und Krapf, Heating and Ventilating Engineers GmbH, Sales Office, Vienna 1B, Franz-Josef-Kai."

"A good location. The Franz-Josef-Kai borders the fashionable Inner City, and lies on the Danube Canal. Visitors often mistake this waterway for the real Danube, but it is just a narrow creek. We want you to focus chiefly on the area between this arm and the main river. From your office you have, within walking distance or a short tram ride, first of all the Leopoldstadt, the Jewish ghetto."

The high Nazi functionary snorted like a leaking lavatory cistern at the very thought of this affront to the purity of Aryan blood. He went on: "Breathing there is an impediment. To the north of this and separated by railway yards and the Augarten Park lies the Brigittenau, a working class district, where the Marxist City Council have erected extensive housing and packed them with communists, trade unionists and red banner wavers. They must be winkled out or brought into our fold and instilled with hatred of the Jewish-Bolshevik-Capitalist conspiracy who betrayed our triumphant armies. They must be taught to yearn for Austria's union with Germany."

"Sieg heil!"

"The young Führer lived in the Brigittenau," Smaliz babbled on, "in the Meldemannstrasse. You will have the good fortune to pay homage to his erstwhile abode. And to the south you have the Prater Amusement Park with its Chinaman Kalafati Carousel and the Giant Wheel, the *Riesenrad*. The Viennese are fond of their Giant Wheel. They are a sentimental lot. Politically they are divided between the Jewish-led Social Democrats with their paramilitaries the *Schutzbund*;

and the papal-led, clerical Christian Socials with their troops the *Heimwehr*. These two factions model themselves on our SA. Laughable, but they do shoot at each other, and we encourage this. It can start a riot, as happened when their Ministry of Justice burnt down."

"Good fires serve us well."

"A judiciously placed bomb, a Jewish Marxist Schutzbund member removed, a Heimwehr office ransacked, one side blames the other, we step in and reap the benefit. We'll put you in contact with our leading members; we have key men in the transport and printing businesses. They will be useful when you need to move men or material, or when there is a call for counterfeit documents. Keep a low profile vis-à-vis the present government until it is removed. Our supporters are yet confused. Indecisions are Viennese hallmarks. Your task is to liaise with us, to steer the Vienna Party towards the Führer's goals, to dispatch dissidents. A *Parteigenosse*, a party member, who does not accept in mind, body and soul unreservedly the leadership of Adolf Hitler is a traitor."

"Heil Hitler!"

"You will find enemies and spies within our ranks associating with Jews and non-Aryans. They must be dealt with, that is, they must be obliterated. Always remember the Jewish threat to the German Reich, for, as in the Führer's words: the Jew is like a bedbug that sucks our blood. It sucks our blood today, it will suck our blood tomorrow. It is of no avail to appeal to the better nature of the bedbug. The only course is to crush it. We are raising you to SA Officer *Obersturmführer*. You'll be eleventh in ranking of twenty, and you will report to me, to me only. With a name like Hildebrandt you will not disappoint me."

Smaliz struck his knee, a signal that the meeting was drawing to a close. "I mentioned the Augarten," he added with elongated lips to impart pleasantries to the ending of the conference. "It is a walled-in parkland of some considerable size, and a paradise for lovers, especially in the wilder, wooded areas. And Viennese young boys, and girls, are not to be sneered at."

After wishing each other success in their respective, mapped-out destinies, the newly promoted SA officer rose, placed his cap on his head, and executed an exemplary Heil Hitler salute. He did so with

38

the perfection acquired by a virtuoso committed to repetitive practice, so that the shooting out of his arm, the clicking of his heels, and the voicing of the 't' in Hitler synchronised to a nanosecond.

The older man raised his arm in slow, controlled motion and said, "Hitler."

Hildebrandt flinched at this exhibition of laxity. Searching for a reason, he convinced himself that whilst men of lower rank were required to enunciate "Heil Hitler" in clear diction at the risk of ruthless castigation, men near the top were privileged to utter "Hitler" only, since as leaders they laid the track and saw the terrain and appreciated the high philosophy which the word Hitler by itself embraced totally. As if to underline the veracity of this analysis, Smaliz's hands gripped Hildebrandt's midriff and shook it in a gesture which meant to say, "We understand each other, *Parteigenosse.*"

CHAPTER FOUR (1930)

To the Soup, to the Soup

Aunt Rosa, Brigitte's second sister, believed that misadventure came in clusters of three.

She said when one calamity happened, it was pointless trying to stave off the other two, for they would come, the truth of it borne out by weight of experience. Brigitte listened to the accounts of triple woes, of how her sister had been unable to man the market stall for two weeks due to having gone down with influenza, of how Uncle Toni had been sent home from his casual labouring work, and how Mizzi, Rosa's cat, had slid along an icy patch against an oncoming bicycle with painful consequences for animal and rider, all three adversities following one another during the snows of the previous winter. Brigitte felt compelled to slip a bottle of milk in addition to the usual flour and sugar into Rimowski's meagre shopping basket.

The frequency of Aunt Rosa's visits to the Anzendrechs fluctuated with the depths of her business crises. Next time round, she narrated how two days without selling a sepia had culminated in a stack of twelve falling into the street mire; how Uncle Toni, who now helped along at the stall, and Herr Schreiber had clashed over the removal of a dead rat found in the narrow gangway between their booths; and how she herself had missed a winning lottery number by one, the three mishaps taking place during the course of one week. Uncle Hans, also a frequent visitor to the Anzendrech household, remarked, not for the first time, that the single greatest misfortune besetting Aunt Rosa lay in the nature of her trade.

"The housewives from the dwellings near the Hannover Square Market," he said, "are out shopping for potatoes and spinach. They are unlikely to be buying crimped-edged postcards of Vienna scenes in sepia, simply to send greetings to their loved ones left behind at home."

Why not, he went on to suggest, change the merchandise to the more viable commodity of salamis?

To which Aunt Rosa retorted that hers was the only fancy notepaper-cum-sepia postcard outlet in the whole market, and thus enjoyed a monopoly. Her life-long know-how, she reminded everyone, rested in lively stationeries and not in dead meats, thank you very much. And by the way, yesterday she had dropped ten groschen onto the pavement and it had rolled away through the grating of a drain cover. Then, when dismantling the booth, the support pole had tipped over and hit her in the thigh, and to top it all, Uncle Toni had left two eggs, which had already been paid for, on the dairy counter, only to find on his return that they had gone.

One afternoon Rudolf, having finished his tramway shift early, dozed on a white- painted chair. Aunt Rosa came visiting and soon she was in full swing: she had overslept that morning, Uncle Toni cut himself nastily when shaving, and the milk boiled over, all within the span of one hour. This was augmented by more proof of bad luck's bias towards the number three: running after a tram and failing to catch it, splashing through a puddle in the process, and at the same time shaking Toni's *Mohnstrudel,* into a mohncrumble.

Rudolf, roused by her narration, said, "Rosa, look. You can walk from here to Klosterneuburg and you will pass a lot of lampposts. Now let's say you take several paint pots with you. You can paint the first three lampposts red, the next three blue, the next three green, and so on. You would have sets of three. The lampposts would be in sets of three. But if the fancy takes you, you can paint the first four red, the next four blue, the next four green, and so on. You would have sets of four. Or you can choose to paint them in sets of two. There's plenty of bad luck about, and there are many lamp- posts. But neither bad luck nor the colour of lampposts fall naturally into sets of three. It depends on how you paint them. Do you see?"

To which Aunt Rosa replied that walking from here to Klosterneuburg was not her scene, at any rate not during the day when her rightful place was behind sepias and note-papers, and furthermore not at night either, on account of standing at the Hannover Square market all day swelled her legs. And even if she were to undertake the expedition during the hours of darkness she wouldn't be able to *see* because many lampposts were broken and didn't light up.

Alexander, now aged five, had lived long enough to learn that whatever affected his elders, affected him also. If, for instance, swallowing large quantities of water on top of large quantities of cherries gave brother Rudi a bellyache, a similar diet did not spare his stomach. So if misfortune visited Aunt Rosa in groups of three, he feared it would pay its respects to him in the same numerical quantity, especially so in the presence of the doctrine's chief disciple herself.

Aunt Rosa called on Brigitte on a warm, sunny Sunday morning in April of 1930, just before the river reached high water, and she let herself be persuaded to come along together with Aunt Anna's family, the Jarabeks, on the first outing of the year to their very-own-wee-little-place on the Danube Meadow, the long stretch of grassland hugging the river. The procession consisted of Brigitte underneath an enormous rucksack, Aunt Anna and Uncle Hans Jarabek burdened with hefty backpacks, Rudi strapped into a home-made bag in size proportional to his shoulder width, Pauli carrying a large, open can of sweet apple compote, Xandi, and cousins Robert and Big Xandi. Big Xandi was so called not because of his excessive height, but because of a need to resolve an identity problem vis-à-vis Brigitte's youngest, who in the presence of his cousins assumed the name of Little Xandi.

Rudi and Big Xandi began tossing the to-the-soup, to-the-soup rubber ball to each other on the pedestrian walkway of the Northrailway Bridge. Steel railings guarded against bulky articles falling into the river, but were totally inadequate against small, loose ones, and especially against small, loose, flying objects. Little Xandi expressed alarm. Brigitte told Rudi to heed his brother's apprehension. Rudi replied that they were throwing the ball very gently and were taking great care in keeping it to the confines of the pedestrian walk.

Little Xandi cried out: "Mammi, our to-the-soup, to-the-soup ball's going to fall in the Danube!"

Robert, as oldest, felt called upon to shield Little Xandi from mental as well as physical distress. He grabbed hold of his brother's right hand. Big Xandi threw the ball with his left. It was a poor throw. Rudi jerked his foot out to impede the low flight past him. The sudden movement brought him into collision with Pauli, who stumbled sideways. The can of sweet apple compote struck the iron railing and left his fist. It toppled over on the pavement, and the drink dissipated to cool the asphalt of the Northrailway Bridge pedestrian walkway: to Little Xandi, a disaster.

Their very-own-wee-little-place consisted of a slightly raised hump half way between the Northrailway Bridge and the Floridsdorf Bridge, close to the rebuilt refreshment hut and the river bank. Its location below the point where the Floridsdorf sewer emptied putrid sewage into the Danube meant fewer people and more space for ball games. As the spot came within sight, they saw a young man sitting on it.

At this time of year the Danube reflected clear, blue skies and so lived up to its waltz reputation. All creation relished the joys of living, cynics marvelled at the wonder of a dandelion, friendship and love were hosts, people everywhere took advantage of the German linguistic trick of hooking a simple syllable onto the ends of words to infuse an endearing quality to all manner of things, animate and inanimate.

There is no English equivalent for this; the nearest is in infant talk, when dog becomes doggy and doll, dolly, or in words like booklet or wavelet, the ending signifying diminution. The Vienna dialect is particularly adaptable to this mode of expression. No native of the city would ever call his favourite, frequented spot on the Danube Meadow anything other than my *Platzerl,* my very-own-wee-little-place. People became passionately attached to their very-own-wee-little-places. And since visitors to the Danube Meadow within the vicinity of the bridges, colloquially known as *Zwischenbrücken,* Twixtbridges, were mostly regulars from the Milk and Cocoa Housing Blocks, they had sorted out their very-own-wee-little-places long ago, and few infringements occurred. If the rare, alien occupation chanced to happen, a few words like "Now look here, you're sitting on our very-own-wee-little-place, perhaps you wouldn't mind moving along a wee-little-step" usually sufficed. The unwitting intruder understood, observed the unwritten law, and moved on.

The present situation differed in that the trespasser squatted on the Anzendrech-Jarabek's very-own-wee-little-place in full knowledge of their claim. He knew them and they knew him. He was Herr Marschalek, who, with Frau Marschalek, owned the revamped refreshment hut, and with whom the blossoming of a neighbourly bond had been frustrated. Uncle Hans had purchased a pickled gherkin, and after biting one end off, had discovered mildew on it. Frau Marschalek had refused replacement or refund, insisting that the offending refreshment had originated from a source other than her display of pristine victuals. The resulting strained relationship ended in outright hostility when Frau Marschalek was heard to blame Alexander Anzendrech for the hut's reduction to charred timbers by lightning. The logic of her reasoning being suspect, she justified it to her regular customers by darkly hinting that werewolves were born, not made.

Now, seeing them coming, Herr Marschalek had deposited himself on their patch with mischievous intent. Little Xandi sensed this heralded the second blow in the trilogy of gloom.

Uncle Hans began choosing amicable words to enlighten the intruder of the error of his ways. Instead of moving on, Herr Marschalek became obstinately uncooperative.

"Will you shift please," said Uncle Hans, his pleasant words ebbing away.

"You must be joking," said Herr Marschalek.

"The Meadow's big. Sit yourself elsewhere on it. This is our very-own-wee-little-place."

"That's right. The Meadow is big. Which stimulates my curiosity beyond endurance to discover the reason for your motivation in molesting me."

"You are sitting on our very-own-wee-little-place!" Uncle Hans said with rising heat.

"I was here first."

"We've always been sitting here. We've been sitting here when you were still shitting in your nappies!"

"You've bought the place?" replied Herr Marschalek, keeping remarkably cool. "If you've bought the place, perhaps you've got the deeds to it, in which case I'd be pleased to examine the documents, on account of seeing is believing!"

He lay back, placed his arms under his neck and blinked into the sun.

"Go and move your arse elsewhere," shouted Uncle Hans in vexation.

"Tell you what: you lick mine."

If duelling had been the order of the day, Uncle Hans would have challenged the refreshment hut fellow to a fight to the finish. As it was, he called on Aunt Anna and Brigitte to bring over the rucksacks.

He pulled blankets from the voluminous interiors, and signalled to the boys to spread them out around the uninvited guest. They dropped their gear and themselves onto them. Aunt Anna and Brigitte commenced disrobing into their bathing apparel according to time-honoured Danube Meadow routine. The women were ill at ease, but at the same time ready to endure the trial, since they felt right was on their side. Herr Marschalek sat up and finding himself in the centre of this activity, bore a look of bewilderment mingled with contempt.

Next in the families' timetable was feeding. To raise the situation onto a more civilised tableau, Aunt Rosa, who knew little of the refreshment hut dispute, offered the encircled man a slice of *Schmalzbrot.*

"You know what you can do with that!" Herr Marschalek's responded belligerently.

"What?" demanded Uncle Hans.

"You can rub the *schmalz* on your backsides against sunburn. And she can smear it into her ample cleavage. To say the least, it'll improve the perfume all round."

Uncle Hans' lower lip quivered. Just then Frau Marschalek appeared by the side of the refreshment hut and hollered: "Franzl!"

The families realised this heralded the solution to the rapidly deteriorating impasse. But Herr Marschalek remained motionless so as to impress upon them he would not retreat at the first easy opportunity.

"Franz Marschalek!"

"What do you want?" he yelled back.

"We need fresh water."

"In case of fire?"

"With the werewolf around, yeah. And for drinking."

"Fetch it yourself."

"You out of your mind? I'm needed here to look after the trade. It's time you moved your idle buttocks, you lazy bastard."

The man rose, feigned reluctance and departed.

The third upheaval loomed when Uncle Hans, to placate the lingering ill humour, said, "Come on, to the soup, to the soup."

His words stirred Little Xandi to a high pitch of excitement. Even Robert's comment that he had seen the Skeleton, the mounted policeman, on duty, did little to allay it. The game's preparation, utensils and rules were simple: an easily recognisable mark on the meadow, achieved by pulling out a tuft of grass, served as the soup pot. A small rubber ball represented the dumpling. The players crowded round the soup pot with outstretched hands hovering over it and the dumpling. One player, the caller, stood a little way off, and recited the following rhyme:

"*Zur Suppm, zur Suppm, die Knedln san hass,*
Sie siedn, sie kochn, sie lossn an Schass.
To the soup, to the soup, the dumplings are starting
To simmer, to boil, and now they're farting."

Upon completion of this verse, and after a suitably dramatic pause to build up tension, he called out a name, at which everybody dispersed with explosive speed, except the one thus called, who reached for the ball and hurled it at any receding target of his choice. A hit meant that the person struck became the new caller; a miss meant a repetition without change.

The Skeleton set spurs to his horse from a point obscured by the refreshment hut, and the Marschaleks withheld warnings of his approach. So the mounted policeman pulled up unexpectedly.

"What might you be doing?" The query, emanating from a robot face attached to a body clad in uniform and set high on a horse, should have, by tradition, inspired trembling in swimwear-attired laymen.

Uncle Hans replied. "We are playing to the soup, to the soup, the dumplings are starting to simmer, to boil, and now they're farting."

The horse pranced a few steps to one side, and the Skeleton unhurriedly brought it back under control. "Playing ball games on Inundation Land is against the law."

Rudi, who had acquired a reputation for quick repartee, answered, "It's not really a ball game. According to the poem, it should be played with a dumpling. Only we don't have a dumpling."

The Skeleton caused his steed to rise on its rear legs and neigh.

"Are you being funny?"

"Oh no," Rudi replied, "we learned about the origin of the game in school. It dates back to our pagan forefathers. The soup pot represents a sacred burial ground, and the dumpling the entrails of a sacrifice. Our ancestors believed anyone coming into contact with the animal guts would die an agonising death. The farting is symbolic of their groans."

"Are you taking the mickey?"

Rudi kept a straight face: "It's from pre-Roman history. Our headmaster told us to practise the ancient games as part of our curriculum."

The policeman's confidence was giving way; the boy spoke with authority on the subject. "You can't play a ball game on the Danube Meadow," he snarled.

"Actually," Rudi went on, "we usually play it with an old rag knotted together. Coming over the Northrailway Bridge, my young brother, Little Xandi, stepped into a pile of soft dog's muck. We had to unknot the rag and clean him up. We threw the rag into the Danube because it stank. That's why, this time, we played the game with a ball."

"Ball games are forbidden on the Danube Meadow!"

"Are we allowed to play it with a dumpling?"

The Skeleton, towering above them on his high seat, could not determine whether Rudi poked fun at him or not. He noted names and addresses of the offenders, turned his horse towards the smallest and said, "You know what we do to little boys who break the law."

He rode off with the rubber ball, leaving Little Xandi duly frightened at what policemen planned to do to him.

The Skeleton

"You peel the skin off him and you see nothing but bare bones," said Big Xandi.

The words explaining the rationale behind the Skeleton's name was the reason why Little Xandi dreamt the following night that, equipped with Mummy's potato peeler, he sneaked up on the dreaded policeman chained to a "No Ball Games" sign. But before any experimental wee-little scraping off the incapacitated cheeks could be carried out, the policeman broke loose, used the signpost as a giant hobby-horse and galloped after Little Xandi, flourishing an enormous potato peeler. The little boy claimed that the wet sheets upon sudden waking were due to excessive perspiration.

The Skeleton patrolled the Danube Meadow on horseback in the summer, and the Zwischenbrücken district on foot during other seasons and when surplus river water swirled over the Meadow. The yearly flooding of this man-made strip of land, some fifteen kilometres long, was the sole reason for its existence. The stretch of the Hubertus Dam prevented the inundation of low-lying Floridsdorf. Green grass provided feed for cattle and recreational space for people, creating ideal opportunities for kicking balls about. This, of course, motivated the city authorities to erect notice boards stipulating "No Ball Games" on particularly flat stretches and near the stairways to the bridges. They deployed mounted police to ensure observance. However, this deterred no one, because the moment people sighted the equestrian, they signalled warnings to neighbours, and awareness of the policeman's approach travelled half a kilometre ahead of him.

The Skeleton outshone all other uniformed men in enforcing this decree. His orders were to stop ball games, and orders were orders. To outmanoeuvre the Danubian early warning system, he frequently dismounted and, hidden from view behind his horse, led the animal by the reins so that it appeared to be innocently grazing, swung himself into the saddle, galloped into the midst of the offenders, scattered them into all directions and went for the ball. He would pursue any fugitive, who, through lack of presence of mind or experience, had chosen an escape route leading nowhere except to the open expanse of the meadow. Having caught up with him, the upholder of law ceremoniously wrote his name and address in a black notebook, and trotted off to distant parts, there to straighten his uniform, force the point of his bayonet through the ball, and discard the flabby shell. In spite of his cunning, he remained unaware of transgressors reviving his murdered booty. Even the sight of a bright red patch on grubby rubber skin did not deflect his routine.

Normal measures against a Skeleton surprise attack saw hardened ball players race to the stairways leading up to a bridge. The bridge afforded asylum as the horse could not tackle the granite steps, and the policeman could not leave his horse. The Skeleton's idiosyncrasy required lingering below some while so as not to lose face, whilst the uprooted teams engaged in sending down verbal scurrility, along with fluid abuse from mouths and lower parts of their anatomies.

Six weeks had elapsed since the to-the-soup incident, the Danube Meadow resembled a quagmire after lying under floodwater for a month, and the Skeleton had yet to remount his horse. One day during Whitsun the Anzendrech boys, their cousins and Berti Spagola crawled through the tear in the wire barrier surrounding the Danube Coke Yards. Beyond this opening a narrow gap between the fence and a stack of semi-rotting timber boards allowed their thin and agile bodies to wriggle to the top of the pile. Crouching low, they could spy through the chink of a small, frosted, partly open glass window into the company's building. The boys waited to glimpse the appearance of a body covered in floral fabric, then arm movements followed by a lowering torso; and after a period of stillness, in reverse order, a rising torso followed by arm movements, and hearing the gurgling of rushing water.

After witnessing what they had come to see, the boys departed and headed for the derelict buildings along the Handelskai, there to set up headquarters in the remnants of a workman's hut and to think up what to do for the rest of the day. They found a rival gang already installed, and as its members were numerous and looked wild, the boys did not challenge their title to the hut. Instead they amused themselves at hurling debris lying on the ground at debris standing up. They aimed at broken glass stuck in corners of broken windows.

Some way off, the rival gang followed their example. A little later, a chunk of cement fell at Pauli's feet. Cousin Robert decided to call it a stray. But when another, and then another came whizzing over, no doubt remained that the missiles had been deliberately pitched. Robert pushed Little Xandi behind a mound of earth, the others returned shot for shot. As the gang advanced, the weaponry grew in size according to an instinctive distance-weight ratio. The skirmish proceeded without speech until a member from the aggressive camp called out:

"Skeleton!"

Robert and Rudi hauled Little Xandi from his hiding place and both attackers and attacked fled, knowing that mutual destruction, or merely instigating bleeding shins, contravened the law. Little Xandi hared away, fearful what the law would do to him if caught.

The Anzendrech-Jarabek contingent ran past the boiler tube dump into the Children's Free Open Air Lido on the far side of the

Floridsdorf Bridge, and as their clothing consisted of swimming trunks and singlets only, they quickly mingled with the noisy multitude in the basin. Relying on safety in numbers, they watched the Skeleton engage in earnest conference with a white-attired attendant. The policeman repeatedly glanced at the huge Lido clock, and finally walked away.

"If I were you, I'd keep out of his sight," the attendant warned the boys as they approached the exit cautiously. "He's after your guts."

"Who?" asked Pauli.

"Who? The Skeleton. You're lucky he didn't fish for you in the pool. He was in a hurry."

The boys decided not to venture far from the security of the swimming pool. They headed to the nearest place of interest, the waste ground overgrown with thistles and nettles, upon which an assortment of obsolete boiler tubes of diverse lengths and circumferences had been laid to rest. The larger tubes offered shelter from wet weather and isolation from unwanted spectators and were also the source of many discoveries. They had come across a white comb, a chocolate bar complete with wrapping, the brown stains along the edges of the silver paper pointing to a history of alternating liquefaction and solidification, and once they had found a two groschen piece. On this occasion streetwise Robert and Big Xandi spotted a thin, oblong, sock-like sleeve, which set them off giggling.

Pauli, balancing on the narrow bit of an oval shaped pipe, showed Little Xandi how to waggle his toes to feel the red powdered rust trickle through. Rudi, Robert and Big Xandi tugged at a man-high barrel so it began to roll towards remnants of corrugated fencing. Berti wandered off along a railway track hidden under vegetation until he reached a set of points. He heaved at the lever.

"I can't shift it," he cried, "it's stuck."

The other boys hurried over. The combined muscle power of the three eldest matched the resistance of the dried up pivots, and they watched as the pair of long, gradually thinning rail ends flipped over.

A shrill hiss. They looked up. A locomotive, its whistle blowing, filled the entrance to a scrap metal yard. The boys pulled at the lever in reverse. In vain. The rusty steel spars remained lodged where they had come to rest. The engine advanced.

Robert yelled out, "Stand back!"

Stunned, the youngsters hid in the green, uncurbed growth of weeds.

The slowly rotating wheels drove the locomotive into the boiler tube sanctuary. There they locked. The mighty mass shuddered to a standstill. The engine driver climbed down from his cabin. He gazed at the colossus standing on the uncanny rails. A workman rushed across from the scrap metal yard. Both men stared at the points, looked about for an explanation. Their eyes fell on fragments of heads obscured by wild vegetation.

The boys fled. But Berti reacted slowly. The workman caught him and held him. The others stopped some way off and surveyed the situation. Berti in captivity was not a good omen. Berti lacked the expertise of wriggling out of predicaments; he did not possess Rudi's quick wit and language. The older boys thought it would be in everybody's interest to go back. One behind the other in descending order of age, first Robert, then Rudi, then Big Xandi, then Pauli, then Little Xandi, they returned to the scene of their misdemeanour, where Berti sobbed once between every three breaths.

"You cripples!" the workman shouted at them. "What the hell d'you think you were playing at?"

"We didn't know the loco was coming. We were going to put the points back," mumbled Robert.

"You could have caused a major accident! You know that!"

"That's why we came back," said Rudi, "to see what damage has been done."

"I'm arresting you. The lot of you. It's a criminal offence to tamper with railway installations."

Rudi said, "Is that wise?"

"Is that wise? Is what wise? Are you a wise guy? I'll show you what's wise!"

"I mean is it wise to allow public access to railway installations?"

"You can ask the Skeleton your wise questions. I'm taking you to the Engerthstrasse Police Station."

"Is it wise for the Railway Authorities to forego issuing instructions to engine drivers to the effect that they must examine all points that are open to public access, to see that they are correctly set, immediately before a locomotive rolls over them?" asked Rudi.

The silence that followed boosted his boldness. "The Skeleton would be interested to hear of a case of negligence."

"I shall see that your teachers know of this," the workman said a little less ferociously, whilst the engine driver walked back to his cabin.

"We've been learning in school about what constitutes negligence, and how the law deals with such negligence."

"Let's have your names and addresses," demanded the workman. He released his captive. Berti trotted over to his friends' side.

"Surely," said Rudi. "Perhaps you'll give us your name and address also and the engine driver's to make sure there hasn't been a case of negligence."

The workman glared at the boys and retraced his steps to the scrap metal yard. The locomotive followed him slowly.

The boys could not bring themselves to celebrate their victory; the tension had sapped their emotions. They looked for a quiet venue for recovery from the shock.

A Car on the Handelskai

"I know. The Northwestrailway Bridge," said Pauli.

"Trains don't to go over it no more," said Berti, "it'll collapse, it's that weak."

"The pier, dimwit. The top of the pier. Nobody'll see us there. The Skeleton won't find us there."

They tramped one kilometre along the deserted, pot-holed upper end of the Handelskai to their chosen place of tranquillity. The recesses between the rectangular granite blocks were just wide enough to fit the bare toes of boys. Helping hands from brothers and cousins hauled Little Xandi to the top where crisscrossing steel and round pipes abounded. They sniffed sharp smells, and gazed upon grey bird droppings speckled along the maze of girders. Big Xandi crawled away along a bulky duct. He vanished from view. Contrary to Berti's assertion, a train thundered overhead, rocking their hold and showering them with droplets and grit.

"I hope Big Xandi manages to hold on okay."

He did. He reappeared, grimy, grinning at having been where no one had been before. He said he had crept over the railway marshalling yards, saw the shunting trains below, pushed on as far as the Danube and had looked down on the eddying brown river bubbling like boiling chocolate between the quay and the wide-bellied coal barges moored to it.

Little Xandi wished he could have been party to such sights.

Robert made a sudden hand movement to his lips, then pointed downwards. "He's looking for us," he whispered.

The Skeleton stood below on the street. He turned his head from side to side as if indeed in search of lawbreakers. In the distance a black dot grew larger. A motorcar travelling on this portion of the Handelskai seemed to the boys an event as rare as an ice floe floating down the Danube in July. But a motor car it was. It stopped alongside the Skeleton. A door opened and the policeman stepped in. The car drove off in the direction of Nussdorf.

"He's seen us!"

"He can't get up here like we can. He's too gawky."

"He's gone to collect crampons and an alpenstock."

Apprehensive that the Skeleton might indeed be planning to return reinforced for an assault on the pier, Robert suggested retreating to the still partly waterlogged Danube Meadow.

"Good idea," said Rudi. "He won't follow us there. He'll get stuck in the mud like a praying mantis in a mishmash of hymn books."

"Very clever," said Robert, "you didn't think that up yourself."

"Like an ant in an elephant's arse," from Big Xandi to prove Jarabek's parity in metaphoric invention.

"Like a bedbug sucking Frau Czarnikow's blue varicose veins," from Pauli.

Little Xandi couldn't stop shaking with laugher at this.

"Listen," said Rudi, "or like us in a motor boat. You know the ferry past Nussdorf just before the Leopoldsberg."

"Yeah?"

Rudi then pieced together the framework of a tale designed to secure a free passage: Father worked as conductor on the Jedlesee tramway. The terminus was situated a little way beyond the Hubertus Dam in direct line with the Danube Meadow ferry stage. They had been sent by Mother to await Father's arrival there to tell him that this evening's chess tournament had been moved from the Wirtshaus *Zur Weintraube* near their home in the Engerthstrasse to the Kaffeehaus *Am Spitz* in Floridsdorf. Father was playing for the Vienna

Tramway Men; the opposition consisted of music students from Berlin. To secure victory necessitated Father's participation. The time interval between the cessation of his work and the commencement of the contest allowed one tram journey across the Danube. Travelling to the Weintraube and back again to the Kaffeehaus Am Spitz would mean late arrival and disqualification. They had intended to reach Jedlesee via the Northwestrailway Bridge, but as everybody knew, it was in poor repair. Half way over the Danube they had been stopped by missing planks making up the timber walkway. Mother had expressly forbidden crossing such dangerous paving especially in company with Little Xandi, who could not swim. A detour back over the Floridsdorf Bridge would have added extra kilometres and the legs of the youngest would have crumbled under the strain. To drive home this point Little Xandi was to squat on Robert's shoulders during the recital.

The ferryman, a supporter of the Vienna football club *Rapid,* understood the need of winning, notably when poised against a team from the capital of the other German-speaking nation. He had no option but to allow the youngsters' access to his boat.

Sauntering along the path to Jedlesee empty stomachs signalled that the day had advanced, and that a fair distance separated them from their meal pots. Just then Big Xandi spied a weird, open receptacle enmeshed in shrubbery.

"It's a pram," cried Pauli.

"It's got no wheels," said Berti.

"They'll be washed up somewhere near Budapest," said Robert. "Jump in, Xandi."

They removed wet earth from its interior and pushed it along the thick grass with Little Xandi lolling inside. It slid along like a sledge on snow.

"It'll whistle down the dam a treat," asserted Pauli.

"I'm first. I saw it first," said Big Xandi.

"Now, now, we'll take turns. Oldest one first."

When at last it came to Little Xandi's go, Robert ran alongside, ready to pull him out in the event of the contraption hitting a high resistance zone. Then Rudi queried the effect on speed if, according to the theory of frictional pressure relative to area of contact, the perambulator's bottom touched intermittently the corners of the nearby stone steps on its downward journey.

"It'll go slower because the edges dig in," said Robert.

"No. There's only narrow bits of granite wanting to stop it."

"Let's try it then."

"Somebody must be inside, it's got to have the right weight."

Big Xandi volunteered. He elected to stand in it. A slow start gave way to rapid acceleration, and when the thing turned sideways and began to display erratic pulsations, he jumped out, continued to race down whilst the perambulator careered after him, bouncing from step to step. Not expecting the impact on his calves, he lost balance, stumbled, fell, scrambled to his feet and held his hands against a reddening forehead.

When at last homeward bound, Little Xandi's outstretched hand pointed to a wireless set in a cracked wooden housing, with knobs, and tangles of wire. It lay embedded in clay near the river's edge. Berti ousted it and bent over the high water to cleanse it.

"You let it go, butterfingers!" Big Xandi called out.

"It wouldn't have worked anyway."

"Daddy can make it work," cried Little Xandi.

Stones hurled into the eddies beyond the floating gadget in the hope that the ripples would steer it to the shore proved of no avail. So Big Xandi stripped off his tee shirt, dived in and retrieved it, and washed away the dried blood from his face.

An eerie emptiness confronted them as they entered the Milk Block. The concrete platform in the middle of the courtyard lay void of shrieking children. The chess tables gaped at them from vacant space. The boards seating card players hovered parallel above ground in the absence of hefty behinds. Only Frau Bitmann sat on the step to Staircase 10. She focussed on the boys before they reached her spot, her toothless gums performing chewing motions. As they passed, she raised her face so that the remaining light falling on her withered skin revealed a patchwork of black lines, which reminded Little Xandi of the cracks in the sun-baked mud on the higher ground of the Danube Meadow.

"Your folks waiting for you up number thirteen," she said.

"Where *is* everybody?"

"Eating their supper, I wager. What have you done to your head?" She asked Big Xandi.

"Fell over, on the Danube Meadow."

"Children drown on the Danube Meadow when it's under flood."

"Flood's finished," said Robert.

"Children drown. And the Municipality pays for the funerals. Councillor Herr Dufft'll tell you that's right."

"True," observed Herr Dufft walking up from Staircase 13. "Last year, no fewer than three." Turning to the children he said: "Your mothers are very worried. Hurry, show you're still alive."

"Folks waiting for you up number thirteen."

The Anzendrech's unlucky address had never bothered any member of the family. But the bewitched number voiced by the witch-like mouth carried an ominous ring, and the boys decided to stay together, and together face the storm.

Herr Dufft caught up with them. "Here," he said producing a bag of eucalyptus candy and checking it contained enough to go round, "to sweeten the pill."

Rudi rang the bell. Surprisingly Frau Spagola opened the door. She separated her son from his friends and delivered him a resounding slap on his cheek.

Waiting in the kitchen stood Brigitte, Aunt Anna, Uncle Hans and Frau Rosenfinger, all looking very solemn.

"What time d'you think it is?" asked Aunt Anna.

"Another half hour and we would have been on our way to the police station to tell the Skeleton to look for you."

Big Xandi pointed to the wireless set, anticipating mitigation at the sight of the trophy. Brigitte took it from Pauli's hands and placed it into a box earmarked for household waste.

"You were supposed to be back home by one o'clock," Frau Spagola scolded Berti. "We were supposed to visit your uncle Simon. Poldi cried her eyes out because we couldn't go."

"No supper for any of you," Uncle Hans announced.

The bigger boys counted on their ability to survive a hungry evening on a eucalyptus sweet; Little Xandi counted on Mummy's inability to see it through.

CHAPTER FIVE (1931)

Heil Schicklgruber

Impatiently Smaliz raised his voice. "If people follow what they're taught in churches, target the priests. And you know, a Reverend Father found in bed with the local butcher makes good propaganda and brings converts to the Movement. Simple. What of the police?"

Hildebrandt moved the mouthpiece closer to his lips to make sure his reply reached his mentor loud and clear. "Coming over to our side in droves."

"You know, the cost of the Nussdorf convention ..."

"We laid on cars and taxis. We collected men on duty. We registered one hundred and one recruits. Unofficially because Austrian law..."

"Schools?"

"We're organising symposiums for teachers."

"Good, excellent. Concentrate on the boys. The Valhalla Heroes. Like that Alexander what's-his-name. Remember? Anzendrech. They're our future. The press?"

Hildebrandt's reply came a fraction late. His hesitation convinced Smaliz that a fault line ran through Vienna's newspapers. "Run by Jews, we know. Eliminate Jewish editors and reporters. You achieve that, we move forward, H-H."

Silence. Hildebrandt hung up, vexed because he didn't know whether the parting "H-H" had been an amiable shortening of his own name or an abbreviated "Heil Hitler", which, at the end of tapped telephone conversations, was a safe way to express homage to the Führer within politically hostile Austria.

He looked out of the window. The tramway rails made a sharp bend after the bridge, then curved away into the terminus loop. Shrieking streetcar wheels grated on his temples, aggravating his irritation, inflaming it yet more by the three-arrow emblems of the Social Democrats fluttering on the trams below. The sight of the decrepit paddle steamer *Budapest* wheezing in the narrow Danube Canal, her once-white paint flaking of to reveal brown, rusting metal, was almost the last straw. Naturally, the vessel belonged to the

Jewish Danube Coke Company. There could be one end for such eyesores, he thought, and pictured her disintegrating at the bottom of the river.

As Smaliz had said, this city was a dung heap. Take yesterday: an Aryan collides with a grey-bearded Hebrew wearing a caftan. The Aryan shouts, "Out of my way, Yid," pushes the Israelite into the gutter and, believe it or not, walks into Isaak Grünspan's Delicatessen and purchases a pickled herring!

And as Smaliz had warned, even National Socialists showed laxity and no respect for discipline, like the party member, *Parteigenosse* Brunner from the Municipal Laundry, running propaganda at the Party's Brigittenau Branch. This man must be brought into line.

The telephone rang. He lifted the receiver. A voice said, "Heil Schicklgruber."

Hildebrandt held the earpiece whilst his scar metamorphosed into the colour of an erupting volcano. He replaced the receiver, banged his desk, missed a brown, oval insect that had strayed from a neighbouring apartment, and said aloud to the bedbug, "Time will come when such callers will be traced, will be placed into institutions where telephones are not on the list of amenities."

He had heard of the Schicklgruber saga. Some busybody journalists, Jews, nosing around and spreading the story that Hitler's pater was a born Schicklgruber.

He told his secretary that he would be away for the rest of the day. When stepping out into the street, he decided that a cup of hot Vienna coffee would calm his ruffled nerves before setting off on the long-planned pilgrimage. He entered the Kaffeehaus Adler and aimed for his familiar table in an alcove. A tram conductor sat there. Groups of men clustering around other tables stared at chessboards.

He saw the tram conductor sifting through a newspaper held in a polished cane frame. Hildebrandt had learnt that this Viennese innovation enabled easier page turning, and clearer display. The frames hung from their coiled handles on a piece of furniture something like a coat stand, and the overall effect resembled a modern-day interpretation of a Christmas tree.

Hildebrandt walked up to the newspaper fount. It was completely stripped. Then he saw a spare copy lying on the table in the alcove.

He pointed to the paper. "Excuse me, are you reading this? May

I?"

"Please do," replied the conductor. "I guess by your accent you are from Frankfurt, no?"

"From Düsseldorf. I went to school in Frankfurt," said Hildebrandt.

"I travelled to Frankfurt as a baker's journey-man," explained the tramway man.

Hildebrandt's eyes searched for an empty table without success.

"Sit with me," offered the tramway conductor, his eyes fixed briefly on Hildebrandt's scar. "I'm on duty shortly. I come in here during a break."

Hildebrandt sat down and introduced himself. "Heinrich Hildebrandt."

"Rudolf Anzendrech."

"No! Not the father of the Valhalla Hero?"

"Excuse me?"

"Alexander Anzendrech, a four-year-old, miraculously escaped being struck by lightning?"

Rudolf smiled as he recalled the incident. "In the refreshment hut. On the Danube Meadow a couple of years ago. It was in the papers. Xandi, my youngest, was heart-broken over his lost railway set from my American friends. Brand new it was."

The waiter brought a large cup of coffee on a silver tray. "Your usual, sir?" He indicated the steaming refreshment, *"Eeine Mélange."*

Hildebrandt took it and said to Rudolf, "Anzendrech is a truly Nordic name." He placed a finger on his newspaper and continued, "I see they are setting up soup kitchens in New York. Your American friends, are they standing in line also?"

"It's the depression: over there, over here. How long will it last?"

"It won't last long in Germany once Adolf Hitler takes control. But it's playing havoc in the USA, the so-called land of the free!"

Rudolf said, "People *are* free over there. What I like most about America is that everybody is a mister there. No dukes, no barons, no titles of any sort. Everybody is free and has a chance."

"A chance to starve, whilst Jews are getting fatter, and Negroes breed like rats?"

The tram conductor reacted with surprise to the racist slur, but dismissed it as stemming from ignorance. "Americans are generous people. And do you know who I found the most obliging? The black

59

community. I tell you, I never felt threatened in Harlem, I never heard an insulting word there."

"You don't say. You've been to New York?"

Rudolf looked at the scarred face; it needed enlightenment. "Let me tell you how I came to the New World. After Frankfurt, I had spent a year with bakers in Hamburg and I felt it was time to cross the ocean. I didn't have the money for the passage, so I signed on as a ship's baker. When we docked in New York I aimed to leave the ship, but walking off with a suitcase would have looked suspicious."

"You wanted to join your American friends?"

"I didn't have any at the time. I put on everything I possessed: four shirts, five pairs of socks, umpteen underpants, three pairs of trousers, two jackets, an overcoat; and I waddled down the waterfront out of sight like an overcooked *Zwetschkenknödl,* a prune dumpling".

"Zwetschke is not a Germanic word. Why do Viennese insist on bastardising the German language?"

Ignoring the interjection, Rudolf and went on, "You know the crazy luck I had? I stood in the busy street, underneath all that gear, not knowing a word of English apart from how-do-you-do, with a few dollars in my outermost trouser pocket. People dashed by, the roadway teemed with automobiles, horses, trams. I heard German words spoken, two men and a girl passing me, speaking German."

"In ten years German will be spoken all over the world."

"I hurried after them. 'Excuse me,' I said, and explained my plight, how I worked on the ship, how I walked off with all my belongings hanging on me, how I didn't know a soul, how I didn't know what to do, where to go, and could they suggest something. The girl, a pretty young thing she was, looked at me, and her eyes grew bigger and bigger the longer I spoke. One of the men said, 'What's your trade, mister?' So I said, 'I'm a baker.' The man turns to his mate and says, 'D'you hear that? He's a baker.' And the other slaps his hand on his buttocks, tells me they are bakers and in a spot of trouble because their man quit an hour ago, and if I was agreeable could I help them out straight away, and I could stay with them until I found a place."

Rudolf laughed at the memory, and Hildebrandt said, "German comradeship. A true German always helps another German."

"They showed me the ovens, the dough was inside, growing by

the minute, and needed to be taken out, and there was I, stripping off coat after coat in the heat, and the owners rushing in and out, fearful their bread would get ruined, shouting in desperation each time: 'What, another shirt? God Almighty, not another pair of trousers!'" Rudolf laughed again. "That's how it was then, in America."

"Now the German Reich hails us."

"I remained with the bakers for four years, got on with them like a house on fire. Could have married Gretl, the daughter, become a partner. And what do I do, silly fool that I am? I hear the Kaiser's pardon for the draft dodgers, I get a bout of homesickness for the Wiener Prater, and I buy a ticket for the whole stretch. I tell Gretl I'll be back soon, but no sooner had I arrived in Vienna than the war breaks out, and I'm stoking the ovens of the field bakeries for another four years."

"And Gretl?" Hildebrandt could not resist the question.

"She met someone else. Four years is a long time to wait. But we stayed friends. They're Americans and the most generous people I've ever known."

"They're true Germans."

"Yes. Originally they came from Leipzig. They asked me to the wedding. I didn't go. I heard it was a grandiose affair. There wasn't room for everybody in the synagogue."

"She married a Jew?"

"They were Jews, all of them. Bride and bridegroom, and the rest."

Hildebrandt looked aghast: "Jews are not Germans."

"I know many German Jews, contradicted Rudolf, irritated by his listener's repetitious innuendo. He pointed to the middle of his newspaper. "The man who made up this joke is Jewish; one side of his family comes from Germany."

Hildebrandt pulled the paper towards him; his eyes skimmed over the passage:

DUFFT'S COMMENT OF THE DAY

The Changing scene in politics:

First citizen: 'Once a Jew, always a Jew.'

Second citizen: 'Once known by a name, always known by that name.'

Third citizen: 'Heil Schicklgruber.'

Fourth citizen: 'Heil Stalin.'

Rudolf expected his companion to show amusement, but instead he saw twitching cheeks and the scar turning blue. Perhaps the German who'd gone to school in Frankfurt hadn't been in Vienna long enough to appreciate the native humour. He explained, "Stalin rolls more easily over the tongue than Schicklgruber, never mind their respective politics."

Hildebrandt made a mental note of the journalist's name. "A joke is funniest when it backfires on the joker," he said dryly. "Do you know this Dufft?"

"I know of him." Rudolf recalled Brigitte's words never to get involved in politics with strangers. She had spoken of fanatics beating people up if disagreeing with their views. He said, "Everybody knows of him."

"Let me tell you this: Adolf Hitler is the keenest thinker the world has known, and commands respect from every German. I do not tolerate abuse directed at him. Can you show me the way to the Meldemannstrasse?"

"The Meldemannstrasse? We used to live in the Meldemannstrasse." The words slipped out before he could stop himself.

Hildebrandt's face brightened. "What a coincidence. Or is it providence?"

Rudolf wanted to disengage himself from his new acquaintance but his natural desire to help prevailed. "Come with me. Tram thirty-one takes you there."

Hildebrandt's Pilgrimage

Hildebrandt took measured steps along the broken surface of the Meldemannstrasse towards the outline of the distant gasometer. The still air, the absence of any form of life, the hazy sunrays, the knowledge that he walked on hallowed ground, compacted into a narcotic aura, and sent him into a semi-conscious trance. The tickling sensation inside the back of his head assured him that fate propelled him along.

He discovered he was heading in the wrong direction, but this did not dispel the sanctity of the moment. He turned and eventually came to a halt in front of Number 27, a tall structure in better repair than neighbouring buildings. The black rectangle of the open entrance contrasted with the obliquely sun-lit facade. Gazing into the dark interior, knowing that here had beaten the heart of the Führer, his Führer, heightened the inebriation. He shut his eyes. On this spot it was the right thing to do: to abandon the mind to free meditation, to imagine the young Hitler battling to survive in the wilderness, like another figure had done elsewhere two thousand years earlier propounding another but outmoded doctrine, but who still commanded a huge following now ripe for mobilising into the Greater Cause. He recalled Smaliz' words, that men of stature needed to be hardened by fire. The vision of himself leading stern-faced, brown-shirted men in a straight line through burning debris towards the blond, white-robed damsels in the misty, white edifices returned. Yes, here was destiny.

"Are you all right, mister?"

He opened his eyes and saw a slightly tanned young woman in her early twenties, dressed in white, standing in front of him. The girl repeated her concern: "D' you feel all right?"

Hildebrandt forced himself out of the stupor. "A great man used to walk through this doorway."

The girl laughed unashamedly. "Great men walking through here? You must be a comedian. Of all the men coming and going through this hostel none would qualify to a title beyond that of total insignificance, except perhaps my own father."

"Your father?" In spite of having regained self-control, his voice faltered. "What's your name, Fräulein?'

"My name? Everybody here knows my name. I'm Vikki Huber."

It could not be. One of the white-robed damsel of his vision? His daughter? No. Fate? "What did you say your name was?"

"Why, Vikki Huber." The girl laughed again. She felt drawn to this odd character with the dashing scar on his cheek speaking in the strange accent.

The drops of perspiration on Hildebrandt's forehead cooled down. He had misheard. Her name was not Schicklgruber. It was Vikki Huber. Yet destiny *played* a part here: a near miss, but to score a near miss the aim must have been at the target.

"You look as if you could do with a pick-me-up," said Vikki.

Hildebrandt studied her more closely. White-robed she was, and pretty, very pretty, but not of blond hair. A blacker hue could not be imagined. Another near miss.

"I live just up the road on the other side of the Marchfeldstrasse. I have some cognac at home." Her anxiety about his wellbeing was genuine, although the possibility of a new client did not escape her. He showed no sign of moving from the spot, so she urged, "There's nothing to see here."

His gaze shifted from the girl back to the sombre entrance. "I sense his presence. His former presence. I tell you, momentous happenings are taking place, right here and now."

Vikki stared at him in incomprehension.

"I met a man who resided in this street," he enunciated solemnly.

Was he a nut case?

"A tram conductor ..."

"So?"

"His name is Anzendrech, father of a Valhalla Hero."

"He lived on our stairs," She exclaimed. I see him now and again punching my ticket on the number thirty-one."

"Destiny. His young son, you know him too?"

"Which one? Alexander? He was still a baby when they moved out."

"The street has a powerful pull. Do you feel it? The Führer's personality lingers on, reverberates between the houses. Today's events are fusing together with prophetic significance. That toddler Alexander was born under a benign star. He's got the gift, the gift of survival. His father too is exceptional."

"Herr Anzendrech exceptional?" The girl chuckled. "Yes, he's exceptional. He's the only man I know who had a crush on me but never made a pass at me."

"He lived in this historic street. He flaunts his Aryan name Anzendrech, yet he favours Jews and Negroes."

"We all have our quirks," Vikki said ironically. "Take the Council. They said they'll demolish these houses and put up an extension to the Engels Block and make it larger than the Karl Marx Block. But here I am, still living in the ramshackle old place. I do think you need a revitaliser from whatever's upset you."

"I tell you this, Miss Huber, there comes a day not far ahead when these housing blocks you mentioned will have different names!"

"Are you a fortune teller too? We can read each other's hands!" She started to walk, and so did he.

She pushed her arm through his, as a token of lending physical support, not as a sign that she would not object to him making a pass at her. She had matured. Years of fortune telling had taught her much about women, and everything about men. Clients wanted to hear about their fortunes in love, a few were obsessed with their professions. Strangely these career zealots usually became infatuated with her. The phenomenon presented an occupational hazard, but it assured continuity of income. She did not fear the male gender; although she knew that some men would go for her if given half a chance. So she exercised care to give only a quarter. They aspired to touch her skin, and holding hands was part of the service. They reached for her arm, her shoulders or neck after the second or third session, but there it stopped. She had the power to predict the future, and who was to say, also the power to influence it. She could tell men what they liked to hear, and she could divulge what they did not want to listen to. Some believed she was able to put a curse on people.

Therefore she had nothing to fear.

Hildebrandt's Tutorial

Hands dived into pockets and emerged with small boxes in whose velvet, purple interiors reposed, like miniature corpses, silver swastikas on long pins.

Obersturmführer Hildebrandt, guest speaker and emissary from the German Mother Party, here to inspire political awareness, entered. Hildebrandt's swastika was minute, smaller than anyone else's. Although never written or decreed, it was understood that the size of the badge was symbolic, in inverse proportion, to the eminence of its wearer.

Arms shot out, heels clicked, and voices ejaculated in unison. "Heil Hitler!"

Hildebrandt raised his arm in a relaxed, controlled motion and replied, "Hitler," very much in the manner he had observed Smaliz do.

He viewed the assembled Austro-Germans of the Brigittenau Branch with satisfaction. He was the only Germ-German in the gathering, and his chest filled with the glow of self-importance. His gaze came to rest upon the lapel of Parteigenosse Brunner from the Engerthstrasse Laundry, responsible for propaganda. This man had displayed, on Hildebrandt's first appearance, a yet smaller swastika.

"You!" Hildebrandt had accosted Brunner. "Do you not feel obliged to conform to wearing the insignia of our Movement?"

"Very much so," Bruner had replied, pushing his hand under his lapel, and thrusting it forward towards the scar on the visitor's face.

"I, and the citizens of Vienna to be won over to our Movement, are not in the habit of carrying magnifying glasses."

"Action is what counts."

"Precisely. The first action of the lower ranks of our Movement is to display badges that can be seen."

The Obersturmführer had felt Brunner's resentment hitting back like a rock, but discipline had to be established.

Now Hildebrandt's face muscles tensed, which caused a slight curvature in his cheeks and gave the impression that his scar was grinning. But he was not amused. Brunner wore a replacement emblem of elephantine proportions.

Brunner, for his part, did not take kindly to being categorised of lower rank. Responsibility for propaganda was an important post. Content only when in control of people, like over his laundry women, he had quickly gained a leading position in the Party branch. It was early days yet, politics had a long way to go, but he viewed the scarred face from Germany with begrudging distaste, which, after subsequent encounters, grew into downright hatred.

Hildebrandt's tutorial hovered around the National Socialist Party's doctrine of Jewish-Bolshevik-Capitalist global conspiracy as the cause of Austro-German post-war wretchedness. "Every defeat, every setback, every crisis is engineered by Jews, the mortal threat to the Reich. As the Führer puts it: the Jew is like a bed bug, the bedbug sucks our blood today, it sucks our blood tomorrow. It is of no avail to appeal to its better nature. The only solution is to crush the bedbug."

"Sieg heil! Sieg heil! Sieg heil! Sieg heil! Sieg heil! Sieg heil! Sieg heil!"

"We must burn out the Jewish plague, which is operating in the Marxist Schutzbund, and is evident in the collusion of Hebrew finance in the clerical Heimwehr. We must Aryanise the newspapers. The treaty of Versailles must be annulled. German Austria must return to the great German Mother Country."

"Sieg heil! Sieg heil! Sieg heil! Sieg heil! Sieg heil! Sieg heil! Sieg heil!"

Hildebrandt raised his hand to calm the frenzy. "Jews, Gypsies, Slavs, Poles, natives from the trees in the Congo ..." he paused to gauge the effect of his gift for jocular utterance and was duly rewarded by raucous guffaws, "... are inferior. Aryan culture, Aryan history, Aryan philosophy, Aryan words, Aryan names, Aryan art, Aryan science are the highest achievements of the human race."

Brunner approved the words of the German speaker, but was irked at the same time because he held he was amply qualified to deliver them himself, and better.

"We National Socialists have an unshakable faith in the superiority of the Germanic Aryan race. We do not degrade our blood with that of lesser species, and we deal pitilessly with Aryans who do."

"Sieg heil!" Brunner's solitary shout reverberated through the meeting.

The Obersturmführer nodded at the laundry man to show appreciation where it was due. "As Adolf Hitler writes in *Mein Kampf.* We believe in strength, power and force. Like a woman, who does not respond emotionally to abstract reasoning but longs for decisive force, who prefers to bow to one strong arm rather than to dominate weaklings herself ..."

Here, the laundry man's concentration drifted as words of a woman's preferences reached his ears.

"...so the mass of the people are drawn to a decisive leader and to a doctrine tolerating no other beside itself, rather than to a petitioner granting liberalistic freedoms. Our slogan is: One People, One Nation, One Leader. We pledge our unreserved loyalty and obedience unto death to our Führer, Adolf Hitler."

"Sieg heil! Sieg heil! Sieg heil! Sieg heil! Sieg heil! Sieg heil! Sieg heil!"

Like men under hypnosis imagining a pile of rotting potato peels to represent haut cuisine, they absorbed this verbal garbage as if it was an invigorating, all-embracing, life-giving elixir. They identified with the strong, powerful, superior Aryan Germanics. The unfamiliar vowel sounds from the speaker's mouth brought on a surge of pride on being favoured to hear the elitist accent.

The exception was the man from the Engerthstrasse Laundry. He savoured other things as, with his eyes closed, the women in his life, all fully Aryans, pranced by: the widow Schurmbard, the sisters Rabotski, Frau Kleingeld, Lutschi Fritzer, Brigitte Anzendrech - wait, she's holding out. She scorned him. He'll get her through her little treasures. Her youngest, Alexander. She'll open her legs if it means saving the brat. For the moment, there's this new one, this fresh one. In his fantasy his fingers, again and again, undid the suspender belt of blond-haired, wide eyed, freckled faced Gusti Spagola, drawing it out from under her long skirt and discarding it, his hand returning, again and again, slipping underneath elastic....

"Parteigenosse Brunner!" Hildebrandt had finished his educational dissertation and had walked up to the propaganda chief. "You carry a far-away look. Are you dreaming of our glorious future? Our task as yet is to deal with the present."

Brunner gazed at the guest speaker with cold eyes.

"Our task," Hildebrandt went on, "is to rouse the Aryan masses, so they hit out at Jewish treachery. Jews in Germany have been claiming to be Germans. Not for much longer. Any liaison between Aryans and non-Aryans must be stamped out."

"I don't know which crime is worse," replied Brunner coldly, "a Jew screwing an Aryan or an Aryan having it off with a Jew. Both should carry the death penalty."

"The Führer is preparing the way along that route in Berlin. Let us do our bit to prepare the way for the Führer here in Vienna. Run a campaign on that score, leaflets and so on, and at the same time attack Jewish newspapers. Your main target will be ..."

"I know what to do," said Brunner.

"...the neighbourhood between the Danube and Danube Canal, Brigittenau, Zwischenbrücken. The police in these areas are increasingly sympathetic to our cause. Concentrate on the municipal housing blocks."

"The men in the municipal housing blocks are Reds. We have

distributed leaflets there. A few knocks on the heads will bring them to their senses quicker. The coke heaps in my laundry are perfect hiding places for explosives."

"That too is on the agenda. Who is the fuel supplier for your boiler plant?"

"We get the coke from the Danube depot. The Danube Coke Company depot."

"We know it. The head office is in Regensburg. It's run by Hebrews. What's more, Reibeisen, their man managing the Vienna business, has been actively campaigning against us. Change to an Aryan business."

Brunner shook his head. "The Municipality do the buying. And the Council are in the hands of the Schutzbund, and the Schutzbund lick the Jews' arses. They need to be brought to their senses with a bang."

"Who's stopping you? What about the quality of the fuel? Hm?"

"What about it? Coke's coke," said Brunner, "some days it burns better, sometimes it's worse. Depends on the weather!"

"Have you never heard of contamination? Foreign non-combustible material mixed into it. We National Socialists use our initiative. Our boys in Düsseldorf tipped lorry loads of slag and other dross, looks like coal but has the calorific value of black ice, into a Jewish coal merchant's yard. That Jewish coal merchant is no longer in business."

"Such an operation needs organising and it needs money."

"Our job is to generate enthusiasm and to raise finance. Both are achieved if conviction and will are there. We use our power. You know, laxity is the problem with the Austrian attitude towards politics."

Brunner took exception to the admonition. He stood for power, wielding it, less so yielding to it. A flicker of nationalistic resentment was contained from flaring into a conflagration by the knowledge that Hitler himself had sprung from Austrian soil, and by the expectation that one day, he, Brunner, would be sporting a smaller swastika than this German scar-face.

"You Austrians," Hildebrandt said, "should study the habits of German leaders and German discipline. This will expose flaws and weaknesses in your approach."

Studying the habits of you, Obersturmführer, could expose a few flaws in your approach, Brunner thought, but he said: "We have our own way of doing things."

"I received good news today. My company, Klug und Krapf, has been selected by the City Authorities to service the civic boiler plants. The Engerthstrasse laundry is on the list. This means that you and I will be able to meet inconspicuously, and this will give me ample opportunities to pass on to you at close quarters our strategies relating to propaganda and other matters. You are a lucky fellow, Brunner."

Maybe I am, reflected the laundry man, mindful of the ample opportunities this would give him to study at close quarters this Obersturmführer and his habits.

Hildebrandt's Secret

Heinrich Hildebrandt clung to the doctrine that Jews, Gypsies, Slavs and descendants of anyone other than the Aryan race were inferior, and that because of this they needed to be despised, dehumanised, hounded, persecuted, abused, dispossessed, done away with.

Yet in spite of his superior Aryan station stemming from his superior Aryan name, he, like anyone from any ancestry, Jews, Gypsies, Slavs, etc, etc, ate, drank, farted, defecated, urinated, slept, felt pain when pinched, and became slave to nature's drive for propagation, that is, being heterosexual, fell for a person of the opposite sex. Fate decreed, with habitual irony, that for him the chosen one was Vikki Huber. At the end of their first encounter, he wanted to see her again in spite of her bronze complexion and alien, black hair. After each visit his longing escalated until desire reached dizzy heights. Vikki, however, restricted physical contact to professional holding of hands and stroking of palms. She would not allow him to air his feelings, so he gave vent to the dream in his mind and to the fluid in his body at the first opportunity when privately closeted. His passion for the girl and the nature of his relief constituted his secret.

He endured weeks of eyeballing the tantalising bulges behind her white blouse. He fantasised the light brown skin underneath violet transparent fabric transmuting into pink circles with the hard centres pressing against silk, there to be touched, first lightly with the tip of his smallest finger, then stroked, then gently pressed, then the shoulder strap lowered and his lips at the pliable, red, cylindrical excrescences. He took to wearing two pairs of underpants lest his vision became too vivid and he lost control whilst she played with his palm, read his past, his present except his innermost secret, and his future.

Her insight was phenomenal. She saw in his hands past successes and setbacks in his professional and ethereal pursuits. She prophesied a period of triumph interrupted by a black, personal disaster. True to her words, orders for steam plants in electricity generating stations and contracts for servicing boilers in laundries filled his filing cabinet. At the same time, his glowing reports to Smaliz attested that his craving to banging desks in political frustration had waned.

Then the dark prophecy reared its ugly head.

It happened on a day earmarked for one of his regular expeditions to the Meldemannstrasse. The morning began satisfactorily enough. From the window of the 31 tram he saw streets strewn with leaflets bearing the message:

JEWS OUT. HITLER FOR AUSTRIA. JEWISH NEWSPAPERS TELL JEWISH LIES.

And Jewish shop windows were smeared with the caption: PERISH THE JEW.

He smiled. He had primed the rumour that Parteigenosse Kristopp, also from the Engerthstrasse, would excel as chief of propaganda in the Brigittenau branch, and this had brought the wayward laundry man Brunner into line.

He approached Vikki's rooms in high spirits. Playing down the black hair and off-white exterior, he resolved to emancipate her into a white-robed damsel of his vision, reach for her breasts and declare his love.

He stood dumbfounded in front of her door, his eyes fixed on crudely daubed words:

GYPSY WHORE.

The door opened and there stood Vikki, dressed in white: beautiful, desirable, angry. "This is the work of your political hooligans. Go and order them to clean it off! They left this." She thrust into his hand a swastika made from black card some five centimetres across.

The emblem slipped from his fingers. He picked it up. A conspiracy! Traitors within the Movement collaborating with men sniffing around. Men with dribbling noses sniffing around. Like that fellow Dufft of the Schicklgruber saga. Yet …

"Are you? Are you..." he stammered and stopped.

"A whore?"

"A Gypsy?"

"What if I am? I am half-Gypsy. Who cares? You care?"

"I care..." He was going to say "I care for you" but the last two words stuck in his throat. He felt unsteady; he swayed. He found himself being pulled into her room where she sat him down and poured out a cognac.

"Let's see what the future has in store for us," he heard her saying.

His hand ceased shaking when his skin felt her touch. He noticed her anger ebb away; after all he was a well-paying client. She gazed hard at the lines in his palms, traced them with her long, sensual fingers right up to his wrist.

She leant forward so that his eyes filled the space between her neck and dipping raiment. He spied what previously his fantasy only had conjured up.

Those resilient curves. The pressure in his groin.

He heard her soft voice: "A black disaster followed by ups and downs. Ups and downs. Then a surge of success."

He reacted uncontrollably to her music of ups and downs. Then the surge. Aaah! He shivered. The wet lining of his underpants clung to his skin. He staggered to his feet; his hands trembled. He walked round the table and looked down on her. She returned his stare with steady eyes.

The beautiful, black eyes of a half-Gypsy!

My oath to the Führer, my desire for this half-breed. My destiny stands at a crossroad. I want both. I was born under a benign star like Alexander the Great, like that Valhalla Hero Alexander Anzendrech. I am a leader. With special needs. I can see the terrain. I look at something I fancy. My Führer, help me.

He marched to the door, closed it behind him. The empty anticlimax gave way to pride. *I have withstood the temptation. I have remained loyal to my Führer. I have defeated the cunning treachery of inferior blood.*

But contrary to expectations, two days later when sitting on the lavatory pan, her black eyes and black hair stormed into his brain. With them the soft-violet, transparent fabric, the lightly tanned skin transmuting into dark, pink circles and thrusting nipples.

The clash between emotion and dogma proliferated. Her image sprang into his mind, uninvited, when writing out a quotation for a boiler, when sipping coffee in the Kaffeehaus Adler, when urinating in a pissoir, when listening to light chat between his secretary and other occupants of the office building, when travelling on a tram, when speaking on the telephone to Smaliz.

He responded with intensified concentration on his Führer's tenets. He engaged in extra invective against all things non-Aryan. And he felt like swimming in seas of satisfaction when picturing what he'd do to the joker with the five-centimetre, black swastika, as fervent hope transposed into a compulsive conviction that providence, sooner or later, would drop that charlatan, that double-crossing hypocrite, be he Jew or Aryan, into his hands.

Ups and downs. When down he spent sleepless nights, went off his food, lost weight. A political fellow traveller in the medical profession diagnosed a deficiency of essential nutriments such as those found in fruit and vegetables and advised embarking on a daily intake of generous portions of greens, especially spinach.

CHAPTER SIX (1932)

Spinach

Brigitte reasoned that if nature's sunlight fortified the exterior of a child's body, so nature's produce should toughen the interior.

She cooked carrots, kale, cauliflower, cabbage, spinach, leeks, peas, beans, tomatoes, sprouts, and added, wherever practical, nourishing ingredients like milk. She then hid slices of spicy sausage or crusty pieces of pork below the surface of the mix, and battled with her boys to stop angling for the meat, gobbling it up and lingering over the rest until it got cold. Sometimes she moulded the vegetables into flattened shapes, fried them and postulated that the preparation not only looked, but also tasted like *Schnitzels.* These protestations carried little conviction; the boys scraped off the crispy outer layer, and poked about in the soft middle.

Rudi scorned all vegetables other than raw onions. And since Pauli and Xandi liked and disliked whatever the eldest brother liked and disliked, Brigitte faced a prodigious challenge. Rudi's chief vegetative aversion equated with the one heading the list for goodness. Brigitte proclaimed, rolling her eyes in ecstasy, that spinach was rich in iron. Xandi failed to understand why a base metal bore the accolade of riches when at all other times that distinction singled out gold, or why he never succeeded in digging up a nail, screw or a lump of the crude element when spreading the green mass to the rim of his plate, hoping thereby it would look less.

Rudi's biology teacher, Herr Echenblatt, who lived in the Milk Block and frequently played chess with Herr Anzendrech, believed in all-round education. He outlined the two methods of solid matter propulsion within the digestive system. Firstly, swallowing: a conscious act of muscular contractions that transported the chewed, saliva-imbued food via the taste buds from mouth to stomach. Secondly the unconscious, totally unfelt movements of the intestines, which propelled the increasingly digested, increasingly unpleasant material towards the rectum from whence, through conscious muscular exertion, it returned to the outside world.

The class resounded in boisterous uproar when the pupil

Katzenhofer, in a somewhat loud whisper, assigned the colloquial terms to the increasingly unpleasant material and its port of exit.

Rudi knew from physics lessons that, given sufficient pressure, stationary matter could be set into motion and made to overcome all manner of obstacles. He judged that swallowing represented a kind of obstacle, and he resolved to put to the test an idea designed to conquer the disagreeable taste of vegetables. He initiated Pauli into his scheme, the experiment to be carried out on the next spinach day. But when Rudi saw masses of green leaves spilling over Brigitte's shopping basket, his stomach contracted in cramp-like spasms. He stayed in bed and ate nothing whilst Brigitte administered to him the lesser torment of chamomile tea. In the meantime, the green leaves were bubbling away in the stewing pot.

"Xandi," Pauli said, contemplating his yet untouched spinach, "you don't really love me, do you?"

"I do. I do love you."

"But I tease you."

"I don't love you when you tease me."

"I'm teasing you now. You ran naked after fire engines, you ran naked after fire engines."

"That was a long time ago."

"And you still wet your bed."

"I don't"

"You do. When you dreamt the Skeleton chased you with a potato peeler. Xandi wets his be-ed, Xandi wets his be-ed."

Near to tears, Xandi cried, "I'll tell..."

"Who? You'll tell Poldi? Xandi has a girlfriend, Xandi has a girlfriend. Would you like to slap my cheek?"

"Yes."

"Well, you can."

"But you'll hit back,"

"No, I won't," reassured Pauli, acting in accordance with Rudi's instructions. "You can slap my cheek to punish me because I've teased you. As a matter of fact, you can slap both my cheeks, but you must do it at the same time. You can hit as hard as you like. I promise I won't hit back. Wait till I tell you."

Pauli spooned a great quantity of spinach into his mouth, so that his face became a balloon and resembled that of a musician about to commence the "Trumpet Voluntary".

"Mm mm mm mm mm mm mm mm mm mm," he mumbled which Xandi understood as meaning: "Now hit as hard as you can with both hands."

Xandi stood up, leant over his plate, and as hard as he could, with both hands, lashed out at Pauli's full cheeks. But contrary to Rudi's forecast that the stuff would slip down the gullet unimpeded and totally unfelt and untasted, a green stream of tepid spinach shot from Pauli's mouth and impinged on Xandi's forehead, nose, mouth and chin, settled there for a while then slowly separated and dripped onto his plate.

As Brigitte rushed from her sick boy's bedside to see to Xandi's wailing, Rudi knew that further theories and experiments were needed to tackle the spinach problem. However, the hot summer and the Danube Meadow pushed activities on that score into second place.

The Blue-rimmed, White-enamelled Tin Mugs

"I'm ready for a dip," announced Uncle Hans.

The boys set off at once. Aunt Anna responded by pulling the pink and orange striped portions of her voluminous bathing costume down to her knees, and the neckline up to her chin. Brigitte needed cajoling before yielding to the lure, primarily because leaving their belongings unattended presented complications. Covering the rucksacks and scattered clutter with blankets and rugs did not allay anxieties, and asking Frau Refreshment Hut Marschalek to keep an eye on their things had ceased to be an option. Eventually a deeply tanned don't-get-wet sun lover at his nearby very-own-wee-little-place, lying on his back with closed eyes, acquiesced to assume guardianship of their property, and Brigitte joined the bathing party.

The air quivered over the hot, yellow grass. Food debris, soggy paper pulp and brown human waste floated down the river, and increased in density to where it belched out as a thick, black concentrate just this side of the Floridsdorf Bridge. Uncle Hans remarked that its smell could flatten an unsuspecting army. But it always attracted a crowd of onlookers who defied the overpowering odour. They awaited the arrival of a swimmer, who, by mischance or unfamiliarity with the local drainage system, had missed the point of no return. He or she would fight a desperate struggle to beat the river's current, as otherwise it meant traversing the noxious fluid, or floating down in midstream two or three kilometres to allow for its dilution. And great the reward, the spectators responding with cheering, whistling and holding of noses, when an unfortunate victim had committed him- or herself, could neither gain the river's clean bank nor its middle, and was swept into the quick to emerge blackened with filth.

Further upstream the river sparkled clear. There the steep slope of the embankment ended in a level stretch of granites, on which no one lingered as its temperature approached that of a sizzling frying pan. People crossed it by sprinting on tiptoe to minimize duration and area of contact. Beyond this the stones dropped away, irregularly thrown together. Waves generated by passing steamships, and splashing from bathers, cooled these slabs to body warmth. However, progress over them presented difficulties due to the many inclined surfaces and sharp corners. Uncle Hans' keen sense of balance overcame these impediments as he skipped to the river edge carrying Little Xandi. There he immersed him three or four times, wedged him between two boulders and waited for the safe arrival of Brigitte and Aunt Anna.

Nature had deprived the two mothers of any sense of balance whatsoever. Their downward trek began with the selection of two suitably large slabs on the level portion, and they would sit on these, gradually acclimating their bottoms to the heat by alternatively rolling from one buttock to the other. The descent proper continued in this squatting position, legs in front and hands behind acting like lifting jacks raising posteriors and manoeuvering them to hopefully flat granites on which to set them down. If by misfortune no flat granites lay in their paths, there was nothing for it but to grin and bear it, as reversing in this manner on all fives was impracticable.

Once in the water, movement became easy. Brigitte and Aunt Anna turned over onto their bellies, clung with their fingernails to the edges of stones, their nostrils held above the ripples, their bodies and legs stretched out into the river, and grunted like happy alligators. Every joint and muscle could be flexed without the encumbrance of supporting weight.

"You know," Brigitte said, "ducking under the water in the Danube don't just cool you down, it's a cure for rheumatism, because Danube water contains radium, and radium is nature's element for healing. The ache in my hip's gone and I feel ten years younger."

Little Xandi took up a position between mother and aunt, and felt as secure as when hanging on to Robert's shoulders in midstream. He preferred hanging on to Robert's shoulders, but this was only possible in his mother's absence.

Uncle Hans and the four bigger boys walked up to the point where a mud-flanked inlet led to the *Zinkerbacherl,* the first of a series of lakes strung along the original riverbed, collectively known as the Old Danube. Here no boulders obstructed the way forward. They waded out into the waxing force of the current, and when no longer able to withstand its pull, they let themselves be swept away, and exclaimed to be *in den siebenten Himmel,* in seventh heaven. They commenced their fast crawl back to the bank to rendezvous with Brigitte and Aunt Anna's toes. This produced a great deal of screeching, followed by prolonged laughter, as the mothers explained that they had thought carp were nibbling at their extremities.

They returned to their very-own-wee-place to find the disposition of rucksacks and sunbather unchanged. Food and drink were laid out, followed by a hunt for four blue-rimmed, white-enamelled tin mugs. Brigitte said that she must have left them at home, but subsequent searching in all rooms failed to bring them to light.

A few days later, as they passed the refreshment hut, they saw, hanging in a row on hooks, four blue-rimmed, white-enamelled tin mugs.

The Fizzy-drink Bottle

Pauli found it.

Contention erupted over the measure of orange-pink liquid inside. Big Xandi, never one for lengthy disputation, put the bottle to his lips. Robert knocked it away.

"You great camel! It's gone bad. Look at the dirt on it."

"Hasn't gone bad."

"You can catch cancer of the stomach if you drink that!"

"Still got the fizz in it," remonstrated Big Xandi.

"Could have been poisoned." Robert poured the colourful drops onto the grass.

"There's two groschen deposit on the bottle," mused Rudi.

"We can buy a box of matches for two groschen."

"I've seen heaps of old wood on the Mistgstettn," observed Robert.

"If the Skeleton catches us..."

"He don't go on the Mistgstettn."

"A hollow brick," said Rudi, "makes a first class crucible." Knowing that Little Xandi's grasp of scientific terminology was restricted, he turned to his young brother. "You heat things in a crucible. If you heat glass in a crucible it goes soft like rubber."

"And silver goes soft like schmalz," said Big Xandi.

"And gold goes soft like butter," augmented Robert.

"And pooh goes ... what happens if we put a pooh sausage in a crucible?" asked Pauli.

The consensus ruled that the finder should be the claimant, who would then have first choice as to the nature of the substance for the crucible experiment. Pauli marched up to the refreshment hut, placed the bottle on the counter and said, "I want two groschen."

Frau Marschalek, far from happy with legions of ants radiating from it towards stacks of *Wurstsemmels*, Vienna-style bread rolls filled with cold meats, grasped the thing by its neck and bellowed, "You misbegotten son of a werewolf bitch! Scoot off before I pulp you into meat puree and spread you over the Mistgstettn for the benefit of the resident rats."

She hurled the bottle after the bolting Pauli. She missed. It fell onto grass, somersaulted, hit a rusted bucket and came to rest. Outrage gripped the boys at the injustice and violence. Furthermore, the bottle had sustained a visible crack across its cylindrical portion, so that its refund value had diminished. They accepted as pointless any attempt in recuperating the two groschen from another shop, and weighed up the implications of reporting the matter to the Skeleton. But the mounted policeman was nowhere in sight. Whilst debating the point, they stood the bottle on the aging bucket and threw stones at it until Big Xandi's direct hit spelled its end. They then realized that without an exhibit their case would make no impact on the law, and considered alternative ways to exact retribution.

They knew the refreshment hut routine: Frau Marschalek, or Herr Marschalek, or both, with Rolli, their ancient Alsatian, arrived about eleven o'clock in the morning, pushing a handcart on two bicycle wheels, piled high with chocolate wafers, pickled gherkins, lemonades, *Wurstsemmels* and *Schusterlaberls,* another type of Viennese bread roll. The route followed the path leading from the Hubertus Dam near the Floridsdorf Bridge diagonally across the meadow to the steps of the Northrailway Bridge.

Next morning the boys collected the pieces from the shattered bottle, added extra pieces from other extinct glassware, and embedded them across the path so that sharp edges pointed skywards. They then lay flat on their stomachs a safe distance away and waited for the arrival of the handcart.

The sight of a stout, middle-aged man on a bicycle caused some consternation among the boys. The fact that disinterested parties might also use the path had escaped their planning. One hissing sound followed another. The man zigzagged, leapt off and pranced around for balance. Then he squeezed the flabby tyres, looked at the barrier, saw boys in flight. He swore an oath, likening them to the deformed issue of depraved coitus, and gave chase. Had Robert's presence of mind not prevailed by gripping Little Xandi's elbow and bumping him along, the day could have had a sad ending. As it was, the man, out of breath half way to the Zinkerbacherl, recognized the futility of his attempt to catch up with the younger legs. He also realized that his bicycle, though impaired but nevertheless rideable by a passing desperado like a Mistgstettn gypsy, lay unattended or arguably abandoned, a considerable way off. He returned to the scene of willful transgression, there neutralized the barrier by kicking the glass pieces into the grass and turned his bicycle upside down on its handlebars and saddle. The boys retreated to the Floridsdorf Bridge, and watched with empathy the laborious separation of tyres from rims. They would have given assistance gladly.

Their impulse to hit back at the refreshment hut waned, and they were ready to forgive and forget.

The Flying Schusterlaberl

Rudi came up with a new game called "Driving Back the Enemy". Two sides were required to throw a suitable article, like the hardened *Schusterlaberl* they found lying near the refreshment hut, back and forth to each other. The spot where the object hit the earth became the mark for flinging it back. The party gaining ground and reaching a predetermined line, for example the Floridsdorf Bridge versus the Northrailway Bridge, declared victory. Robert and Rudi possessed the strongest arms, and were on opposite sides. Since winning was paramount, a great deal of argument as to the democratic principle of taking turns fairly ensued, and this, as well as noisy disputes over the exact points of impact, alerted Frau Marschalek. But it wasn't the noise, which caused her distress. The sight of the slowly disintegrating *Schusterlaberl*, bouncing nearer and nearer to the refreshments on display, would have given the meekest victual seller strained blood vessels.

The entire range of edibles lay vulnerable, and trade itself was threatened by potential customers comparing the flying bread roll with the baker's goods, or worse, of equating their respective ages. And when, to crown it all, the smallest boy stood himself unashamedly, legs astride, in full view of the hut, fumbled with his swimming trunks and weed in a wide arc, she could tolerate no more. She roused the drowsy Rolli, pointed to Little Xandi and urged the old Alsatian to "catch the thief," implying thereby that she had not entirely renounced ownership of the missile.

She expected that the waddling dog would scare the boy off. Uninformed of the difficulty of running while observing the call of nature, and having no inkling of the inadequacy of little boys to shut off the flow in midstream, she saw the animal dig its nose into Little Xandi's rear, and push. The result: concentrated ignominy. The boys laughed. But then it dawned upon Rudi that the dignity of a member of the family had been abused. He inspected his damaged, wet, crying brother, and solemnly declared that the act of setting Rolli on him had been a gross violation of family honour, and something needed to be done.

The Nailed-up Refreshment Hut

Although boarded up when empty to deny uninvited traders use of the counter, the refreshment hut had no lock. There was never anything left inside, and the Marschaleks realized that a lock would invite thieves to break down the door, or steal the lock. Locks with keys that didn't fit had been known to circulate on the more dubious markets.

A brief visit to the Mistgstettn equipped the boys with a selection of nails in various degrees of deformation and degradation, but still viable for rendering the refreshment hut permanently closed. With the aid of small boulders from the Danube embankment, they hammered the nails straight and drove them through the outer edge of the door into the support post.

They finished in time to see Frau Marschalek, handcart and Rolli, negotiate the steep path leading down from the dam. The boys hid in a sandpit, where Little Xandi's giggling at the anticipated pleasure of witnessing Frau Marschalek's frustrated tugging at the door had to be continuously hushed. Wholly unexpected, but in conformity with his reputation to appear when least wanted, the Skeleton emerged from underneath the Northrailway Bridge. Spying refreshments en route, he steered his horse in the direction of the hut. The boys thought it prudent once again to retreat to safer observation from the Floridsdorf Bridge.

The Skeleton's status prevented him lending physical assistance in solving Frau Marschalek's dilemma. But issuing verbal directives from his elevated position was permissible. He pointed to the specially constructed pocket on the side of the cart holding a small black trowel used for transporting undesirable accretions from the corners of the hut to the river, there to mingle with similar substances from the sewer.

"Wriggle the flat end of your *Scheiss-schaufel,* your shit shovel, under the heads of the nails. Now twist."

His advice proved workable, and Frau Marschalek eventually carried on business. On the Anzendrech-Jarabek's next visit to their very-own-wee-place the site displayed a heap of stale black shovel matter plus a fresh pile, which looked very much like having belonged to Rolli not long ago.

The boys decided that this act of vagrancy called for further reprisals.

Danube Boulders

Xandi was posted as lookout on the hump of their very-own-wee-place, whilst the bigger boys lugged boulders from the river up the embankment into the hut until sight of the floor had vanished.

"They're coming, they're coming!"

The boys hid in their favourite sandpit, their eyes glued on Frau Marschalek as she maneuvered the cart into position prior to pushing it through the door. Her hand remained on the door latch as she opened up. She looked. The ancient Alsatian looked, sniffed, entered and cocked up his leg on the nearest rock. Frau Marschalek's attempt to lift one failed. She walked to the river embankment, peered down, then up at the sky. Finally she harnessed herself to the handcart, and with refreshments and dog retraced her steps.

The boys celebrated by dancing victory rites on the stones, round about the hut, on its roof. They acted as if their adversaries had been vanquished forever, and neglected to take even the most elementary precautions against the likelihood of their return. The shower of earth clots and obscenities hurled at them by the red-faced, rapidly advancing Herr Marschalek brought them face to face with reality, and drove them to flight. They regrouped in a hollow far enough away to escape to the bridge, yet close enough to savour the sight of bulging sinews on arms and necks as the traders hauled boulder after boulder onto the cart, wheeled it to the edge of the embankment, and tipped the contents down the slope.

The following Sunday the Anzendrech and Jarabek families noticed from the bridge that a whole tribe had taken over their very-own-wee-little-place. Due to the overspill, encirclement was not an option. The prospect of dislodgement by appealing to the intruders' humanity met with zero expectation as the families recognized a link between the trespassers and the refreshment hut. Frau Marschalek chatted to them, and Herr Marschalek carried over refreshments. The families ceded defeat. They searched for another place nearby, feeling like refugees in an alien land. To make matters worse the juvenile members of the clan deliberately and provokingly flaunted themselves in front of the uprooted camp. They rolled about, they lolled about, they stuck out their tongues. The families knew that the Marschaleks had engineered the whole thing.

Flypapers

Some days later Rudi suggested combing the Mistgstettn for spent flypapers. He had overheard Uncle Hans' outburst after walking headfirst into the dangling mixture of pink goo and black fly corpses hanging in Brigitte's kitchen. Apparently, the experience was worse than Judgment Day punishment for a sinner who had indulged in a lifetime of orgies. On a heavily overcast morning, the boys amassed vast quantities, and constructed a web with string and wire inside the hut extending from door to counter, from floor to roof.

"I'd rather scuffle up the Floridsdorf sewer than grapple through this," said Robert surveying the completed handiwork underneath the darkening sky.

"They'll wish flies hadn't been invented," observed Big Xandi accompanied by a distant thunder roll.

"They'll wish we'd filled the hut with pooh instead," said Pauli.

The heavens opened before they reached their observation hollow. Water streamed off Little Xandi's hair as he ruefully recalled the loss of his railway set during a previous cloudburst. The boys possessed the sagacity to realize that no sane mortal would hanker after Danube Meadow refreshments in a downpour orchestrated by disgruntled gods, and that therefore their antagonists would abort the day's trade, and that it would be futile to await their arrival.

After the thunderstorm came endless rain, turning grassland into squelchy swamp. When sunshine returned, and allowing a day or two for drying out, the boys ventured out to find the refreshment hut in working order, remnants of torn flypapers nearby hinting at unhappy toil. Once again, they were ready to forgive and forget.

The Reddening of Xandi's Cheek

"Herr Brunner gave it me," said Berti carrying a multi-coloured ball.

"Herr Brunner's awful," said Pauli, harbouring a vague memory of the scene when his little brother had been recipient of a wet rag in the Milk Block laundry.

"But Herr Dufft's nice," said Little Xandi.

"Herr Brunner likes your mum," said Rudi to Berti.

"Herr Dufft likes your mum as well," said Pauli to Berti.

"I like your mum," mimicked Big Xandi in a high pitched voice, "but right now I'd like to play football. We've got enough for three-aside."

Robert organized the goal posts: Berti's shoes, a stone, which on an earlier occasion had fallen off the handcart, and the rusty bucket, which had witnessed the demise of the fizzy drink bottle. Little Xandi manned the goal nearest the hut, Berti the other.

The game progressed.

"You thieving werewolf!" The refreshment hut woman suddenly fell upon Little Xandi. "You stole our bucket."

Little Xandi protested his innocence: "Robert took it."

"Shut up. You filled the hut with them rocks! You plastered it with them flypapers!"

The vivid recollections of the travail in rendering the booth fit for business sent her blood pressure soaring. She reached out and struck the boy's cheek with a force the impact of which cut through the summer air like a rifle shot, dwarfing Little Xandi's screeching in response to it.

"I'll have the mounted policeman on you! I've told him about you! You werewolves," she shouted, carrying the bucket off with her and putting it down nearer the hut.

"We'll have the policeman on her," said Robert.

"Striking little boys is against the law," confirmed Rudi. His attitude towards Little Xandi's cheeks receiving slaps was not altogether disapproving, since his brother's tears had often led to smacks on his own cheeks administered by Father. But it depended on who doled out the chastisement and under what circumstances.

"Let's go find the Skeleton," said Pauli.

"He gets free *Wurstsemmels*, he's her beau," said Big Xandi, "he won't do nothing for us."

"Best report the matter to the Engerthstrasse police station," said Robert.

They crossed the river to register their complaint. On the bridge Rudi suggested reddening Little Xandi's cheek before presenting it to the policemen for tactical reasons. The others agreed; Little Xandi agreed. So they smacked away without fear of retribution. Little Xandi bore the ordeal bravely. He didn't make a sound, until suddenly he let out a loud howl.

"What's the matter?" asked Rudi. "We're doing it for your own good."

"You - hit - the - wrong - cheek!"

When the right cheek attained the glow of a polished tomato, they hurried to the entrance of the police station.

"Stop!"

They halted.

"I just thought," said Rudi, "they'll ask us why the woman walloped him. And we'll have to say because we moved the old bucket."

"That's not a crime," said Robert.

"And that we played football."

That was. The notice boards said so, and the Skeleton had already taken their names for a ball game offence.

"S' truth," agreed Robert.

"We'd better leave it."

At this Little Xandi began to howl again. "I got hit for nothing."

"We can say we took the bucket to fetch water so we could wet the sand to make it firm for building Little Xandi a sandcastle with the ball sitting on top," said Pauli.

"That's what we were going to do anyway, afterwards," said Big Xandi.

Little Xandi offered his cheek gratefully for further colour enrichment.

Chief Police Officer Sessl eyed them with a blank face, whilst Rudi told the story with his lucidity of language. He heard him out, then raised a long arm and pointed to the door. That was that. But they had not walked far when Sessl had second thoughts and directed Officer Breitwinkl to catch up with them. Breitwinkl spoke to Robert, the tallest, in the grown-up fashion, addressing him with 'you' instead of 'thou', equivalent to saying Sir to an English twelve-year old.

"Sir," he said, "the Floridsdorf Police have a medical unit. If you report the matter there, they'll examine the boy. A charge against the perpetrator will be levelled if an injury is established."

Berti had no idea what perpetrator meant, and thinking it referred to him as owner of the ball, and recalling the unhappy ending of consorting with his Anzendrech-Jarabek friends beyond mid-day, said he must go home, and left.

The boys had arranged to meet their mothers at their very-own-wee-place around one o'clock for bread-and-schmalz. They thought they had plenty of time, and decided to proceed to Floridsdorf as directed. Indeed they could do no other since the policeman's "sir" had infused the matter with an intractable importance.

They were ushered into a large room surrounded by apple-green walls, their bare soles glided on polished, dark brown linoleum. They sat down in huge black leather chairs. A policeman in a corner pounded a typewriter. He looked at them for a moment with benign curiosity and went on pounding. The rat-a-tat of the machine resounded in the otherwise dramatic hush. Little Xandi sat on Robert's knees, mesmerized by the bouncing levers.

The big cousin whispered into his ear, "Look, how they jumpty-dumpty."

The silliness of the remark, uttered in a setting where merrymaking was out of place, started Little Xandi giggling. The policeman looked up, and with the same benign expression asked, "What's so funny, my little man?"

Rudi explained that the amusement stemmed from Alexander's first encounter with a typewriter.

"Have you seen this? I carry a magic inkwell in my pocket."

Rudi said his brother had seen a fountain pen before, so the policeman returned it to his pocket. Little Xandi felt sorry for him, because the man looked friendly, but was obliged to forgo a demonstration of the pen's miraculous properties.

In another room, smiling men in everyday clothes listened enthralled to Rudi's narrative. A little later, a policeman led Robert and Little Xandi into a white surgery where a doctor shone bright lights into the boy's ear, followed by talking and writing, and the pronouncement that Alexander Anzendrech had sustained a slight swelling in the inner ear.

Brigitte and Aunt Anna, quite naturally, thought the worst had happened when by mid-afternoon, they saw their children arrive in the company of a severe-looking policeman. The boys had told the officers in Floridsdorf that the rusty bucket, Frau Marschalek and their mothers were all to be found near the refreshment hut, so that the matter could be settled on the spot in one go.

Seven weeks later the case came up in court. Washed, scrubbed, brushed, put into polished shoes and sailor suits presented by Rudolf's American friends when on a recent visit to Vienna, Alexander and his brothers bore the expression of pure innocence. They sat in the waiting room. A man called out, "Alexander Anzendrech." Another relayed it: "Alexander Anzendrech." And once more another: "Alexander Anzendrech!"

Brigitte pulled her youngest along. They stood in front of the magistrate. Sombre men and women everywhere, sombre looks everywhere.

"Why did the woman slap your cheek?" asked the magistrate.

Alexander didn't know what to say, so he said, "I don't know."

The magistrate was appalled, "The child does not even know why he was hit! Preposterous."

Frau Marschalek broke in. "He knows why. He said Robert took it. Took the bucket, I mean. They've done other things to us. They're werewolves. They've..."

"Silence. You struck the little boy because the children made use of a rusted bucket while playing. You chose to hit out at the smallest, the weakest. I fine you fifteen schillings or one day's imprisonment."

CHAPTER SEVEN (1933)

Poldi

Unkind people spoke of Poldi as a pea on a pumpkin, because she carried a small round head on a massive round body. When walking, her haunches made swishing sounds as the extensive areas of skin rubbed against each other. She liked playing with children several years younger than herself, which the unkind people put down to her backwardness.

She liked playing with Xandi.

They became best friends, and frequently the little boy ate dinner at Poldi's, especially when Gusti cooked *Reisfleisch*; and conversely Poldi shared Xandi's meals, especially when Brigitte made *Pallatschinken*, pancakes filled with chocolate-flavoured custard.

The smaller of the two bedrooms in the Anzendrech household was Rudolf's. It contained a table of very pliant wood on which Rudolf built his inventions. Xandi discovered that he could make a groove by pressing a blunt pencil into the soft top. Pushing the pencil lightly, it followed the groove wherever it led, just like a tram on rails. Whenever he had access to the table, he extended the grooves, added curves, points and crossings, until the top featured a network of lines with sidings, loops, termini and depots.

Poldi took to the game like a moth to lamplight. The first time she saw it she hopped up and down, begging to have a go. Xandi went in search of a second pencil, but Brigitte firmly refused him the loan of the indelible ink pencil that lay in the drawer of the oblong, inlaid chessboard table amidst cotton reels and buttons, and which was cast for the role of being at hand in an emergency.

Xandi put his elbows on the soft wood, his chin in his hands and said, "Let's think."

Poldi adopted the same posture and said: "Let's think."

After a while Xandi cried, "I know!"

"What do you know, Xandi? Come on, tell me, what do you know?"

"Let's do it with matchsticks."

"Yes, let's do it with matchsticks." The idea earned him a hug.

They knew very well that in accordance with the oft-recited rhyme:

Scissors, gas, light, fire hot
Are for little children not,

access to the hidden matchbox would also be denied them. So Xandi suggested used matches, and Poldi ran down into the courtyard in a quest for discarded ones.

She returned carrying a fistful of matches and a wad of pamphlets, sucking a sweet.

"Herr Dufft gave me two," she said, dumping a eucalyptus sweet and a pile of leaflets on the table. "Look at the funny pictures," she whispered.

Xandi popped the confection into his mouth whilst Poldi pointed to a dark brown image of a bearded face with a crooked nose and drops dripping from it above a printed verse.

"What's the writing say, Xandi, tell me what it says."

Xandi spelt out each word:

"Ein-Volk-ein-Reich-ein-Führer
Das-Volk-wird-immer-dürrer
Die-Juden-immer-frecher
Heil-Hitler-unser-Retter.

One nation one people one leader
The people are getting leaner
The Jews are getting greedier
Heil Hitler our redeemer."

Bewildered, Poldi stared at her friend. "What does it mean, Xandi? Tell me what it means."

"Are you lean, Poldi?" he asked after a while.

"No, I'm fat," replied the girl, laughing.

"I'm lean. Because I don't eat the spinach. These are bits of spinach running down the man's face, like they did mine when I slapped Pauli's cheeks and he spat all over me."

"I love spinach," said Poldi. "What shall we do with the pictures, Xandi?"

"Hide them. Because if my mummy sees them, she'll go and buy more spinach."

Poldi pushed the papers down her blouse over her flat-chested front, where they caused an outward bulge, which looked as if she had one central breast.

The children got on with their game. Xandi discovered that licking the used matchsticks enhanced their performance, so he and Poldi were soon competing over whose saliva possessed the better lubricating properties. They propelled their matchsticks along the predestined grooves, Xandi exploiting curves and loops, Poldi repeatedly arriving at dead ends, and suffering derailments in the process.

Rudolf came home unexpectedly. His work schedule had allowed him a longer than usual rest period, and he had planned to assemble his latest detector radio set. The components were to be mounted on a piece of ceramic tile, which he had searched for and found on the Mistgstettn. Anticipating an hour's relaxation he arrived in good humour, but when he saw his worktable occupied, he felt a little discomfited. He knew ousting the children would incur Brigitte's disapproval.

She brought them slices of bread and *schmalz* garnished with raw onion. He watched large chunks disappear down Poldi's throat, and knowing that good-natured or malicious remarks had no effect on the child's understanding, he said, "Poldi, if a fraction of the food you eat nourished your mind and not your buttocks, we would have you outpacing Einstein."

"No, not me," cried Poldi in reply, laughing and at the same time releasing a shower of chewed breadcrumbs.

"What are you playing?"

"Trams!" Another spray of food particles rained onto the table-top.

Rudolf shook his head in incomprehension that anyone could derive pleasure from the very things provoking his daily irritation.

"I've never been a-riding on a real tram in my 'ole living life," Poldi added. But the hint – if there had been a hint - left him unmoved.

He said to Brigitte, "The Nazis are at it again. Leaflets everywhere."

"Herr Rosenfinger wants to call a meeting. He wants Richard Dufft to speak. Frau Dufft doesn't like the idea."

"It could be worse. Look at Germany: they're saddled with Hitler."

Averse to harbouring unpleasant thoughts for long, Rudolf went on, "Listen to the funny thing that happened today. The tram rolls up to the Wallensteinplatz, and there waiting for it is Lutschi Fritzer, you know, Lutschi from Morgenthau's over the road. She has a large suitcase by the side of her. The platform of my tramcar is nearest her, so I thought, poor young thing struggling with the heavy suitcase, here's a chance to show off my muscles."

"Poor young thing indeed! What about poor Frau...." Brigitte's lip contortions were lost on Rudolf, although he did briefly wonder why she was suddenly imitating a fish gasping for air.

"What?" he asked.

Brigitte punched the air with her finger towards Poldi's back, and again moved her lips in silent speech. Rudolf reflected what it could mean.

"Fräulein Fritzer's suitcase was empty," he said, then he realised he'd given away the punch line of his anecdote. "Now you've spoilt the whole story."

"I have?"

"You made me say the suitcase was empty."

"What's so particular about an empty suitcase?"

"Nothing, if you'd only listen without constantly interrupting."

"Interrupting? I was only saying, Frau...." and Brigitte added in a low whisper, "Spagola."

"What's Frau Spagola got to do with my story?" Rudolf retorted, almost shouting, in vexation.

"Sssh - Poldi."

"It's beyond human comprehension why you must always create riddles. I'm telling you something, and you butt in with remarks that have nothing to do with the topic. And you always say 'no'."

"I haven't said 'no'."

"At other times you always say 'no'. D'you want to hear the story, or don't you?" asked Rudolf.

Brigitte remained silent. If he didn't know what the whole of the Milk and Cocoa Blocks knew, that Karl and Lutschi were having an affair, it wasn't her fault.

"I don't know why I bother to come home during break. The kids are at my table, and it's more profitable to converse with a *Pinzgauer* horse than with you."

After a strained silence, which seemed to last forever, Brigitte asked, "Do you want some malt coffee?"

"All right."

"Bread and *schmalz*? I'll cut you another crust."

Rudolf recognised the peace overture. Vienna bread came in round loaves resembling solid cartwheels. Cutting it along parallel lines of latitude produced first and last pieces with abundant crust, and middle slices with little. He was passionately fond of crunchy crusts, but the rest of the family favoured these also, and since a loaf cut in this fashion yielded only two, luck in timing decided who got them. Brigitte took charge of bread slicing; men were too much at risk of self-mutilation. The art required holding the loaf vertically against the ribs with one hand, and working the knife through it. The danger came not only at the end of the knife's travel, when its sudden release caused its acceleration towards the heart, but also from the tendency of loaves to slide sideways, and here women held undisputed advantage of slip prevention in both directions.

Brigitte would not, under normal circumstances, commence a second line of cut at an odd angle to produce a second crust, for much the same reason that no one in the family would eat an apple by taking indiscriminate bites at it from all sides, instead of eating round it from one starting point. Only on special occasions, during illness or on birthdays, would she waive the rule. Rudolf was neither ill, nor was it his birthday. Brigitte's offer to slice off another crust represented therefore an attempt at conciliation. He laid his hand on hers and squeezed it gently.

"Aren't you going to tell me the tale?" she asked.

"As I was saying, there's young Lutschi waiting at the stop with this enormous suitcase. So I go up to her and say, 'Allow me, Fräulein Fritzer.' And I stand myself next to the suitcase, and I clasp the handle with both hands, and with a mighty heave I yank it onto the open platform of the tramcar. And *hoopla* the suitcase goes flying over the platform, and tumbles onto the street on the other side. Ha-ha-ha. You see, I thought it was heavy, but there was nothing in it. She was bringing it home from the pawnbrokers."

Rudolf's laughter infected Xandi, and his infected Poldi.

"Did it tumble off the other side of the tram?" the little boy asked, the spoken words adding lustre to the mental picture.

93

"Yes, I threw it right over the open platform. Don't you think it's funny?" he said, turning to his wife.

"I don't believe it," replied Brigitte.

"It went sailing across the platform and came down on the cobblestones the other side."

"No, I don't believe it."

"What don't you believe?"

"There's railings on the platform so that people don't fall off."

"I tell you, the suitcase went flying over the railing an' all."

"Never."

"It did, Briggi."

"No."

"I'm telling you, I threw it over the open platform." He felt exasperation growing. But the children laughed, and it mollified his temper.

"Well, if you think it's funny…" Brigitte shrugged her shoulders. "You could have damaged the suitcase. Didn't she say something?"

"She laughed too, and later on she cried."

"Cried?"

"She said she'd be going away."

"What? To have it in secret?"

"To have what in secret?"

"What? Everybody knows what." And she mouthed something like " 'ees 'ild".

He looked perplexed at yet another of his wife's riddles, but before he could pursue the point, Xandi climbed upon his knees and pleaded, "Tell us another story, another funny one."

How lucky to have little boys who appreciate a comical situation.

"Another funny tram story."

Rudolf wetted his lips. "As a matter of fact, the other day something funny did happen. Did I tell you about the Yank and his daughter?"

He was pretty sure he had told the yarn before, but he thought his wife wouldn't mind hearing it again.

"The other day, the tram was very crowded," he said, pulling Xandi closer, "We were travelling along the Ringstrasse, when a man in a chequered suit and his tall daughter climbed into my carriage. I could see a map of the city clutched in his hand, and I heard them speak English with an American accent – I know English, because I lived in New York when I was a young man. And I tell you New York is a little different from our happy-go-lucky Vienna town. All hustle and bustle, rush rush, quick quick, over there. The Americans are like that. So I go to collect their fares. We've hardly moved a stone's throw when he says to me in broken German, 'Pliss, ze Falkenstrass, where is?' Now I've seen it somewhere, but just at that moment I couldn't think where. So I fetch out my little green book, the street guide, and sure enough, I read the Falkenstrasse is opposite the Museum. We're just passing the Museum, the tram slows down for the next stop, and there I see Falkenstrasse written on the street sign, and a little way down I see these big blue letters, American Express. 'Pliss, the Falkenstrass, where is?' he says again. So I put my little green book away, and I look at the American and his daughter, and I smile, because they haven't been on the tram for longer than half a minute, and I say in English: 'There you are, sir, over on the other side is the Falkenstrasse, and further along is the American Express, can you see the sign with the blue letters?' You should have seen their faces! 'Oh yas,' they said in amazement at the speed we do things in Vienna! And he and his daughter stumble off the tram thinking the Vienna tram conductors are wizards, getting all that and the English from the little green book."

"Now that *is* funny," Brigitte remarked.

"I've never been on a tram in all my living life," said Poldi.

"When you're grown up and much bigger," Rudolf said mischievously, his happy frame of mind restored, "and earning pots of money in the Prater for being the Prettiest Lady In The World, you'll be able to afford a special reinforced tram car all to yourself, and you'll be able to ride around in it all day."

"Will I?" Poldi's face lit up. She paused as if pondering which was the brighter prospect: riding the trams or being the prettiest lady. She whispered coyly. "Herr Dufft says I'm pretty."

"You know Poldi, when you smile, you remind me of Herr Dufft."

Brigitte intervened, "Don't say these silly things to the child."

"Poldi don't mind. Do you, Poldi?" "

"No."

"She'll go and repeat the things you say to her."

"Poldi forgets anything I say to her in a couple of ticks. Don't you,

Poldi?"

"Yes."

He placed his red-trimmed tram conductor's cap on the girl's head. It fell down to her nose, which Xandi found very funny. But Rudolf said, "Now you are a real pretty tramway lady! Bim-bim, off we go, and don't forget to call out the stops: Engerthstrasse! Engelsplatz! Danube Meadow! Hubertus Dam! Floridsdorf! All fares please. If an inspector comes along, and he finds a passenger who hasn't paid his fare, he'll have you. You get a fine."

The Tram Ride

Rudolf erred in assuming that Poldi forgot everything he said to her, for he sparkled in her eyes as Apollo did in the eyes of Ancient Greeks. With a real tramway cap on her head, her dream of being a real tram conductor like Herr Anzendrech came a step nearer to fulfilment. So words flowing from his lips carried special significance. She had some difficulty in making sense of his remark: 'We could have you outpace Einstein,' but finally came to the conclusion that it meant running past the Stone. This was a reasonable interpretation, since 'ein Stein' is German for 'one stone'.

The large concrete slab, dubbed The Stone, dominated the centre of the Milk Block courtyard. Originally it had been laid as a base for a monument to the Socialist pioneer Lassalle, but due to diminishing funds, then to forgetfulness, later to a shift in political fervour, and finally to the council committee's realisation that another monument to Lassalle had, in the meantime, been successfully erected on the nearby Lassalleplatz, the project remained a slab of concrete. It served not only for a castle to countless juvenile kings, and a battleground between kings and pretenders, but also as a favoured place for rendezvous. Even Brigitte would say to the impatient Rudolf, when after lengthy preparations for a stroll round the block the call of nature had still to be attended to, "Go on ahead, I'll catch you up by The Stone."

So Poldi took to sprinting past this monument to municipal ineptitude. And since she grew breathless after a few steps, her puffing attracted the courtyard's attention. Besides the multitude of boisterous children, the elderly sat on sunny benches; the chess players occupied a shaded corner, the right to it won by unchallenged precedent; the card players slung cards and ten groschens upon home-made, collapsible tables; Frau Bitmann reposed in front of Staircase No 10.

The children believed Poldi played at steam engines. Herr Dufft, a frequently visiting chess player, watched Poldi's solo races with fascination. He handed her a bag of sugar fish from Morgenthau's, saying she'd won first prize. Herr Junge, a World War veteran who hobbled on one leg aided by crutches, remarked whilst shuffling cards, that Poldi had looked into a mirror, and in consequence had embarked on a slimming programme. A gang of men, commissioned by the council to paint some weatherworn benches, declared she had found herself a boyfriend. Immediately the names of two qualifying suitors floated from pernicious lips: Isidor, the local cinema attendant, whose mental age equalled his physical years divided by five, and who had been caught in the act of ogling at her, and Herr 'Raken, The Thinnest Man In All Christendom', a universally known attraction featuring in the entertainment programme of the Prater.

Poldi, unaware of the speculations flourishing on her behalf, pulled up sharply in front of Xandi on a warm, sunny, Sunday morning in spring. She opened her fist and said, "Look."

Xandi saw three silvery coins lying in her palm.

"Them's thirty groschen," said Poldi. "Manni Czarnikow said I've earned the money because I let him," she giggled, "see me in my birthday suit. Don't know why he wanted to do that. I told Herr Dufft I can earn money and he said I'm a Fräulein full of ideas. I've got an idea: Let's go on a tram, Xandi. Let's go on the tram what goes to Engerthstrasse! Engelsplatz! Danube Meadow! Hubertus Dam! Floridsdorf!"

"On a tram over the Danube?"

"Yes."

The engineering feat of taming the Danube had long ago risen to folklore status, and had become a chapter in Vienna's collection of grandeur, such as the defeat of the Turkish sieges, the St Stephan's Cathedral, the elevated City Railway, and the Giant Wheel.

Not to be conspicuous waiting for the number 11 in front of their home, they decided to walk to the Engelsplatz to catch the Floridsdorf tram.

Here stood the Milk Block, solid, square, secure. Here sparkled the windows of Morgenthau's shop with toys and watches, and inside, on work days, smiling Lutschi who gave Xandi three sugar fish instead of two when he had one groschen to spend, and sometimes told him snippets of fairy stories. Here boys and girls played games with shiny, coloured marbles, rolling them into hemispherical depressions that they had carved into the earth with their heels. A player would roll marbles one after another into a designated hole until he missed, when the next player would take took over. The one who sank the last marble would claim all the others in the hole. Further down the street, no longer pockmarked by holes for marbles, older tenement houses with large, Gothic doorways and Roman numerals on oval plates, signalled the beginning of adventure.

Xandi had been away from the Milk Block many times before, but on those occasions mother or father or brothers and cousins had been there to protect him. But now, was Poldi to look after him, or he to look after her?

They walked past the green door of the magic lantern show, and on the corner of the Hellwagstrasse stood the Cinema, where people with money could see *The Journey to the Moon*. Poldi told of its bewitching marvel, even greater than the magic lantern show. She had been in the cinema once for a whole ten minutes. Isidor, the doorman, had let her sneak in.

After crossing the Hellwagstrasse the pavements of hard grit dug into their bare soles. Grass grew between the glistening stones laid in narrow rows alongside the tram rails. The gutter gratings stood out beautifully browned with rust. They knew the Northrailway Viaduct sheltered witches. They held their breaths and looked straight ahead as they ran through. They marched quickly past the Engerthstrasse Police Station in case the Skeleton popped out to ask where they were going. Finally they reached the Engelsplatz tram stop. Xandi saw the huge, grey-green arches of the Floridsdorf Bridge and his pulse quickened with the anticipation of an explorer. The tram arrived, unconcerned about Poldi and Xandi and their anticipations. They selected a window seat.

Poldi said, "We must hide Gugi, or the conductor will want to give him a ticket an' all."

They shoved the yellow cloth doll between their bodies. And then came the moment when movement began. The cobblestones slipped backwards, one by one, then two by two, then too fast for the eye to catch. The wheels thumped over the rail joints: boom-boom, boom-boom. They looked down into the fast flowing Danube, its waters swelled by melting snow in the Alps. They passed the covered staircase leading down to the Danube Meadow, they saw the Zinkerbacherl, which had already overflowed and drowned the shrub land near its banks.

The conductor chatted to people on the platform and came inside when they approached Floridsdorf. Poldi handed him her thirty groschen.

"What's this? Tin money? That won't buy you no tickets." The conductor looked at the children severely.

They didn't know what to say.

"You know you can get into real trouble if you pass on fake money? Big girl like you!"

"Manni Czarnikow gave me it," Poldi said at last.

"Well, you give it straight back to him, because it's tin. Where you going?"

"Engerthstrasse! Engelsplatz! Danube Meadow! Hubertus Dam! Floridsdorf!" Poldi replied.

"Where are you from?"

"The Milk Block."

"Does your mother know you are riding on the tram?"

Poldi became very coy and started to giggle.

"I have a good mind to hand you over to a policeman," said the tram conductor. "You get off here, and take your little brother straight back to the Milk Block. You walk back over the bridge, do you hear, not across the meadow, because it's flooding. Come on now, quick."

Poldi hurried to alight. Xandi followed.

The big girl stumbled, leapt about on one leg and said, "I hurt my toe a bit jumping off the tram. Anyway, we had a good ride, didn't we? Even if the money's no good."

"Yes," said Xandi.

"He thought you was my brother!" Poldi found this very amusing. But she stopped laughing when she blundered against the curb as she limped to the pavement. She sat down and examined the red trickle running over her foot.

"I ain't lucky with my big toe today," she remarked as she squeezed together the split skin.

She dipped her foot into a puddle holding on to Xandi's shoulder. The injured toe developed an affinity for large stones like a magnet for iron. They sat down and applied crumpled-up weeds to soak up the blood.

"Does it hurt?"

"A bit."

"It's quicker across the meadow," said Xandi, when at last they reached the Dam.

He thought wading through the many large pools would ease the girl's pain. Disaster struck when, splashing through a deep depression full of murky water, her foot hit the edge of a squashed metal drum hidden from view. A gush of blood spouted from her toe. She struggled onto dry grass, flopped to the ground and pressed the wound together with both hands.

"Xandi, Xandi," she stammered.

The boy had to do something. The refreshment hut, boarded up for the anticipated flood, stood nearby. Although fully aware of Frau Marschalek's acrimony towards him, Xandi raced to it. As he came near, he heard voices. He couldn't shift the door, but he saw a peephole near the top. The contentious rusted bucket lay a few steps away. He fetched it, stood on it and looked through.

"Make it last, make it last," he heard a woman say.

The dark interior revealed the movement of figures in deep shadow. A moment later the door flew open, knocking over the bucket and the little boy.

"You bastard, filthy brat! You peeping Tom! Is that what you do because we feed you *Reisfleisch?*"

Xandi saw raw wrath in Herr Spagola's eyes. Alarm about Poldi's toe evaporated like spittle on a hot iron. He scrambled to his feet and ran.

The Search Party

When Berti Spagola called for Poldi, Brigitte said, "She isn't here. She's with Xandi. They're playing in the Kindergarten."

"No. They're not. My mum says the potato soup's ready."

Brigitte hurried down the staircase to check for herself. She sought out Frau Bitmann. Martha, a flaxen-haired girl of the same age as Xandi, traced her rosy fingers along the wrinkles on her grandmother's face.

"Poldi and Xandi walked through the passage into the street. It's bin a good hour and three quarter since I've seen them go," said Frau Bitmann. "Children are playing marbles in the street."

"They haven't come back?"

Frau Bitmann urged Martha to run and see whether they were with the marble players. Martha came back shaking her head.

Frau Spagola appeared. Word of the missing children spread. People gathered around the two mothers. Rudi, Pauli and Berti hurried off to search the boiler tube sanctuary and other haunts along the Handelskai. Boys and girls were hailed off The Stone and detailed to look over the Milk and Cocoa Blocks. They did this with much fervour. The thrill of sudden importance went to Manni Czarnikow's head. He lifted the lids off all the dustbins, a performance which other children immediately copied. It created a mighty clatter.

"What d'you expect to find in there, you silly toads?" cried Frau Czarnikow.

"We've looked into every nook and cranny," replied Manni, "and we can't find them nowhere."

"Never mind nooks and crannies. Be searching in crates and craters," observed the one-legged, war-disabled, Herr Junge. He leant on his crutches, grinned open-mouthed at his wit, scanned people's faces to see whether any registered appreciation at his slant on Poldi's size, feigned loss of balance, an act that he tended to execute in proximity to ladies of his choice, and groped for support on Frau Rosenfinger's lower torso.

"She had thirty groschen," observed Herr Dufft thoughtfully. "Poldi told me she had thirty groschen."

"Wager they're in Morgenthau's buying up sugar fish," said Herr Rosenfinger.

Little Martha rolled her eyes in imaginary delight.

As if conjured up by mentioning his name, Herr Morgenthau loomed in the passage surrounded by several children. He carried the air of a messenger with information of some weight, but Herr Kristopp, the artist living in a studio flat on the top floor of Staircase 13, sneered and said, *"Von seiner alten Bude kommt Morgenthau, der Jude,* from his hovel comes Morgenthau the Jew."

"Kids are saying Poldi Spagola's run off?" Herr Morgenthau queried, seeking verification.

"Poldi and my Xandi can't be found," replied Brigitte, "have you seen them?"

"Ay."

"Where?"

"Looking into the shop window. I came out because the boy Ferdinand Trapfen insisted I still had marbles in the bracelet section. How they got amongst the jewellery, I don't know. And I don't mind telling you it's been a pressing morning with customers, no other recreational establishment in the whole of Zwischenbrücken opening on a Sunday, and everybody wanting clay marbles. Could have sold a sack of clay marbles, but I didn't have none, because last week they wouldn't look at nothing except *Dradiwaberls,* spinning tops. Yes, I saw them and I overheard them."

"Out with it then, you old stink bomb," muttered Herr Kristopp.

"The little lad wanted blue sugar fish, he insisted on blue being his favourite colour, but the girl Poldi said they mustn't buy none because they needed the money for the journey."

"Journey? What journey?"

"I don't know what journey. I don't belong to the profession of clairvoyants. Not my business to probe into the comings and goings of customers, especially on a morning when I myself don't know whether I'm coming or going, what with Lutschi having the day off, and the urchins clamouring for marbles, and the shelves lined with *Dradiwaberls* in all colours. I don't know what journey, didn't ask them."

"Journey to the Prater?" suggested Frau Czarnikow.

"Journey to the Moon," said Manni Czarnikow, parroting the title of the film showing at the Hellwagstrasse Cinema.

"Perhaps they've gone to look at the Danube Meadow," remarked Herr Trapfen, who, like many of the Zwischenbrücken people, was awaiting the flooding of the meadow in spring with the same ardour as the falling of the first snow in autumn.

"Jesus-Mary-'nd-Joseph!" Gusti Spagola cried out and understandably her apprehension had substance. "I'm going over to see."

The two mothers and several men were about to set off when Herr Brunner, having been informed of the situation, came up with a troop from the card tables.

"Hold your horses!" he directed. "No point everybody going to the same place. I and Frau Spagola will look for the little treasures on the Danube Meadow; the rest of you split up and search other places."

"They've been abducted." The speaker, a thin-faced chess crony by name of Posidl, a locksmith by trade, who preferred watching the game to playing it, cherished the habit of remaining aloof to deliver bombshells at decisive moments.

"Police. Call the police." Frau Bitmann shook her head and chewed vigorously.

Brigitte said, "Yes. Frau Spagola, first the police. You'll come with us, won't you, Herr Dufft. My Rudolf's working on the trams."

"Herr Dufft?" the laundry supervisor jibed, "Dufft? Haven't we got enough of it in the yard already?" Herr Kristopp and his wife sniggered because *Duft* is German for odour. "I'll come along with you; I am on friendly terms with the police officers." He touched Gusti's elbow.

"We know that. Thank you all the same. We'll go with the Councillor, Herr Dufft," insisted Brigitte.

"Who needs a Jew?" asked Herr Kristopp in a low tone.

"Personally I'd be seeking the company of a crocodile rather than of a Jew," was Herr Brunner's response.

"When trouble visits you, Herr Brunner, we'll give you a ticket for the zoo."

The retort stung, especially as Herr Rosenfinger grinned all over his face. Brunner gave Brigitte a piercing look, which meant to say, "You'll pay for this, sweetheart, no one scoffs at me!" He folded his arms across his chest and standing with his legs astride, turned to Gusti. "Frau Spagola has the good sense to let one of her own kith and kin accompany her."

"Spagola's away on ship," replied Gusti.

"Someone of your race. I'll escort you to the police station."

"We'll be better heard in the presence of a councillor," insisted

103

Brigitte.

Gusti sensed the beginning of a tug-of-war between Brigitte and Brunner, with herself the rope. "Holy Jesus, I've left the potato soup on the gas! I won't be a second. You go on, Frau Anzendrech, I'll catch you up."

She ran off to rectify the oversight, whilst Brigitte and Herr Dufft hurried away to the Engerthstrasse Police Station.

"Now isn't that a typical Vienna touch: to start deliberating anti-Semitic sentiments at a time when every minute counts, and shilly-shallying could mean trouble for the lost children. I mean what is the difference who goes along with the ladies? A darkie born in Timbuktu could do the job as well as anybody here. I could do it, only I've seen the Engerthstrasse police cell from inside and it might prejudice the case." The speaker, Herr Kranitschek, a big man, referred to the time when he had been spokesman for the power station strikers. "Or we could all go, or perhaps Frau Anzendrech and Frau Spagola don't need nobody when it comes to it, but it would be more in keeping with the principle of solidarity if one of us menfolk does. Now Frau Anzendrech expressed the wish for Herr Dufft to undertake the task, and who am I to quarrel with that? I mean the thought of the kiddies lost, not that I am saying they are lost. I mean children these days get up to all sorts of tricks. It's wise to prepare for all eventualities..."

"Aptly spoken, we are all in the same boat, Frau Anzendrech," interrupted his wife. Small as her husband was tall, she stood in the middle of the crowd and had not noticed that Brigitte and Her Dufft had already departed. "Could have happened to any kid. And the Jews have the same feelings as us Christians. Ask Herr Dufft if that isn't Gospel."

Frau Czarnikow chipped in. "The Jews turn up their noses when they sniff a *Schweinsschnitzel*, a pork cutlet, in the frying pan."

Frau Kristopp thought this funny and once again responded with a giggle. Frau Czarnikow went on: "The Jews wouldn't lift a finger to pull out a child a-drowning in a street puddle if it happens to fall in on a Saturday, the Jews' Sabbath."

"That's a load of rubbish!" exclaimed Frau Rosenfinger.

Herr Junge placed his crutches and himself near to Frau Kristopp and murmured that Jews, being renowned for sagacity, would not waste energy, Sabbath or no, if the child in question resembled

Poldi's build, which in order to lift from said street puddle would require an effort equivalent to raising the Stone off its foundation. "Hoopla," he added, grasping the lady's waist, as his wooden support slid away from under him.

"I'm looking for the kids on the Danube Meadow," said Herr Rosenfinger. "Who's coming?"

Several men separated from the knot of people. Just then a chess game came to its end. The players had been engrossed in a battle in which Herr Bergmeister, a railway worker, had relentlessly outmanoeuvred the schoolteacher, Herr Echenblatt. They saw card players mingle with tenants, and enquired about the cause of the commotion, bringing the search party to a halt. And since they held the notion that coping with the complicated moves of knights and bishops required loftier minds than those distinguishing between clubs and spades, they offered instant advice.

Herr Bergmeister, still smiling at his success, said, "Poldi and Xandi? They're bound to be noticed and brought back home."

"They're not tiny infants," retorted Herr Echenblatt. "Why should anyone notice them? The girl's big enough to pass for the little lad's mother."

"They've been abducted," repeated Herr Posidl.

Frau Kristopp butted in. "We were in the woods on the *Hermannskogel* last Sunday, my man and I, the sun was setting, and do you know we saw this man with a horrible face following us behind trees. And he carried a sword."

Herr Kristopp acted as if he hadn't heard. His wife frequently caused him embarrassment.

"What the bandits won't do these days," someone remarked.

Frau Czarnikow said, "Wouldn't stop at nothing nor for as little as thirty groschen."

"Thirty groschen or thirty silver pieces, comes to the same thing," said Brunner. He lowered his arms from his chest. "A crime's a crime. And we know who the perpetrator was. Judas. Did the man in the wood exhibit the likeness of a crooked nose?"

"Yes," cried Frau Kristopp, delighted that her fable had generated a response.

"The sooner the Jewish race is abolished..."

"Let it be, Brunner, let it be!" Herr Rosenfinger raised his voice.

"Don't drag your infantile politics into this matter. We don't abolish people. Our Chancellor Dollfuss can abolish parliament, but we're still democrats here."

Frau Czarnikow remarked, "The Jews threw the bomb through the Danube Coke office window."

"Reibeisen is the manager there. He's a Jew himself!"

"The Heimwehr did it."

"The Schutzbund."

Herr Rosenfinger turned on the crowd fiercely. "That bomb was the work of the German Nazis!"

"It was a Social Democrat, who joined the Christian Socials, then became a German Nazi Jew," observed Herr Junge who felt the situation needed a calming wisecrack. However, the joke acted like oil rather than water on fire, for the laundry man flared up and advanced upon the war veteran.

"You listen to me: there are Bolshevik Jews, and there are financier Jews, and there are lousy Jews. There are no German Jews and there are no Austrian Jews. We Austrians are Aryans. And in case you've forgotten, the Jews were responsible for Versailles and your absent leg."

"You'll do well to remember that!" from Herr Kristopp.

Herr Junge stumbled backwards on his crutches. "All right, all right, keep the heat down. I'm no Jew, and I'm no German, and I didn't get my leg shot off for no Jew nor for no German. I lost it because I've got a soft spot for the old Vienna town, that's why. And for the rest of the politicals there isn't much to choose between any of them, be it Dollfuss or Mussolini or Hitler, except when things go wrong, then it's always the fault of either the Jew or the pedal-cyclist."

Frau Kistopp gawked at the war invalid in astonishment: "The pedal-cyclist? Why the pedal-cyclist?"

"Good question that. Perhaps Herr Dufft, when he comes back, will tell you why the pedal-cyclist if you tell him why the Jew."

Herr Rosenfinger moved off with the search party to look for the children on the Danube Meadow.

Dufft's Prayer

Gusti Spagola turned off the gas underneath the bubbling potato soup, went into the bedroom and knelt down below Karli's crucifix.

She prayed to the Holy Virgin to spare Poldi. And Xandi. The terrifying idea came to her that God had called Poldi to Him in punishment for living in sin. Her heart beat faster as she prevailed upon God: "If You spare Poldi, I'll sin no more. Karli can have me again when we are wed properly. And if that means waiting until his real wife passes away, so be it."

At the back of her mind sat the irksome question of how to convey this to Spagola.

She hurried down the stairs to catch up with Frau Anzendrech and Richard Dufft. Before darting over the last few steps she caught a glimpse of two sturdy legs, planted astride, attached to the lower part of Brunner's torso. "He stands there like the woman-eating panther that he is, preying to pounce on me." She turned and softly fled upstairs. The attic door stood open. She entered into a maze of passages with rows of timbered storage cubicles. The stream of tenants putting inner window frames, stoves and stovepipes away for the summer meant that the attic remained temporarily unlocked.

She descended by another staircase.

The Sunday dragged on. The Danube Meadow party returned without the children. The Jarabek family arrived. Rudi, Pauli, Robert, Big Xandi, Berti continued searching. Uncle Hans and Herr Dufft peered into shops. Brigitte and Gusti sporadically rushed down into the street and questioned anybody passing by. Nothing from the police. By mid-afternoon, exhausted, they sat in the Anzendrechs' home, waited.

"No news is good news," Aunt Anna remarked.

"They were inseparable," retorted Gusti, "she never stopped telling me how she loved playing on Xandi's railway table."

"Trams, he knows all about trams," murmured Brigitte, unlike Gusti, using the present tense.

"The Lord's taken Poldi," said Gusti. "For my sins."

"We are all sinners," said Aunt Anna.

"I've been living in sin," Gusti persisted. "For most of my life."

Richard Dufft grasped her wrists. He hadn't touched her since her teenage years. The present situation warranted physical contact: "Gusti, girl, listen. There are two billion souls living on this earth. Every hour of the day the world adds two billion more sins to its collection."

"Spagola isn't my man. Poldi isn't his child."

Brigitte thought, *Rudolf is my man, and Xandi is his child, so why is He punishing me?*

Richard Dufft glanced at Gusti's sun-coloured freckles, which suggested merriment, and contrasted with her dry, taught skin. He remembered their teenage love: the incident in the Augarten, which could have made him more than an onlooker now. *If you'd given me a child,* went through his mind, *I'd have liked a boy like Alexander. He'd have played tram and railway games too, and I would have taken him for rides everywhere.*

He said to her, "So you have sins. So you go to confession. Today is Sunday. You've been to confession?"

Brigitte turned to the Jewish agnostic. "You don't believe in confession?"

He hunched his shoulders as if he had been found out and could offer no explanation. But he thought, *Religion is the opium for the people. A little medicinal opium now and again may be a good thing.*

Gusti said, "She'll go to heaven, the innocent lamb, and when my time comes, I'll be going to the other place."

In spite of the grave moment, Dufft could not suppress a smile.

"It's no laughing matter," Aunt Anna reprimanded. "No reason to be amused."

"I am not amused." His smile had been a reaction to Gusti's naïvety, which he had always found captivating.

"Why the smirking? Don't Jews go to heaven or hell?"

"Oh yes," replied Dufft, "throughout the ages many Jews have gone to the latter place, mostly before their demise."

Brigitte said, "Herr Dufft is a free-thinker."

"No reason to laugh at us."

Richard Dufft apologised, and felt ill at ease. Should he go?

"Perhaps they have strayed into the Allerheiligenkirche," said Aunt Anna, "and got locked up in a chapel."

The words fell like a lifeline on the mothers' ears. It had to be true, it would make sense. They felt fresh hope. They hurried out.

Dufft followed, not wishing to stay behind with Anna Jarabek. The church stood at the east end of the Allerheiligenpark. People went in and out through the wide-open doors. The incense in the interior pressed on Dufft's shoulders. He hadn't been in a place of worship for years. Though he would not admit it, he feared religious ritual lest it should rob him of his faith in agnosticism. His needed doubts. God, to him, represented a concept like infinity: any number, however large or small, stood in equal proportion to infinity. So any faith, and for that matter any individual, shared the same relationship to God. But he was unsure whether to believe this also.

The children had not stumbled into the church. He saw Gusti fall prostrate in front of a gilded figure and cry out beseechingly. A little later Brigitte knelt down quietly. Silent words passed through Dufft's mind: *God, for God there ought to be, though not like this, nor like any other. God, though I don't know what You are, where You are, if You are. God, if You are, forgive me if I say if, I can't help it, You have made me that way. God, if You are, save their children.*

CHAPTER EIGHT (1933)

The Confrontation

Brunner waited for Gusti at the bottom of Staircase No 9.

Time slipped by. What goes up must come down. Eventually doubt crept in. He ascended to the fourth floor, turned the butterfly grip on Spagola's doorbell. No one responded. He turned it and turned it again, oblivious of the reverberations through the staircase.

He carried on ringing until glancing up he saw the attic door ajar. This brought on the notion that what goes up must come down, but not necessarily in the same spot. He climbed the short flight of steps. Small windows sat in the outside wall of the attic, rows of cubicles filled the interior. Tiles and bricks, planks of wood and remnants of piping, which the builders had left years ago and nobody had removed, lay scattered on the rough timber floor. He looked out to the east at the river encroaching on low lying parts of the Danube Meadow, at the three bridges upstream and two downstream, at the coke mountains alongside the river bank. His eyes scanned the coal yards until they came to rest on the shattered glass of the Danube Coke Company office. Men moved about inside, unusual for a Sunday. He guessed they were clearing up the mess of the bomb blast. He picked up a length of bent piping, held it to his face in the manner of a rifle, and trained the barrel at a figure he took to be Herr Reibeisen.

He ambled to the northern side of the rectangular Milk Block, where he could see the viaduct carrying the Northrailway line over the Engerthstrasse, the tracks curving away south towards the Prater. Beyond the viaduct. heavy traffic headed for the Floridsdorf Bridge. Once again he raised the pipe and played it on vehicles and trams. He inclined the tube to an acute angle and peppered the socialist Engels Block with imaginary bullets. The sport fascinated him. He sauntered to a west-facing window, from where the tall spire of St Stephan's Cathedral came under fire. To the south the Giant Wheel succumbed to the assault. He completed the circuit and looked out again at the river. The pools on the Danube Meadow had grown larger.

A column of Milk Block people on the pedestrian walk of the

Northrailway Bridge drew his attention. He lifted the piping and singled out the heavy bulk of Herr Kranitschek who, together with Herr Rosenfinger, had fostered the Floridsdorf Power Station strike with the result that the Zwischenbrücken districts had lain in darkness for three days. He pulled the imaginary trigger, and said, "Got you". He watched as the men came down from the bridge to the riverbank and talked to a gang of navvies. Evidently the little treasures had not been found. Now the search party went into the coal yards and became hidden from view.

The boarded-up refreshment hut standing on a strip of dry meadow was just visible behind the arches of the Northrailway Bridge. Brunner selected it as his next target. Whilst picturing the wooden structure disintegrating into a thousand splinters, he noticed two figures, one larger than the other, emerge from the covered staircase leading down from the Floridsdorf Bridge. He could not distinguish details. He lowered the piping to watch their progress more clearly. They walked around puddles towards the refreshment hut, disappeared behind it, and did not reappear.

Brunner left the attic and made his way to the Danube Meadow.

After some fifteen minutes he reached the deep pool at the foot of the Northrailway Bridge stairs. He viewed it with distaste. He waded through it to get to the higher ground near the refreshment hut. He was shaking water off his shoes and trouser bottoms, when Alexander Anzendrech came racing towards him from the hut, followed by the bare-chested Herr Spagola.

Brunner blocked the way, and the boy bounded into his belly. The laundryman's fist firmly embedded itself into Xandi's hair and held fast. The two men came face to face.

"Is your girl in the hut also?" Brunner spoke first.

The question stunned Spagola into stupefaction. A misunderstanding was inevitable.

"Who wants to know?" he asked belligerently.

"Who wants to know? The whole Milk Block is in turmoil."

"The whole Milk Block can bloody well mind its own business."

"And Frau Spagola needs cajoling as she's slowly going demented."

"What's that? You keep your paws off her or you'll get a taste of mine in your grub hole. Frau Spagola is my business."

111

Brunner shrugged his shoulders. "The boy isn't your business."

"Neither is he yours!"

"Neither is stealing away with the little treasures to the flooding Danube Meadow a feat of intelligence. They've gone to the police."

"What?"

Brunner noted a withdrawal of colour from Spagola's face.

The captive Xandi cried out: "Poldi's hurt her toe!"

The vicelike hold of the laundryman did not allow movement of the boy's head, and Xandi could not turn to check on the state of his injured friend. The men ignored him.

"What did you say?" Spagola queried.

"You heard. But for your peace of mind, I'll tell you further. Your missus and Frau Anzendrech together with their kosher boyfriend Dufft shot off to the Engerthstrasse Police Station. The Skeleton with a posse of law enforcement officers will be swarming to this place any moment."

Karl Spagola's brain threw up fragments of confused thought. Beads of perspiration gathered on his forehead.

The laundry supervisor, pleased with the effect of his words but somewhat mystified at producing it, said: "You ponder that." He released Xandi's hair and gripped his arm instead. "I'm getting out of here before we get washed away. I'm taking the brat."

He walked off, dragging Xandi along. Karl returned to the hut.

Xandi pulled at Herr Brunner's hand and pointed towards the black heap in the distance: "Poldi's hurt her toe!"

Brunner jerked him back. "Cut that out, will you. She's his problem."

The reply satisfied Xandi, as he believed it meant that Herr Spagola would take care of Poldi.

Brunner's Triumph

"He's found them. Herr Brunner's found them!" Berti Spagola came running shouting the news as Brigitte, Gusti and Herr Dufft left the Allerheiligenkirche.

In the Milk Block courtyard the laundry supervisor savoured his triumphant entry. He adopted his favourite stance: legs astride and arms folded across his chest. Not speaking, he moved his head up and down in a manner designed to convey to his audience some undefined virtue of which he alone had possession.

Xandi ran to his mother the moment she appeared.

"What happened, Xandi? Where have you been?"

"On the tram."

"Where?"

"Poldi hurt her toe."

"Where did you find them, Herr Brunner?" asked Brigitte.

The laundry supervisor elected to ignore the question.

"Where's my Poldi?" asked Gusti.

Xandi traced lines across his mud-caked bare foot. "Blood came out here and it ran over her whole foot. Then pointing at Brunner, he said, "He pulled me away. He pulled me away by my hair."

"What's happened to my Poldi?"

The connection between trams, blood, and being pulled away led Frau Kristopp to exclaim, "Run over by a tram!"

A wild rumour started. Herr Jungle declared that a special coffin would have to be constructed on account of the victim's shape, and Frau Bitmann commented, somewhat ruefully, on the need to start a collection for floral tributes.

Little Martha Bitmann stroked Xandi's shins, and asked in a clear, silvery voice, "Have you been to the moon?"

Brunner enjoyed the scene. He levelled a supercilious smile at Brigitte.

"Has something happened to Poldi?" Gusti's voice rose in pitch.

Herr Dufft turned to the laundryman: "Do you know where Frau Spagola's daughter is? Why don't you say?"

Xandi cried out, "Poldi is still there, on the Danube Meadow. She's Herr Spagola's problem."

"The girl's with her father." Brunner condescended to endorse Xandi's statement.

"With Spagola?" Gusti asked incredulously.

"With the very same."

"But Spagola is away on board a ship. In Budapest."

Xandi said, "Herr Spagola chased after me."

"He must have come back a day early. Why didn't he say? I've got nothing ready for him to eat."

Xandi said, "We went to Floridsdorf on the tram. We walked back over the Danube Meadow."

"They were in the refreshment hut with the flood water swirling in the ditches," added Brunner.

Herr Rosenfinger shook his head. "We looked inside the hut. Nobody there."

"You didn't see Herr Spagola? You can't have looked very hard."

"Holy cross of Jerusalem, Spagola's gone crazy! What's he doing in the refreshment hut? What's he doing taking the children to play chasing games on the Danube Meadow when the flood's rising? He told me he'd be away all Sunday, in Budapest. Did he speak to you, Herr Brunner?"

"He did speak to me."

"What did he say to you?"

"I don't recall his exact words, but the gist of his verbal pronouncement was to mind my own business. It seems scoffing at my concern for your little treasures is a common trait of your families. So I brought back the boy on his own, although it meant the soaking of my trousers and the ruin of my shoes, and the risk of Frau Anzendrech's tongue in telling me also to mind my own business."

"Oh no, Herr Brunner," Brigitte replied, "we are very much indebted to you," and she thought how much better it would have been if somebody else had found the children.

"People come to their senses when it's too late," he said and told himself, *she thinks I did this for the love of her boy.*

"All's well that ends well," Frau Kristopp's remarked, reflecting the mood of the courtyard. It put an end to further speculation.

"I'll tell them at the police station," said Brigitte as she led Xandi home.

The tenants dispersed whilst Gusti looked alternatively at Brunner and Dufft; both had remained by her side. "He said he would be away on board a ship. It's not like him to go off with the children without telling me."

"It *is* odd," remarked Dufft. "Something doesn't fit. The lad said Poldi was hurt? Perhaps she and Herr Spagola need help."

"He didn't strike me as wanting help," said Brunner. "He radiated virility from his bare chest."

"Spagola takes his shirt off at the first glimpse of sunshine," explained Gusti.

"We ought to make sure," insisted Dufft.

"I said he needs no help. Do you doubt my word? Do you call me a liar?"

"Herr Brunner, the issue is not about my doubts. I have plenty of doubts. The issue is about the wellbeing of a child."

"And I have no doubt at all," the laundryman said, "that Frau Spagola is getting tired of your interference in her affairs. Herr Spagola didn't need my assistance; I can't imagine why he should want any from an Israelite."

Dufft waited for a signal from Gusti. But she was confused, she did not know what to think. Was Poldi safe with Spagola? What was the matter with Spagola? She remained motionless.

Dufft decided to investigate and walked off.

Gusti wanted to follow, but Brunner grabbed her sleeve. When the journalist was out of earshot, he twisted the fabric and growled, "You gave me the slip. You ran across the attic."

The woman-eating panther, still preying on me for passion, flashed through her mind.

"Am I not good enough for you? Do you roll your eyeballs at the Hebrew?" Brunner jibed.

"I roll my eyes at nobody."

"That Jew boy is after you. Tell him to emigrate to Palestine if he ever bothers you. Or tell me. I'll turn him into mincemeat."

"I've known Richard since we were children."

"Take my advice: learn to un-know him."

"I'll do no such thing."

"Do you know what I think of you?"

"What?"

"You are one in a million. Get shot of your old man, I'll receive you in my arms. Yes, I would, because you turn me on. You really and truly turn me on."

"You haven't got me mixed up with one of the water taps in the wash house?"

"Does that mean I turn *you* on? That's what I like about you. Your sense of fun. The first time I set eyes on you, you said you were as fresh as the bread straight from the oven. D'you remember? And I said to myself back then: that's the girl to satisfy my craving."

How many thirty-three-year old women would not feel their

hearts miss a beat when called "girl"? She replied, "I'm sure you say that to all your lady friends, Herr Brunner."

"I have none."

"You can tell that to the natives of *Schlaraffenland,* the Never-never-land. I've seen you trying to chat up Frau Anzendrech."

"Frau Anzendrech? That arse-crawling Jew lover?"

"And Lutschi Fritzer?"

"Lutschi Fritzer is an infant. I like my women to be mature, experienced."

"She gets the number two dryer, and the best ironing table."

"I wake up at night clutching my pillow, thinking my face lies buried in your breasts."

"I can't stop you thinking."

"When was the last time you visited the Kratzmayer Heurigen pub in Grinzing?"

Gusti shook her head. Clearly, visiting the drinking booths catering for Viennese joviality did not feature in her calendar.

"What d'you say to a night out when your old man's away on the ships?"

"Spagola is supposed to be away on a ship today," she said expressing lingering anxiety, not in potential acquiescence to Brunner's proposition.

"He isn't," said Brunner, "he's in the refreshment hut on the Danube Meadow with your oversize fat ball. Anyway tonight's no good, I need to attend a meeting. On the other hand we could go into the boiler house for half an hour."

"To end up like Lutschi Fritzer, on a heap of coke?"

"Gusti, I could eat you. You're different. "

Magic words from the woman-eating tiger's mouth. But for Gusti they meant no more. And indeed she was different. For better or worse, she had made a bargain with God, and if she would sin no more with Spagola, she would not rush into an affair with this wanton, seductive wild creature, however much masculinity he threw at her. Alarmed that she had already gone too far, she wrenched herself free of his grip. She left him abruptly and hastened, almost ran, to see for herself what was going on in the refreshment hut on the Danube Meadow.

The Rescue

Gusti reached the pedestrian walk of the Northrailway Bridge and saw Richard walking on ahead. She slowed her steps: if Spagola came up with Poldi from the Danube Meadow, it would be better she met him by herself. But Richard's sixth sense, or simply chance, caused him to turn his head. He waited.

He said, "I'm sure Poldi is somewhere safe with Herr Spagola, but I thought I'd look into the refreshment hut, just in case."

Gusti surveyed the swelling waters on the Meadow. She felt certain Spagola couldn't be still roaming there and she was glad to have Richard at her side.

She smiled at him: "I'm sorry Herr Brunner used those words. You're doing such a lot for people. I don't understand why they get at you."

"If we understood what motivates people, we could build paradise on earth. Or hell. Take that lunatic in Germany. He knows how to manipulate people."

"Germany is a long way off."

"The Danube Press commissioned me to go to Berlin. To pick up local political jokes, to see whether Berliners still retain a sense of humour. I'm leaving tomorrow."

"Richard, be careful." A wave of sympathy for her childhood sweetheart rolled over her. She took his hand and gave it a gentle squeeze as she had done fifteen years ago, but not since. "Germans don't welcome Jews, Richard."

"Herr Brunner doesn't welcome Jews. He doesn't welcome me much, but he seems to go for you."

The laundry man's flattery rang in her ears. She motioned as if to withdraw her hand, but he held firm.

He glanced at her, said, "But it was noble of him to bring back the Anzendrech boy. How do you get on with Karl Spagola these days?"

"Spagola? We get on all right. He never lets us starve; he never beats us. He disappears for a spell now and then, but he always comes back. Now I have a problem, which I don't mind telling you for old time's sake: I've resolved not to be like a wife to him any more, not until I'm his real wife."

She returned his pained look with her large, wide-spaced eyes set in her freckled face. He thought, *How damned attractive you are.*

She continued, "His real wife isn't well. She may pass away at any time. But Spagola's been saying that for years."

"Do you want to be his real wife?" asked Richard.

After a little while she said, "I have two children. They need a father."

Richard thought, *I'd love to act as their father.* He detected a faint throbbing in the hand that still nestled in his. "I used to call you *Zuckerrüberl,* wee little sugar beet, because when you were six you ate raw, sugared carrots. Do you remember? Do you remember the orchards where the Engels Block stands now? You and me up in the apple trees?"

Gusti had not forgotten. "We had no worries then."

He said, "The gardener caught us. I wanted to run away, you held me back, and you said to him, 'These are gorgeous apples, taste one.' He went into his hut and brought us a plateful of plums. I believed I'd never be able to live without you by my side. You were so full of fun then."

"Full of fun! Have you tried looking after a sweet but clumsy girl and a rowdy boy for twenty- four hours a day, every day, and a man who, although he never beats or starves his family, is no saint?"

"Gusti, I don't get much chance to speak to you, and I don't want to upset your life. I'm a one-woman man. Mama says it's stupid of me, but that's how it is. You and I, we have different backgrounds, different outlooks. So what? I would have liked a child. Your child."

In his mind he saw, as always when imagining *their* child, a boy like Alexander Anzendrech for whose wellbeing he had "sacrificed" umbrella wrecks from this very spot on the bridge.

"What's past is past," she said. "Things don't always turn out as you want them to. Not if you're a woman."

"You haven't forgotten? I was wearing my new uniform, we were strolling in the Augarten, and we went deep into the trees..."

"Don't," said Gusti.

"...we sat down, we lay down, I unbuttoned your blouse. I had been dreaming of doing this, but I had never mustered enough courage before. It was a pale blue dirndl blouse with tiny dark blue flowers on the sleeves and I couldn't manage the fastenings of your bra on your back. You helped me. I don't know how it happened, but

I was inside you."

But he knew how it had happened: she resisted, said "No, don't, please don't," but he pressed on because he wanted her, and he believed she wanted him. She said "No," and his body moved on its own and she said "Yes, yes," and just before the climax, her muscles tightened and she said, "No we mustn't. It's a sin, a mortal sin. We must wait until we're married." And he withdrew, laid his stiff member on her belly and flooded her navel. And he told her of his love. And she said, "Yes, I love you too." And he said, "Mama wants me to marry Violetta. But I shan't. I'll tell Mama how things are, and you and I will wed as soon as this war is over."

Such was his recollection. The sight of the dying Antonius Freiherr flashed through his mind, the friend who took the secret of Poldi's birth to his grave, and spoilt Gusti's life. And his.

He said, "I shouldn't have asked Antonius to stay that night."

"Antonius. I can't explain. I don't remember him doing anything to me."

"Perhaps he did it because he had broken up with Fanni, you know, his fiancée."

"I really remember nothing, believe me," said Gusti.

"We had too much to drink. We were pissed as newts. I remember nothing either. The last thing I recall is falling over the doorstep."

"Did Antonius ever speak to you about me?" asked Gusti.

He reflected, if there had been no Antonius and consequently no Poldi, he could now be walking next to Frau Richard Dufft; or, if Antonius had survived, would she have become Frau Freiherr?

Richard said, "We should have gone the way nature had intended, that afternoon in the Augarten. We would be looking for *our* child now."

"You would have scorned me afterwards."

"We would be man and wife now."

"Did Antonius speak to you about me before he was killed?"

Should he tell her that Antonius had never once mentioned her, but had spoken of reconciliation with Fanni and that they had planned to marry after his release from the army?

"He said he loved you." Richard heard himself whispering. Why did he tell the lie? Because *he* loved her and wanted to spare her feelings?

"Antonius behaved abominably. Anyone taking advantage of a girl who lost control through alcohol is a cheat who's sold himself to the devil." She withdrew her hand. "If Spagola sees us like this, he'll throw a fit. How are we going to get through this water?"

"Gusti, before we tackle that problem, let me say this to you: You'll always be my Zuckerrüberl. I've no desire to look at another girl. That's the situation. I won't make it difficult for you. You're with Karl. But if circumstances change, if you need me, or if you need help, now or at any other time..."

"All right," she said and reached for his hand again. The third admirer, the one she had left in the Milk Block, never entered her mind.

Dufft took off his shoes and socks and rolled up his trousers. Frau Spagola tucked the hem of her skirt into her knickers. They waded gingerly through the floodwater at the bottom of the steps. Further away from the bridge the ground rose and progress became easier but a vast, moving lake surrounded them. They knew of the Meadow's many holes and ditches. Holding hands once more, they advanced step-by-step, ankle deep, towards the refreshment hut.

Inside, on top of the counter, on a ramshackle chair, her generous flesh overhanging both sides, sat Poldi, softly whimpering. Her foot was wrapped in bloodstained pink cloth.

"Where's Spagola?" her mother asked impassively, as if coming upon her marooned daughter occurred every day.

"Haven't seen him," replied Poldi equally composed.

Frau Spagola sent a knowing glance at Dufft. "I thought all the time she hasn't seen him. Because do you know why? Because he's on ship in Budapest."

"I've been unlucky with my big toe," said Poldi.

Frau Spagola removed the stained cloth, which turned out to be the child's voluminous bloomers. Steadying herself on Dufft's shoulders, and with the aid of his pocket knife, she cut and tore strips of linen from her petticoat and wound them tightly round the wound. Poldi watched with intense curiosity, and at the same time recounted her adventure with Xandi.

"You went for a ride on the tram?" her mother said sternly. "If I catch you running off again..."

"And we were afraid the conductor would give a ticket to Gugi, but he told us to get off the tram."

"Promise me, never, never to do that again."

"Yes, Mum. And Xandi, he helped me walking. He is such a good walker, Mum. He is the best walker I've seen all my living life. Where's Xandi now, Mum?"

Dufft cleared his throat as he posed the questions: "If Herr Spagola wasn't with the children, who was? And why did he, whoever he was, leave her here?"

"Who was the man playing with you and Xandi?" Frau Spagola asked, her first aid finished.

"No one was playing with us, Mum."

"No one molested you? No one touched you? No one cuddled you?"

"I cuddled Xandi, because I love Xandi."

"Who was chasing Xandi?" asked Herr Dufft.

"The tram conductor chased us off the tram. He said we had fake money, but I didn't know that, because Manni Czarnikow gave it to me."

The contradicting eyewitness accounts gave Richard Dufft no peace. "Brunner says he spoke to Herr Spagola. Xandi says Herr Spagola chased him. She says she hasn't seen him."

"Herr Brunner must have been mistaken. Spagola wouldn't walk away and leave her. Spagola is in Budapest."

With one arm round her mother's neck and the other round Herr Dufft's, Poldi limped through deepening water to the safety of the bridge. Aware that he had helped rescue the child of his freckle-faced, wide-eyed, yesterday's Zuckerrüberl, Richard was filled with quiet contentment. His eyes went to Gusti, and she returned his look. He felt the warmth of Poldi's body penetrate his clothes. He agonised, if not a boy like Alexander, it would have been gratifying had Gusti borne his daughter, even one like Poldi.

Gusti, in turn, wondered what life would have been like as Frau Dufft. His injury? It must have healed. If he asked ask her now, she would say yes. Yes, but what of Berti, and what of Spagola?

"Mum, we left Gugi in the hut."

"We can't go back now, there's too much water, Poldi."

"Mum!"

"Listen, Poldi. The fire engines."

They could hear and see the red vehicles racing over the neighbouring Floridsdorf Bridge. The sight and sound distracted Poldi from the loss of her toy.

"Where's the fire, Mum?"

Dufft said, "They aren't going to a fire. They're carrying a boat. Somebody must be in difficulties on the Meadow."

The mystery of Karl Spagola's whereabouts troubled Dufft and Gusti for the rest of the day.

During the ensuing night Gusti slept badly. Towards dawn she rose, made herself a hot drink, sat by the window and found it restful to watch the fast flowing water of the Danube in flood.

CHAPTER NINE (1933)

Stolen Jewellery

Karl Spagola could reach only one conclusion, yet it was erroneous.

Inside the hut Lutschi Fritzer tidied herself up, and put on her brassiere, bracelets and necklaces. As he entered, she lifted a sagging chair back onto the counter. That done, she placed her arms round his waist, her head against his chest.

"What did Herr Brunner want?" she asked and kissed him on his chin. "And the Anzendrech boy?" She laughed. "He loves me, you know."

Karl stepped aside. "He's still after you? I'll make mincemeat of him."

"The boy. I mean the boy. It's because I slip him the extra sugar fish when he comes into the shop to buy two for a groschen."

"Did you steal the things from Morgenthau?" Karl nodded towards a small bag made from heavy, embroidered cloth with two handles.

"How do you think I got them?" She drew him back and kissed him on his ear.

"He gave them to you? Like he gave you that fat sapphire? Why would he give that to you? Because of your sterling gift for selling sugar fish? Or because you let him maul you?"

Lutschi involuntarily turned her hand so that the blue stone on her finger lay hidden from view. She continued fondling him but made no reply.

"Did you take things from my missus?"

She relaxed her hold. "Of course I didn't. What do you think I am? I wouldn't so much as look at any of her possessions, never mind touch them."

"And none from the Anzendrechs?"

"They haven't got nothing to take."

"Is Morgenthau a Jew?"

"Yes, he is. Why the interrogation?"

"You took the jewellery and he suspects you?"

"No. I carry the key to the shop, and I go back in, after he's locked up."

"I saw it coming, the calamity." Karl breathed a heavy sigh. He wriggled into his shirt and sleeveless, green pullover with a giant red heart stitched on the front, which Lutschi consistently eyed with jealousy. "You must have been crazy to think you'd get away with it," he added.

He opened the bag and looked at a collection of glittering objects: a bracelet, necklaces, rings, brooches, candlesticks, a watch, a silver chain.

"There's enough in it for Budapest?" Her voice betrayed anxiety.

Karl scratched his head: enough for a couple of Hungarian goulashes! The whole business of Budapest had run out of control. What had started as a daydream to be shared with the girl during moments of delight, and later used to deflect the inevitable reality, stared him in the face in the shape of the pilfered articles.

"You haven't sold any of this to anybody?" he asked.

"No."

"Given any away?"

"No."

"Lost any? It's important you tell me."

"No." She wavered, unsure and beginning to feel anxious. "A couple of days before your birthday, I just come out of the shop, Frau Anzendrech runs after me and hands me your watch."

"My watch?"

"The one on your wrist. The one I gave you on your birthday. The Riesenrad watch."

Karl's timepiece depicted the outline of the Giant Wheel, twelve of its suspended cars in place of numbers. The unique design had aroused curiosity among Milk Block tenants.

He said, "What's Frau Anzendrech got to do with my watch?"

"I dropped it coming out of the shop."

"Holy Jesus! I told Gusti my workmates gave it me. That's it," Karl moaned, "that figures."

"What? What is it, Karl?" She snuggled up to him again, against Gusti's pullover.

"They know."

"Who? Who knows? Who knows what?"

"The whole Milk Block knows. About us. About you and me."

"So? You're not married to her." Her nose was two centimetres away from the red heart; she smelled it.

"About you thieving the stuff. And besides the Milk Block, the police know as well. They'll be here any moment, because that old washerwoman Brunner won't keep the secret to himself, having found us. It figures. Frau Anzendrech tells my missus the Riesenrad watch came from you. Together they go and see Morgenthau. He finds the watch is missing, and the other bits and pieces as well, and Brunner sets the Anzendrech brat to spy on us."

"Herr Brunner told you that?"

"It figures all right." Karl Spagola began to think hard. His love life was one thing, going to prison for receiving stolen goods another. "How are you fixed with Morgenthau?"

Lutschi looked into his eyes, shrugged her shoulders.

"He *does* fancy you?"

"I don't care for him. I love you, Karli."

"Listen, if the police ask you where you got all of this from, you tell them Morgenthau gave it to you. Like he gave you the sapphire. He still gives you presents?"

"No. You see Frau Kristopp comes into the shop and shoves this paper into my face. I take it off her. It's a leaflet, and there's this rhyme on it. It went: One people, one nation, one leader, the Jews are getting greedier, the people are getting leaner, Heil Hitler, our redeemer."

"That's the political stuff Brunner plays around with," said Karl.

"And there's this ugly, brown head on the leaflet, with a beard and a crooked nose and dribbles running from it. Somebody's drawn a noose round the neck and pencilled Morgenthau on it. So I was holding the leaflet, and Morgenthau himself trots up. Frau Kristopp runs off, and before I could do anything, Morgenthau takes the paper from my hand. He never says a word. I tell him I had nothing to do with it, but he walks away."

"Now he's after your guts?" Karl considered the implications. "Or is he still making passes at you? Sticks his spout into you for instance?"

"Karli, I love you."

"That sapphire wasn't given for nothing. And that washerwoman Brunner? How does he fit into the picture?"

"Herr Brunner's been threatening to beat up Herr Morgenthau."

"Has Brunner made love to you?"

Lutschi Fritzer, her heart beating fast, not in memory of a past event in a boiler room, but at the turn of events now, murmured, "It was never like that."

Karl's jealousy waned as he contemplated the contents of the embroidered bag. "It might be a good idea to dump the lot."

"Can we hide it somewhere? On your ship? Until this blows over? Karli?"

"Let's go."

A narrow strip of dry grassland separated the hut from the river. The floodwater had already overflowed the edge of the bank where the fast current became evident. Feeling his way with one foot, Karl located the exact drop of the sloping embankment. Lutschi followed him, not noticing that her shoes were swamped after a few steps.

"It won't make any difference, Karli, to us? We can still go to Budapest?"

He realised with relief that discarding the tinny jewellery would let him off the Budapest hook.

"She has betrayed you," Lutschi went on.

"Gusti? Yes. And the things I've done for her! I took her and her brood in, you know, fed them and clothed them. Her camel-brained lump of suet is none of my doing, you know. And her everlasting praying. Gusti can pray the tail off the devil, if she sets her mind to it. The Old Man up in the clouds grants her wishes just to get a bit of peace and quiet. It goes on all through the night. You'd think she'd show some consideration for me, especially after a session."

"Karli!"

"I suppose hearing about you and me got her mad. There's no knowing what a woman won't do bitten by the bug."

"A bed bug?" Lutschi asked without thinking. Her mind was on other things.

"The jealousy bug, ninny."

Lutschi saw her world dissolve like a lump of lard melting away in a frying pan. Karl swung his arm, the embroidered bag hanging from his hand. She said, "Karli, the bag itself, it's mine."

He stopped the pendulum motion and opened the bag. "If I had known you were stealing all this."

"I only did it so we can go to Budapest."

He took out a silvery chain, fingered it for a while. "If they catch us with this, we are in the clink."

He hurled it into the Danube, and thereafter quickly threw the rest of the items into the water.

"You won't leave me, Karli?"

"Come on." He handed her the empty bag. "It's getting wet here."

They walked in silence towards the covered staircase of the Floridsdorf Bridge. Karl's main concern revolved around a story for Gusti. But a convincing excuse just would not take shape. Play the tactics of attack, come home drunk, knock her and the children about? No, he wasn't that type of cad. And what to do with Lutschi Fritzer? Take her back with him, to live as a threesome? After all, Gusti was no angel in spite of her praying, what with Richard Dufft, and that *Leutnant*, Poldi's father, now dead. And who knows who else, the laundry man Brunner?

He can't bring Lutschi home with him: the nagging of one woman was enough. He'll think of something.

Lutschi shivered from head to toe as he lifted her off the ground to carry her across the water-filled ditch to the covered staircase. She felt safe whilst in his arms, but on the bridge a trembling weakness diffused into her legs.

"Suppose the policemen are waiting for me outside my door, Karli?"

"Say you know nothing. The stuff's gone, they can't prove nothing."

"You will look after us, Karli? I'm not a thief really. I only did it for you. Hide me on your ship. Take me to Budapest."

"I can't. Not now."

"I'll be giving birth to the baby in prison."

"Baby?" What a time to bring that up. Just like a woman.

A burst of anger hit Lutschi. "Baby. Yes, baby. Your baby. It's all right for you. You have your fun and you get your pleasure. Well, what about me? What about me now? What have I got left? I won't have a job to go to tomorrow. Where am I going to get money from? What's to become of my baby?"

"Calm down," said Karl. "We'll think of something."

She leant over the railings. The fast flowing current made it appear as if the river stood still, and the bridge and she were receding at top speed, away from it all. If only it could be so. She sent an imploring look at Karl.

"God, I'm dry," he said, "I'm as dry as a roasted peanut in the middle of the Sahara at mid-day. I could do with a beer."

Lutschi's heart sank. Only a few weeks ago she had been playing the affair with Karli like a merry game where she knew all the rules. Now everything depended on the whims of the man. It wasn't a game any more, none of the old rules applied.

She pleaded once more: "You're not wed to her. You're wed to the one in Tulln, and she is poorly. You said she wouldn't live long. You don't care for one or the other! You promised you'll marry me. Do something about it."

Below in the river a faded white pleasure steamer pulled her funnel flat against the deck to clear the underbelly of the bridge. Her paddle wheels lashed the water but the vessel made slow headway against the current. The man and girl on the bridge, glad of the diversion, watched as the boat approached. They read the name of the vessel: *Budapest*. Lutschi let out a self-mocking laugh. On the ship a ruddy-cheeked man in traditional *Lederhosen*, pulled at an accordion, and people stood around clapping to the rhythm of the melody.

Lutschi raised her head when the steamer slipped away under the bridge. The Danube Meadow had given way to the rising river; only a small area around the refreshment hut showed grass.

"Look!" She pointed to the green patch where a dark object moved towards the hut.

"It's an animal," said Karl "Rolly the Alsatian belongs to the refreshment hut."

"We left the door open. It's crawling in. It'll drown in there. I'm going back."

"Are you meshugga?" Karl used the Jewish words for crazy, a frequent custom to underline the seriousness of a lunacy. But Lutschi was determined. The action would distract her from thinking about her prevailing predicament, if only for a short spell.

Karl also needed a change of situation. He held her back by her dress and said, "Wait here. I'll go."

He set off at a lively pace and immediately became aware of

several things: two constables in dark green uniform approaching from the city end of the bridge, and another two men of the same ilk looming up from the Floridsdorf end; Lutschi's stolen watch with its unusual face still girdling his wrist and very visible; the clatter of a trotting horse and jolting wheels hitting him from behind. His first impulse was to deliver the watch to the Danube and meet up with the policemen. But he could not dislodge the leather strap from the buckle. He glanced back at Lutschi: her eyes were fixed on the refreshment hut; he glanced at the horse and cart on the other side of the roadway heading for Floridsdorf.

Lutschi and the Policemen

"Fräulein!"

Startled, Lutschi spun round and faced two policemen. She had not noticed their approach. She braced herself for the inquisition.

"Nasty sight, the Danube in flood," said the taller of the two. His prominent cheekbones and sunken flesh gave his features the look of decay. Lutschi recognised the Skeleton.

"People drown in the Danube," said Breitwinkl, his companion, a friendlier looking policeman.

"Nasty sight a young woman drowned. What are you doing?" from the Skeleton.

"I'm looking for my friend."

"Where? Down there?"

Lutschi cast her eyes along the bridge, where she saw two more constables, no one else. She turned to the empty meadow. "He must be on the stairway."

"It's an offence loitering in the covered staircase," observed the Skeleton. "That's where it starts. We've known it to end with the young mother washed ashore below Vienna at Fischamend. We're going down the stairs ourselves. If we had found him and you in there, loitering in a public place, we'd have arrested you."

"You are arresting me now?" asked Lutschi.

"No," Breitwinkl laughed. "We are restricted to arresting people for illegal activity."

"One day we'll have the ability to see into people's minds," added the Skeleton, "we shall then arrest people for illegal thoughts. Suicide is illegal."

It dawned upon Lutschi that the policemen were not investigating the Morgenthau thefts, or that they did not connect her with them. She noticed the other two officers turning into the covered staircase.

The Skeleton continued to fire questions at her. "This friend of yours, what's he doing on the stairs?"

"He's going back to the refreshment hut, because there's a dog in it."

"A dog?"

"Yes, we saw it crawling in."

"Your dog?"

"No, the old Alsatian from the hut."

"You saw it from here? The hut is some way off. Are you sure it was a dog? Could it have been a child? Or two children?" the Skeleton asked.

"My friend's gone to see. Will the policemen go instead?"

Just then the two officers emerged from the covered staircase, and the parties joined up. They greeted one another by name, and Lutschi heard that the Skeleton was called Halbkrank.

The Skeleton explained: "The young woman says she saw something crawl into the hut. The man on the stairs, did he throw any light on the matter?"

"Man? What man? There's no man there."

The policemen turned to Lutschi for an explanation, but she had none. She felt desperately anxious to free herself from the overpowering presence of the many dark green uniforms. Now the thought occurred to her that Karli had simply dived headfirst into the Danube to escape the pincer movement of the police. Or perhaps somebody had fallen overboard from the steamer, and he had flung himself into the river to save the drowning person. Karli would do that. Had he not pulled out young Khan from the Zinkerbacherl last summer, and Khan's father creating for him a two kilo *Schlagobersbiskotentorte,* a cream biscuit-wafer cake, in gratitude?

Officer Breitwinkel watched as the last fleck of green around the refreshment hut vanished. "It's a job for the fire brigade. They'll have to bring a boat."

"Fräulein, come along with us." The Skeleton indicated the direction towards the Engerthstrasse police station. "We need a

130

statement about this creature you and your mysteriously vanished friend observed creeping into the hut."

Karl's Disappearance

Karl Spagola took three long strides and hoisted himself up onto the tailboard of the speeding cart, whereupon the policemen and Lutschi diminished in size and importance. He kept an eye forward, because not every coachman endorsed the principle of providing free conveyance for those who could not, or would not, raise the money for a tram ride. Lashing out with whips at uninvited hangers-on happened frequently. This one, however, did not know or did not care about his passenger, and Karl stayed on the vehicle until it slowed down in the busy streets of Floridsdorf. There he jumped off and wandered about feeling a cad. To let Lutschi face the policemen alone seemed like the action of a coward. But he was no coward. He just did not believe in going down with a sinking ship. He told himself he had had no choice. The Riesenrad watch would have proved a giveaway and made matters worse for Lutschi. Now she had a fighting chance of talking herself out of the hole. He hoped that she would have enough sense, if questioned, to endow him with a false name. Yet in spite of these arguments, he felt a cad.

He walked the streets. He needed time to work things out. Tired and mentally exhausted he stepped into a wine-and-beer cellar. He drank and regurgitated the unsettling thoughts: why has Gusti betrayed him? Because of his affair with Lutschi? Or was the laundry man mixed up in this? That womaniser had been hovering round Gusti. Or her Jewish childhood lover, caught red-handed? Or any of the unemployed hanging around all day in the Milk Block courtyard? Why was he shovelling coke into sacks, when other men played cards? Why did he always get the rough deal? Same with Susanne, his estranged wife. It wasn't his fault she contracted tuberculosis. And just because he went out to have a little fun, she shut the door on him, and posted her monstrous brothers to stand guard. All right, he looked for a bit on the side. So? What man doesn't, or fantasises about it? At least he had the guts to act out his impulses. And now Lutschi, she goes completely crazy over a moonshine story about Budapest, and on top of that gets herself pregnant!

To crown it all, Gusti sets the police on him. And all the things he had done for her, for her schmalz-barrelled daughter, for her boy who, for all he knew, had also sprung from another man. And for the friends of her children, the Anzendrech crew: Alexander comes to eat Reisfleisch, which he provides!

His eyes went watery from self-pity and wine. He requested another bottle; the barman declined to oblige unless he produced money. Karl placed all the coins from his pocket on the table. The barman told him a lot more were needed.

"Never you mind," Karl slurred, "I tell you what we shall do. You bring me a half a litre *Heurigen*, put it right here. And, whilst you bring me the wine, I shall divest myself of my beautiful pullover with the love heart, the red, bleeding love heart. It was knitted for me by the woman I cherished. But she let herself be dragged down into the gutter, by a laundry supervisor, and by a newspaper man, and by ... just about anybody. I'll put the pullover down in part exchange, how's that?"

He began to strip off. The barman called for assistance and when Karl realised they meant to march him off the premises, he said, "I have a better idea. You take my watch. It's a watch in a million. It features the Riesenrad, see? I have the *Heurigen*, you have the watch."

Karl struggled with the wristband, managed in the end to release the clasp, and handed the watch over. The barman examined it, and quietly put it in his pocket. He brought the wine.

Night was well advanced when Karl tottered along the street with no knowledge of his whereabouts. He congratulated himself on his sagacity for bartering the incriminating watch against the evening's drink. He staggered on aimlessly, and eventually found himself on a stretch of gravel road that he knew. It ended at the bank of the Old Danube Lake, continued as a footpath alongside the Northrailway Line to the dam of the Danube Meadow. The pedestrian walk of the Northrailway Bridge lay in darkness, but the water covering the Danube Meadow glistened in a silver sheen. He distinguished the outlines of the Milk and Cocoa Blocks on the other side of the river. He saw windows lit up, amongst them one behind which Gusti and Brunner celebrated...in bed? He'd get even with the swine! He decided to spend the rest of the night in the yards of his employers, and have another go at working things out in the morning.

He groped for the gap in the wire fencing through which he had seen Berti and his Anzendrech friends slither. He scrambled through, crept along the timber stack and stumbled in pitch black to his familiar patch. He scooped out a niche in a small coke mountain, lined it with sacks, and laid himself in it, waiting for the natural warmth of coke to penetrate through. But he registered no rise in temperature. He thought it strange. He fingered a few lumps to ascertain the reason, but whilst doing this, fell asleep.

He dreamt he was removing Reisfleisch from the Peeping Tom, Alexander Anzendrech, who in turn was throwing wet ten-shilling notes at his cheeks. He woke with a start as cold pieces of material from the coke mound skidded into his face. Stiff and shivering, surrounded by the grey light of early morning, he brushed debris off his head, chest and legs. He set off running towards the Reichsbridge to stimulate his circulation. As his quickening heartbeat generated heat, he noticed the *Budapest* steaming downstream very near the bank. Karl thought it an omen. Why not, indeed, hide away on a ship and start a new life in Budapest?

But fate decreed otherwise.

Shipwreck

The vessel commenced the turning manoeuvre to head against the current for docking at the Reichsbridge landing stage. Her bow pointed directly at Karl, when movement ceased. In this configuration, at right angles to the river, her paddles locked. The ship floated helplessly on. Wide-eyed, still running, Karl witnessed the *Budapest* strike the first supporting pillar of the Reichsbridge.

Men fell into the river. The vessel hovered on the pier like a giant sausage pronged in the middle. Then she broke into two. The rudder end vanished. The front portion turned turtle, and ended up with the ship's open belly wedged into the girders of the bridge, the bow seemingly embedded into the river bed. Karl spied a man's head flat against the side of the wreck, holding on, defying the force of the water.

Indeed, coward he was not. He stripped off his jacket, dived into the Danube, and his powerful stroke soon brought him in line with the broken vessel. Lying on his back, he cushioned the impact against the hulk with his feet. He grasped broken protrusions, realising that one false move and he would be swept beyond hope of rescuing his fellow creature, or be knocked against metal and so himself become a victim. He inched his way towards the man's head. His progress was suddenly impeded as if he were held back. Gingerly he turned his head, and knew without seeing properly that the point of a snapped railing lay entangled in his pullover. He cursed his foolishness for not having discarded it before jumping into the water. Twisting and contorting, clinging with one hand onto the end of a steel rope, he managed to slip his head through the garment. He freed one arm. Wriggling out of the other, he lost his grip. At once he was sucked towards a tangle of railings. With a calculated push, he escaped their mauling action, and threw one arm round the neck of the gasping man. Both heads hit the ship's side, Karl's centimetres from the razor edge of ripped steel. Both men went under; Karl had anticipated it and taken a deep breath. On surfacing, he applied his life-saving hold on the other's limp body.

He dragged the victim ashore some way below the landing stage, and became immediately aware that the man was dead, either from drowning or the deep gash across the throat from which blood poured out. He also realised that not a soul had witnessed the accident, but that this state would not last, that in spite of the early hour people would come rushing in. So what to do? To report the matter would mean throwing himself deliberately into the hands of the police, and this for a dead person of no connection, when only yesterday he had escaped their clutches in abandoning a very much alive person of very close connection. The man was gone. Nothing could restore his life. The Danube had claimed him, so let the Danube have him. But before rolling the body back into the water, Karl went through the man's pockets. To his astonishment they were packed with soaking wads of banknotes. He remembered the wet ten shillings thrown into his face when he woke on the coke heap: 'that boy's got the magic touch. It pays to dream of him!' And he pushed the money into his pockets.

The river swallowed the corpse in an instant. Karl washed away all traces of diluted blood from the bank and his own person. He left the spot unobserved and headed for the nearby woods and fields of the Kriau.

Chief Police Officer Sessl

Chief Police Officer Sessl was no fool.

But he wished he could be serving an institution in which a policeman's lot depended on performance rather than on one's aptitude for not being a fool. He recognised the importance of law, and excelled in administering it: in apprehending thieves, in arresting ringleaders of strikes and members of illegal organisations, in tracking down loiterers in public places, in retrieving lost children, in name-taking of ball-players on forbidden grass. He envied his counterparts in other lands: Sherlock Holmes' mastery of criminology had not been hampered by changing politics, in which the wrong allegiance today could mean the end of one's career tomorrow. The Vienna police teemed with Nazi sympathisers; some were known to attend secret meetings even during duty hours. And across the border they were travelling on a one-way ticket into their Third Reich. Austria could be sucked into the slipstream by the flick of a political switch. And then what?

The bomb attack on the Danube Coke Company pointed to Nazi fanatics, so was it wise to track down the insurgents? Local men like Brunner and Kristopp, or men from Germany running branches of German businesses? Or would it be better to question a few prominent Schutzbund and Heimwehr activists? Or pull up the mentally retarded Isidor Kuhspiegel of the Milkblock? It would be simple to parade Isidor with a grudge against the company, say, having been chastised for lifting coke? No, he shied away from the corrupt thought. Best get away with doing nothing.

He had planned to spend the Sunday evening in the Gasthof *Waldhäusl,* the wee-little forest inn, tucked away on the slopes of Neuwaldegg, a wooded Vienna suburb, where no one knew him as a policeman, where he could enjoy wine and sentimental Viennese waltzes, where he could make eyes at pretty waitresses in their dirndl costumes, pat their firm buttocks and, if in luck, let his palm linger thereon for a second, where he could participate in controversial chat with his convivial table companions. The afternoon drew to a close. He was in a sour mood. The report of the two lost children, together with the items the fire brigade had unearthed in the waterlogged refreshment hut, meant that Neuwaldegg faded as fast as the daylight.

He opened a cupboard and removed from it a yellow object, shapeless and threadbare. He had been baffled by it, until Constable Breitwinkel, father of a four- year old, recognised in it the remains of a cuddly toy. He placed it on his desk, returned to the cupboard and took out an enormous pair of pink bloomers speckled with red stains.

"The wearer must resemble a gasometer," he muttered to himself.

He spread the garment out on the floor in the manner of a hearth rug, sat down and rested his eyes upon it, seeking inspiration for a connection between it and the missing children. The facts, as he saw them, were these: one eight-year-old boy, Alexander Anzendrech, and one fifteen-year-old girl, Poldi Spagola, walk away from the municipal housing block in the Engerthstrasse at around eleven a.m. A young woman, Lyudmila Fritzer, reports that she witnessed the entry of a creature, human or beast, into a trader's hut on the flooded Inundation Land at about two p.m. Her companion allegedly sees the said creature also, and sets out for the hut to investigate. He cannot subsequently be located. The fire service reaches the hut by boat at three thirty p.m. and finds in it a yellow, weather-worn cuddly toy plus an outsize, blood-stained lady's undergarment.

Sessl decided on visiting the mothers of the lost children himself. At the same time, the policeman Halbkrank, known even in the station as the Skeleton, entered.

"Frau Anzendrech's here. The children have turned up."

Sessl prepared to set off for Neuwaldegg.

CHAPTER TEN (1933)

The Pullover with the Red Heart

From her window, Gusti Spagola saw the steamer *Budapest* strike the pier of the Reichsbridge. She woke Poldi, told her sleep-befuddled daughter she would be back soon, and hurried to the bridge. People were coming from everywhere. She fought her way through the crowd, and looked down into the open belly of the wreck. A pullover with a bright red heart pierced by a spike from twisted metal beckoned her.

"That's my man's sweater," she cried, and at that instant she understood the devastating reality, the solution to the mystery of Spagola's whereabouts. He had told her he would be away on ship in Budapest. He must have said that he would be away on the ship *Budapest*.

"My man is on that steamer," Gusti screamed and appealed to a police officer, but he and other constables carried orders to clear the bridge so it could be cordoned off.

Gusti struggled. "That's my man's pullover."

"The fire brigade men will get it," they told her and dragged her away.

The fire brigade had little idea what to do. Their dilemma ceased, however, when amidst thundering shudders, the half wreck rolled over, disintegrated, and vanished from view.

Hope that Spagola had survived did not enter Gusti's mind. She recalled the incident on the day of Alexander Anzendrech's birth, when she had overheard his words flirting with Vikki Huber and drawing blood from his finger. And the reason for his death came in direct consequence of her bargain with God: she would live in sin no more if He would save Poldi. Poldi had been saved, and the only way the bargain could be kept meant either her own demise or Spagola's. She had been spared. Spagola had not.

She rushed back to her children. They looked at her with alarm. She cuddled them, spread extra schmalz on their bread, told them nothing. The harsh truth could wait until later, when Berti finished school. She kept her daughter in bed because the injured toe throbbed and ached. Gusti's mind could not latch onto the story of *Aschenbrödel, the* Austrian Cinderella, which Poldi wanted to hear, twice. First time round had been spoilt by too many long pauses.

How will she clothe and feed the children without Spagola's shillings? Yesterday Richard Dufft had told her if she needed help, he would be there. She knew she must act before the shock of the catastrophe struck her. As she walked to the Cocoa Block, men carrying bundles of newspapers ran past, shouting, "Special Edition! Special Edition! 'The *Budapest* slams into the Reichsbridge. All aboard feared drowned..."

Frau Dufft opened the door.

"I'd like to speak to Herr Richard," said Gusti.

"He's not here. He is away for a few days."

"Oh yes. Berlin. I forgot. Spagola's dead."

Richard's mother breathed in and grew visibly larger. "Well. My condolences. What was the matter with him?"

"Drowned. Gone down with the *Budapest*. The steamship *Budapest*. She sank after hitting the Reichsbridge. Have you not heard?"

Frau Dufft shook her head. "Why do you want to speak to Richard?"

Now, the reality, like black treacle, crept into every corner of Gusti's being: 'Gone. He's gone.'

"I am sorry about your misfortune," said Frau Dufft.

Gusti said noting.

"Richard has his own problems," said Frau Dufft.

Gusti sensed resentment streaming from Richard's mother.

"I am sorry," said Frau Dufft.

Why the distorted smile on Gusti's lips? Because the bitter sweetness of disaster is heightened by total disaster?

She met Xandi on her way back to the Milk Block.

"Is Poldi's toe better?" he asked.

"Come and see."

"I got to get sour milk and rice for Mummy first."

Will there ever be another Reisfleisch day? Gusti wondered.

Echinopsis and Rhipsallis

The day promised to be sunny and warm, and in such weather sunbathing would not rouse suspicion.

Around midday Karl Spagola slipped into shapeless trousers, and stowed away six hundred and eighty, dried shilling notes. With this sudden wealth nestling in his pocket and his hand over it, yesterday's problems of Lutschi, Gusti and Brunner receded to a century ago. He needed new clothes, he needed a new abode, he needed a new face, he needed a new woman.

All these things, with the exception of the growth of a beard, came to him in a short time. Shrewd enough to avoid purchasing an entire new outfit in one swoop, he bought a shirt here, a pair of trousers there, socks and shoes elsewhere. He selected the Wirtshaus Volksprater on the Danube Canal and noticed Reisfleisch on the menu. He ordered a large portion with a large beer. Having quelled the rebellion in his stomach, he scanned the framed photographs of cigar- shaped flying ships decorating the walls. A little later his gaze wandered over to the forest of cacti on the windowsills. Empty chairs had become fewer and conversations louder. Comments relating to the *Budapest* accident travelled to his ears from all quarters of the room.

Returning from a toilet visit to his half-empty glass, he found seats next to his occupied by two women.

"Oh, excuse us," said one of them, "we thought the table was free."

"I claim the wee-little space my posterior needs to sit on, the rest of the world is entirely at your disposal."

"We don't wish to infringe on your privacy."

"Infringement by two such charming ladies as yourselves can only be a delight."

"Thank you," said the older-looking woman, "it's a real treat to hear a gentleman's compliment."

"What will you drink, Fräuleins?" Karl produced a fistful of banknotes, selected one and hailed the waiter.

"Have you robbed a bank, or do you own one?" asked the younger woman, who wore her hair in pigtails.

"Sold up everything," replied Karl.

"Don't you squander your savings on a pair of Prater women."

"Shut up, Lisl, he just wants to be courteous," remonstrated the pigtailed one.

"As a matter of fact," said Karl, "I'm celebrating the last day before my departure. I've got a passage on the *Graf Zeppelin* to America."

The two women goggled at him, half in admiration, half in disbelief.

"To help my cousin grow cactuses. He's got fields over there, bigger than the whole of Vienna, and on them nothing but cactuses." Karl's imagination boomed: a Zeppelin flight to America for cacti cultivation made a far more interesting tale than the shuttle to the Handelskai for filling sacks with coke.

The women quaked, enraptured. Karl learned that their professional activities also connected them with gas-filled space vehicles, although theirs evinced less glamour than the flying ship *Zeppelin*. They told him laughingly of their Prater pitch, at which they could be seen touting for custom, selling their collection of many-coloured, sky-clamouring balloons. The younger, pig-tailed one said her name was Steffi.

"Ottakrink, Karl Ottakrink."

A boy came in selling special newspaper editions. People snapped them up, eager to read the latest about the *Budapest* disaster. His last two sheets went to Steffi and Lisl.

"Dreadful business," remarked Lisl, "not one survivor, everyone washed away." Looking up from her news-sheet, she said to Karl, "The fire brigade struggled to salvage a pullover hanging from a broken rail. One pullover."

He savoured her large blue eyes.

She went on: "The ship broke up before they got to it"

"It says here," Steffi took over the story, "sabotage can't be ruled out."

Lisl raised her eyes again, and beckoned to another woman who had just entered.

"Meet Herr Ottakrink," she hailed the newcomer, "our friend of today, who's off to America tomorrow," and to Karl: "This is Madame Fleurie, the best soothsayer in the Prater."

Karl's throat felt as if a football was forcing its way down as his eyes picked out a young woman whose tanned features, framed by black hair, contrasted with her white costume.

"Herr Ottakrink's business is in cactuses," Lisl with the blue eyes volunteered further.

"Yes? Echinopsis? Rhipsallis?" asked the black-haired vision.

Karl swallowed hard, and said quickly, "Let me get you a drink, Madam Fleurie. But first, come, let me show you."

The two balloon ladies watched, surprised, as Karl led the fortune teller to the cacti by the window. But they plied their attention again to the special editions.

"It says here," Lisl observed, "that there was a scuffle with policemen. A woman recognised the pullover as her husband's. She said she recognised the red heart stitched into it."

"Poor woman," said Steffi, shaking her head, which sent the pigtails swinging like pendulums.

At the window the black-haired beauty asked Karl, "Since when Herr Ottakrink?"

"Since today. I need to be known by a different name."

"Why?"

"I had a dream. I dreamt of Poldi's friend Alexander Anzendrech. You remember the little brat? He's got a special gift. I dreamt he threw money at me. The dream came true. Up your street really if you haven't changed your trade. It's a long story and rather boring. So what about you, Vikki, since when Madame Fleurie?"

"My professional name."

"You're still in the fortune telling business?"

"I am. I still tell people what they tell me, and what they want to hear."

"What's all this about Echinopsis and Reposes or whatever?"

"Rhipsallis. They are cacti."

"You're studying botany?"

"It pays to know these things if you're a fortune teller. I know about Saint Assisi, I know who Caravaggio was, I know what elephants' shit looks like, I even know the difference between ordinary steam and superheated steam for boilers. But that's boring too. Where have you been all this time?"

"Nowhere much. And you?"

"When I recovered from the upset that you threw me over for the

141

Morgenthau girl, I moved from the Meldemannstrasse. Clients don't like calling on derelict places. Of course you didn't know. But that's not why you haven't been to see me? And now you are off to America? I don't really believe that."

"I could change my mind," said Karl.

Coincidences Happen All the Time

"Xandi," said Herr Dufft, "which way is the best to the Northrailway Station?"

The little boy helped out happily. "Take the number five tram from the Taborplatz to the Praterstern."

"Thanks." Dufft extracted from his pocket a bag of eucalyptus sweets, which he had bought for sucking away the tedium of the impending journey, and placed three in Xandi's hand.

Twenty minutes later, with a rucksack containing five days' clothing, toiletry and note books, Dufft had waited for a longer than normal time at the number 5 tram stop when a *Sonderwagen, a* tram out of service, rattled past without stopping.

"Verdammte Sauwirtschaft!"

Dufft glanced at a face marred by a scar across the left cheek and said light-heartedly, "Looks like the tramway men are on extended siesta. Looks like I'll have to spend the night here. Should have packed a tent."

The reply came over in a German accent. "A fine start to your holiday."

"I'm on an occupational trip. I carry the rucksack because I need my hands free to scribble down notes."

"Scribble a note to the Transport Authority. Enclose a feather pillow to sweeten their dreams. Attached to a can of explosives to wake them up."

"Or filled with a nest of thirsty bedbugs," Dufft warmed to the banter. "I shouldn't have listened to my wonder boy. I should have taken the A-tram from the Reichsbridge."

"You have a wonder boy?"

"He carries the entire tram network in his head."

"My wonder boy is a Valhalla hero who's got the gift of staving off disaster. We need him here now."

Eventually a tram did arrive. Dufft reached his destination. He bought a newspaper and entered the railway station.

His new acquaintance stood at a vacant ticket counter. "I should have brought a tent as well."

"It's my lucky day," replied Dufft, "the Berlin train don't leave for another ninety minutes. This fills me with hope; when the ticket man's siesta is over, there's still time for a beer and goulash."

"You're indeed lucky travelling to Berlin. You'll be needing free hands to jot down plenty of notes. You'll find slipshod management isn't tolerated in Germany's new regime."

"Here he comes," said Dufft, his eyes on the scurrying station official. "By the relief on his face he must have been caught short, managed it just in time."

"By the relief of his face," the other sneered at the ticket clerk's thick lips and flat nose, "he needs to be chased back to the Congo."

Dufft thought: *The man's a whacky racist.*

A few minutes later, outside the Wirtshaus Praterstern, he heard the now familiar accent behind him: "What do you think the chances are that we'll find the barmen asleep in here?"

"Ah, we meet again," said Dufft with little enthusiasm.

"What a coincidence. Or is it providence?"

"In my profession coincidences happen all the time, especially when nobody's aware of them," lectured Dufft.

"Like strangers unknowingly paying homage to the same gigantic man?"

"Or to the same insignificant boy," said Dufft for the fun of confounding this pompous person.

"Or strangers conversing, unaware they share the same political aspiration."

"Or strangers conversing, unaware that one of them respects human dignity," said Dufft.

He opened the door to the Wirtshaus Praterstern, ignorant of the totally irrelevant coincidence that Karl Spagola stepped into the Wirtshaus Volksprater at the same moment.

"Are you German?"

Duff replied, "I'm Viennese, through and through."

"I have friends in Berlin," said the man with the scar on his face.

"Fingers crossed I won't encounter too many foes."

143

"You'll see a difference in the new Germany. There the heat's been turned on to spark off a future for the *Deutsche Volk*, the German people. I wish I could come with you. Unfortunately I'm obliged to turn the heat on to kindle a future for your *Volk* here."

"The people here could do with a bit of extra heat, especially in winter."

"Very funny. Talking about heat: my business is heating engineering."

"Mine's writing funny stories for newspapers."

Dufft located an empty table.

"That is interesting. Perhaps you won't object if I sit with you."

Politeness dictated Dufft's assent.

"I am Hildebrandt, Heinrich Hildebrandt, Director, Vienna Branch of Klug und Krapf." He reminisced in thought: *Two years ago I shared a table with a stranger, a tram conductor, and that led to Vikki. An omen. Vikki! Your white blouses, your bulges. The olive skin, the pink circles...* He sat down and continued fantasising: *... the pointed nipples. No. My Führer! You command, I obey.* He fidgeted on his chair, countered the phantasm, as he had trained himself to do, with political endeavour. "The people need journalists not afraid to spell out the truth of Hitler's National Socialist Movement."

"I shall spell out the truth of Hitler's National Socialist Movement," said Dufft.

"Good. Good. You will be visiting the exhibition *Der Ewige Jude*, The Everlasting Jew, in Berlin?"

"I was told better jokes can be seen and heard at the Katakombe."

"A hot bed of Jewish decadence. The Katakombe cabaret and the Exhibition show the Jew in his true light. Do you write about Jews?"

"About Austrians, Germans, Poles, Chinese, Gypsies, Red Indians, Jews. About anybody and anything that tickles our sense of the ludicrous. Last week I wrote about the Jew who converted to Catholicism, and a month later to Protestantism."

"An example of Jewish duplicity."

"An example of Jewish self-preservation. He reckons if National Socialism comes this way, and he's asked. 'What is your religion?' he answers 'Protestant'. And if he's asked, 'What was your religion before that?' he truthfully says 'Catholic'."

"Laughable indeed," said Hildebrandt. "If he changes his religion a thousand times, we'd still be able to tell he's a Jew. We can smell a Jew three kilometres away in a hurricane, can't we, Herr..."

"Dufft, Richard Dufft. I write funny, satirical stories. My immediate job is to unearth amusing tales from Berlin, and from my journey thither, like now."

A student of facial physiognomy would have construed that the onset of rapid twitching and discolouring in Hildebrandt's scar stemmed from a meteoric collapse of metabolism. Hildebrandt mentally stitched together the new situation. *So here sits this Dufft, this meddler in the Schicklgruber saga, this Hebrew, this sample of vermin who sniffs and snoops around. Well, well, well. Give me a chance to show who is master here.*

"What a coincidence," escaped from his lips. "Or is it providence?"

"To what do you refer?" asked Dufft.

Hildebrandt pulled himself out of his mental frenzy. His thinking was clear. "Our meeting. I said I have colleagues in Berlin. They can assist you in your quest. They know the German capital from end to end, they know the right places where you can laugh your head off, they know the right people who understand a joke. Let me give you names and telephone numbers. Better still, tell me the hotel you are staying at, and I'll ask them to get in touch with you."

The waiter stood at their table. Dufft hesitated between Hungarian goulash and Reisfleisch, but in the end chose the Magyar dish. He glanced at his newspaper. He read in the stop press column: *The pleasure steamer* Budapest *sinks in the Danube. The ship collides with the Reichsbridge pier.*

"Holy wall of Jerusalem! Do you know anything about this?"

"They're selling Special Editions. I can hear them outside. They'll be in here any moment," replied the waiter, ready to take down the other man's order.

Hildebrandt looked at his watch. "I can't stop. I just wanted a quick beer. Haven't got time now. My train leaves in a few minutes. Oh, Dufft. The name of your hotel."

"Hotel Osterhof, Heerenstrasse."

"Ha! Another coincidence. I know people at the Hotel Osterhof. I'll contact them. They'll make your stay memorable in Berlin, I assure you." With that he left.

Hildebrandt had ample time before the departure of his train for

Korneuburg, a small town a little way beyond Bisamberg. He walked up and down the platform glowing with joy. Revenge is sweet. His eyes fell on a young woman in a white blouse. Vikki? He casually passed her. No, not she. Before delivering his pep talk to Korneuburg's Parteigenossen, he telephoned Berlin HQ of the SA with instructions to organise a special reception, a very special reception, for the Jewish resident Dufft at the Hotel Osterhof, Heerenstrasse.

Left alone the journalist looked forward to his goulash. Just as he was about to raise his hand to hail the boy shouting, "Special Edition, Special Edition," he had a fearful thought. He reached for his wallet instead. His passport was OK. Then the paper with the list of hotels, a cross marked against the one he had booked. Reassured, he sat back. He looked for the Special Edition seller, but the boy had gone. Never mind, disasters were hardly a good source of amusing anecdotes; a few satirical comments at best. Still he must not allow himself to be deflected from the task ahead. The next few days belonged to Berlin, not to Vienna. He ate his meal, mentally planning his trip from the doors of the Hotel le Meridien to the Katakombe.

CHAPTER ELEVEN (1933)

An Unforeseen Turn of Events

God is punishing me, Gusti decided after Xandi had sped off for sour milk and rice. *I asked for it. Now that he's gone, what am I to do? I did love him, in spite of his women. Spagola, what am I to do for money? There's Richard. He, with or without his dreadful mother, still wants me? Do I still love him? Shall I snuggle up to him when he's back from Berlin? Better than earning a groschen peddling for people's laundry? Laundry! There's the laundry man, the woman-eating panther. What now?*

"I've been dreaming of you every night," said Brunner, clad in his khaki boiler suit, stepping into her path. "I've been dreaming of you and me ..."

"Spagola's gone," she interrupted.

He took her hands: "He's run off? Makes things simpler for us."

She freed herself. "I saw his ship hit the bridge. He drowned."

"What, he was on the *Budapest*? Sorry to hear that."

"I'm to blame. I killed him."

Brunner laughed. "What a funny notion. I'll tell you who's to blame, sweetheart: the Jews. The Jews sank that rusty tin can to get rich on the insurance."

"I made a bargain with God. It's His punishment."

"Punishment? We'll punish the Jew; believe you me, my pet. If a Jew smells dosh anywhere, he's on the spot. I bet Israelite Dufft will show up, pretending to be on your side." He reached for her hands again. "He'll call you sweet names, but in reality he's like a bedbug. He'll suck you dry."

"Richard's not like that." She shook off his hand.

"Stay clear of him. I warn you, stay clear of him. If your old man went down with the *Budapest*..." He faltered, how could Karl Spagola have been on board that ship coming down river from Tulln, when on the previous day he himself had exchanged angry words with him on the Danube Meadow? "You'll be getting money, compensation money. I tell you again: Jew Dufft will be after you, for the shillings. If he sees he can't make headway, he'll change his tack. He'll work with the company so they can avoid paying out, so he collects his cut that way. Stay clear of him." He reached for her again.

Gusti, for the second time, retracted her hands. "Richard wouldn't do that."

"No? If I see him pestering you, I'll render him impotent for the rest of his life."

"I'll speak to whom I please."

"What makes you think your old man was on the ship?"

"Spagola told me he'd be away on the *Budapest*. I saw his pullover hanging on the wreck. The green one with the red heart." A solitary tear massed in her eye.

Brunner, like all residents from the Milk and Cocoa Blocks, had seen Karl wearing the garment. He said, "Couldn't it have been a lookalike pullover?"

"There's only one like that. I knitted it. Spagola drowned. And a Gypsy woman foretold he'd drown."

"The day before, on the Danube Meadow, he and I ..." Brunner stopped. Not his problem to figure out how her husband got onto the ship.

"The day before, you said you spoke to him on the Danube Meadow?"

The laundryman's thinking performed a somersault. Nothing to be gained by sticking to the factual story. A drowned husband pointed to compensation money for Gusti. And Gusti with cash meant a worthier catch than Gusti without.

He replied, "Coming to think of it I didn't speak to your old man. No, I talked to somebody else who looked like your husband. Don't worry; I'll see you're all right. I've said before, you get shot of your old man, I'll step into his place."

"I loved Spagola," said Gusti and burst into tears.

"You'll get over it. We'll put in a compensation claim."

"Compensation goes to Spagola's widow."

Brunner signalled assent. "Sure. You'll get it."

"His widow lives in Tulln. I ... was never his wife."

Brunner's chin dropped. This turn of events he had not foreseen.

After a while he said, "You are a bit of a sly filly, aren't you? All this time I took you for a married woman." He pondered, Gusti, single and without prospect of compensation, called for a new strategy. If he cooled off now, she'd turn to the Jew Dufft. This must not happen.

Dufft's Faux Pas

Richard Dufft came back with only a few jokes in his notebook, most of these told by a political fugitive he had sat next to on his return journey. The man was a font of information, and appropriately his name was "Quelle", which translates to Fountain.

His first call was Gusti. She greeted him, and immediately expressed concern about Brunner's threat.

"Listen," replied Richard, "I put up with intimidation coming from your Karl, understandable, but I don't care a donkey's turd what that despicable Nazi has to say on the matter. If he wants a showdown, I'd be happy to oblige him. How's Poldi?"

"She's over at the Anzendrechs, playing tram games with Xandi. Keeps her mind off it. It's touched Berti more."

Richard wondered why Poldi's swollen toe should affect her half-brother to any great extent, but he shrugged it off. "How did Herr Spagola explain why he left her in the hut?"

Gusti's silence and quivering lips suggested something besides Brunner's threats troubled her. He produced a small box in shiny gold paper: "I haven't given you anything for a long time. I thought after our venture rescuing Poldi, I might be forgiven for bringing you something back from Berlin."

He delighted in watching her agile fingers undo the wrapping and reflected that it was how she moved them when she was seventeen. She lifted the dainty lid.

"Earrings!" She held them against her lobes, went into the bedroom to peep into her mirror, came back to him and stood on tiptoe to raise her mouth level to his.

"If Karl sees them, say..." Dufft shrugged his shoulders.

"What?"

"Tell him.... well, only wear them when he's away on his ships."

Gusti fell back onto her heels. "That's a horrible thing to say."

Not understanding her reaction, he spluttered, "You think he'll jiggle a knees-up when he sees them dangling from your ears?"

"Even Herr Brunner wouldn't make such a remark."

"Herr Brunner! What's he got to do with it?"

"At least he said he was sorry."

"Whatever are you talking about?"

"Spagola's been a good man."

"Spagola, Brunner! Never me! My God, I wish they were both dead."

"I think you'd better go."

The Official Version

Each day Rudolf Anzendrech, the tram conductor, bought for one groschen a one-day-old *Neues Wiener Journal,* a leading Vienna newspaper, from the Gasthof Am Spitz in Floridsdorf. This kept the Anzendrechs informed of world events. When the *Budapest* sank, Brigitte could not wait twenty-four hours for the latest reports and the habit of a lifetime for cheap reading was temporarily suspended. Every member of the family scurried to sift through the pages; even Xandi devoured the words although he did not understand them all.

The official investigation revealed that the *Budapest* took on fuel on Saturday, and on the following morning called at the Reichsbridge landing stage, where passengers embarked for a leisure cruise up-river to Tulln and through the Wachau to Krems, Melk and Linz. Due to the fierce current and a fault in the boiler system, the vessel arrived at Tulln three hours late. The captain decided to discontinue the trip; all passengers were taken off, and the ship left for the repair docks in the Winterhafen at the lower end of Vienna at first light the next day. On the way down the vessel was to land at the Reichsbridge jetty to enable one member of the crew to disembark for the nearby Danube Coke Office with documents and ready cash, as the recent bomb blast on the company's premises had disrupted normal working procedure. Power and steering control collapsed during the docking manoeuvre. The force of the floodwater swept the *Budapest* broadside against the Reichsbridge pier. The steamer broke in two. One half sank and vanished, the other half remained wedged under the bridge for some forty minutes before it rolled over and disintegrated. There were no survivors. Danube Coke, owners of the *Budapest*, confirmed that once legal matters had been finalised, compensation to the widows, or in the absence of widows, to the dependants of the perished crew, would receive attention.

Subsequently a newspaper carried the scoop that contaminated coke, amounting to ninety per cent slag, had been located in the company's yard. A Nazi publication claimed that the disaster had been engineered by the Jewish owners, deliberately burning dross and thus starving the vessel of sufficient steam power, which led to the tragic deaths of stalwart Aryan sailors. The devilish deed was intended to reap high profits from excessive insurance cover against the loss of a rusting, worthless ship. And the bomb attack on the company's offices preceding this Jewish atrocity had apparently been a demonstration by local Aryan citizens in response to having had to put up with non-burning coke supplied by these devilish Jews during the past winter.

Danube Coke Company announced that management had no previous knowledge of the presence of the inferior fuel, that it could not have been deposited through normal unloading operations by crane from moored barges, and that it must have been delivered clandestinely by road transport. The matter, they declared, had been placed in the hands of the police.

Lutschi's Fears

Lutschi Fritzer lived through an agony of uncertainties. Karl had been with her on the Floridsdorf Bridge, and he had vanished.

Did he jump into the river, and get onto the ship? No, the *Budapest* steamed upstream, Karl would have been carried downstream. Perhaps when he emerged from the covered staircase he hid behind the pier to avoid the policemen. Then, after they had gone, he caught the train to Tulln to deliberate with his wife as she, Lutschi herself, had requested. There, he saw the *Budapest* tied up at the landing stage, and discovered that the partly disabled vessel would return to Vienna in the morning. The ship's crew invited him aboard. So Karli journeyed back on the stricken boat and drowned, and she was bearing his child, and Herr Morgenthau would charge her with theft. And Herr Morgenthau could say she had stolen the blue sapphire ring on her finger. She lay in her tiny room staring at the ceiling, not eating, not drinking, not sleeping. Her one thought, which had worn a groove into her brain so she could think no other, brought her to the bridge: to follow Karli into oblivion. She would spare his child a life of misery.

But other thoughts did squeeze into the groove when Herr Morgenthau called to ascertain whether illness accounted for her absence from the shop. Finding her indeed unwell, he prepared weak coffee and left to come back with an aromatic bunch of violets, two oranges and a *Punchkrapferl,* a Vienna speciality of a small sugar-coated sponge cake laced with rum.

"The young Anzendrech lad's been asking where you were," he said. "I'll tell him I'm looking after you."

She had not expected this. Did he want to hustle in? Their philandering days ceased when Karl and real love came upon the scene.

"I'm pregnant," she said.

"That's been my worry. I knew, I knew the day would come when you'd say that. I'm a married man. Ruth wouldn't believe me. I don't want to give up my family. You are bringing a child into the world. Don't say I'm the father. This is terrible; I don't know how to put it. Look, this man, this man Spagola. He died in the *Budapest* accident. I know you were fond of him. Say he was the father. Your job is safe with Morgenthau's."

Lutschi looked at her employer in astonishment. Had he not learnt about the birds and bees? Or could it be that he imagined, when on one occasion after he had presented her with the sapphire, she had let him embrace her, and she had felt his manhood pressing against her abdomen, first rigid then soft, that he imagined this was it? She gave vent to a fit of laughter: to complete the comedy Herr Brunner needed to march in and pick a fight with Morgenthau over the baby! But the outburst came as a reaction to the many hours fixation with Karli's disappearance. She calmed down. She realised that Morgenthau's words contained the germ of an opportunity, which hitherto had not entered her thinking.

The owner of the toy-cum-jewellery shop viewed the situation with dismay. The question whether Lutschi would heap the parental role upon him now that Karl Spagola was dead tortured his mind. He had fancied Lutschi, he had showered her with gifts, and he had held her in his arms and had found orgasmic relief whilst fully clothed. Seen as a wealthy man in Engerthstrasse eyes, the young, attractive Lutschi had always displayed his presents with a flourish. She now faced shame. Would it not be tempting for the girl to point her finger at him?

"If you say I'm the father," he said in low voice, "it would be your word against mine. Your Catholic word against my Jewish word. Get well fast. We have a lot to do in the shop. I've caught Ferdinand Trapfen dipping his fingers into the sugar fish bowl. I said nothing because I didn't want a scene. You know how it is: a Jew is very wrong when he is wrong, and wrong when he is right."

"I'll keep my eyes open," said Lutschi.

"He's not the only one. And in the jewellery department too. Things have gone missing. Many things. The Riesenrad watch is gone. I don't remember selling it."

CHAPTER TWELVE (1933)

Dufft's Dismay

The flood receded, and people resorted to spending easy hours in their very-own-wee-little-places. However, easy hours did not feature in Dufft's diary. He learnt of the *Budapest* accident and of Karl Spagola's fate, and rushed to see Gusti, but found Brunner was with her. He felt like twisting the new admirer's genitalia into knots.

He waylaid her coming out from a crowded service in the Allerheiligenkirche. "Last time I saw you," he said, "I didn't know. Karl's passing has come as a shock to you and me. I think of you every day of my life, and even more so now, almost constantly since I found out what happened to Karl. I want to talk to you about us, about the future, our future."

"Here? All these people."

"Let's go to your flat."

Brunner was there with the children, so she said, "I've got a splitting headache. Another time."

"How are you managing for money? There's a little library job going, calling on borrowers who've failed to return their books. You could do that any time during the day or evening. It doesn't pay a lot, but it's better than nothing. It's run by the Social Democrats. I'll see the job comes your way, if you want it."

"Yes. Please."

"One thing you must let me do: take up the case for your compensation. You and the children were dependants, although there's a living widow. We must clear up the niggling contradictions."

"I know." She placed a hand on her temple.

"We'll talk about our future later. I'll speak to Mama."

"Your mother doesn't like me."

"I'll make her like you." He pulled out his wallet. "Take this to tie you over. Pay me back when you can, or don't, it doesn't matter."

"No, Richard. Not yet anyway. I'll ask when there's a need."

"Gusti, I love you. We'll emigrate to America. What I've seen in Germany frightens me. If we get it here, it won't be just Jews. Everybody will be in the mire. We'll talk about all this, when you feel better. Yes, my darling, my Zuckerrüberl?"

"All right."

In search of facts concerning Karl Spagola's past employment, he called on Reibeisen of Danube Coke. What he learnt there wrapped him in utter dismay.

Towards the end of the meeting the manager said, "I'm quitting. Next time a bomb explodes it'll be in my home. My kids live there. I've managed to get all the papers together for me and my family to emigrate to the New World. Just in time, because not only am I on the Nazi death list, but somebody spread the rumour that I'm a contact man acting for a clandestine escape organisation."

"Not, what did he call it, the Purple Pimpernel? I met this fellow, coming back from Berlin just a few days ago. He was on the run, from the Nazis. He mentioned the Purple Pimpernel. They keep safe houses and help people cross the border."

"The least said about such things the better. I'm getting out legally. In a fortnight I'll be on the high seas. Dufft, do the same."

"I intend to."

On his way home, the funny story journalist racked his brains on how to deal with Gusti's compensation claim. It seemed a hopeless case.

A Can of Worms

The vicinity of the refreshment hut, where Karl Spagola had been seen last, could yield a clue. Dufft sat down next to the Anzendrech and Jarabek families at their very-own-we-little-place.

"The fact that Gusti wasn't married to him," he observed, "wouldn't be critical if it were shown she and her children were his dependants. But a crucial aspect is that *he* has been married to somebody else, and according to law, compensation goes to his legal widow."

"Perhaps they can split the money between the two," Aunt Anna suggested.

"That's not all. Reibeisen showed me Spagola's employment contract. His job title reads 'casual labourer in the coal yards'. Reibeisen says Spagola had no official business to be on any ship, that if he had been a passenger on the *Budapest* he would have been taken off in Tulln and offered travel to his destination by train. That didn't happen, therefore the only way he could have been on board at the time of the accident was as a stowaway, in which case the company disclaims liability."

"He was on board, his pullover was hanging on the wreck," said Aunt Anna.

"He was here, near this very spot, the day before, at the time the *Budapest* steamed up river," countered Dufft, dejected that the facts pointed in the wrong direction. "How do we explain the feat of Karl Spagola transporting himself from here onto a vessel in the middle of the river?"

"They say the rusty steamer was falling apart, and that she'd been insured for three times her value," said Uncle Hans. "The whole business is a can of worms."

Brigitte turned her face away from the setting sun and addressed Dufft: "I spoke to Frau Spagola the other day. She says Brunner was mistaken. She says he didn't meet Herr Spagola that day, she says he met another man."

Dufft raised his eyebrows. Nodding at the boys returning from the last bathing expedition of the day, he asked, "Didn't your Xandi see Herr Spagola here also?"

Brigitte hailed her youngest: "Xandi, when Poldi hurt her foot, when Herr Brunner brought you home, Herr Spagola played chasing games with you?"

Xandi blushed and didn't answer.

"Well, go on, answer," Uncle Hans urged. "Did you see Herr Spagola?"

Xandi shook his head.

"You didn't? Who was it you saw, then?"

"I... I don't remember."

"You don't remember? I can't believe that."

Xandi ran off. Uncle Hans soon caught him and brought him back. "What's the matter? There's nothing to be frightened of."

Xandi's words came out in a garbled rush, "H-he told me I must s-say."

"Who told you? And what mustn't you say?"

"He told me if I said anything I won't go to heaven and nasty things will happen to me."

"Who told you that?"

Xandi sniffed. "Herr Brunner."

Brigitte drew the boy towards her: "Nothing nasty will happen to you, Xandi. Herr Brunner is just a mean man."

"He gave me a chocolate bar," said Xandi.

Uncle Hans persisted: "Was Herr Spagola here with you on that day?"

Xandi nodded. "Yes, he was."

Dufft said dolefully, "If Karl Spagola was here on the meadow, he can't have been on the ship. If he wasn't on the ship, he can't have drowned in the accident. If he hasn't perished, he's around somewhere. In other words he's done a bunk."

"This man Brunner swaps stories," Uncle Hans proposed, "so it becomes credible that Karl Spagola *was* on board."

"Gusti genuinely believes he was, because of the pullover," added Dufft.

"Brunner tells a different tale because he's after her," interjected Brigitte, "he wants to lay his hands on the compensation cash if she gets it. Hardly a day passes without him knocking on her door."

Richard cursed inaudibly. Cursed the world, cursed his fate. Why was he still pursuing his childhood sweetheart? True, she reciprocated his affection then and still does now, but in between she became mixed up with his soldier friend and bore his offspring, and later she fell for this bullshitter Karl and carried his child. And now she's entangled with this despicable Nazi. If she gets pregnant by this lout... Dufft sent a prayer to the god of agnostics that Brunner would walk into a tram, fall off the Northrailway Bridge, catch diphtheria, and/or swallow a poisonous toadstool.

He returned to the Milk Block yard and strolled up and down until by chance she appeared. "Zuckerrüberl, listen: this business about compensation."

She interrupted, "If Brunner catches you talking to me..."

"Blast Brunner to hell!" Richard exploded.

"I'm scared. Really scared. He means it."

"This is a serious matter, Zuckerrüberl. We must get to the bottom of it."

"I-I can see Brunner now," she stammered.

"Listen. Blow the compensation. Blow Brunner. Blow Spagola." He breathed heavily. "You, the children, me and Mama..."

"Another time." Gusti rushed away.

"America."

A Patch of Worms

That Sunday, Uncle Hans did his best to dawdle through the last hour on the Danube Meadow. He knew that his overalls would be waiting for him, hanging on the door of the living room, ready to remind him of work on Monday, which might be the last before the dole queue. He was in no rush to get home.

The sky changed to a pale pink and the distant wooded hills to a dark purple; the warm air thrummed with the hum of the river. The boys' brown skin glistened, highlighting the soft fluff of short white hairs round their necks and down their spines.

Brigitte said, "You can keep your stately homes and your palaces. Just give me my very-own-wee-little-place here on the Danube Meadow and a view of the Vienna Woods, and I want for nothing else."

Aunt Anna said, "If only we could stop time."

Uncle Hans remarked, "If you are planning to do that, hold on for a second until I finish an argument with this mosquito."

With a precision-aimed stroke he slapped his thigh, accompanied by a grunt of satisfaction. Everybody became aware of the insect raid and swatted away.

"Let's light a fire," Uncle Hans suggested. "The smoke will see the mosquitoes off."

Old newspapers and paper bags lay scattered on vacated very-own-wee-little-places; dry, decayed sticks, leftovers from the flood, formed a long line near the riverbank. The boys collected a great pile, and Uncle Hans struck the match.

Combustion held Little Xandi spellbound. He watched each sheet of newspaper, in his imagination the facade of a towering building, turn brown before erupting into a roaring inferno. Whilst thus engrossed, a dark shadow fell over him. Looking up he saw the underbelly of a horse with the Skeleton on top. The recollection of the policeman's threat of what happens to little boys who break the law, galloped through his head. The steaming nostrils of the animal barred flight to the protection of his mother. Instead his reflex for escape propelled his footsteps in a direct line to the stairway of the Northrailway Bridge.

It so happened that this route traversed a patch measuring some twelve metres across, which was shunned by mankind. For reasons apparent only to flying May beetles, this stretch of meadow had been chosen for their breeding ground. The earth there lay barren; all vegetation had been stripped by thousands of white, three-centimetre-long larvae that had survived the flood. As the grass roots had been eaten away, so the quest for food had forced the grubs, which normally spend their four-year life cycle out of sight underground, upwards and finally onto the surface. This vertical mass migration had broken up the soil into a sandy consistency, in which the round, maggoty creatures with short brown legs and brown heads lay loosely embedded.

A few days earlier Rudi had dared Big Xandi to cross the area for two groschen. It had proved a precarious operation, involving the pre-selection of each minute clear space on which to lower his toes so as not to squash the semi-circular bodies, not in consideration of future cockchafer generations, but because defiling bare soles with May beetle grub matter was considered worse than stepping into excrement from animal or man. Big Xandi had come to a standstill after three steps, taken a mighty leap back, and owed Rudi two groschen.

Little Xandi had penetrated several metres into this densely populated patch before he realised that the Skeleton wasn't following him. Simultaneously, it dawned on him exactly where *he* himself was. He stopped and froze at the sight of the wriggling creatures and at the thought that he must have already flattened hordes, and felt a distinct tickling under his heels.

As he considered what to do, several options occurred to him in quick succession. He could stop breathing in the hope he would die, but somehow he knew this would end in failure. He could pray to an archangel to lift him clear, but archangels had a long way to fly, and response was uncertain. He could scream until his mother came to his rescue, but this meant waiting for an eternity in this wreathing, white-brown hell with the dreaded likelihood of a multitude of worms climbing up his ankles and shins. Or he could shut his eyes and run back the way he'd come.

He shut his eyes and ran back the way he'd come.

The Skeleton reached for his notebook. To his annoyance the culprits, caught red-handed, showed a singular lack of awe. They focused all their attention on a boy fleeing wildly from the scene of the felony, who suddenly stopped, and then retraced his steps with equal abandon.

"Nail me to the crucifix!" exclaimed Uncle Hans just before Little Xandi started on his return sprint. "They'll gobble him up alive."

Sympathies were with Little Xandi. Compared to his experience, the Skeleton's imminent name taking was a trifling matter. Brigitte hurried to meet him. The others followed, leaving the Skeleton alone to contemplate the black ashes of the exhausted blaze and the empty page in his notebook.

Safe in his mother's embrace Little Xandi first checked that his body had survived unblemished, that no brown heads peeped out from his feet, legs, belly, chest, arms, face; that none had tunnelled from toes to knees; that none, dead or alive, had attached themselves to his skin anywhere. He shook himself as a dog after a bath, partly reacting with nausea, and partly to fling off any grubs hanging on in unseeable, unreachable places. Then he succumbed to the shock.

"Mummy, Mummy! The worms. The worms!"

The Skeleton drew up on his horse. "What's going on here? It's illegal to light fires on Inundation Land."

The policeman's trite remark in the face of her nephew's predicament overturned Aunt Anna's gentle temperament. With a vehemence that Uncle Hans knew she reserved only for the most extreme provocations, she let fly at the Skeleton. It surprised everybody, including herself.

"What are you worrying about? We are collecting scrap paper. We are tidying up the meadow. We are burning the rubbish. We are rendering a service to the community! It's a lot more than what the police and civic authorities do! Look at this. Look at it. Look at this heaving mass of worms. What are you doing about it? It's a disgrace. Who knows what disease they harbour. They'll lay eggs and multiply and they'll eat up the whole meadow before something's done about it! Why don't you make a note of that instead of harassing peace-loving folk?"

Rudi yearned to correct Aunt Anna for academic reasons that the heaving mass constituted larvae, not worms, and that neither worms nor larvae laid eggs. But he had learned enough of the ways of the world to know that it was often better to serve wisdom than knowledge.

The Skeleton seemed impressed, not so much by Aunt Anna's outburst, but by what he saw. He cantered around the infested area to estimate its length and breadth. He fell into deep thought. What if history was to repeat itself, and to re-enact the dramas of ancient Egypt? According to acquaintances from his *Heurigen* table, the city already reeled under the influence of the Jewish International World Conspiracy! Herr Brunner, the Milk Block Laundry supervisor, had specifically asserted that this conspiracy would not stop at breeding vermin to lay waste Aryan lands. And now this woman said the same. What if these grubs were indeed to multiply and turn into avaricious insects, like giant locusts or bedbugs, devouring all? What if he, the Equestrian of the Danube Meadow, could nip this dastardly plot in the bud? He would become the most famous policeman in Vienna. He forced himself to restrain his fancy taking flight into the future, when name taking of bonfire lawbreakers would be delegated to his existing chief, Sessl, serving under him. He must be vigilant. He must keep an eye on this nest and watch how it developed.

And so, over the ensuing days, the Skeleton hovered near the refreshment hut to the irritation of regular ball-players there. Frau Marschalek offered gifts of refreshments, less for reasons of compassion with the policeman's lot in his tightly buttoned uniform under the sweltering sun, more for reasons of strategy, for in these days of political uncertainty a policeman indebted to you could prove a good investment.

Her action, however, led to the waxing of prevailing disagreements between herself and Herr Marschalek, when after the first gratuitous lemonade, the Skeleton interpreted the extra favour as a precedent escalating into free Wurstsemmels. Herr Marschalek felt that the Skeleton was the type of man, who, encouraged by a little finger, wanted not only the whole hand, but had designs on the entire body. The warring in the refreshment hut delighted the families at their very-own-wee-little-place, and compensated for the suspension of playing "to-the-soup, to-the-soup".

The Skeleton's professional ambition to oust his superior had yet to wait. Constant sunshine and the complete absence of nutrition began to take their toll. The grubs in the centre of the nest shrivelled up first, thereafter decomposition spread rapidly towards the periphery. Then the crows from the nearby Mistgstettn displayed a liking for a change of diet, and after a morning that saw great flocks of black birds screech over the refreshment hut, only a bald, sandy patch remained.

A Bloodied Nose

The Anzendrech's neighbour, Herr Rosenfinger. organised a collection for Karl Spagola's funeral to take place as soon as his body was recovered from the Danube. People brought little presents for the children who had lost their father. Brigitte invited Poldi and Berti to join them for meals. Xandi asked her to cook his favourite, Reisfleisch.

The attention heaped upon the deceased's offspring played on Manni Czarnikow's sense of self-esteem. Crouching low behind shrubs in the courtyard near the bench on which Poldi sat, he kneaded a ball of wet earth.

Xandi walked past. Poldi stretched out her hand and said, "Don't sit here."

"Why not?"

"Because of this, look..."

She showed him parallel brown streaks on the flowery frock covering her broad backside: "The men have been working with the paintbrushes again," she explained. "Herr Dufft gave me a eucalyptus sweet because I was crying."

"Why were you crying, Poldi?"

"Because my new dad'll give me arse a basting so he can watch it wobble, when he sees the paint on the dress." She removed a bright red disc the size of a ten-groschen piece from her mouth, and handed it to Xandi. "You can finish it if you want."

Xandi pushed it between his lips and asked, "Is Herr Brunner your new dad?"

Poldi burst into tears. "I wish Herr Dufft was my new dad."

Xandi did not know how to ease his friend's misery. He looked around for ideas and saw Manni working at a clod of earth. The big boy fashioned it to his satisfaction, firm and coalescent, and aimed it at Poldi, a target difficult to miss. He sang out:

"Here's a riddle: why's Poldi's middle
Half the size of an omnibus?
Because she eats too much, and shits too liddle."

Poldi took a suck at her yellow doll Gugi for comfort, and when a second earth clot hit her, she waved the toy at him in protest. Manni strolled up, snatched Gugi from her hand and kicked it against the side of The Stone where it dropped, limp, to the ground. Several children were playing marbles nearby. Xandi rushed over to collect the cloth doll and restore it to its owner. As he bent down to pick it up, Manni snatched it away from under his hands, and set about to kick it again against The Stone.

"You!" Xandi shouted, "Stop kicking Gugi."

Manni, twice the weight of his adversary, collected Poldi's toy. "You want it?"

Xandi, still innocent of the two-facedness of the older world, nodded.

"Come and git it, you little arse 'ole."

Xandi began to learn fast. Poldi stopped crying, Berti clenched his fists. Little Martha Bitmann, the one with the silvery voice, clenched her rosy fists also. When within hitting distance, Manni struck out at Xandi's face with Gugi.

"D'you like that? Want some more?"

The smaller boy stood his ground, and Manni, faced with such an easy target, lashed out at his the cheeks, left, right, left, right.

"Say when you've had enough."

Xandi didn't answer. Then, with a sudden liberation of energy, his arms whirled like the sails of a windmill in a tornado. His fists landed on Manni's shoulders, chest, chin and face. Before the big, surly boy could gather his wits, blood poured from his nostrils. It ran down over his lips onto his chin where it separated into two thinner streams, and splashed onto his grubby tee shirt, his shorts and knees. Manni put his tongue out to sample the flavour, and realised the red fluid originated from his nose. He ran home, howling, his hands smearing the blood from ear to ear. By the time he reached Staircase

163

no 13 his face resembled tomato puree. Frau Czarnikow emerged from her ground floor flat.

"The Anzendrechs are trying to murder me," he screamed.

Frau Czarnikow postponed questioning, cleaning her son's face or exclamations of shock. She immediately hauled him up the stairs to demand restitution from the parents of her son's attackers. They met Herr Brunner coming down from one of his frequent visits to the Kristopp's studio.

"Good grief," said the laundry man, "what's happened?"

The staircase filled with people, enticed forth by Manni's noise.

"The Anzendrech boys did that," said Frau Czarnikow.

"Three against one. Yes, the Anzendrechs lick Jews' arses and that's the consequence," spluttered Brunner.

"It wasn't three," the silvery voice of little Martha rang out from below. "It was only Xandi. And Manni started it."

Brigitte's Compromise

Rudi won first prize, a bicycle, in the Vienna schools poetry competition on the subject of "Bread". He promised Xandi rides on the crossbar if his little brother recited in public the seventeen verses of the ballad. The older boy wanted to revel in hearing it broadcast, and also to poke fun at Xandi's stammering. But Xandi had the last laugh, because he knew the words by heart, having listened to incessant repetitions during the evenings of its creation. He balanced on the edge of the Engerthstrasse kerb-stone, and swaying in time with its meter, rattled the verses off in one unbroken swell.

"Bread.

> In such a paltry word as bread
> Lies many a sorrow hidden
> They know who do the treadmill tread
> To whom to be free is forbidden."

The poem continued in the same vein, carrying the same message, composed in innocuous innocence of any political overtone. It had won first prize because of its lyrical merit, helped along by the liberal views of the assessing committee's chairman. Xandi did not grasp much of its meaning as he hurled the words into the winds. But the last verse arrested Frau Kristopp's attention.

"And the windswept sheaf on Austria's lands
Let it stand for peaceful accord:
That men reach out for each other's hands
That these hands guide the plough, not the sword."

Frau Kristopp remarked that listening to Alexander Anzendrech speak the poem was worth a milli'n schillin', a comment of unspecified grandeur, because in Frau Kristopp's numeracy anything larger than a single figure sum leapt straight into the million bracket. Thus a linen tablecloth bore the same price tag as a Danube steamer trip to Tulln; and both were worth a milli'n schillin'.

Uncle Hans called to inspect the sparkling chrome handlebars of the bicycle. He arrived on his own contraption, which he rode to and from work; it was as heavy as a tank, built with the same lumbering lack of finesse, and styled for economy by the absence of a freewheeling device.

Having enjoyed pedalling side by side with his nephew and his sons by virtue of Rudi's generosity, his fantasy raced away at top bicycle speed. He was due to decorate the flat during his week's summer holidays, and he reckoned he could speed things up by borrowing his workmate's paint roller instead of using a regular paint brush. Saving a day would mean there would be time for a family trip on bicycles into the country. The problems of accommodating little Xandi and sharing two bicycles between seven riders deemed secondary to the major obstacle, that Brigitte and Aunt Anna had yet to master the art of cycling. Uncle Hans tackled these difficulties with Trojan determination.

"I'll make a seat for little Xandi and clamp it to my crossbar. Big Xandi has a birthday coming and I promised to buy him a bicycle. I've seen some cheap ones advertised and I'll knock them down a schilling or two because they belong to men out of work and they need the money, but don't need no bike to ride to no work. That gives us three machines. The rest we can hire from the dealer in the Welistrasse. But the most important thing is to teach the mothers to sit up straight, and we only got six weeks, and that don't give us much time for training and practising, so the sooner we start, the better."

Brigitte viewed the prospect with misgivings. But she realised Uncle Hans' proposition contained the germ of victory in a lifelong battle, and she announced the following compromise: "If the boys eat my spinach once a week, I am prepared to give it a go."

In the past, whenever Uncle Hans had been able to induce Brigitte or Aunt Anna to mount his mammoth machine, neither had progressed beyond the first stage, when Robert acted as anchor to the handlebars, Pauli held the saddle, Rudi and Big Xandi bolstered up hips on opposite sides, and Uncle Hans dashed from side to side to act as a support ram for correcting growing slants. This complicated system of propped-up instability, with little Xandi hanging on to the rear mudguard, moved off at a snail's pace, the feminine bulk deposited on the contraption like a sack of potatoes, feet pressing hard into the frighteningly rotating pedals, eyes fixed in terror on the fleeting rubber tyre, and mouth shrieking, "I'm falling!"

Undeterred, they pursued with the learning process and surprisingly, after several sessions, the mothers advanced to slowly rolling, completely detached, along the empty Handelskai at no faster than trotting speed because turning and stopping unaided had yet to be mastered. A masculine presence remained necessary on both sides. The hazards were numerous, the short, narrow trench between road and pavement that exerted a pull on the front wheel as if a stretched elastic band connected the handlebars to the ditch, the occasional other cyclist, and the treacherous double railway tracks crossing the roadway linking the derelict warehouses with the main line. The gap between the double rails had been expressly designed to fit the widths of bicycle wheels. Once caught, escape was impossible, even for circus cycle virtuosi.

In time Aunt Anna attained a degree of proficiency, which allowed her to hold a limited conversation with the breathless troupe, evidence that automatic reflexes were taking over. And Brigitte no longer panicked when sighting a horse-drawn vehicle on the distant horizon. With increased skill came encouragement for increased speed and longer runs.

Uncle Hans commenced the tuition of steering in semicircles so that catching the pupils for dismounting could be done from the launching spot. Unattended starts and homings still belonged to the future, since the crossbar proved an insurmountable impediment to female legs, hampered by thick skirts, passing from one side of the saddle to the other. However, the adaption of Rudolf's and Uncle

Hans' second-best trousers had commenced.

Learning to cross the railway tracks featured next on the programme. Uncle Hans outlined the somewhat complicated procedure. "When you see the rails ahead, depending which way they go, either starting off on the near side of the road and finishing on the far side, or vice versa, because they always run oblique-like across the roadway, the thing to do is to prepare yourself beforehand so the wheels hit the rails head-on square like that." He placed the edge of his left hand at right angles over the edge of his right. "Now then, if the rails start off on the opposite side of the road, the thing is easy: turn towards them for the crossing, but don't leave it too late, or you'll be squeezed into the narrow gap, which won't give you much room for manoeuvring. If the rails start off on the near side, you got to ride into the middle of the road first and then turn into them."

Uncle Hans demonstrated the action with perfect timing and big Xandi gracefully swept over the rails without the use of hands, earning him guffaws of admiration. The big moment came. Aunt Anna rode in front, Brigitte followed, determined to do exactly what her sister did. Uncle Hans ran alongside, shouting what to do. The bicycles approached a railway track starting off from the near side of the road. Aunt Anna dutifully manoeuvred towards the middle when called upon but failed to steer towards the rails, so that her wheels approached the obstacle like a circle does to a tangent. The cry went up: "Turn, turn!"

But instead of turning into the rails she turned away from them, either through misinterpreting the instructions or through a sudden impulse to postpone the experiment to another day. She made a U-turn and terminated in Roberts arms. The unexpected curves travelled by the leading bicycle threw Brigitte into confusion. The frantic screams of "Turn! Turn!" conveyed little meaning. She did not comprehend which way she should turn: follow her sister, or steer over the rusty-brown bands of unfriendly steel. In consequence she did neither. Uncle Hans hoped, prayed, that Brigitte's natural wobble would bridge the tyre over the gap. It proved a vain hope.

Nursing bruises from shoulder to ankles, Brigitte declared that if she were required to participate in the summer venture, Uncle Hans would have to obtain a three-wheeler.

Rudi's new bicycle was carried to the Welistrasse repair workshop to fix a twisted front wheel, and spinach continued to be a sore subject in the Anzendrech household.

CHAPTER THIRTEEN (1933)

Karl's Remorse

Karl Spagola moved into the Schmelzgasse, Leopoldstadt, lodging with Vikki and the two balloon girls.

He slept on the floor in the tiny kitchenette, and was up and washed by seven o'clock. Now and then Vikki took time off being Madame Fleurie to have the apartment to themselves. But the arrangement lacked lustre because both flatmates tended to appear separately under more or less believable pretexts; for instance Lisl to change shoes as the ones on her feet were killing her, Steffi to equip herself with a fresh supply of blue balloons.

Vikki located alternative accommodation for Karl in the Kleene Mohrengasse, near enough to take to him supplies, as he needed to remain in hiding. Two young men from Przemysl, in Hungary, who spoke only limited Yiddish-German, occupied the same room. Karl's new beard grew and blurred his features and this gave him confidence to step out into the street. Immediately a mass of papers whirled around his feet. He picked one up and read:

"When German knife drips Jewish Blood
The Aryan people say Good, Good, Good.

He paid little heed to the leaflet and others displaying crude drawings of faces with bent, dribbling noses, beyond thinking that from a purely poetic and artistic point of view, he could do better. The thought led to him sketching out the drawing of a handsome woman holding a man's palm next to a catchy rhyme, advertising the brilliance of Madame Fleurie. Afterwards he complimented a female visitor to the men from Przemysl on her good looks, mentioning at the same time that he needed a duplicating machine. To his pleasant surprise the young lady led him into a basement stuffed with clattering machinery, where she stood him next to a primitive apparatus and told him, if he turned the handle himself, he could run off two hundred copies for the price of the paper.

Assured that his new name and facial hair would protect him from recognition, he posted the flyers into letterboxes of shops and businesses in main streets running up to and alongside the Danube

Canal, and began to concentrate on his new enterprise of Ottakrink's Salted Grey Radishes. He had still sufficient cash to acquire a second-hand, two-wheeled street barrow and other necessary utensils for plying his trade. Vikki and the balloon girls vied with one another to introduce him to Prater personalities and Prater routines, and he himself struck up new acquaintances quickly. On wet days of empty streets, he bought a bottle of wine, wheeled his barrow to Madam Fleurie's shack, and slowly drained it with Vikki. If a fortune-seeking customer called during such spells, Vikki advised the client through the keyhole of the locked door to wait a wee-little-moment whilst Karl retired to the adjoining chamber, where he listened to the soothsaying with suppressed giggles. Afterwards he and Vikki laughed together and finished the drink.

Then an unexpected thing happened. He felt a new, uncomfortable sensation. Vikki, who had acquired knowledge from her clients in such matters, said dryly he carried a guilty conscience. Yes, he suffered remorse. He felt sorry for Lutschi. He missed Gusti, although he told himself, having betrayed him, she did not deserve his sympathy. He missed Berti. He even missed Poldi. He envied men of a stable family like the Anzendrechs. Their *Reisfleisch*-gulping son Alexander would have a better chance in life than his own Berti. He stuffed eighty-five schillings into an envelope, addressed it to Frau Augustine Spagola, pushed sixty shillings into another envelope earmarked for Fräulein Lyudmila Fritzer, and went with both to the posting box. There he decided that sending the money was not a good idea.

Had he posted the letters, the recipients would have concluded that the sender could be none other than Karl Spagola. The brawl in the Milk Block Laundry would never have taken place.

The Brawl

The report of the incident lay on Police Officer Sessl's desk.

"Women scratching their eyes out over a man that's alive, understandable. But over one that's dead?" Sessl leant back in his chair, his hands clasped behind his neck, and inclined his head towards Constable Breitwinkel.

"Danube Coke disputes the man's dead," Breitwinkel replied.

"Hm. This character's name is Spagola?"

"It is."

"And one of the feuding ladies is Frau Spagola?"

"She goes under the name of Frau Spagola, although legally she's single. Her real status is Fräulein Augustine Schattzburger. The other combatant in the affray was Fräulein Lyudmila Fritzer."

Sessl closed his eyes and said, "We know them both. Missing children, and mislaid boyfriend." Sessl touched the papers. "I've looked through this briefly. What's it all about?"

"The brawl took place inside the Engerthstrasse Laundry. It began when women there disputed the exact details of the sinking of to the *Budapest*. Then, according to eyewitnesses, our two ladies, each asserting to be a legitimate claimant for compensation on account of having been dependent on this man Spagola, threw wet laundry at one other. This escalated into a battle to submerge each other's head in a tub of household linen. Then a Frau Anzendrech intervened, with the result that other women joined in and took sides."

"Anzendrech," said Sessl, "we know that name as well."

"A string of incidents on the Danube Meadow."

"Alexander. One of the missing children. He had a tussle with the refreshment hut. We sent him over to Floridsdorf. I followed the court case, was impressed that the little street urchin won it. Breitwinkel, in a few years' time, what'll become of the scallywag, and others like him, if Superman over the border has his way?"

"Best left to the will of the gods."

"Right. Carry on."

"Herr Brunner, the laundry manager, aims to restore order. Fräulein Fritzer lies on the floor. Frau Echenblatt calls us and summons an ambulance. The laundry manager carries the sobbing Fräulein Schattzburger off to her tenement. Fräulein Fritzer is taken to the Samaritan Hospital in Floridsdorf. The hospital finds no permanent bodily injury, but establishes she is in the advanced stages of pregnancy."

"The father is Herr Spagola? Or the missing boyfriend?"

"She was discharged without information on that score being recorded."

"I have a hunch that Herr Spagola and the missing boyfriend have been or are wearing the same boots."

"Yes. The two women believe he drowned when the ship broke into two."

Sessl tapped his fingers on the edge of his desk. "Danube Coke says Spagola was not crew. His body has not been *recovered*. Two women, not related to the man, but with knowledge of his body *uncovered,* engage in a skirmish. There is the question of his pullover seen on the wreck. If missing boyfriend and Herr Spagola are one and the same, according to Lyudmila Fritzer, he was on the Floridsdorf Bridge when the *Budapest* steamed up river below. The pullover could have been dropped onto the ship then. Why has missing boyfriend, that is Spagola, disappeared from that moment in history? Could it be that confronted with the arduousness of a two-women affair he longs to dissolve into thin air? Fräulein Fritzer tells us he went onto the flooding meadow to see to a distressed animal in the refreshment hut. She further tells us he was a champion swimmer. So once on the meadow, he sees his chance. The *Budapest* isn't making much headway. He runs upstream past her, swims to the ship, climbs on board. If he's seen he'll explain he's done it to retrieve his pullover. As it is, he hides himself away, perhaps somewhere in the engine room near the boilers to dry out. He would be familiar with the layout, having worked in the coal yards and attended when ships take on fuel, and having pestered Danube Coke to be transferred to ships. He aims to do a vanishing trick in Linz. But the steamer stops at Tulln. He gets locked in. So he stays on the ship and is on the ship when she hits the Reichsbridge pier. And that spells the end of Herr Spagola. His body isn't washed up because it's trapped in the machinery. Does that make sense?"

Breitwinkel saw the logic in his superior's analysis, and voiced no contrary opinion.

Sessl pursued his analysis further. "We know this individual Spagola wanted to work on the ships, and we can reasonably conclude that he bore a grudge against manager Reibeisen for keeping him in the yards. Assuming he did pass over into a saner world, we can argue without fear of contradiction that this grudge grew strong enough to incite him to bomb the company's office. How does he get hold of explosives? He lived in the Milk Block, Council property, and that's where political factions hide their arsenal."

Breitwinkel shrugged his shoulders.

Both men reached the same conclusion, but neither put voice to it: 'This lets us off the hook for having to track down the Nazi conspirators, or frame local simpletons like Isidor, the cinema attendant.'

The Riesenrad Watch

Lutschi left the hospital with extra items she did not have on admission: three plasters attached to her forehead, a certificate for examination on the progress of her pregnancy in four weeks' time, and fifty groschen with the directive to travel back by tram.

She did not take the tram. People who are desperate for money walk. How did she know Herr Morgenthau would keep his word and pay her a wage, once she was a mother and had written 'Karl Spagola' on the birth certificate, and needed time off to feed her baby?

She remembered her employer's fear. She could whisper to Frau Kristopp that not Karl Spagola but Herr Morgenthau... or better still, she could drop a hint to her boss that she intended to accuse him after all, at the same time asking for a few things. Nothing more than a signed statement securing her job, or a bonus, or... Nasty thoughts, blackmail. But she was only thinking them for her baby's sake. If compensation came to be paid to Karli's widow, she wondered how much it would be. Several thousand shillings? But what if it were to be claimed by his dependants? Surely she headed the list of dependants, if only she could prove the unborn child was Karli's, and that he had promised to marry her.

Thinking all this dried her throat. A glass of strong liquor would do her good, and she needed to sit down somewhere and put her thoughts into perspective. She had the tramway money, and she was passing a wine-and-beer cellar.

The bar held one solitary old man. She selected a table not far from this person and ordered a shot of rum. She sipped slowly to prolong her stay. The waiter hummed the latest hit tune '*Komm schwarzer Zigeuner,* Come, black Gypsy,' whilst cleaning the table tops. When he came to hers, she lifted her drink, and suddenly, without warning, she grasped his wrist and her glass went flying.

"Holy horse shit! Lady, you need chaperoning or you'll run away

173

with your wits!" He surveyed the disorder on the floor, then glared at her. Women should not be allowed to visit drinking dens by themselves, and especially not one in her condition.

"Your watch. How did you get it?" Lutschi's voice shook in agitation.

The waiter ignored the question, went off to fetch a rag and applied it to the sticky, wet floorboards.

"That's the Riesenrad watch," Lutschi said. "How did you come by it?"

"Madam, that old watch? Drives me up the wall like my old woman. It used to complain once every month in its younger days, now it's stopped functioning altogether. See?" He raised the watch, together with the rum-soaked cloth, close to Lutschi's eyes and continued poking fun at her. "Old watches are like old rags and old rags are like old people. You can't imagine they've ever been young. You accept them for what they are. They happen to be there. What they were in their youth, where they came from, who knows? Who cares?" He turned to the other patron: "Ain't that so?"

"Spot on," said the old man.

"There aren't many Riesenrad watches about. Yours isn't old. Did you find it?"

"I didn't steal it," said the waiter, becoming concerned that he'd let his sense of humour run too far.

The old man realised that Lutschi's disturbed state emanated from causes other than alcohol. He explained, "A young gentleman came in, drank late into the night, more than he could pay for. He left the watch here, in lieu of cash."

"That's correct," confirmed the waiter. "Normally we don't trade in barter. But that young gentleman nearly drained the house dry. The tinny children's watch here isn't worth half the quantity of liquor he carried away inside him. Frankly I would rather he'd walked off minus his picturesque pullover as he wanted to do at first."

"His pullover? A green one with a great big red heart stitched on?"

"Since you mention it, yes. I remember that wacky heart."

"This took place on the night before the *Budapest* sank?" asked Lutschi.

"Could be. Listen, if you know the young gentleman, tell him he can collect his watch for thirteen schillings. That's the amount he owes as far as I remember. Or, since you are here, I'll give it you at a discount. Ten schillings."

Lutschi had neither the money nor the inclination to accept the offer.

She came to terms with the situation: Karli had left her standing on the bridge surrounded by policemen whilst he had gone drinking himself silly. He had not taken the train to Tulln; he had not become a victim of the *Budapest* tragedy. He had no remorse; he was hiding somewhere to escape the responsibility of fatherhood. And that snivelling Frau Spagola seeing a green, red-hearted pullover waving from the wrecked ship, had suffered hallucinations or dreamt it up.

On the Northrailway Bridge a group of five boys with two bicycles followed behind her.

"Xandi," she overheard their chatter, "with that money you could buy five million sugar fish."

"No," replied Xandi. "I'd get seven million five hundred. Because Lutschi always gives me an extra one."

"Here I am." Lutschi turned round and managed to laugh. "If I had to count that many, I'd be an old woman before I finished. What you talking about?"

"Danube Coke compensation payout," explained Rudi Anzendrech. "They say it'll be twenty-five thousand schillings. We read it in the newspaper."

Well, there wouldn't be any payout to Karli's wife, or to Gusti Spagola, or to herself; that was for certain.

"Or you could go on everything in the Prater a thousand times," said Robert to Little Xandi.

"Including the Riesenrad?"

The Prater Girl in the Shimmering Green Costume

The older generation trooped to the Prater for the Strauss waltzes and the sentimental Viennese waltz tunes played on the merry-go-round organs and over loudspeakers; for Kalafati, the grotesque Chinaman figure, already ancient when they had been young; and for the open-air restaurants with the rough wooden tables underneath the heavy horse chestnut trees, where you took the family, bought beers, and laid out a brought-in picnic.

The unemployed thronged to the fairground to escape the boredom of doing nothing. There, Vienna style slot machines offered them a morning's occupation for an outlay of a few groschens with the never ceasing hope of profit. The idea was to flip the coin to soar over the very wide 'no-return' slot, so that it would drop into the very narrow 'pay-double' slot, or at least into the overshooting 'have-another-go' slot. Or they could set up business with the three card gambling game: two losing diamond aces and the winning queen of spades, and within another hour retrieve their ten groschen losses on the machines. In the afternoon they could spend a further hour outside the cinema entrance pleading for a loan of two groschen from clients with sufficient funds to purchase tickets for the *White Hell of Pitzpalü*. And the last hour of the day they could spend in the nearby woods of the Kriau to experience the mysteries of love, but only to learn that these mysteries, like hard facts, depended on hard cash for ultimate success.

To the young, the Prater represented the very pinnacle of existence. Even more so to the young like Xandi, whom the mysteries of economics had denied the means of direct participation. Did not the pleasure of watching others disappear into the tunnels of the Grotto Train, or through the swinging doors of the Ghost Buggies, or down the dips of the Scenic Railway, or into the shrubbery of the Lilliput Railway Line, or into the coaches of the Giant Wheel, surpass the pleasure of personal involvement? Passing through a tunnel lasts five seconds, but you can spend a lifetime imagining it is you!

And when a party of rich visitors toured the Prater, and pulled along a regiment of onlookers? And when such visitors came from foreign lands, like the group of Parisians who attracted almost the entire populace including the hands from the Bombs Over Monte Carlo booth, to jeer at the Parlez-Vous-Francais struggle and stumble on the fast-moving conveyor belt of the Toboggan? Or when some fine Dutch ladies invited Xandi to go with them on the Train-Rapide as a substitute for one timid member of their group succumbing to panic at the sight of the open, fragile car? But crowning everything was the long-standing saga of a body of Americans, who, one fine Sunday, simply hired a couple of barefooted urchins who happened to be tagging along, bade them to be their guides, and gave them free rides on everything. Since that day every barefooted urchin dreamt of being scooped up by such a God-like party of Americans.

An outing to the Prater promised the excitement of new adventure mixed with the security of long-established ritual. Rudolf set the whole process in motion announcing, "Tell you what, let's all go to the *Perevater.*"

His habit of lengthening words when in good mood signified that, by augmenting Prater to *Perevater,* he was in excellent spirits. Xandi took a flying leap at his neck, clasped his hands firmly round it and shouted; "You are so perfect!"

But Brigitte grumbled, "Now he tells us."

To her an outing to Vienna's amusement park, the Prater, like an outing to anywhere else, meant an eternity of preparation: Schmalzbrots to eat, apple compotes to drink, warm clothes in case of a change in the weather, blankets in case they found a grassy wee-little-place to sit on, newspapers in case Rudolf wanted to read, balls in case the children wanted a kick-around.

"Tell you what," said Rudolf, "leave everything, and we'll eat in the restaurant."

"Yes! Let's!" The instantaneous cry of the boys.

Brigitte feigned reluctance: to pay three times the grocer's prices for a few pieces of bread and frankfurters. But the thought of ambling along between the amusement stalls without the drag of the rucksack, of white-smocked waiters balancing above their heads trays of twenty beers waiting on her, exerted a powerful pull. Once in a while, she too, had moments of extravagance.

The first stage along the Engerthstrasse was spent in bliss of expectancy. The three boys, with Xandi in the middle, skipped in front, Rudolf and Brigitte, arm-in-arm, followed behind. In the Mortara Park Rudi's agile mind sought diversions. It had rained the previous day and large puddles covered the uneven pavements. A carpet of drowned earthworms lay at the bottom of these watery depressions. Rudi picked up a stick. Pauli and Xandi retreated. Rudi went for a particular long specimen, dangled it from the end of the stick and flicked it in Xandi's direction. Xandi screamed.

"What's wrong?" asked Dad coming upon the scene.

"Nothing," said Rudi.

"If nothing's wrong, he wouldn't have cried out. What's he done to you, Xandi?"

Xandi pressed his lips together. He didn't want his father to take sides. But a sob surfaced all the same. Anger overcame Rudolf.

"I saw you teasing him," he shouted.

Another sob burst from Xandi's throat. Rudi thought he did it on purpose, but his brother would have bartered the Prater outing for the skill of suppressing it.

"I want to know what he's done to you," said Rudolf threateningly, "or we'll all go back home."

At this threat Pauli caved in: "He threw an earthworm at Xandi."

Rudolf saw the wet, red, S-shaped, lifeless form on the pavement. He struck Rudi's cheek: thwack. Xandi shivered.

It needed the stretch to the Dresdnerstrasse to work off the irritation, and when passing the imposing edifice of the Northrailway Station, the thought of the choc shop at the corner of the Praterstern finally bleached away any lingering stain of the earthworm episode.

The choc shop marked the border: on this side - the humdrum of everyday life; beyond - the vibrancy of the Prater, where the roar of rhythms, marches, waltzes, hurdy-gurdies, of shouting and scraps of jokes hit the ear like invisible explosions. Excitement at once rose to fever pitch. Rudolf stopped at the tobacconist-cum-picture postcard kiosk, which also specialised in outsize chunks of hard, dark, thick, cut-price chocolate. It could be neither broken nor bitten into. To tackle it meant scraping the lower set of front teeth against the broad flank of chocolate. This removed a thin layer sufficient to stimulate the palate, yet hardly diminishing the size of the confection.

To begin with, they headed for the Show of The World, where, upon a raised platform two clowns performed. The first clown briefly surveyed the scene from his lofty position. Addressing an individual on top of the far-off Kahlenberg, he began shouting against the vociferation of neighbouring clowns, the screams from the Ghost Train, the staccato tunes of the roundabouts: "I am going to recite a poem!"

The second clown took the cue, and addressing another individual on the distant Leopoldsberg, shouted in reply, "You are going to recite a poem!"

"I am going to recite a poem!"

"He is going to recite a poem!" This was shouted to the captivated crowd below.

"The fisherman took off his pants
To bathe underneath the stars.
The night was warm, the water cool
It reached up to his knees."

After a pause the second clown yelled, "You said you were going to recite a poem."

"So I did, so I did. I recited a poem."

"It's not a poem. It don't rhyme. Stars and knees don't rhyme."

"It was low tide. At high tide it rhymes."

At the nearby Kaiser Theater a musician, The Phenomenon, produced a broom upon which one solitary string had been strung along its long handle. To Xandi's supreme wonder the Phenomenon played on it most beautifully the well-known melody: *Mei Mutterl war a Wienerin,* my wee-little-mother she was Viennese. The manager, in husky efforts to overcome guttural fatigue, croaked that what the public heard here outside were mere squeaks compared to the orgies of sound that the Phenomenon would draw from the broom inside the theatre.

And at every booth the comedians and entertainers bellowed and cajoled, all for the purpose of softening up the money-tight mass of spectators, pledging funnier, more side-splitting, more extraordinary feats on the stages inside, not for fifty groschen, nor even for forty groschen, nor thirty nor twenty, but for only ten groschen, ten groschen for mums and dads, five groschen for the nippers. The trickle that filed past the ticket kiosks to be entertained inside, emerged from a rear exit a few minutes later, disillusioned but wiser. The bulk remained immobile, to witness another free repeat performance outside.

Next stop: the Toboggan, the king size helter-skelter, promising young and old not only the exhilarating, longest slide-down in the world, but the panorama of all Vienna from its height, and the never-to-be-forgotten fun of the moving conveyor belt up to the first platform. On this belt, the inexperienced, like the party of Parisians, clung in desperation to the handrail, whilst their legs were whisked upwards, out of control, to make writhing horizontals of their bodies. Experienced young males, on the other hand, rode the belt in perfect balance, using both hands to straighten their straight ties, to comb their combed hair. Sometimes the inexperienced turned out to be the man from the *Kasperltheater,* the Punch and Judy show nearby, but who was to know, and in any case the real fun was to be with the crowd, and laugh with it.

From the Toboggan to the high Scenic Railway, its supporting structure hidden behind massive papier-mâché rocks, its screaming cars shooting down the awful dips into tunnels. It hypnotised. Xandi stood and watched, one screeching car after another. Past the Moon Rocket, not taken quite seriously yet, but heralding a coming age. Past the ancient carousel with the central Chinaman Kalafati painted in colourful reds and yellows, dominating everything with his huge, square jaw, seeing everything with his huge, elongated eyes. Past the great community swings, which absorbed twenty to thirty people at a time, swinging higher and higher, stopping, screaming, in the near upside-down position. Past the autodromes, bumper cars, caterpillar trains, sideshows, more clowns, to the horse-drawn roundabout. Here Brigitte halted and remembered her own electric motor-free, internal combustion engine-free, childhood. "Look you here, isn't that something. Real horses, real horses," she said.

Past the cinema, and wouldn't it be perfection if Father said, 'Let's go in to see *The White Hell of Pitzpalü*. But he never did.

Past the Giant Wheel. It belonged to another world. The fifty-groschen fare made the ride as unattainable as the stars towards which the gently rocking cubicles ascended.

The boys could choose one go each, one ten groschen go. Rudi chose the Laughter Kabinet, a chamber built of wooden planks, upon the hoardings of which grotesquely distorted, brightly painted ladies and gentlemen enticed the public into the hilarities of the mirror curvatures. Rudi chose it for reasons of scientific amusement. Pauli sat himself in one of a ring of white chamber pots suspended from a horizontal wheel, was whirled round and felt sick. Xandi went on the horse-drawn roundabout to please his mother.

Past the shack encompassing Lolo the Fattest Lady in the World, and Herr Raken the Thinnest Man in Christendom. A pink and green portrait of Lolo's voluptuous flesh roused Xandi's curiosity as to whether anybody could be fatter than Poldi, but Brigitte walked quickly by. She would not subscribe to a spectacle insulting the dignity of man. Past Madame Fleurie's Fortune Telling Establishment.

Now came the debate about where to go for food and drink. Xandi favoured the *Kuchenstuberl*, the Wee-Little-Cake Room, but it ended, as always, with the decision to visit The *Walfisch*, whose entrance was a pair of real giant whale jawbones. The familiar table was vacant; they sat down underneath the familiar tree in whose branches a loudspeaker played the familiar Blue Danube Waltz.

Xandi's eyes fell on a neighbouring table. There a man and a woman ate potato-size, grey radishes sliced thinly into spirals and liberally sprinkled with salt. His mouth watered. But grey, spiralled, salted radishes did not feature on the Anzendrech programme. Peace and harmony prevailed nevertheless. Hot frankfurters with mustard, beer and fizzy lemonade. And Xandi languishing after grey, spiralled, salted radishes became indelibly engraved in his memory, for it is the yearning after that counts, less so the fulfilment.

The eating and drinking was followed by a pleasant spell of tooth picking and watching people drift by and seeing everything lighting up. Then one more tour round the stalls offering prizes for the skill of hurling cloth balls at stacks of tin cans. At the Bombs Over Monte Carlo shack, life-size dolls could be won for clearing away all the cans, but neither the entirety of cans nor any of the giant dolls ever left their shelves. A cynic suggested that the bottom row of cans were nailed to the wood, an insinuation the proprietor immediately proved groundless by lifting them off one by one. The boys knew however that the lower cans were filled with cement.

A final stroll to the Dragon Train grinding out deafening, eerie organ chords, situated in a square near the edge of the amusement park, where the expanse of wild meadow and woodland began. Adolescent boys and girls, with beating hearts, crossed the area, no longer interested in the mechanics of the fair. They took little heed of the dragon's flashing eyes, and no heed at all of the entertainers performing on the open stage of The Emporium.

A young woman pounced upon Xandi and wound the end of a balloon string round his trouser button.

"No, no, no, no," protested Brigitte.

Xandi's eyes noticed a wheeled conveyance displaying grey, spiralled, salted radishes standing in a corner of the square.

"But go along w' you," pleaded the balloon seller, "look at him, the dear little fella. How he loves to have the balloon. You gonna break his dear wee-little-heart if you take the balloon away."

"We don't need no balloon, we've spent enough already," said Brigitte.

"Ten groschen. Only ten groschen."

Brigitte objected to the principle. You are being pushed around by authority all your life, she told herself, surely you deserve a break from Prater balloon vendors.

Rudolf advanced a compromise. "If he wants the balloon he can have it, but if he wants something else for the ten groschen, you take the balloon away."

"Sure he wants it. The dear boy loves to have the balloon. Don't you, Hansi?"

Rudi urged his younger brother to keep it. His curiosity of how the gas inside would react to a flame climbing up the string already intrigued him. But Xandi was angry; his name wasn't Hansi. He took a few steps towards the grey radishes preparatory to declaring that they represented his choice. Inexplicably the bearded man in attendance turned his back on the group and wheeled the stall away. The radishes vanished in a horizontal direction; the balloon, having worked free, soared up in a vertical.

"Ten groschen," demanded the balloon girl.

"T'was none of our doing," replied Brigitte.

"The stupid brat let the balloon go."

"You wound the string round his button."

"Herr Ottakrink! Herr Ottakrink!" the balloon seller called out and hastened after the retreating cart. But the radish man paid no heed to the young woman's shouts. The spectators who had turned away from The Emporium to take sides in the looming dispute were left standing, disappointed.

The men on the stage raised their voices to draw their audience back. But even with full lungs they could not. The Dragon Train amplifiers gushed out dragon roars from left and right, and The Emporium stood at their focal point. The entertainers' faces grimaced to their dialogue, they were probably telling funny stories, but not one word, not one, arrived intact at the straining ears below.

Having lost the chance to taste spiralled, grey, salted radishes, Xandi felt sorry for himself, and also sorry for the fellow sufferers up on the Emporium stage. Luck was not on his or their sides. The spectators drifted away, one by one, until only seven were left. When Rudi and Pauli departed to look at the flashing eyes of the dragon to determine what made them flash, the number dwindled to five.

The silent show continued. The soundless words conveyed a sad melancholy. Xandi's mother and father sauntered up and down the path leading to the grassland, unaware of the drama played out between the Emporium clowns and their youngest. Xandi could not understand the heartlessness of people in so abandoning their fellow creatures. And when, as a last resort to extract a molecule of response from the hostile, noisy, empty world, a beautiful, dark-haired, dark-eyed, girl in a shimmering green costume appeared on the platform, his heart went out to her in compassion and love. She smiled a forlorn smile with sad lips curving downwards. Her eyes, at first full of movement, settled steadily on the clown whose mouth was speaking without sound, so hopeless, yet still resolved in the pretence.

The performance went on to the bitter end. Then the entertainers departed as quietly as they had played. A man came out from the theatre. He switched off the lights over the entrance, switched off the lights in the ticket booth, jumped onto the stage and switched off the row of coloured lights above it. The ethereal girl in the shimmering green costume was engulfed in darkness.

Oh, if Xandi were rich! He would buy a hundred tickets, see the show inside, and on his way out he would leave an envelope at the ticket booth. He would stuff a ten-schilling note into the envelope and he would give it to the beautiful actress in the shimmering green costume. Then he would disappear into the night, to return years later, to watch from afar her glory and acclaim by all the world. For love, true love, does not seek the advancement of self.

CHAPTER FOURTEEN (1933)

Water Balloons

"It'll be the ruination of my business." Herr Morgenthau muttered to himself. "Today they want water balloons. I could have sold a mountain of water balloons. Yesterday they wouldn't look at anything but clay marbles. What am I going to do with my two sacks of clay marbles?"

In its raw state the water balloon resembled a baby's dummy, colloquially known as a *Lutscher*. Its function, far from comforting an infant's gums or expanding its own gummy skin with innocent air, was to turn itself into a bloated bladder by forcing capricious water into it. A clay marble, inserted into the interior, settled against the port of exit, thus forming with the narrow throat an effective stop-valve. Dislodging the marble from its seat through finger manipulation resulted in the ejection of fine or voluminous water jets. In the hands of boys, water balloons became formidable weapons, which could be aimed at the necks of young women without fear of reprisal, as the only defence against the cowardly attacks was to run. Attempts at confronting the assailants exposed eyes, nose and mouth so that ultimate victory invariably went to the wielders of water.

Water balloons also served to satisfy repressed impulses by creating dank, short-lived graffiti on walls and pavements. When held between legs with their spouts pointing upward, manipulating the marble resulted in a parabolic, sparkling arc indistinguishable from a masculine feat rarely performed in public.

Manni Czarnikow put his extra-large water balloon to use in tormenting the Wirtshaus Zur Weintraube's grey cat. The animal fled through a hole in the hedge enclosing the Kindergarten, so Manni set aim on the flaxen-haired Martha Bitmann. The girl, like the cat before her, ran for cover. She chose Xandi's somewhat bigger frame than her own to shelter behind. Manni approached, the snout of his loaded water cannon pointing at Xandi's face, his forefinger and thumb tickling the clay marble.

"Shift yourself, I want to give her a ducking," he said. "Shift, or I'll pump the water straight through you."

Xandi clenched his fists. But they did not land on Manni's nose, because the water impinging on his eyes forced their closure, so that for a second he could not see. Manni dashed away, and chasing him was impeded by Martha's delicate fists embedded in the lower part of Xandi's shorts.

To retaliate immediately against a water offensive with a fist-swinging counter-attack would have been permissible; however, the unwritten rule demanded that deferred reprisals be carried out solely in kind. Thus, if somebody spat in your face, you could, two or three days later, without the risk of commencing an entirely new conflict, spit back. Xandi did not own a water balloon, and other boys close enough in kin or friendship to lend him theirs, no longer had one.

His cousins' water balloon had come to grief when Big Xandi and Robert, both having mastered the art of catching without spilling a drop, had been tossing it at each other in their home. As usual Robert had heeded Uncle Hans's request to stop, but Big Xandi had not. In consequence Robert, not expecting another throw, had moved out of its way, so that it had landed on the table, bounced onto a chair, fallen onto the floor and leapt around, at each impact jettisoning a portion of its fill, dousing the screws and nuts in Uncle Hans' tool kit tray, and Aunt Anna. Uncle Hans had opened the soap and toothbrush cupboard, removed his razor, and castrated the offending thing.

Berti's water balloon had come to a premature end when he, Manni, Xandi and Poldi had been playing soldiers. Manni had proposed that Berti's water balloon be a bomb, and he had girdled it to Poldi's waist belt in such a manner that it hung suspended over her vast backside. He had then ordered a fast retreat into the bunkers, battling against advancing Jews, which in practical terms meant running backwards into the perpendicular wall of the Stone. Manni's ensuing laughter revealed that he had foreseen the result.

Xandi needed a water balloon to hit back at Manni. The price of the cheapest stood at ten groschen. And then came the sudden switch to pea shooters. Morgenthau's stock of rubber dummies amounted to three virgin boxes. In a frenzied effort to catch the tail end of the crumbling market, he scaled down the price to seven groschen each. Xandi possessed four groschen. Poldi had three.

Forgetting their promise not to leave the Milk Block courtyard, they headed for the toy shop, where Herr Morgenthau counted blue, red and golden pea shooters.

"A *Lutscher*, please," said Xandi.

Herr Morgenthau, engrossed in his activity, thought they wanted to see Lutschi. He had reached seventeen; he went on counting. The children gazed at the exciting things, there to look at, none to have: tin soldiers, farm animals, teddy bears, dolls, boxes with pictures of railway trains, *dradiwaberls* spinning tops, squeaky ducks, coloured crayons, the great bowl filled with many coloured sugar fish.

Lutschi reposed on a chair in the jewellery section. She watched the children absentmindedly. Her thoughts, which had occupied her mind since she had seen the Riesenrad watch, revolved around Karli's possible hiding places. She liked children, and for the sake of her own child to come, Karli must be found. She hoped for an event out of the blue, a miracle that would reveal his whereabouts.

Xandi's eyes rested on a bunch of blown-up air balloons. "I've seen your dad," he said to Poldi.

"You've seen my dad? Where have you seen him, Xandi?"

"I've seen him when my balloon flew up into the sky. He was selling salted radishes on a barrow."

Herr Morgenthau raised his head, called into the adjacent section, "Lutschi, children here asking for you."

Lutschi got off her chair, wondered what they wanted.

"A *Lutscher*, please."

"Where have you seen him, Xandi?" Poldi asked again.

"In the Prater where the Emporium is."

"A big one or regular one?" Lutschi enquired.

"A *Lutscher* for seven groschen."

Lutschi disappeared into the storeroom, the depository of merchandise in low demand.

"If you see him again, Xandi, tell him to come back. Because I'm not fond of Herr Brunner. He's not quite my new dad yet, but..."

Lutschi placed the requested article on the counter. "You like the Prater? You see all sort of exciting, unexpected things there, don't you?" she said.

At the Engerthstrasse watering trough for horses, neither Xandi nor Poldi had the strength to stretch the stiffly resilient rubber throat over the cast-iron spout of the hydrant. They enlisted Berti's help against a promise to let him have first go. The balloon grew to a frightful size before he pulled it off. Xandi and Poldi stepped aside to fulfil their part of the bargain, but instead of getting on with the execution of first go, Berti tucked the swollen sack under his arm, and raced with it into the Milk Block. Xandi set off in pursuit and challenged him in the courtyard: "Gimme it back!"

"Be quiet, Xandi. I shan't keep it forever. I want to have first go as you said. Watch me."

He lifted the bulging water balloon above his head, and crept quietly towards the Stone, where Manni Czarnikow devoted his attention to directing his giant-sized peashooter at the Wirtshaus Zur Weintraube's grey cat. Berti tiptoed upon the unsuspecting victim from behind. Xandi understood that his friend also needed to inflict reprisal upon Manni for his sister's drenched knickers. Martha Bitmann ceased skipping so that she could witness better the outcome of Berti's approach. Other children stopped whatever they were doing. Even the grown-ups beckoned one another. Herr Junge's lips parted in ecstatic expectancy. And Frau Posidl broke off whispering to Frau Bergmeister that she had heard the rumour that Karl Spagola had been involved in the Danube Coke bombing.

When Berti began to impel the sagging vesicle forward, due to increased hand pressure, it split apart. The unexpected cascade onto his own head shocked him into inertia.

Manni turned round and said, "Great Kalafati!"

Herr Junge's body oscillated in gay abandon. Frau Bitmann chewed air and muttered something about "he who diggeth pits". Frau Czarnikow came out from Staircase No 13, shaking a fist. Frau Spagola slapped Berti's wet cheek and led him away to dry out.

Xandi and Poldi contemplated the shrivelled-up shape of the remains of the *Lutscher*, a total loss.

Spirals

Rudi had chosen Spirals as the subject for his summer holiday homework. Aware of high expectations set by his school, and full of high importance himself, he insisted on absolute quiet whilst engaged on thesis work.

Pauli drew Danube ships during one such soundless spell, and Xandi thought up rhymes, as speaking in verse had mushroomed amongst the Anzendrech juveniles. Brigitte brewed chamomile tea next door to calm one of the Rosenfingers' regular stomach upsets. Rudolf and Herr Dufft had arrived at a decisive stage in a chess game, Rudolf engrossed in prolonged thought. Herr Dufft, in a rare winning position and unaware of Rudi's strict dedication to silence, turned to the boy for friendly chat.

"I hear you're working on spirals."

"That is so," said Rudi, raising his eyes reluctantly from his papers.

"I've always found the circle fascinating, and the never-ending number pi."

"You can draw circles and ellipses with the aid of instruments," said Rudi, "but there is no instrument or gadget that produces a spiral."

After a moment's awe-inspired pause, which the pronouncement called for, Xandi, said, "There is."

"And I shall prove," Rudi shot a look of contempt in his young brother's direction, "in my thesis, that no such instrument or gadget can be invented."

"There is," Xandi repeated.

"Of course he knows better." Rudi took a deep breath and delivered a two-liner to crush the interceptor:

"Why does my brother tire all,
When nil he knows of the spiral?"

He returned his attention to his papers, and Herr Dufft returned his to the chessboard. During the ensuing stillness Xandi opened the drawer of his mother's oblong sewing table and rummaged about in it.

The chess game entered a phase when neither Rudolf nor Herr Dufft took their eyes off the board. A sudden stir and Rudolf's cheeks gave way to a broad smile. Herr Dufft left his seat and said he would never have believed it.

Rudi had finished for the day, and Xandi laid a cotton reel, Brigitte's indelible ink pencil, and a piece of brown paper upon the thesis book. Then he recited in a thin voice:

"What shape, my brother, do you think
Drawn here with cotton reel and ink?"

Everybody gathered round: a perfect spiral. Rudi, dumbfounded at first, slapped Xandi on the shoulder, and proclaimed that ingenuity from whatever quarter must be recognised. He promised he would add a rider to the end of his paper spelling out that an Archimedes Spiral can be generated with an instrument in the form of a drawing implement attached to the end of a stretched cord unwinding from a fixed cylinder, and he would credit the method to one Alexander Anzendrech, aged eight years and five months.

$2 + 2 = 4$

Brigitte came back from the neighbours and listened to the tale of the spiral before lighting the gas under the coffee pot.

Herr Dufft turned to her for sympathy: "What can I say about your husband? I held him in a vice. I was tightening the screw with every move, and suddenly: snap! He had me by my throat. I shall seek out a new partner. Frau Anzendrech, do you play chess?"

"Chess?" Brigitte laughed. "Chess isn't a woman's pursuit."

"We have women writers and women doctors. Why shouldn't we have women chess grand masters? Joan of Arc was a woman general."

"If I was a general," said Brigitte, "I would put the governments at the front. That would stop wars quickly enough. They're wrapped up in blankets."

Rudolf's forehead became a sea of wrinkles. "Wrapped up in blankets?"

"To keep warm."

"The generals?"

"Our next-door neighbours."

"We were talking about governments and generals."

"Haven't I just been over to the Rosenfingers? They ate pig's trotters yesterday."

Rudolf said, "We were talking about women generals!"

Brigitte burst out laughing and said, "Herr Dufft, do you know what he did last winter? He walked home from the Wex Strasse, his new tram depot. All the way he had the feeling his left foot was shorter than his right. Was it poor blood circulation, or bone shrinkage, or something to do with the nerves? And when he arrived home he was sick with fear he'd contracted a serious disease. He told me all about the symptoms and the possible causes. And I looked down at his feet, and he had his right foot stuck in an overshoe, and the left one was without!"

Rudolf chuckled. The image of absent-mindedness suggested an air of professorship. "Hark who's talking! The other day I was lying in bed - I sleep during the day if tram duty starts early in the morning – and I was listening to the detector radio to lull me into dreamland. We don't have a licence because we don't run a loudspeaker on the electricity, only the detector with earphones, and to get good reception I connect the earth wire to the water tap. Consequently, a telltale wire trails from the kitchen into my room. Half asleep I am, when suddenly the door flies open, and she bounces in, and I get a bundle of wire in my face with the shout: 'Radio!' I'm supposed to know what that means. She doesn't say 'the radio people are here,' or even 'Radio inspectors,' No. Just: 'Radio.'"

Brigitte fetched home-baked *Powidlbuchtels,* buns filled with prune jam. "He's forever making radios," she said. "D'you know his latest? He's built one into a matchbox."

"Well," said Rudolf, "no inspector will think of looking into a matchbox!"

He pulled one out from his pocket, and opened it to reveal a tiny, brown Bakelite base supporting a crystal and a cardboard cross with copper wire wound round it.

"Does it work?" asked Herr Dufft.

"I'll make you one," offered Rudolf.

"Ah, *Powidlbuchtels,*" said Herr Dufft, as Brigitte pushed a plateful in front of him. He lifted one into his mouth: "Must get Mamma to learn the art of baking them. They're miles better than the ones at the Kuchenstuberl in the Prater. I could eat them all day."

"In our household you have to," said Rudolf. "Briggi makes wonderful *Powidlbuchtels*. But it takes forever to convince Briggi to bake them. There are moments when the thought of just one *Powidlbuchtel* makes my mouth twitch like a man's lost in the Sahara desert dreaming of a cool, clear glass of Vienna high-Alpine-spring water. And then comes the deluge. I don't mean of water, but of buns. We're eating *Powidlbuchtels* for breakfast, they're here in basinfuls at midday, they come trooping on the table six abreast for supper. Look there!"

Herr Dufft followed Rudolf's outstretched hand pointing to the top of the crockery cupboard. There, in neat rows, stood an army of *Powidlbuchtels*.

"You've seen nothing yet. Rudolf went to open the door to the family bedroom. The two wardrobes strained under the weight of buns.

He returned to his chair and wetted his lips three or four times, the usual preamble to the narration of an anecdote. "Talking of *Powidlbuchtels*, when I was apprenticed as a baker," he began, then stopped whilst reaching for his smoking gear and prodded tobacco into his pipe. Herr Dufft, open mouthed, watched a performance with a giant gas lighter held in one hand close to an aspirin bottle held in the other.

"What in the name of ..."

A spark ignited a gigantic flame on the wick poking out from the bottle. It ended in a column of black smoke. Rudolf twisted his pipe towards the fire and inhaled. Herr Dufft quaked in fear that the pipe and the face attached to it might burn to cinders.

"Ah!" A sigh of satisfaction escaped Rudolf as he took his first puff. "Talking of *Powidlbuchtels*, I lived in Prague and worked as a baker's apprentice... "

"How do you put it out?" cried Herr Dufft, his eyes pinned on the blazing aspirin bottle.

Rudolf shook it, got up and placed it flat on the tiled section of the kitchen floor, and trod on it. He squeezed the life out of the flame, but left a black blot on the tile. Brigitte came with a damp rag and wiped it clean.

"The bottle is freshly filled," he explained, "and the fuel overflowed a bit. Usually the flame is no more than six centimetres high."

"Six centimetres!"

"It's a safety lighter," explained Rudolf. "I carry the spark maker in one pocket, and the fuel reservoir in the other. With other lighters you have the spark maker attached to the petrol container. If you were to accidently rub against the wheel whilst the lighter sits in your pocket, you go up in flames."

"Holy Abraham! I shudder when I think of fatalities through

combustion from accidentally ignited cigarette lighters residing in their owners' pockets."

"Don't you think it's a good idea?" asked Rudolf. "I thought I'd patent it. It's never failed to light first time. I'm making another from a shampoo bottle. That should last a year without having to refill it."

"Dad, the story," Xandi urged.

"Ah yes. When I was in the bakery trade, every morning the delivery van went out with bread and cakes for the shops. One morning, however, it's getting late, and the coachman hasn't turned up. The master baker runs outside every minute to look for him. The bread's ready, the shops are open, but no coachman. In desperation he comes to us apprentices. 'Anzendrech,' he says, 'can you handle a horse?' Well, I thought, this might be a chance to get away from the ovens into the fresh air. So I says, 'Depends what you mean by handling.'"

"Handle with your hands?" asked Xandi, climbing onto his father's lap.

"'It's easy,' says the master baker, 'the horse knows where to go. He'll stop outside the shops on his own. All you have to do is carry in the orders according to what's written on the paper, and when you're ready to move on, pull gently on the reins and say 'hoo'. Can you do that?' It seemed simple enough. I climb up into the driver's high seat. I take the reins in my hands, give a gentle pull and say 'hoo'. Sure enough, the horse trots out of the yard, turns into the road. And I'm ready to enjoy the crisp morning. We haven't gone very far when the master baker comes panting after us. 'Listen,' he cries, 'I forgot to tell you, this is important. Don't use the whip! On no account use the whip!'"

"No animal should be whipped," said Brigitte.

"'It's all right,' I says, 'I won't.' Well, everything runs like clockwork, the horse stops outside the shops one after the other, and I carry in the bread and the cakes. By the time we're finished, the sun is up, people are about, and the horse must have been glad to be on his way home for a bit of hay. And I, sitting in the coachman's seat, have a little time for thinking. I've always been cursed with an insatiable curiosity. Why, for instance, did the master baker tell me so emphatically not to use the whip? What would happen if I did? I mean I wouldn't lash out at the beast, just touch it gently like. Once that thought gets in my head it sticks there. So in the end I pull the whip out of the holder, and stroke the horse with it on his backside. Heavens above and hellfire below! The horse sticks his tail up at the sky, and his nose goes up likewise. He neighs as if he's sighted a whole cavalry of willing mares. And down the hill we go, in a gallop that puts the charge at the battle of Austerlitz to shame. We overtake a tram. My hair stands on end, I hold on to the reins like grim death. I shout 'hoo' and 'haa' and 'hee', and as we come level with the tram, who is standing on the open platform? It's the master baker, his eyes as big as a church clock. His finger raised, he yells over to me: 'Didn't I tell you not to use the whip!'"

Everybody laughed and Brigitte said, "Go and play us something."

Rudolf fetched his mandolin. He played it by ear and Brigitte loved listening to the tunes and joining in with her marvellous deep voice when she remembered the words. And above all, she loved watching his grimaces, each note demanding a different contortion. Uncle Hans once remarked that in the event of deafness, he would still be able to enjoy Rudolf's music, as he would hear the tunes from the faces he pulled.

Herr Dufft, seized with wonder, looked alternatively at Rudolf and at Xandi. Rudolf played a Strauss waltz, then a German student song, then a few other popular airs before deciding on an interlude. He placed the mandolin carefully on the floor, and Herr Dufft introduced a topic that was gnawing at his guts.

"I spoke to Herr Morgenthau. Lutschi Fritzer told him Karl Spagola's alive."

"She goes and seeks Herr Spagola," replied Brigitte, "because he's the father of her unborn baby."

"She says she has cast iron proof he's alive. And I have this problem with Gusti. She won't listen. She's fallen under the spell of the laundry supervisor. He eggs her on to claim compensation. It's hard for her to face the facts. On top of her misery she's going to make a fool of herself."

"Lutschi has got to parade Karl Spagola in front of our eyes. We see him in the flesh, we have a fact we can't deny, like two and two make four," said Rudolf.

He reached again for his mandolin when Pauli chipped in, "What happens if two and two make five?"

"Two and two are four," his father retorted. "Nobody can make two and two equal five."

"Nobody?"

"Nobody."

"Not even a magician?"

"No."

"Not even God?"

"Not God either."

"Don't say such things," objected Brigitte.

Rudolf, at ease that no blasphemy had been committed to any deity, struck up a merry melody. He saw his wife's unhappy face, so he put the instrument down once more, wetted his lips, and everybody knew that another dissertation was on its way. Herr Dufft shifted in his chair to sit more comfortably.

"Let's say I put two *Powidlbuchtels* on the table and then another two *Powidlbuchtels*," Rudolf commenced, demonstrating the proposition. "If I end up with five *Powidlbuchtels* on the table, it means that God has created one, but it doesn't follow that two and two make five. The equation is: two-and-two plus one created by God make five."

"Yes, the Almighty can make two-and-two equal five," said Brigitte.

Rudolf tried another approach. "Two-and-two is just another name for four. Like this here *Tisch* is this here *table* in English." He pointed to the oblong piece of furniture. "I can't throw this here *Tisch* out of the window, and leave this here *table* standing in the room, if this *Tisch* and this *table* are the same object."

"Why on earth would you want to throw my table out of the window? You could kill somebody."

"Your name is Brigitte Anzendrech; I call you Brigitte. Now let's say Brigitte is cooking a potato goulash. Herr Dufft calls you Frau Anzendrech, so Frau Anzendrech must also, at the same time, be cooking a potato goulash; and can't, at that same time, be darning my socks."

"I often cook and darn your socks at the same time," replied Brigitte.

"I didn't mean it that way," said Rudolf, a little nettled at failing to make his point. "Let's say you, as Brigitte, are cooking a potato

194

goulash here in the kitchen, then you, as Frau Anzendrech, can't be darning my socks on top of Mount Everest, at the same time."

"Why should I be darning your socks on top of Mount Everest? The Kahlenberg is much nearer," Brigitte asked, looking at Xandi to see whether he agreed.

"I don't deny that God can create a second Brigitte Anzendrech, so one Brigitte Anzendrech cooks potato goulash in the kitchen, and another Brigitte Anzendrech darns socks on top of Mount Everest. But that's not the same as separating Brigitte from Frau Anzendrech if they are the names of one and the same person."

Xandi said, "Daddy means you are my mummy and you are my mother, and I love you both."

Herr Dufft laughed. He carried on laughing until everybody else laughed too. Xandi didn't know why everybody laughed, but he was happy because everybody else was happy.

Rudolf picked up his mandolin and Herr Dufft looked alternatively from father to son. In the middle of a melody, Rudolf stopped.

"Xandi," he said, "why are you pulling these silly faces? Is my playing that bad?"

Rudi sang out immediately:

"When Father plays the mandolin,
His nostrils bend, now out, now in.
My brother's nose through facial miming
Keeps in tune in perfect timing."

CHAPTER FIFTEEN (1933)

Luncheon on the Kahlenberg

Hildebrandt arrived at the Kahlenberg restaurant at the appointed hour.

Smaliz, the bald patch on his head having increased in the same proportion to the circumference of his waist, was not alone. Vivian, his companion, a tall beauty attired in a white trouser suit, her short flaxen hair coiffured in the style of a *bubikopf*, was the very epitome of a modern, white-robed damsel. The three selected a table in a corner, which commanded an extensive view over the city. The head waiter recommended *Schweinsbraten*, roast pork Vienna style, and wine from a special Langenlois vintage. The two Nazis acquiesced, Vivian chose a *Naturschnitzel*, Schnitzel prepared without breadcrumbs, from veal. A trio consisting of violin, clarinet and accordion played a selection of Lehár's Gold and Silver waltzes. After coffee, the conversation touched upon Viennese composers before shifting to Wagner.

"His works and the Reich coalesce," observed Smaliz, "They are peppered with Valhalla Heroes."

Hildebrandt recalled their conversation in Düsseldorf, four years ago: "Like our mutual friend, Alexander Anzendrech, born under an auspicious star."

"I remember speaking of the boy. Destinies *are* shaped by stars. The Führer consults the stars. My business here today is to speak to you about our destiny of tomorrow."

Vivian rose and left to wander alone in the restaurant gardens. The men ordered another bottle of the special vintage.

"May I congratulate the German Party," said Hildebrandt. "Objective number one has been achieved. Adolf Hitler occupies 'the throne' in the *Reichstag.*"

"Now we come to objective number two. The pathetic dwarf, the Austrian Chancellor Dollfuss, has the impertinence to ban the Austrian National Socialist Party. He makes us laugh. We National Socialists use our initiative. If our men in Germany had been prevented from parading in their brown SA uniforms, they would have worn shorts and white socks. However. The German Third Reich is expanding. Nothing can stop it. We are here to clear the detritus from the pathways to minimise scratching and bruising. Little Dollfuss is a piece of detritus. His removal is on the agenda. We shall require firepower. We shall commence shipments to Vienna shortly. We need you to organise collection, transportation, safe keeping and distribution at a moment's notice."

"When will it take place?"

"Shipments for the provinces are already in progress. Vienna has been slower. You know this town now, a shit house of indecision."

"I mean when are we to receive the go-ahead to put the Führer in the Vienna *Rathaus,* the Town Hall?"

"This is not for us to know. The Führer knows. You must be ready when his finger hits the button. And there'll be no place in our ranks for weaklings and men prone to make mistakes."

"I'm weeding out the parasites."

"Mistakes like sending a fighting force to the wrong location."

"Firing squad if such a blunder turns victory into defeat."

"Like transmitting the wrong logistics."

"Same," Hildebrand said glibly.

"Like telephoning through false intelligence."

"Same."

"What do you think of Vivian? Whatever we say about the Austrians, we cannot deny that they produce good music, excellent Schweinsbraten, exquisite wine and splendid boys and girls."

Smaliz gulped down several mouthfuls of the Langenlois, belched, which he found hilarious, so much so that he placed his hands on Hildebrandt's thigh to constrain himself. "Pity Vivian couldn't eat Schweinsbraten."

"Yes, indeed. Why couldn't she?"

Smaliz broke into guffaws of laughter. "This is good wine. Vivian is missing out. Shall we call Vivian? Perhaps not."

"Why?"

"Vivian enjoys solitude."

"Why couldn't Vivian eat the Schweinsbraten?"

"Why does an officer of our movement fornicate with a gypsy?"

The vacant look on Hildebrandt's face prompted Smaliz to exhibit further amusement followed by emptying his glass.

"A gypsy fortune teller by the name of Vikki Huber."

Hildebrandt jumped to his feet. "I disclaim ..."

"Sit down, Hildebrandt, sit down." Smaliz tilted the bottle over his glass, only a trickle flowed out. "We need a refill."

"Whoever meddled ..."

"Sit down. Join the club. Stick to the rules. Waiter, another Langenlois, same vintage." Smaliz' face glowed as he fixed his gaze back upon the young zealot. "We're the leaders, we lay the tracks. We see the terrain. We look around, we find a Jew. Before we bury him we remove his gold teeth. Or we find something we fancy, maybe something taboo. Drink up. We don't shout it from the rooftops. The rank and file don't understand the needs of their leaders. We, the leaders are special. Amongst the specials there are special specials, who enjoy taking risks, who find forbidden fruit tastes sweeter. Gauleiter Stohmeyer was a foolish man."

"Gauleiter Stohmeyer was shot. By a rank and file SA man!" Hildebrandt's tight lips ejaculated.

"There are two sets of club rules. Rule One: equip the inflammatory object with credentials. Failing that, and if the situation gets too hot, operate Rule Two: discard the inflammatory object and point to the corruption of the inferior races, to their treachery of infatuating us, of casting spells over us. Gauleiter Stohmeyer didn't do either. He protected his Jewish mistress. You look like a ghost. Has the Schweinsbraten disagreed with you? Have more wine."

"No intimacy between Fräulein Huber and myself has taken place. I have not entered her establishment for two years. I have kept to the Führer's edicts. A lying traitor fabricated this."

"Hildebrandt, Hildebrandt. I kept you under observation. That is how the system works. Cheers."

"A lying traitor collaborating with Jewish journalists; collaborating with Jews like this son of a bitch Dufft. But I shall get him, I shall get him by his balls."

Smaliz moved his head up and down slowly. "You're doing an excellent job, we hold you in high esteem in spite of your gaffe about the Hotel Osterhof. We prefer to do without such incidents. Try to avoid them or somebody high up could construe a case of passing on false intelligence. Actually it was quite comical." The senior Gruppenführer chuckled and spluttered wine mixed with saliva upon

Hildebrandt's lapels. "When our troupe arrived to give this Jew the once over, the receptionist couldn't locate a Dufft, but they had a Duffy staying. So our men set about this individual who turned out to be Mr Duffy from England studying German illuminated manuscripts. We had quite a rumpus with the British Embassy, and only when we produced a miniature camera with film of sensitive German documents did they calm down. Duffy's back in England. He said he preferred English hospital treatment to ours. Silly Mr Duffy."

Hildebrandt brushed away the sweat that had accumulated on his forehead during his mentor's recital.

Smaliz leant forward to be nearer to his disciple's ear and spoke softly: "With respect to Rule One: do you think one of our men whose name might be Hildebrandt born in Düsseldorf, and who operates in an aircraft factory in Bristol, England, is known there as Mr Hildebrandt? No. He might be known as Mr Jones or Mr Smith or Mr Duffy born in Swindon, and he has a British passport. Vivian's papers specify pure Aryan ancestry. Vivian happens not to favour pork. Silly Vivian."

He leant back in his chair; his mouth fell open and emitted rasping snores.

Confused, disorientated, Hildebrandt felt the urge to relieve himself, so he staggered to the gents toilet. Before he had finished urinating, a tall man in a white suit stood himself against the wall and said, "Fast asleep. He can't take his liquor. I do apologise."

Hildebrandt's eyes travelled from the blond bubikopf down to the flat chest. How on earth had he not noticed before?

"When he wakes up," said Vivian, "he'll be sober, but he won't remember a thing."

Hildebrandt, a Wiser Man

Hildebrandt returned from the Kahlenberg luncheon a wiser man. He had learnt several lessons.

Firstly, never allow alcohol to blur your senses to the extent of divulging your secrets: Vivian, well, well, well. Smaliz, upon recovering unimpaired sobriety, was, as Vivian had predicted, totally oblivious of the conversation embracing club rules. So Smaliz did not know that he, Hildebrandt, knew. Such knowledge shared would inevitably lead to complications, held singly would fuel his destiny.

Secondly, Dufft had outwitted him, was alive and well. That had to be rectified.

Thirdly, if Vivian's papers stipulated pure Aryanship, Vikki's could do likewise.

Finally, he recognised he had failed to appreciate the special needs of the leadership to which he belonged, and that his naïvety had prevented the pursuit of his passion under Club Rule One, fitting her out with papers specifying pure Aryan ancestry.

His erotic craving detonated like fireworks. His fantasies reasserted themselves to the full lustiness of the days when he came within grasp of the bulges underneath Vikki's white blouse. He had glimpsed the curvature of those swellings, and the tantalising urge to see and feel them unprotected by fabric grated his flesh against his bones.

Her prophecy of a black disaster had come true: the years without Vikki.

Now it was over. But he must observe strict secrecy until implementing Club Rule One has been finalised.

He set off for the Meldemannstrasse. As he alighted from the tram a curious rush of unease subdued his spirits. He approached Vikki's dwelling and saw a gap in the row of tenement houses. Men behave irrationally when needing to conceal an emotional secret. Had he not suffered from the forbidden infatuation, he, in his capacity as a leading Nazi, would have had the fortune teller's new address on his desk in a matter of days. Instead he visited other soothsayers, conversed with them about rival establishments, only to find that many of the female visionaries, intrigued by the sight of his scar and sound of his voice, were willing to go beyond the holding of palms, but of a Vikki Huber fortune telling salon they knew nothing.

Then memory threw up a lifesaver. Vikki had spoken of the tram conductor, Herr Anzendrech, father of the Valhalla Hero. This tramway man had a crush on her but had never made a pass at her. This same man, who had been to New York, was a man of the world. Whether or not he had made a pass at Vikki since, he would know where to find her. This tram conductor had to be located to establish her whereabouts, and, if necessary, to eliminate any rivalry for her affection. Furthermore, the opportunity of contact with the wonder boy Alexander presented itself.

He hastened to the Kaffeehaus Adler, more than once. No Herr Anzendrech. He took rides on the 31 tram, but did not meet with his man. A direct enquiry to the tramway authorities appeared too careless to his obsessed mind, which imagined an open enquiry would reveal its ultimate design. Hildebrandt, in spite of his pure Aryan superiority, was vulnerable to human imperfection, especially when applied to the gift of reason. Providence needed to intervene.

The Black Swastika

"Under here," Brunner indicated the large piles of coke, "or under the sand. We keep the sand in case of fire. It could easily hide two or three crates."

The laundry man pointed to an obscure alcove. He found a shovel and began to dig, creating a channel about half a metre wide. Hildebrandt advanced gingerly, observing the growing depth in the sand with interest. Then Brunner's forward stroke came to an abrupt halt. The shovel had hit something solid, which after a spell of high expectancy, turned out to be a wooden crate, very similar in shape and size to the ones planned for burial. Brunner prised the lid off with the blade of the shovel. Neatly stacked inside lay eight rifles and about two dozen boxes of ammunition.

"Well, well, well," said Hildebrandt, "well, well, well."

"Must be the Schutzbund."

"You didn't know this was here?"

"No." Brunner, annoyed, felt the question implied that he should have known.

"Who has keys to this place?"

"I have."

"Anyone else?"

"I believe the chairman of the tenants committee keeps a set."

"His name?"

"Rosenfinger."

"Is he one of us?"

The laundry supervisor shook his head.

"Well?"

With mounting irritation at the conduct of the interrogation,

Brunner said, "He's a Red. A Bolshevik Socialist."

"A Jew?" And after a while in a tone of rebuke, "Do you not know?"

"Not every man who is a Jew goes around shouting he's a Jew," Brunner replied vexedly, "just as not every woman who is a Gypsy goes around shouting she's a Gypsy."

A pause, then: "What do you mean by that?"

"I'm stating a fact." Brunner's distaste of Hildebrandt's overbearing attitude had reached bursting point. "Did Gauleiter Stohmeyer know his woman was Jewish?"

"What are you saying?"

"Last night's meeting was full of it. Another Jewish ploy: Jews poisoning the Movement through perverse attachments! They put her away, and Stohmeyer is no more. An ordinary, patriotic SA man saw to that. So we got to watch out whom we pick for a bit of the other. Gauleiter Stohmeyer may not be the only one of high rank to have defiled Aryan blood. Have you got an opinion on that, Obersturmführer?"

Hildebrandt's scar twitched furiously. He strained to keep calm.

"Let's get on," he managed not to splutter. "This isn't the place to hold a conference about renegades. What do you know about this Rosenfinger, who is he in cahoots with?"

"Who d'you think?" Brunner subdued the impulse to rub a fistful of sand on the pulsating, purple disfigurement confronting him. "With the rest of the tenants. They're Reds, all of them. Bar one or two exceptions. Then there's that journalist Dufft, lives in the Cocoa Block next to us. He writes for Socialist newspapers. He *is* a Jew. And his cohorts are the Anzendrechs, who live next door to the Rosenfingers."

Like a flip of a coin, Hildebrandt's troubled brain catapulted into a pirouette of excitement when this intelligence bounced onto his ears. Dufft! Anzendrech! All this happening at once. Yes, destiny was operating here.

"Anzendrech?" His voice revealed a faint rise in pitch. He could not stop his scar indulging in a further routine of twitching. "What's his job?"

"You know him?"

"I asked: what's his job?"

"Tram conductor."

"And Dufft is the journalist who pokes fun at us?"

"Sticks his crooked nose into everything. And his prick into Aryan women! I bet he knows how these guns got under the sand."

"You've uncovered quite a conspiracy, Parteigenosse Brunner. Well done." Hildebrandt's show of approval aimed to dispel any lingering concern over the Gypsy insinuation. "We find who plots against us. Who else comes in here?"

"No one without my knowledge enters these premises during the week when the laundry's working. But on Sundays, like today, anybody with a key can come in unobserved."

"We nurture the ability to turn a detrimental event to our advantage. We located some weapons. Maybe there are more. Find out. We shall leave them here hidden away, so enemies of the Reich will not know they have been discovered. But we know where they are, come the time they are needed. And that time is not far off. Your pathetic dwarf Dollfuss can put a ban on the Party here in Austria now, but he cannot stop our gigantic Reichsführer Hitler marching on, and the road leads straight to Vienna! Our men in Germany, if prevented from wearing their brown uniforms, would wear shorts and white socks! We shall fit an additional lock to the door. It will not be noticed. Only you will have a key. You will keep it unlocked until necessity demands otherwise. In that way we gain control of access. In the meantime keep an eye on who enters here on Sundays."

"Hm. That would be easy with the eyes of Kalafati."

"Kalafati? Who's Kalafati?"

Tartly, Brunner explained: "There's a roundabout in the Prater that everyone knows. In the centre is this figure of a Chinaman, Kalafati. He keeps turning with the merry-go-round and sees everything around him."

"Interesting. You must take me there and show me. You can find out whether the Reich's enemy has been in here on a Sunday by pasting a thread across the door and the wall in an unobtrusive position. If the thread is broken, you know someone has entered and you will be alerted accordingly. We National Socialists use our initiative."

Brunner cringed. He had requested the German Obersturmführer to endorse the proposal of an arms repository in his boiler room. He should be giving the orders and asking the questions on his own territory. Yet, after a brief spell of gaining the upper hand, he continued to be the recipient of inferred criticism and patronage, and was told what to do and not to do. He pondered that if an ordinary, patriotic SA man can dispatch a depraved Gauleiter, what was to prevent an ordinary, patriotic Party man to impose a similar journey upon an equally depraved Obersturmführer? Such sacrifices need to be done to cleanse the Movement from contamination.

Hildebrandt said, "With respect to this Jew reporter, Dufft ..."

In an effort to gain stature, Brunner butted in, "I've got plans for the Jew Dufft. I shall use my own initiative."

"What do you intend doing?"

"Blow him to Kingdom Come. Together with his buddies, the Anzendrechs. A demonstration for the benefit of Jew-lovers," replied Brunner. "Get the youngest, spare the mother, she'll have happy hours for a lifetime."

"Hold your horses." Hildebrandt intervened at once. The Valhalla Hero must not be felled by the laundry man. And the tram conductor must reveal Vikki's whereabouts before entering oblivion. "I want these people alive for further investigation. Don't do anything until I tell you. Understand?"

Brunner made no reply.

Hildebrandt went on, "We are taking delivery of a new design of letter bomb. The device inside the envelope is secure until switched on. After thirty minutes it becomes sensitive to the slightest touch. The contrivances can be activated and placed inside the letter boxes attached to walls adjacent to front doors during the hours of darkness. In the morning, when the occupier touches his correspondence, bang. Dufft and this Anzendrech fellow can be useful targets for site tests after I have finished with them."

Brunner refastened the lid and pushed the crate back to its original position. He said, "And another strike at Danube Coke. They're plotting with Jew Dufft to avoid paying compensation for wrecking the *Budapest*."

"Danube Coke will pay. Our lawyers are working on it. Several crew were staunch supporters of the Movement. The widows will want to show appreciation once they have been recompensed."

Brunner straightened up before shovelling the sand back. "There's the woman known as Frau Spagola. Her common-law partner went down with the ship."

Hildebrandt caressed his scar. "It happens our legal men looked into the Spagola case. As you say, he was not Frau Spagola's husband." He remained pensive for a moment, then added, "But that can be rectified. There's a sum of twenty-five thousand schillings at stake. We'll see to it they pay treble."

"I have some influence over the woman," Brunner was quick to divulge.

"You have? That's good. Persuade her to vouch that she was married to Karl Spagola. We'll procure the documents."

Brunner drove his shovel deep into the sand, a gesture celebrating the turn of events.

"Yes. Make her join the Movement, Brunner. Or better still," he chuckled, "marry her. We'll fix it that the Party, I, you and she benefit."

The laundry man was adamant that any compensation money would benefit him, no one else. For once he agreed with Hildebrand's suggestion, whether meant in jest or otherwise: marriage to Gusti was priority number one, before her traumatised mind decided to hitch up with this Israelite Dufft. He knew what he had to do. The elimination of Dufft, with or without the Obersturmführer's endorsement, was straightforward; that of the Obersturmführer's himself needed postponing until Gusti's fake marriage certificate was procured.

He diverted the conversation back to the original topic. "Danube Coke men strut around in Heimwehr outfits. And Reibeisen hangs out Dollfuss flags."

"You're not keeping up to date with information. Reibeisen slipped through our fingers. He's half way to America. But the company is still run by Jews. Another bomb will show the escape of one Hebrew makes no difference. One Jew running away renders this city one step nearer to becoming *judenfrei,* free of Jews."

"The Klosterneuburg Branch are ready for an operation," said Brunner.

"They'll have to use conventional material until the new letter bombs are available." Hildebrandt changed the subject. "Your next meeting will need to be clandestine since Dollfuss has banned the

Party. As I've said before, if we can't be seen in our brown uniforms, we can wear clandestine shorts and white socks, especially our boys! I have an idea: we ship our clandestine arms consignment by river in a Danube Coke barge. Just for fun. This housing block overlooks the coal yards. I would say that from the top windows you have commanding views over Floridsdorf. And beyond lies the Czechoslovak border."

"I've already checked out the attic. With a few machine guns placed up there we control traffic on the river and on the streets below."

"Good, you've done your homework. See if you can find staunch Party men, family men to blend in with the *Volk*, occupying high story flats overlooking the Danube. Such lucky men can be assured of a promising future."

"I'm working on that."

"Good, good. And work on recording what people in these tenements are doing, saying, thinking. Who are the Jews, the Jew lackeys, the half Aryan Mischlings, the non-Aryans and who associate with them. This knowledge will work wonders in the days immediately following our takeover. And whilst I'm here, I would like to see where the Jew Dufft and this tram conductor Anzendrech live."

Brunner smoothed over the sand to restore a look of innocence to the pile; he was titillated up to his eyebrows that a copious future lay ahead for him with the woman of his choice who'll make him rich, in a domicile of political, military and strategic importance. But to register unimpaired triumph Hildebrandt must be plying future shovels, except when it came to digging his own grave!

For the present the Obersturmführer merely flicked away the grains of sand that had settled on his suit. The action propelled his fingers against the protruding handle of a metallic device sitting on a workbench.

"Ouch!" he exclaimed, "what instrument of torture is this?"

Brunner looked up. "This is my swastika machine. Ideal for pressing out swastikas." He demonstrated by pushing a piece of black card into the throat of the gadget, and pulling down the lever. He handed over a perfectly shaped Nazi emblem, some five centimetres across. "I leave one behind wherever I have completed a mission."

Brunner led the way to Staircase 13 to indicate the Anzendrechs' abode, then to the Cocoa Block to show where Dufft lived. The two men parted, wishing one another success in their immediate ventures and ending with "Heil Hitler."

Back in his office Hildebrandt removed an envelope from a drawer of his desk, where it had lain since his last visit to Vikki. The envelope contained a black swastika identical to the one brought back from Brunner's boiler room. Well, well.

He, too, knew what he had to do.

Intervention of fate manifested itself once more the following day when he received a request from the German Head Office of Klug und Krapf to carry out surveys of random households concerning their needs for heating equipment, such as stoves, for the coming winter. He selected the Anzendrechs for one such study, to be conducted by himself.

It was a hot summer day. He slipped into a smart, light grey business suit with hat to match, took the 31 tram to the Engelsplatz, there changed to the 11 tram down the Engerthstrasse as far as the Milk Block.

The Tarring of the Engerthstrasse

The municipality waited every year until equatorial heat hit Vienna before commencing the tarring of its ballast-paved streets. At the same time Mama Dufft fled to her sister's, mentioning dizziness and weakness in her knees. Brigitte invited Herr Dufft to share the family's meals for the fortnight of his mother's absence.

The high air temperature lowered the tar's viscosity to a treacle-like consistency. The spectacle of the operation was intriguing: a team of four horses, their noses deep in sacks of hay, oblivious to the catastrophes they left behind, pulled, at funeral pace, a black cylindrical tank on wheels. Whether black was chosen to mourn the passing of civilised existence, or to blend with all that followed, was, in Dufft's words, never fully resolved.

The rear of the tank featured a horizontal pipe, which extended half way across the road. The pipe exhibited holes at short intervals from which a continuous flow of the liquorice liquid issued. There was no splashing, no breaking up into droplets. What came out of the holes fell, like solid rods, onto the road, creating continuous, parallel, black lines of tar. The arrangement looked like a giant black comb, combing the street. A few steps behind the tank a row of men completed the procession. The ends of broomsticks lay anchored in their bellies, the broom heads spaced end to end forming one long line of brush. The oily streaks were thus spread over the whole area swept by the brooms. The tar offered considerable resistance and to make progress the men's bodies adopted an inclination of some thirty degrees with the vertical.

Controlled propulsion of the whole assembly was the key to its success. A momentary slowing in the forward motion of the horizontal pipe immediately produced pools of extra tar with a consequent reduction in frictional resistance, and this brought about a speeding up of the forward motion of the brooms. If this was not matched instantaneously by an equal acceleration of all men in unison, the angular incline grew, and there came a point when the broomstick-men configuration lost equilibrium. Every man working on road tarring lived in dread of this eventuality.

The horizontal pipe carried a shut-off valve, which the man leading the horses closed at street corners, usually paved with cobblestones. This in theory freed the population from a life marooned on islands in tar. In practice however, wagon wheels, and the bare feet of boys who delighted in squelching over the black goo, smeared the oil everywhere. There was no escape. The tar was trampled onto pavements, into courtyards, onto staircases, onto timber flooring, onto the linoleum of the more affluent. It found its way onto chairs and tablecloths, shopping baskets, hats and spectacles. It appeared on crockery, bed linen and babies' nappies.

The Engerthstrasse and its side roads came under the pipe. Brigitte covered everything that could be covered with newspaper. Water stood heating on the stove. Carbolic soap, scrubbing brush and tin bath waited ready in the lobby. Herr Dufft sat by the window and contemplated the devastation.

"The Danube is said to be blue, and the Viennese are said to have the gift for easy-going conviviality," he muttered. On the street below the grocer's delivery horse's legs spread-eagled as its hooves failed to get a grip. "Both are myths. If the Danube is blue, the mess out there is pink, and if we Viennese are anything other than flabby jelly, the potatoes in your cooking pot are chunks of iron! In any town of any other country this oil treatment would cause a revolution."

"I wish I had Frau Dufft's problem knees. I'd be away too," observed Brigitte.

"And what do we do? So I ask you, what do we do?"

"I think I can hear my boys."

"If they carried a cauldron into the street, filled it with soup stock, lit a fire underneath, and asked us to stand in line for our turn to jump in, we'd do so without a murmur!"

Brigitte transported steaming water into the lobby as the doorbell rang.

"Mummy," Xandi burst in excitedly, "they're putting the tar on the street."

"Don't," Brigitte commanded in a tone that demanded instant obedience, "walk anywhere before I've scrubbed you."

"We saw Frau Czarnikow go splotch! And her cherries looked like plums."

"Frau Czarnikow went splotch?" Herr Dufft asked as he walked over to the stove to marvel at the inverted pyramid of simmering pots, larger ones sitting on top of smaller ones over a single gas ring for economy, and from which Brigitte had just removed the uppermost containing hot water. "As they say, no thorns without a rose!"

Rudi walked in. "Tar is good for tyres," he called out dragging forth his bicycle, which, still blemished by scratches on handlebar and mudguards, nevertheless remained his pride and joy.

"Give me a ride on the crossbar," pleaded Xandi. "You said you would."

"When did I say that?"

"When I did your Bread Poem in the Engerthstrasse."

"That was a long time ago."

"You said."

Below the Anzendrechs' dwelling, near the tram stop, the Engerthstrasse had developed a small hollow, which on rainy days collected a puddle. Now, having amassed black tar, it was completely filled and hidden. Just as extra depth of oil released the brooms in a sudden forward surge, so it liberated bicycle tyres from lateral hold. Brigitte and Herr Dufft rushed to the window amidst violent jingling of a bell, the clanging of metal and obscene language. They saw Rudi and Xandi rising to their feet, and a pedestrian separating himself from a keeled-over bicycle and a clinging road.

The pedestrian wore a speckled outfit, which, a moment ago, had been a smart, light grey suit. A matching hat lay captured a little way off, and no gust of wind would manage to dislodge it.

Pitch dripped off the man's fingers like black milk from a cow's udders.

Esperanto

"If everybody in the world spoke the same language," Rudolf said to his son Xandi, "nobody would want to go to war. That's why I'm learning Esperanto."

He gladly accepted Dufft's invitation to accompany him to the Convention for European Unity, which featured on its agenda a discussion on the universal language.

The two men took advantage of the warm evening and walked to the meeting along the tree-lined avenues of the Augarten. They came to a spot that jerked Richard Dufft's memory: hidden amongst these trees he and Gusti had lain, and had been within a hair's breadth of a different life. He taunted himself that marriage with Gusti would have faltered, that her pious nature and his broad outlook would have clashed. So why was he still a bachelor? Why had he not romanced with Violetta?

'Because I love *her!*' screamed his soundless lips. He said aloud, "She'll end up in a bloody mess."

"Who are we talking about?" queried Rudolf.

"Do you know what this arse-face, excuse the expression, said to her? He threatened that if he catches us, Gusti and me speaking together, he'd bludgeon me to pulp. You know I am a peaceful man, but frankly I'd welcome a showdown with the bastard. I mean Brunner. He's set to move in with her. And she? She accommodates him. She's scared. She won't talk to me, won't let me put her wise. We came here when we were youngsters, Gusti and I."

A young couple, close together arm in arm, sauntered ahead of them. The aura of the location spelt out this was lovers' territory. It affected Rudolf too. Gretl of New York sprang to his mind and Vikki of the Meldemannstrasse. What had become of them?

"Women and politicians," he sighed, "the flawed institutions of the universe."

"Women, politicians and funny story editors," augmented Dufft, recovered from his vexation. "Have you heard this one? I picked it up in Berlin. A politician visits Vienna. 'What is the percentage of Social Democrats in your city,' he asks. 'About forty-seven percent,' comes the reply. 'And the percentage of Christian Socials?' - 'About forty-five.' - 'And that of the Nazis?' - 'About a hundred percent.'"

Rudolf took a little time before he got the point. "There's truth in it," he said.

"I like it as a joke. The sad fact is the Nazis will put an end to many things, primarily truth. It should make us weep. It should be classified as an anti-joke."

"Like in climax and anti-climax, since we were talking about women." The remark hardly conformed with Rudolf's normal chat, but the optimist in him strove to counter Dufft's cheerless satire.

"Like in Semitism and anti-Semitism, since we were talking about politicians," returned Dufft. "But it's no laughing matter. I've seen it first-hand. The SA hordes run the country over in Germany. They terrorise the Jews, but others as well: Trade Union Officials, Social Democrats, Communists, anyone daring to voice an opinion. They murder in cold blood, and the police and the judiciary look on, doing nothing."

"Let's talk about something else. Let's talk about this Convention for Unity."

"Listen, the Nazis get a majority in the election. The parliament building burns down, if you ask me, torched by the Nazis. They say the Communists did it, so they take steps to avert a Communist putsch, and promptly put an end to freedom. Of speech, of opinion, of the press; telephones are tapped, mail is opened. They set up concentration camps. They call a boycott of Jewish shops, of Jewish doctors, dentists, they even stop Jewish lawyers. All this is done by this self-appointed army of SA oafs, in reprisal for the Jews spreading false horror stories abroad! Like me telling you what I've seen. Let's hope this convention shows the way to foil a Nazi takeover here. But I've got my doubts."

They arrived at the meeting. The hall reverberated with catcalls, shouts, whistles, a terrifying din.

"The National Socialist contingent is here in force," said Dufft.

"Why are they doing this?" Rudolf asked innocently.

The audience craned their necks towards the balcony, from where the vulgarities cascaded.

"It's a needle in a haystack situation. I'll be searching forever to find a funny story here. The chairman himself is a retired general from the Austrian Imperial Army, with distinctions and what-not. He happens to be a Jew, as are other speakers. The Nazis have come to ruin this convention."

Dufft was right.

The orchestrated chorus from the balcony drowned every other ripple of sound.

> "One nation, one people, one leader,
> The Jews are getting greedier.
> The people are getting leaner,
> Heil Hitler, our Redeemer!"

And: "Jew, go home, your matzo ball soup is waiting."

And: "Jew out, Jew out, Jew out."

And: "When German knife drips Jewish blood,
> The Aryan people say good, good, good."

And: "Jewish swine, go to Palestine."

Speaker after speaker battled in vain against the onslaught.

"Ni estas tutaj homoj, we are all human beings." The man on the platform screamed, but he too, and with him the system of the international language, drowned in the torrent of abuse.

A young man with striking red hair mounted the podium, directed blazing eyes at the gallery, drew in masses of air and roared against the pandemonium. "I come to you not as socialist, nor as a communist, not as conservative, free mason, Esperanto linguist, artist, nudist, Rotarian, vegetarian, or barefoot walker, but as a Jew, one who is proud of being a Jew, who doesn't pretend to be anything else, and who doesn't give a damn about not being an Aryan."

Stony silence from the balcony, wild clapping from below. Richard Dufft applauded, Rudolf applauded.

The meeting ended. Dufft became engrossed in conversation with fellow journalists. The hall emptied, Rudolf walked out to wait for his friend. A few metres away from the entrance, underneath a street lamp, a crowd of men filled the roadway, shouting, swearing. Curiosity impelled him to draw near. He discerned youths wearing shorts and white socks, kicking at the red-haired head, chest, groin, and legs of a crumpled figure. It jerked this way and that over dark, red patches on the cobblestones as blows dislodged it from where it had come to rest. Rudolf stopped, aghast.

He felt an iron grip on his shoulder.

"Here's another one," a voice behind him announced. "The Esperanto Jew."

Rudolf tensed his muscles, ready to pounce the instant the approaching young men laid hands on him. He knew it would be a lost cause, he knew he would end up like the person lying in the street.

"No, no, he is no speaker," a voice with a German accent penetrated through the crowd, "he's a tram conductor."

The grip on his shoulder relaxed. A teenager in shorts and white socks indicated the twitching body at his feet. "That's what happens to people who are proud of being Jews and don't care a damn about not being Aryan."

"You can't blame their enthusiasm." The man who had intervened stepped forward. "You have the build of the Esperanto speaker. They mistook you for him. I remember you from our meeting in the Kaffeehaus Adler a couple of years ago."

"Yes," said Rudolf, dazed with aftershock.

He recognised the scarred face, noticed also that Brunner stood nearby.

"We've had an interesting conversation in the Kaffeehaus. I had hoped to speak with you again." Hildebrandt, elated over the chance encounter, said, "Why not pop into my office. Klug und Krapf. Opposite Kaffeehaus Adler. Can't miss it. We'll share a bottle of wine, or some beer. Or a coffee. In a Wirtshaus if you wish."

Rudolf, utterly bewildered, but aware that the German had saved him from a beating, just nodded.

"Good. Tomorrow morning?"

"I'm on tram duty."

"In the afternoon. Tomorrow afternoon?"

"I have a break between twelve and two."

"See you then. Looking forward to it." Turning to the laundry man he said, "Good to see you here, Brunner."

People, amongst them Dufft, emerged from the entrance. Well, well, well, another intervention of fate. He could not have fixed it better. If they fight, one kills the other, both are done for.

The Nazi gang spread out, confronting the cluster leaving the hall. Rudolf found himself among the thugs as if party to their intentions.

"Carry on, Parteigenosse!" Hildebrandt relayed the order to Brunner and retreated, conforming with the established procedure for commanders before a fight.

"Heil Hitler," Brunner shouted after him. Then muttering to himself, "And to hell with you, Gypsy whore worshipper."

Rudolf had no time to reflect on the invitation received by Hildebrandt. He flung himself into the diminishing space between the two advancing groups, raised his arms horizontally into a crucifix pose and cried out, *"Ni estas tutaj homoj."*

The white-socked youths pushed him out of the way.

"What now, Jew? Worried?" jeered Brunner, coming face to face with Dufft.

"Now? I'm not worried about now," returned Dufft. "I'm worried about the future if your lot ever get political power here."

"And so you should, you pathetic *Wanzen*, bedbug," sneered a pimpled, up and coming poet of the Movement in shorts and white socks, *"Du wirst tanzen wie a Wanzen …* you'll be dancing like a bedbug prancing, on a sharpened beetle pin. We shall conquer the world. Hitler has weapons which will wipe out whole cities."

His compatriots burst into song: *"Denn heute gehört uns Deutschland, und morgen die ganze Welt,* for today Germany is ours, and tomorrow the whole world."

"I tell you one thing," said Dufft. "If every city, every human being who disagrees with you, if all of humanity is wiped out, bedbugs will survive."

"You sure of that?" asked the pimpled, up and coming poet of the Movement.

"I'm sure of it. As sure as two and two make four."

"The Führer can make two and two add up to five."

"You'll think two and two is five when we have finished with you," amplified Brunner. He slapped the pimpled boy on his back and pushed him forward.

"I tell you what I think. I think hot air from the drying rooms in your laundry got sucked into your brain," said Dufft.

"You'll find it hot all right and quite a laughing matter, Herr Funny Story Writer. If I were you, I'd start praying."

"I'm ready to take you on. You or any one of your gang, if you possess the basic human integrity of one against one."

Brunner signalled to the white-socked adolescents. He and half a dozen fell upon the journalist.

"Two against two!" yelled Rudolf.

"We are all in this." Dufft's colleagues joined the fracas.

Fists flew. Boys jumped on men's backs. Bodies rolled on the ground. A bright streak flared . A knife. A scream.

Screeching sirens. Chaos.

Suddenly no sign of white socks. Brunner gone too. One of Dufft's friends holds his hand against his chin, blood trickles through his fingers. Policemen everywhere. Ambulance men lift the injured man of the earlier assault onto a stretcher. Others attend to the bleeding man of the knife attack.

Dufft and Rudolf returned home by tram.

"Not a word of this to Brigitte," said Rudolf.

"Nor to Mama," replied Dufft.

"How do we explain our bruises?"

"We slipped and fell when we jumped off the number 31."

"I had boxing lessons when I lived in the orphanage." Rudolf managed a smile.

"I'm picturing the housewives with their baskets of dirty linen outside the laundry when the bandaged supervisor turns up tomorrow."

"Tomorrow," Rudolf said reflectively. "Did you see the man who talked to me, the man with the scar on his cheek? He asked me to meet him."

"He's a Nazi."

"I won't go."

Hildebrandt savoured the soft leather of the taxi, and the pleasant outcome: Dufft taken care of. Tomorrow I'll handle the tram conductor, find out where Vikki is. Destiny has spared me another visit into tar territory. Meeting the wonder boy can wait. First Vikki. Those bulges. Under her skirt, another cleft.

He placed his hand where it itched.

CHAPTER SIXTEEN (1933)

Kalafati

Hildebrandt struck his desk in temper.

Not since he punished this same piece of office furniture over the Schicklgruber revelation had his knuckles endured such torment. His fury stemmed from the newspaper headline:

JOURNALIST THWARTS NAZI ATTACK. GIVES AS GOOD AS HE GETS.

"I'll *get* this Dufft. I'll have him covered in tar and dragged face down the whole length of the Engerthstrasse!"

His secretary announced a visitor: Herr Bader of Bader Transport entered.

Hildebrandt willed his twitching scar to immobility, as he closed the door to the outer office and locked it.

"I'm glad you came early," he said to Bader, "I have another conference scheduled for later. Heil Hitler. Take a seat. I want to speak to you about the shipment of guns."

"Fire away," said Bader at the same time lighting a cigar. He did not offer one to his host. "Try to miss, though, because if you plug me, I might flood your office with fully fermented, half-digested wine of the Wachauer variety. Ha-ha-ha."

Herr Bader's round face exuded joviality. His grey-green Tyrolean headgear with feather matched a grey-green Tyrolean jacket. His Lederhosen threatened to explode whenever he laughed, which happened often. Hildebrandt judged him as a typical specimen of happy-go-lucky Viennese slovenliness, fond of wine, women and song, but who nevertheless had declared himself of similar ilk regarding politics. He provided motor lorries on demand.

"The code name of the operation is Kalafati. The crates of arms will be loaded onto the barge *Helena*," Hildebrandt began.

"Mind if I take notes?" Bader reached for a sheet of folded paper from Hildebrandt's desk.

"Memorise the details."

"Just a few leading words," reassured Bader. "I'll learn them better if I see them written down. I'll eat the paper afterwards, and help it down with a draught of Wachauer. Ha-ha-ha."

"The cargo of coke will be delivered for unloading to the Vienna Danube Coke Company yards."

"We've been there before."

"We'll be there again. But this is different. Our people working for the coal merchant in Germany will issue documents containing discrepancies so that unloading cannot commence until the errors are corrected. This means the barge will be moored for several days beyond the reach of the cranes, near the Northrailway Bridge where there is public access by road. We shall need your transport for removal of the boxes to our base beyond the Leopoldsberg in Klosterneuburg. The operation will take place when the yards are closed for normal business. Nevertheless, you will carry papers showing that you come to collect coke. The crates will be addressed to the Danube Coke Company. So if anything misfires, if the guns are discovered, the finger will point at Jewish Danube Coke for importing illegal weapons."

"Ha-ha-ha."

The men exchanged complimentary comments relating to the triumph at last night's Convention for European Unity. Before Herr Bader departed, he placed the folded sheet of paper back onto the desk, having committed to memory all the key words.

Left alone Hildebrandt indulged in the routine pleasure of picturing brown-shirted men marching towards hazy, white edifices peopled with white-robed damsels. Amongst these misty, blond maidens, one stood out with dark hair. He knew H_2O_2 was an effective bleaching agent. He looked at his watch and fetched a bottle of wine and two glasses, giving free rein to his dancing scar. His agitation stemmed from his rigid belief that the awaited tram conductor knew Vikki intimately.

The advantages of knowing your destiny, your future, are stupendous, he mused. I'll talk to him on this subject; I'll mention there is evidence that his son Alexander has been born under a benign star, and I'll urge him to consult expert fortune tellers of Gypsy stock. He's sure to divulge Vikki's whereabouts. That done, the tramway man has fulfilled his mission on earth.

He consulted his watch again and inspected his correspondence. On top of the pile lay a folded sheet. It must have been pushed into his letterbox with the rest of the mail. He recognised Bader's scribbles. Typical of Viennese sloth to discard such evidence so carelessly. Intent on tearing it up, he first unfolded it and saw a picture of a dark-haired woman holding somebody's hand. He read the accompanying message:

Your life is written in your palm,
Come day of storm, come day of calm,
Reveal the omens in your track,
Fulfil the white, avoid the black,
To the Prater, next to Kalafati, hurry
Let your fortune be read by Madam Fleurie.

Hildebrandt sat quite still. Eventually he muttered, "Destiny."

He had no doubt this was she. He would see her, make love to her. Now. No need any more for the tram conductor.

He left his mail unopened and headed for the Prater, oblivious to the rain. His heart thumped as he turned the gilded doorknob on Madam Fleurie's shack. The entrance was locked. Then he heard a voice, Vikki's voice, no doubt at all, Vikki's voice, from within.

"Would you mind waiting a wee-little-moment?"

A squall of rain whipped his back and legs.

He became completely self-composed now that he had found her. The door opened and there stood Vikki in a white gown, oh yes, a white gown, and a white bodice. Her black hair fell onto the white silk covering her shoulders, and reached the contours of those bulges, oh those bulges.

"Vikki, I have found you."

"Come in."

"I have searched, I have searched. You left the Meldemannstrasse without telling me."

"You are soaked through."

Vikki led him into the chamber, dimly lit by a paraffin lamp. The heavy curtains were drawn, cushions abounded. Ornaments, animals carved in wood, vases, beads, and all the regalia of her trade lined shelves and decorated the velvet furniture.

He had come without raincoat and umbrella. Water dripped off his jacket and trousers. It seeped into the deep pile of the carpet. He saw none of this as his hand clasped her hand, his skin touched her skin.

Vicki said, "Good to see you again. I thought you'd know where to find me." She helped him remove his wet coat and carried it to a stand near the door.

"It was this, a stroke of luck, a stroke of fate." He held out the folded paper and wanted to throw his arms round her body and press his hands over her breasts, but she backed away, took the leaflet from him, fingered it as if to feel his vibrations, smiled and led him to the table and chairs.

"Have your fortune told." She remembered the scene of their last meeting. Had he run off then because he had thought her a Gypsy, or a whore?

He nodded as he sat down. She drew his palm towards her.

He asked: "Do you still see Herr Anzendrech?"

"The tram conductor?" Strange question. "Yes, now and then." She had seen him a few days ago when travelling to the Vienna Woods. "Why do you ask?"

Hildebrandt hallucinated a vision of three corpses: Dufft, Brunner and one clad in tram conductor's uniform.

"Vikki, I love you," he shouted.

She faced a triple dilemma: she had not expected him; she had not expected his declaration of love; Karl Ottakrink, alias Spagola, sat barely two metres away in the adjoining chamber, listening to every word.

She looked at him long and intensely with her black eyes, and said, "The mystical forces flowing between two persons in a sitting depend on tranquil, unruffled, mutually correlated understanding. Highly charged emotions distort the flow of the lines, interfere with the oscillations between us. We must not allow this to happen. We must remain perfectly neutral on a reciprocal level of perception. Have a drink. It will steady your nerves and drive out the rain from your system."

She poured out Karl's rich, red wine. Hildebrandt gulped it down, and she refilled the beaker. Vikki's vocational success hinged on her understanding of human nature. The man facing her, bursting with desire for her, was unlikely to be a great womaniser. If he were he would not behave so frenziedly about any one female in particular.

Therefore the name Helena did not refer to another love of his. Why scribble it on the back of Karl's promotion leaflet together with other words: Kalafati, Coke, Danube, Northrailway Bridge, Crates, Danube Coke?

She held both his hands in hers, turned his fingers upwards and downwards to create and delete crisscrossing folds in his palms. She lowered her eyelids to simulate a trance-like state, but years of practice allowed her to peep through an imperceptibly narrow slit to observe his body language. She let her thumbs caress gently the trembling lines in his skin.

"H-h-h-h," she muttered, "hero, heroics. I see warriors fighting a mighty battle. I see ruins, I see fire, I see devastation, I see water. T-t-t-t, Troy. I see a woman. H-h-h-h, Helen of Troy. Helen, Helena."

Hildebrandt's scar throbbed with the rush of blood entering his face. He nodded slightly without knowing it, freed his right hand and reached for the beaker of wine.

"A woman?"

He shook his head slightly without knowing it.

"No, no, no, not a woman. Water. I see water. A river, a bridge. A ship?"

He nodded slightly towards her drawn eyelids.

"I see a ship. I see the name of the ship. It is *Helena*? It is *Helena*."

Now she opened her eyes fully, saw his beaker required refilling. He nodded again, this time aware of his affirmation.

"It is a white ship?"

"No."

"A black ship. She doesn't carry passengers. She carries something else. Something, something black?"

Hildebrandt began to feel the heat of his racing blood. He needed to cool himself with draughts of wine.

"Coke. But something else?"

Vikki was cruising in top gear. He wavered. He had resolved not to emulate Smaliz' performance on the Kahlenberg. He must remain in control of his wits. *Shall I terminate the sitting or let her go on prophesying the outcome of operation Kalafati. She will unearth the Führer's secret. Those bulges.* He drank more wine.

"Something else..Something in boxes...Something valuable?"

She waited for a sign, perhaps a raised eyebrow, a twitching finger. "I see the ship moored on the Danube by the Northrailway Bridge, and I see packages coming from China ...? No, going to China... No, no, I see a Chinaman... I see Kalafati..."

He mustered his strength to halt the relentless exposé. Destiny or no destiny, allegiance to the things of the Führer went above all. Even her bulges? The surge of activity in his groin reached traumatic proportions. "Yes there will be a barge *Helena* tied up where you see it in your head," he said with forced nonchalance, but slurred all the same. "The vessel will be there for a few days, unattended and quite unimportant. I know about it because some papers relating to a shipment of costumes and gowns for Prater clowns and artistes, Kalafati included, were sent to the Klug und Krapf office in error. You have picked up the residue of vibrations relating to this matter from my hands. But it is totally irrelevant, so let's do something else."

He jumped abruptly from his seat. His chair went flying. He leant over the table. His hands, trembling, reached forward. Vikki drew back. The corner of the table wedged into his groin. His mouth opened in a distorted grimace and let out, not for the first time, a prolonged groan. He stayed fixed for a second or two, then his body slumped onto the table, and slowly slid to the floor.

Excursion - Day One

Uncle Hans proposed a two-day excursion on foot to reach the distant attractions that a one- day cycle ride would have opened up to the families.

For Brigitte the idea of an overnight stay reverberated in a vacuum of the unknown. It needed the passage of time to digest and to marshal together reasons for questioning the wisdom of such an undertaking. "What if we fail to find accommodation? What if we cross the path of vandals? What if we get lost? What if our belongings are stolen? What if one of us steps on an adder? What if we are caught in a thunderstorm?" She remained in a minority of one, and Uncle Hans did his best to dispel her dismal approach by recourse to proverbial persuasion: that nothing ventured, nothing gained; that faint heart never won fair lady; that he who counts all costs will never put plough to earth.

"The jug goes to the well until it breaks," said Xandi.

Brigitte frequently quoted the saying when confronted by her boys' obstinacy. Xandi pictured a brown terra cotta jug with a jolly face, long ears, twinkling blue eyes and short legs skipping to the Engerthstrasse water hydrant, the one that had filled his water balloon, and which was also colloquially known as The Well, until one day it bumped into the cast iron pillar and broke into a thousand brown pieces. The irrelevant nature of Xandi's contribution floored Brigitte's reservations, and the outing was agreed upon.

The families rose at dawn on the appointed day, and saw everything tinted in pale, grey light, evenly spread, casting no shadows. The only sound was the chirping of the sparrows. Uncle Hans said he would be heading in the direction of Mauerbach-Rappoltenkirchen. As a native of Klosterneuburg he had, in his youth, heard of, met relatives from, and even been to the nearby villages scattered in the Vienna Woods. Possessing no maps, he planned to rely on signposts and guidance from natives to reach a farm by late afternoon, where they would be able to stay overnight. And repeating it for the hundredth time, if the worst came to the worst, if they found no farm to put them up, they would search out a haystack. In the event of a thunderstorm, they would simply have to appeal to the mercy of the gendarmerie.

They were all young enough to cope with the calculated risk. In fact this risk, the uncertainty after the point of no return, made the excursion the adventure of a lifetime. Even Brigitte had come to revere it because it took her and her boys closer to nature. Uncle Hans relished it because he liked diversion and in his humdrum factory work there was none. Aunt Anna liked it because he did, and the boys loved it because they were boys.

The first few kilometres followed the familiar route upstream along the Danube and over the low slopes of the vineyards to the hills, which continued in an ever-rising chain of mountains to merge with the Alps. From these heights they looked down on the city lying at their feet. The thin morning mist hung over river and streets, but roofs and church steeples stood out sharp and clear, kissed by horizontal sunbeams. And as the rays became more slanted, the mist lifted. What man, woman or child, born and bred in Vienna, would not point to the 138-metre-high spire of the *Stefansturm,* St Stephan's Cathedral, the Prater's Giant Wheel, the Riesenrad, the golden facade of the Schönbrunn Palace? More than that, they picked out the cream and brown frontages of the Milk and Cocoa Blocks, the red and white trams trundling over the Floridsdorf Bridge. Perhaps Rudolf would be conductor in one of them, but no, he was working on different routes now. The long stretch of the Danube Meadow, the half-moon shape of the Old Danube lake, the Mistgstettn, the dust lorries looking like bedbugs crawling in and out, and the big loop of the elevated city railway, from the carriages of which you could look down onto cobblestoned roadways, or straight into kitchens and bedrooms, and if you were lucky, onto ladies plying lipstick to their lips.

Uncle Hans turned his eyes towards the southwest over a forest of mountains, and there, somewhere in the distance, was the Snow Mountain.

"It is said," Brigitte's abandonment of dialect heralded a statement of some importance, "that only a Sunday child can ever see the Snow Mountain free of cloud."

"Am I a Sunday child?" asked Little Xandi.

"No, you were born on a Friday. But Pauli is. He was born on a Sunday, and he will see the Snow Mountain free of cloud. And it is said, when you see the Snow Mountain free of cloud, it sparkles like a thousand fairy lights dancing on the snow."

Little Xandi envied Pauli's good fortune. He gazed along Uncle Hans' outstretched arm, and saw a purple-coloured hump, no bigger than a peanut, cut in half by a purple coloured-cloud, and that was the Snow Mountain. Uncle Hans said he knew somebody who had been on it.

The excursion led to the clear water of the spring, the Agnes Bründl, where they debated the folklore: if you threw a coin into its man-made basin and made a wish, that wish came true. Actually the depth was not very great; they could see the shimmering one and two-groschen pieces plainly on the bottom, and, it seemed, well within Robert's reach. But when he lowered his hand into it until the water lapped against his cheek, his bare arm shrank to a pitifully short length. Big Xandi proposed a way of draining the well, but Aunt Anna and Brigitte wouldn't hear of it. Uncle Hans would have been game, and laughingly said better the groschens end up in their pockets than in the Agnes Bründl Restaurant's till. Even so, to commemorate the special occasion, he threw a two-groschen piece into the water. They stood round the well and held hands. Little Xandi wished he would see the dark-eyed Pater girl in the shimmering green costume again. Only Brigitte's wish was not trivial. She never lost an opportunity to implore the Almighty for peace and goodwill to all mankind, or if that failed, to shield her family from coming cataclysms. Yesterday a bomb had exploded in a pensioner's dwelling in Linz. People said it had been mistakenly placed, and was meant for a Jew.

A man and woman approached. A wave of discomfiture swept over the families when they realised they could not avoid coming face to face with the couple. The two parties recognised one another, but no greeting passed between them. Frau Marschalek said to her husband as they walked by, "Now I know what to wish for!"

Even Little Xandi's uncomplicated mind grasped the meaning of the woman's utterance. Somewhat downcast he prepared himself to accept stoically any misfortunes coming their way. But Brigitte, her unspoken wish still ringing in her ears, retraced her steps. Xandi followed.

"Frau Marschalek, I bear you no ill feelings. Shall we make peace?"

"Peace? Your thieving werewolf cost me fifteen shillings."

They stared into each other's eyes and seeing no congruence, Brigitte spun round to catch up with her group.

"Frau Anzendrech!"

Brigitte turned once more. Herr Marschalek held out his hand. It was difficult to tell from his wry smile whether his gesture stemmed from willingness to let bygones be bygones or desire to oppose his wife. Brigitte hastened back, but Frau Marschalek seized the hand and forced it away.

By four o' clock the hikers had emerged from tall conifers onto a dusty track curving away into the direction of the sun through meadowland rich with grass and plants, swamped in yellow blossoms and supporting the hum of bees in contrast to the sombre trees. Brigitte's lungs expanded. She recalled an event of her youth, and said to Little Xandi, "You know, when I was a young girl in the service of the Countess, I had never seen fields and wild flowers before, and one afternoon, the governess took me for a walk outside the city, and ..."

"My legs are aching, Mummy, how much further?"

"We'll come to a wee-little-place soon," she reassured him, looking to where the road disappeared over a hill, and seeing no sign of human habitation. "Perhaps we'll sleep in a barn, won't that be fun?"

"What's a barn?"

"It's a big hut in which farmers keep hay for the animals to eat in winter."

"For werewolves?"

"No, Xandi, for cows and little calves."

"But watch out for Rübezahl," said Uncle Hans, rolling his eyes. "He's got wild hair and a red beard like a werewolf, and he roams the country on the look-out for little boys. Ho-ho-ho." Uncle Hans' laugh never went beyond a three-syllable ho.

Brigitte said crossly, "Don't say these silly things, or I'll have to put up with the boy's nightmares. Xandi, listen: Rübezahl lives a long way away in Czechoslovakia, and he is just a poor man who counts beetroots."

"I want a drink, Mummy, I'm thirsty."

"I wouldn't say no to a pitcher of cold ale myself," said Uncle Hans.

"We're all thirsty," said Brigitte.

She crouched down to rest her rucksack on a bank of supple moss, and disengaged the straps, the signal for general sitting and lying down. She dived into the bowels of the rucksack and took out a knife. Then both hands brought forth a huge, deep green, spherical object.

"I forgot all about the water melon," she announced with a mischievous smile.

"Drown me in a whisky barrel!" exclaimed Uncle Hans, "you haven't carried that around all this time?"

But Brigitte had. She knew there would be a need for it. Uncle Hans tested its weight and shook his head in admiration. The liquid spilt over the knife as it cleaved the succulent flesh glistening in the sun. The dark brown kernels clung loosely to the moist surface, ready to be flicked away. Lips embraced the saturated fruit, teeth sliced cleanly through the crisp, deep red flesh, throats gurgled with stilled satisfaction. If in a lifetime there is a moment of bliss, it would be hard to find one surpassing the ecstasy of that watermelon by the dusty roadside.

"You are a martyr, Briggi, but a welcome one," Uncle Hans acknowledged, sucking up the last drop from the boat-shaped, gnawed rind, which reached from ear to ear.

"You can do a bit of martyring now," replied Brigitte, stretching out on the soft, dark green verge. "Go look over the hill to see where we are. It's getting to the time for finding a place for the night."

"We'll look." Robert, Rudi, Pauli and Big Xandi sprang to their feet and ran off.

"Don't know where they get the energy from," said Aunt Anna, her eyes, full of admiration, following the slim bodies.

Uncle Hans placed his wrists under his head and winked at Brigitte. "I thought you were telling us a yarn, Briggi, about your bashful maiden days with the governess, and no doubt a handsome young man thrown in for free."

Did Brigitte blush, or was it the aftermath of the day's spent heat? Uncle Hans, unwittingly, had hit the nail on the head. She remembered... The governess and she resting on a bench in the Beethoven Walk on their way back, strolling on and feeling a touch on her shoulder, turning to face a youth with clear eyes looking straight into hers. "You left your book on the seat," he had said holding out a neatly bound booklet, carefully covered in fancy blue paper. It had been her poetry book, which she had carried with her, and into which she had scribbled her favourite poems, also some of her own. Taking the book she had thanked him, and after a pause had said, "Isn't it a wonderful day?" - "Wonderful," the youth had said, still looking at her, "and so are the poems." She had blushed then also. He had continued looking into her eyes, and his eyes had said more, and her eyes had said more, but the governess had been there, and they had stood looking at each other, and no further word had been spoken. She had returned to the bench on her free afternoons, in vain.

"Can't you recall his name, Briggi?" Uncle Hans teased, as her thoughts were lost in time so long ago. "Or were there too many to remember them all? Come on, out with the secrets!"

"I was telling Xandi," Brigitte replied coolly, "I went with the governess for a walk near the suburb of Döbling between Grinzing and the Danube. We came upon a field full of blue cornflowers. I stood and looked, and looked, and looked. Then I said, 'Oh that is beautiful,' and the governess, who was an educated person, you know, she took my hand, and she said: 'Child, you are an artist.'"

After a moment's silence Uncle Hans said, "Go on, Briggi, tell us the yarn."

Brigitte knew that Uncle Hans would never understand, nor would other men. If she had borne a daughter...

"Sing something, Mummy. Sing *Stürmisch die Nacht und die See geht hoch,*" begged Little Xandi.

And Brigitte in her deep, masculine voice, silenced the humming insects on that summer afternoon, as the melody of "Asleep In The Deep" rolled over the meadows. Sad sounds, sad words of the stormy night, the high seas, the sinking ship. As always, the song brought tears into Little Xandi's eyes.

"You should have been an opera singer," said Aunt Anna, when the last sound died away.

"I know," Brigitte replied earnestly, "people told me so all the while."

Even Uncle Hans could think of no funny comment. Little Xandi, to avoid being discovered in tears, busied himself collecting the rinds of the watermelon, and pushed them along in the dust where they left tracks that looked like tramlines.

The boys came galloping down the road. "There's a big house on the other side of the hill, and we've seen people in the meadow, three men making hay," called out Big Xandi.

"Go on, Hansl, see what you can do," Aunt Anna urged. "We'll get the things together and follow."

The three men in the field dug their scythes into the earth and leaned on them, watching the spectacle of the approaching families, preceded by their young, yet already white-haired patriarch in city Lederhosen. The white hair lent him a look of distinction, and he carried the expression of someone intent on business. The men did not resume their rhythmic swings, but waited patiently for the opening words.

"We are eight heads," Uncle Hans did not bother with a preamble, "three grown ones and five boys. We are on a two-day hike, and we are looking for a night's shelter; hay or straw would suit us fine." He went on to give an account of his work, the families' relationships, their residences, their love for the countryside, and the awful predicament they would be in, especially for little Xandi, if nothing could be found.

The tallest of the men asked: "Was that one of yours, warbling just now?"

"My sister-in-law, Brigitte," Uncle Hans whispered, "famous she was, sang in the Vienna State Opera House. Only don't mention nothing to her about that. Sad business, you know what opera singers are like: *la grande amour*. Best forgotten."

The men nodded as if fully versed with the idiosyncrasies of opera singers and their *grandes amours.*

"Well," said the big farmer, "if you now carry on to the house, say to Frau Preiser that it's all right, Sepp said so, you can bed down on the straw."

"And the cost of it?"

The man waved it aside. "A song or two from the opera singer."

Besides the free use of the barn, the Preisers offered freshly baked bread, freshly churned butter, and fresh milk straight from the cow. Everybody enjoyed the delicious food, except Little Xandi, for whom swallowing warm milk straight from the cow was as gross as swallowing cool worms straight from the grass. He did not speak up because of his reluctance to go against the stream of opinion, which leaned heavily in favour of tepid, odorous milk with yellow froth bubbling on top. The farm people, from Herr and Frau Preiser down to the lowly labourers and maids, were so smitten by the virtue of this thick fluid that refusal to drink it seemed like a sin punishable by instant rejection of himself as a person. So he feigned a stomach-ache and went hungry. Pauli said he had gulped down the melon too greedily. His milk, in a brown jug like the one he imagined breaking into a thousand pieces at The Well, was seized by an adolescent farmhand, and Little Xandi watched it disappear down the young man's gullet with a feeling of aversion and liberation.

The whole labour force assembled to sample the visitors from the city. They persuaded Brigitte to sing. The attention and applause overwhelmed her. Never before had people made such a fuss of her. It was one of the rare occasions when she put everyday cares aside. Little Xandi felt happy in spite of rumbles in his stomach.

Brigitte told another of her early life anecdotes. "Yes, when I was in the service of the countess, one day the governess had a ticket to the opera house, but couldn't go herself because the children of the mansion had taken poorly. She gave the ticket to me. So I went, and it was the first time in the opera house for me."

"But not the last," Herr Preiser said knowingly.

"They were playing the *Fledermaus*," Brigitte went on. The entire gathering hung on every one of her words, "and in the interval people left their seats and went outside, but being on my own I stayed behind, and I remembered the melodies and hardly knowing what I was doing, I sung them softly to myself. When the people came back, I turned around, and I saw a very distinguished-looking man in the row behind me. And he said to me, he said, 'Madam, you should be on the stage.'"

"Gave you encouragement," remarked Herr Preiser.

"But what surprised me," Brigitte said, "next morning the governess showed me the newspaper account of the performance, and there was a picture of the same man. He was the music critic of the paper."

"And that's how it all began?" Herr Preiser asked.

Uncle Hans made signs to the farmer to change the subject, and he himself began to talk of the unemployment, and Herr Preiser retorted with a comment relating to the poor prices for the crops, which led to a general lamentation about the bad times, in which the men outshone one another with examples of more and more depressing detail. Aunt Anna, the optimist, interjected at timely moments that nothing was so bad that it might not have been worse, and that the meal was never eaten as hot as it was cooked, and that the best course in the circumstances was to wait and see. The Preisers couldn't wholly agree with the philosophy of wait and see, and voiced a cure for the ills in joining up with Germany. The turn to serious politics spelt the end of easy conversation, as the families did not share the enthusiasm for such a union with Adolf Hitler in control. Brigitte asked whether they could see their abode for the night. Herr Preiser showed them the barn, and when Uncle Hans collected the rucksacks, Pauli came running up excitedly:

"There's a haystack as high as the Grossglockner in the meadow. Can we climb up on it?"

Rudi and Big Xandi were already enacting the question.

"Climb to your heart's content," said the good-natured farmer, "but be careful not to break your bones."

A mass of loose hay lay piled on the ground at the sides of the stack, and after a challenge to jump into it from the top, Big Xandi did. He vanished completely, and came scrambling out beaming all over his face.

"It's fantastic," he cried, "it don't hurt a bit."

Rudi and Pauli jumped next. Little Xandi struggled to make it to the top on his own, so Robert reached down and hauled him up. Now they wanted to see him jump, and Robert said, "Let's fly down to the centre of the earth together."

He embraced his young cousin from behind, they took off, and they fell, fell, and the warm hay enveloped them like feather cushions.

"Did it feel like you left your stomach behind?" asked Robert.

"Yes," cried Little Xandi, eager to get to the top again for another go.

"If you jump too fast, the stomach actually does stop behind," warned Big Xandi.

"Isn't true," said Little Xandi.

"Is true. You ask Rudi."

Rudi confirmed with solemn face that such was the case. However, it didn't deter the youngest from jumping off on his own whilst his brothers and cousins remained on the top. As he surfaced, they called down:

"Now you've done it."

"What?"

"Your stomach's up here."

"Don't be stupid." But Little Xandi touched his belly, a definite feeling of emptiness.

"The stuff that's in it: melon, bread'n butter, milk," they called out.

"Didn't have no milk," he called back.

"It's the stomach lining," said Robert. "Best come up quick and get it back inside you. It might catch cold if left out too long."

They lay flat on their bellies, their heads peering over the edge, watching Little Xandi climb, driven more by curiosity than conviction that up there lay his endangered digestive organ.

As soon as he pulled up his legs, Robert shouted, "Here goes Little Xandi's stomach, ouwee, down it goes."

And one after the other they leapt, leaving the smallest alone on top.

"You aren't squashing it?" Little Xandi shouted down.

"Hey, I think I left mine behind," said Robert, rubbing his abdomen. "Can you see it up there?"

Little Xandi looked, "No, nothing here."

"I've gone and lost it now," said Robert. "I'd better push yours inside me."

"Don't." Little Xandi quickly joined the others below. "Give it me."

They laughed, and he felt a fool. But Robert took his hand and said, "Let's do the jump again, this time you sitting on my shoulders."

Various other combinations and postures were tried: two together, three together, bottom first, belly first. Then Rudi, always eager to combine play with scholarly endeavour, remembered Galileo and the Leaning Tower of Pisa, and said, "If Robert and Little Xandi jump off at the same time, but separately, who'll reach the ground first?"

Big Xandi immediately opted for his much heavier brother. Robert, who had forgotten about Galileo, but was sly enough to suspect a trick question, deliberately avoided the trap of the seemingly obvious, and replied, "Little Xandi will hit the hay first, because being smaller, he's more slippery against the air."

After rehearsing at synchronisation, the experiment was carried out. Galileo's theorem triumphed, providing a big morale boost for Little Xandi, as coming out equal before the law of gravity, he felt also like an equal before the bigger boys. The newly found confidence served him well when a little later he resisted Rudi's urging to be the guinea pig in another experiment to further science: if descending head first, would the sensation be one of falling or one of flying upwards.

No answer was forthcoming because no one volunteered, not even Big Xandi. Nevertheless the argument went on, during which Little Xandi enjoyed a much needed rest. Lying on the hay, his chin supported on his crossed arms, he surveyed the farm buildings and the surrounding fields in the gathering dusk. His eyes picked out two figures, half hidden behind bushes, sitting side by side, their backs towards the haystack. One was a man, the other a woman judging from the length of hair. Little Xandi accepted as normal bared masculine torsos, but he knew women took great pains to shield from view whatever must remain unseen. He saw here an opportunity to find out, for the woman's back was as devoid of covering as the man's.

A ditch cut across the field, and he reasoned that if he emerged from it as if by chance, the woman would have no time for evasive manoeuvres. He slid down quietly from the haystack.

"Hey, where are you going?" Robert called after him.

"Poos."

"Go the other way. The wind's coming from this direction."

He remembered the layout of the field, and he located the ditch. He crept to the estimated point for surfacing. Crouched on hands and knees, he slowly lifted his head and faced a monstrous reddish beard, a very angry mouth and two fierce, glaring eyes. The woman shrieked and turned her body. He caught a glimpse of her features. His heart nearly missed a beat, for he thought he had recognised the dark eyed Prater girl in the shimmering green costume.

"Scram!" The angry mouth hollered.

Even whilst he ran he remembered his wish at the Agnes Bründl. If he could wish again he would want the man with the big, red beard swallowed up by the earth.

"Maria-nd-Joseph, are you ill?" Brigitte asked when he reached the farmyard, where everybody stood waiting for him.

"There's a man with a big, red beard. There in the field."

"Rübezahl?" Big Xandi queried.

"Ho-ho-ho."

"You've only seen a farmhand," reassured Brigitte.

A sequence of memorable activities followed: climbing up the ladder - about which Brigitte and Aunt Anna made more fuss than if they had been on the moving carpet of the Prater Toboggan; patting down the straw to achieve uniform springiness; spreading out coats and arguing who was to sleep where; and telling each other to hurry in the fading light; Brigitte climbing down again to observe a call of nature, placing a fir cone under her rug whilst occupied outside, suggesting on her return that it was a mouse and calming her down;

Robert calling Big Xandi a wildebeest because he had dragged more than his share of blanket over himself; Aunt Anna losing her comb and Uncle Hans lighting a match to find it heedless of Herr Presser's express warning not to, and Little Xandi afraid they would be engulfed in flames; Uncle Hans inquiring whether any of the Agnes Well wishes had come true; and everybody resolving to rise at five in the morning but nobody possessing a watch; somebody blowing off wind and Pauli and Big Xandi in fits of giggles; Uncle Hans complaining of the smell and Robert saying, "The first to speak let off the squeak."

And Uncle Hans replying according to custom, "The second to tell created the smell."

And Rudi piping in, "The third to start, from him came the fart."

And Robert: "The forth in line was the swine."

Rudi: "The one with that tale made the air so stale."

Having run out of regular rhymes, making up new ones became the theme of the contest. Robert, after thinking hard, said, "It's you I think who caused the stink."

Rudi's reply came quickly, having kept it in reserve: "And I presume you are guilty of the perfume."

"Let's go to sleep," suggested Brigitte.

"Let's go to sleep, Rudi let off the bleep, ho-ho-ho." Uncle Hans came to his son's rescue.

Rudi's tone suggested he could take on father and son. "We are in a coma because of your aroma."

After prolonged thought, Robert had this to offer: "What offends our noses came through your trousers."

Rudi said noses and trousers didn't rhyme. Robert maintained they did. Parents were asked to arbitrate, a delicate matter because Uncle Hans was inclined to uphold Robert's view, right or wrong. Brigitte, who could always be relied upon in moments of crisis, trumpeted a raspberry with her lips and said, "With that rattle I close the battle."

Soon Little Xandi heard regular breathing and rasping. But he couldn't go to sleep. Had his wish really come true? He had seen the girl in the shimmering green costume before, in the Engerthstrasse, sometimes from behind and sometimes at a distance, and when he had run one way or the other so he could pass her face-on, it had always been somebody else.

Excursion - Day Two

Little Xandi opened his eyes and saw motionless figures lying in the straw, lit by lines of yellow sunlight streaming through the slits of the timbered barn. He peeped through, a light brown fawn stood still in the field. Then, perhaps conscious of human eyes, it moved silently into the cover of a spinney. One by one the bodies stirred.

The green handle of the pump in the farmyard dangled just within his stretch. He worked it for everybody. Water squirted from the broad spout in spasms. When it came to his turn to wash away the sleep, he drove the cold, earthy liquid into his mouth to quell the dryness in his throat and fill his empty stomach. Uncle Hans chided the provoking properties of the night's bedding, whilst retrieving flattened lengths of straw from his shirt. He offered the free loan of his hand to Brigitte who tried in vain to reach an itch between her shoulder blades.

"Stand against the pump and move up and down," recommended Aunt Anna treating her own inaccessible places in this manner.

Stepping into the farmhouse to purchase bread and eggs for breakfast, Uncle Hans said, "I hope none of you swallowed pump water, because it isn't high Alpine spring water, you know."

Everybody had heard the story of bygone days when the Austrian Emperor had been hunting on the Snow Mountain. He had cupped his hands under a spring, and had been so thrilled with the crystal-clear water's taste that he had ordered the construction of an aqueduct to the capital, so that all of Vienna's citizens could enjoy the high Alpine spring water. Although by the early 1930s the Snow Mountain snows were inadequate to quench Vienna's thirst without supplement from the nebulous Danube, the treated household supply from the city's taps contained different ingredients to that lifted by green handles of rural pumps. Whilst country folk's intestines had become immune to the spiteful activities of well-water bacteria, town drinkers carried no such protection. By long established axiom, city dwellers must on no account imbibe a drop of country water, or risk dire consequences. Worse than drinking pump water was drinking it on an empty stomach, and worse still on an empty stomach first thing in the morning.

Little Xandi lived through the misfortune of learning this after they had set off on their homeward trek, but he blamed Frau Marschalek's dark wish for the turmoil in his tummy. Brigitte hurried with him into the obscurity of trees, where frightening noises confirmed his plight. Uncle Hans' first impulse was to tease him, but when he saw the white face, he took pity, and to lift his nephew's shaken morale, told the following tale:

"When we was retreating from Bosnia-Herzegovina we were as hungry as wolves on a lonely iceberg. None of us had nibbled at a crust of bread for days. And the order came to halt for rest. I threw the pack onto the ground, and me next to it, and *Himmel, Arsch und Zwirn,* heaven, arse and cotton yarn, what do you think I looked up at? Gooseberries. I was lying under a gooseberry bush. Fact. The berries were as green as peas and hard as peas, but I didn't wait for no order. Them berries went down my food pipe like in a newly patented vacuum cleaner. And do you know, I hadn't been at them for a couple of minutes, when I felt it coming on. You see there was absolutely nothing inside me, and my digestion couldn't cope with the sudden inrush of unripe gooseberries. Like a cloudburst after a drought, the stuff went straight through. I got my trousers down, and holy Jesus, trumpet sounds for quick retreat. And the enemy stood on the hill cracking rifles at us. Everyone ran. And me? I pull up my trousers, pick up my pack and rifle, and run as well. But my rear hadn't finished! I tell you, the things that happen to soldiers in war."

Later in the day, when Little Xandi's stomach acrobatics had quietened down, Brigitte and Aunt Anna queried whether, in the light of Little Xandi's experience and Uncle Hans' story, they had learned their lesson. They had come into a tree-lined avenue of apricot trees. The branches brimmed with yellow apricots. Uncle Hans and the big boys were up amongst the fruit like monkeys. They had learned nothing. They filled their mouths and pockets, and threw handfuls down to Little Xandi. In the enthusiasm no one saw the gendarme until he spoke.

"Well," he propped up his motorbike on its support bracket, "if I were you, I'd come down. Now."

The boys jumped off the trees landing on their feet, Uncle Hans came down on his backside. Aunt Anna rushed to him, but the gendarme was engrossed with the boys.

"I saw you all. You, you, and you."

"These are apricot trees," said Rudi, seeing bluff as the only chance.

"I know that," the gendarme agreed.

"The apricots are ripe for the picking. I don't think many people know the trees are here. They ought to be told, so they can come to harvest the fruit."

"I'll be harvesting you, my boy."

"You can eat them. You taste one. Sweet near the skin, a bit sharp near the stone."

"It's against the law to pick fruit off the highway trees."

Rudi exuded astonishment. "Really?"

"Really! And I saw you up on the trees: you, you, and you. It's no use denying it."

The gendarme turned to Uncle Hans, who had scrambled to his feet, his pockets bulging with apricots. "Now you."

"Me?"

"Are you the father?"

"Father and uncle, aye."

"You saw the boys in the trees. They'd better not deny it."

Uncle Hans' hands were shielding the swells of his pockets.

"We are not denying it," said Rudi. "We picked the apricots because it seemed the obvious thing to do. They'd go rotten otherwise."

"The picking of fruit on country roads is unlawful." And to Uncle Hans: "Did you see the boys up in the trees?"

"Boys will be boys."

"Yes. Well now. You're youngsters, and I give you the benefit of the doubt." Once again turning to Uncle Hans: "It would have been a different matter if you had been picking. You're adult. I would have had to charge you."

Uncle Hans' mouth gaped. Speechless, he nodded meekly.

"All of you, empty your pockets. Come on, boys, the apricots need to be confiscated."

The gendarme produced a canvas bag with yellow stains along its lower seam; it looked like a receptacle specially made for ferrying apricots.

Robert transferred his haul. "Is this the right way to Klosterneuburg?" he asked, not because he was seeking the information, but because he was envious of Rudi having monopolised the parley.

"That's the Klosterneuburg Road right enough," replied the gendarme, watching with moist tongue the accretion of the ingredients for tomorrow's pie. "There's been a bomb in Klosterneuburg. So be on your guard."

"How dreadful," said Aunt Anna.

The gendarme, shaking his head, mounted his motorbike and started the engine. "Don't let me see you up on the trees again!" Then he roared off.

Uncle Hans said, "The man's barmy."

"He mentioned bombs!" said Brigitte.

"He said I wasn't picking. Look. He's barmy. I nearly fell on his head." Uncle Hans removed apricots from his pockets, one by one, a nigh-on endless process.

In spite of lingering apprehension that further explosives might be lurking somewhere, they walked on to Klosterneuburg. Uncle Hans led the way through narrow streets to the insignificant beige walls of the house of his birth. He squeaked with delight when he pointed to the crumbling plaster below the window where his fingers had scraped away the soft mortar between the exposed bricks, digging for treasure. And he stood in the dark passage, inhaling the damp, sweet smell, which evoked memories of Maria and her sweet smell. And he gazed up at the white window from which he had looked down onto a world that had been bomb free and good to live in.

The Red Bunting

Frau Rosenfinger, elected custodian of the Socialist Emblem for Staircase Thirteen, asked the Anzendrech boys to help her carry the heavy red banner to the wash house, where it was passed to willing hands for further transportation to her tub, so that it could be cleaned to hang in pristine condition next year, on May 1st 1934, draping the Milk Block facade from the attic down to first-floor level.

Brunner saw Frau Rosenfinger's trough filled to the brim with crimson cloth, and yards of it spilling over, lying in a heap on the laundry floor. He walked up to it and ruled that only fabrics essential to running a household were permitted to be submerged in municipal hot water.

Frau Rosenfinger dug a pair of pink fists into her hips, and said, "You don't say."

"I do say."

"The Milk Block's solid behind the Schutzbund."

"That piece of filth will use up five tubs full of hot water."

"There ain't nothing in no regulations which stipulates how many tubfuls the likes of us durst or durstn't use. We wash until what we've got is clean. Not that there's much anyway, and the flag here isn't just mine. It belongs to everybody on Staircase Thirteen except the Kristopps and Frau Czarnikow, because everybody on Staircase Thirteen except the Kristopps and Frau Czarnikow paid hard-earned groschen for it and its keep, and because everybody on Staircase Thirteen except the Kristopps and Frau Czarnikow is behind the Social Democrats, and if the Kristopps want to hang out the swastika for Hitler's Nazis, and if Frau Czarnikow wants to hang out the crooked cross for Dollfuss' Christian Socials, the bigger fools they, us being God-fearing Christians ourselves. We have the right to wash our banner."

"I got to cut down on coke. I've started digging into the reserves. You can't have any more water for that rag."

"We'll see about that. I want to book a dryer for the bunting."

"This bunting is going in no dryer."

"You'd tell a different story if it was a Nazi flag!"

"I'm looking after the interest of the Milk and Cocoa Blocks, not after the interests of Jews and Jew-lovers who bribe decent Aryans to hang out red bunting."

Frau Rosenfinger's wrath at this jibe caused her face to match the colour of the cloth clutched in her steaming hands. "You take that back! Us Social Democrats don't know the word bribery. It's the brownshirts' trademark, bribery is. And my man and Herr Dufft look after the interests of the working folk here. They wouldn't, like some I won't mention by name, use the boiler room for their private harem!"

By this time a large contingent of women had gathered round. After Frau Rosenfinger's last remark, several pairs of eyes settled on

Lutschi's abdomen before shifting to Brunner. The laundry supervisor, eager to keep the controversy to the subject of red bunting washing, sunk his fingers into Frau Echenblatt's tub, grabbed the first thing therein, held Herr Echenblatt's dripping long johns above his head and announced, "For this the laundry provides hot water." He plunged them back, raised a length of Frau Rosenfinger's red flag and declared, "For this the laundry does not provide hot water."

And he pulled out the plug of the Social Democrat's trough.

"We'll see about that," shouted Frau Rosenfinger and pounced off.

Herr Brunner adopted the stance of legs astride and arms crossed over his chest, conveying readiness to meet any challenge. He fixed his eyes on Frau Spagola amongst the ladies standing around. Gusti took his stare as an exhibition of courtship.

"Go back to your chores," declared the laundry supervisor at length, "the incident is over."

None of the women moved. They knew Frau Rosenfinger's angry departure heralded the beginning, not the end, of the story. An amicable solution over the red bunting having dissolved like the moistures in the drying cabinets from which it had been banned, Frau Rosenfinger headed straight for the unemployed men in the courtyard. Her husband immediately rushed into the laundry. He requested from Brunner that the issue of banner washing should be decided democratically by washhouse users. The laundry supervisor refused, clinging to his right as manager to manage as he thought fit. Herr Rosenfinger, contemplating the prospect of grubby, creased, red bunting sagging amidst freshly starched Heimwehr and swastika crosses, threatened to collect a band of men and forcibly remove the obstruction to the socialist cause. At this moment Herr Dufft and the heavily built Socialist, Herr Kranitschek, appeared. Herr Brunner began using foul language at the sight of the Jewish journalist, so Herr Kranitschek, conscious of the presence of ladies, pummelled the laundry supervisor into the boiler room, pushed him into a heap of reserve coke, took a bunch of keys from the wall, went back into the wash house, and after spending some time locating the right keys, locked the boiler room door.

More men assembled.

Herr Kranitschek handed the keys to Herr Rosenfinger and said, "Let him sweat in there for a while," then told Frau Rosenfinger to carry on washing the red flag, and returned to the courtyard to gather up the temporarily abandoned king, queen and jack of diamonds together with a bunch of uninteresting black cards.

The captive laundry supervisor drummed on the door, shouted abuse and threatened incarceration in concentration camps for the whole Milk Block. Most women enjoyed the spectacle, but some became apprehensive, and finally Frau Echenblatt observed that enough was enough. Gusti took this as a cue to ask Herr Rosenfinger to let him out. Herr Rosenfinger walked to the door, pushed the key into the lock and turned it. But the door would not open.

The Second Keyhole

The episode came under discussion by the tenants' committee a few days later. Herr Rosenfinger explained that the door remained fastened until Herr Posidl, after examining the lock and finding no fault with it, located an unobtrusive keyhole higher up.

"None of us here on the committee knew a second lock existed," Herr Rosenfinger explained, "and we don't have a key to it. Herr Kranitschek locked it because the key hung on Brunner's bunch. He didn't think it strange at the time. Brunner wasn't in a very responsive mood when let out, but eventually he did say that the lock had always been there, but he had never used it himself."

Committee members who belonged to the Schutzbund stayed behind after the meeting.

Herr Bergmeister said, "This is a fishy business. Brunner's a Nazi. He works for the municipality, but he doesn't like red Vienna. Suppose he stumbled onto our guns stacked away under the sand. Suppose he wants to prevent us using them. All he needs to do is to lock the door with this second key. What's more, the Nazis can lay hands on the guns whenever they want them for their own misbegotten use. We must move the crates to another safe place. The Engels Block will be pleased to have them."

"It'll make the Milk Block a healthier site," mused Herr Rosenfinger who had never been in favour of resorting to weaponry.

For no reason other than mild wonder at coincidences, it should be recorded that the decision was taken at the same time as Brigitte made her wish at the Agnes Bründl.

CHAPTER SEVENTEEN (1933)

Chamomile

Brigitte and her cure-all chamomile tea earned credit for restoring the Rosenfingers' stomachs to normal functioning.

Dufft came to hear of it and wondered how Mama's ailments would respond to the remedy. Brigitte let loose a recitation of nature's medicinal qualities lodged in the yellow-and-white petals, adding that she always kept a glass canister filled with the dried flowers, ready for use at the first sound of a family sneeze. However, she failed to amplify that the stricken family member responded with pressing lips together at the approach of a cupful of the boiled down plants.

Dufft took the jar with him. Brigitte, a few days later, felt like jigging to "Tales from the Vienna Woods" when he returned with two jars of freshly picked chamomiles, saying he must return the gift with interest as Mamma Dufft's dizzy spells had disappeared, and her knees were back to household chore strength. He recommended that Rudolf should take the tea for his insomnia.

Rudolf swallowed his aversion, before swallowing the concoction.

After a week's absorption of the liquor, he slept through the clamour of his alarm clock, and, leaving his breakfast on the table untouched, instead of walking, he jumped on a passing tram to the Wexstrasse Depot. Subsequently he turned the volume on his alarm clock two notches higher. He also developed a partiality for the herbal drink. He became an addict.

The family embraced the brief to pick the plant anywhere it grew, as the daily filling of three mugs necessitated amassment of vast stocks. In times of shortage it became necessary to dilute the brew so that it lost some of its aroma and colour. Uncle Hans remarked when sipping the watered-down version that it had gained in merit, as the stronger flavour and tint would render it indistinguishable from the product of cattle bladders.

Rudolf's belief in the invigorating potency of the plant grew to equal his wife's faith in sun patches. Brigitte understood. She resorted to stuffing pillowcases with the vegetation, asserting the dual advantage of easing the storage problem and of benefiting the sleepers through inhaling the healing vapours. The sweet-warm decomposing smell compensated for the shortcomings of taste, and was not unpleasant if, as Uncle Hans put it, you were trained in the odours of the farmyard.

Diphtheria

An outbreak of diphtheria occurred in Floridsdorf.

Then Rudi went down with the sickness. The authorities traced the origin of the disease to rubbish dumped on the Mistgstettn. The Anzendrechs had been gathering chamomile flowers there. They threw their entire store into the dustbin.

Rudi's condition remained stable for a few days, then deteriorated rapidly. It became bad, then serious, finally very serious. The doctors at the Wilhelmina Hospital engaged in a losing battle. Thoughts of death pressed on the family, but they refused to speak of it. They moved about quietly, they spoke in truncated sentences. Brigitte and Rudolf stood by the window, their backs towards the room, their hands crossed behind them, their fingers touching, their eyes moist.

Xandi sat on Pauli's shoulders and looked over the hospital wall at his brother. Rudi neither waved nor stirred. The drained body lay wrapped in sheets on the solitary bed on the veranda; beside it stood the doctor in a white gown, mesmerised by the laborious gasps for breath. Brigitte beheld the drawn, young face looking like an old man's with no recognition in his eyes. She perceived the crisis: tomorrow those eyes would see no more, or else there would be new sparkle in them. She spoke to no one of this, she bore the ordeal of waiting alone.

The morning broke sunny but cool. Brigitte carried out the breakfast rituals, countless repetition having moulded the end of one movement into the signal for beginning the next. Yet even setting flame to the gas remained an action she would not forget. The closeness of death, like that of birth, lends strangeness to everyday activity. Pace slows down, objects seem remote, familiar things become unfamiliar.

She tidied the rooms, taking care to clear them of every speck of dust. A bedbug clung to the wall. She removed it carefully. When all was done, she set off for the hospital. Summer school holidays were still on, so she took Xandi. She put him under the charge of a blue-cloaked Sister in an enormous white, starched head-covering, and disappeared through a door. Xandi, too, understood that Rudi's homecoming hung by a thread, and that the strength of the thread would be revealed during the next few minutes. The Sister asked him whether he had heard of the wolf who dressed up as grandmother, or of the witch who fattened little boys for the oven, or of the giants, ogres and dragons who infested the land. Xandi confessed knowledge of all these creatures, but their existence caused him small concern. Tragedy in reality differed from calamities in stories, which only ever happened to others. When they happened to your own kin there was no thrill, no excitement, no fear, only a dullness that obliterated all else.

His mother came back. Xandi saw a slight tremble about her mouth. She fumbled with his coat. The sister helped. Brigitte suddenly grasped her gown and wept quietly.

"Na als denn," said the Sister, recognising the tears of exaltation, "has he come through?"

Brigitte nodded.

The door opened and the white-coated doctor entered.

"Doctor Krause, oh Doctor Krause…" Brigitte spoke softly, drying her eyes. "Doctor Krause, I don't know how to thank you."

"Don't thank us. We didn't bring him through. Frau Anzendrech, I have watched terminal cases, and I have seen many unexpected recoveries. We, the doctors and the staff, we do what we can, but we are only the tools of a Greater Will. When someone slips through our fingers, believe me, we feel it. We had given up on your son. There was nothing more we could do."

Doctor Krause stood with a puzzled face. Brigitte sensed his perplexity. She would have liked to hold the grey head to her breast, as a mother would do to her son confronted with a new, difficult experience.

"We didn't cure your son," the doctor went on. "It wasn't his strength, nor was it his will to live that carried him over the crisis. There was something almost miraculous, as if some power had accumulated inside him, and at the point when all else gave in, this power unwound itself like the energy in a spring, and it carried him through."

In Brigitte's soul a revelation leaped and danced, too obscure to be expressed in words. But she had been right. And now nature, the servant of the Almighty, had rewarded her. She thought her thoughts, and locked them away in the innermost of her secret vaults.

On the tram home Xandi said, "We thought Rudi would die."

Brigitte held his hand tightly.

"When's Rudi coming home?" he asked.

"Soon."

Xandi said, "It was you, wasn't it, Mummy? You're always taking our shirts off and pushing us into the sun. That's what made Rudi better, didn't it, mummy?"

Her secret vaults! Brigitte's eyes were shedding tears freely.

Xandi understood then that you can say a prayer with tears.

Sessl's Relief

Chief Police Officer Sessl's days in the Waldhäusl in Neuwaldegg belonged to the past.

A few months ago a table companion had been arrested in the fracas on the day of Hitler's elevation to Chancellor of Germany. The man, along with twenty thousand other Vienna Nazis, had gathered in front of the Rathaus on the Ringstrasse, chanting that Hitler be appointed Führer of Austria as well.

Sessl realised that politics, like sex, were here to stay.

The other day Lyudmila Fritzer, her belly large with impending childbirth, comes bounding into his office, spins a yarn purporting that she can prove Karl Spagola is alive, insisting that any compensation claim for his death on the *Budapest* is fraudulent, and that it is the duty of the police to find him.

This is followed by a letter from America, in which Herr Reibeisen explains that he has just arrived in New York. He encloses copies of documents showing that Karl Spagola has been employed in the Danube Coke yards but not on the *Budapest*. He further writes that he has known, before his departure, from confidential sources, which for reasons of their safety he cannot disclose, that the lorries which have dumped the dross in the coal yards, belong to the transport firm

Bader.

At the same time, a cut-out newspaper article is posted to him, in which a diatribe against Jewish businesses is followed by a statement from Herr and Frau Speelzeug that they were passengers on the *Budapest* trip to Tulln the day prior to the steamer's demise, and that they spoke to the stoker whose name was Karl Spagola.

Sessl's deputy, Breitwinkel, entered, "Some items of information just come through," he said.

"Good or bad? By that I mean non-political or political?" replied Sessl. He knew Breitwinkel to favour an independent Austria, and he felt he could converse with the man without constantly having to watch his words.

"I don't know. What is and what isn't political? The first item concerns Herr Spagola. He hasn't shown up yet?"

"Not to my knowledge."

'Well," said Breitwinkel, "there is a twist in the affair. We found out that Karl Spagola's wife, his real wife, Susanne Spagola, died in Tulln three weeks ago. She had been bedridden for some time. The implications are these: in the absence of a will, and there is the likelihood none exists, if Karl Spagola was employed on the *Budapest* and perished in the accident, compensation money will be due to his wife. She was alive at the time of the accident, and as she has died since, the compensation will be passed on to her legally entitled heirs. On the other hand, if Karl Spagola is still alive, he is due to inherit his wife's estate for what it amounts to. The house was hers."

"That piece of news should winkle a living Spagola from his hole," said Sessl.

"With the consequence ..." said Breitwinkel.

With the consequence that we'll have to think again about the perpetrator of the Danube Coke bombing, Sessl thought. He said, "Best wait and see. What's next?"

"Diphtheria. Two cases in Floridsdorf, one in Brigittenau. The oldest Anzendrech boy. The health authorities ask for our cooperation in tracking outbreaks, especially now that schools are starting shortly."

Sessl responded, purring like a pampered tomcat, relieved to hear of something needing investigation that had nothing to do with politics.

CHAPTER EIGHTEEN (1933)

Tombola

The Tombola was a gigantic, end of summer, pre-bingo-age bingo, taking place in grand style on the Danube Meadow.

A platform, erected on the grass, supported a giant cube-shaped structure, featuring on each face rotatable panels, blank on one side and numbered from one to fifty on the reverse. The numbers were large enough to be readable from any point between the Floridsdorf and Northrailway Bridges. Before play began, a totally bare cube met the punters' gaze. Then, at intervals of several minutes, the process of turning over four identical panels, one from each face, continued until all prizes had been claimed.

Tickets displayed three lines of five numbers. Prizes started to be given out at the checkpoint to ticket holders arriving with two matching numerals in a line, and, as more panels were turned, with three, four and five corresponding digits in the same line, and finally, the one and only star prize, a motor bike, went to the first-come with all fifteen numbers matching. The lower categories carried several prizes varying in splendour. Claimants had first-come, first-served choice. Proximity to the checkpoint and sprinting skill were all-important.

The show attracted multitudes. Conducted in the spirit of a universal holiday, a parachute jump by *Seicherl,* a Viennese newspaper strip cartoon figure, whose purpose in life was to get in and out of scrapes accompanied by Heurigen (Vienna new wine) wit, predominated the entertainment programme.

Brigitte viewed the Tombola as an obscenity: thousands of outsiders, having no respect for nature, churning the earth into dust, augmenting the rubbish with mountains of beer bottles, loudspeakers shrieking into the already brain-wracking, raucous racket of the motor-driven generators, and the wine-besotted clown dangling from the parachute and performing silly somersaults in mid-air.

Uncle Hans conceded that the Danube Meadow could do without the yearly invasion. On the other hand, after days of indecision whether to participate or not, weighing the cost of the tickets against the chance of bringing home a sparkling carpenter's tool set of twenty-four pieces neatly arranged in a polished portable metal case, he savoured the moment when he swung over to go all out for a win. He did not clamour for the motorbike. He aimed to run for the top two-number prize. He had come to believe that he would score by following the rituals of selecting tickets from different blocks; also, he, Robert and Big Xandi would learn their numbers by heart and set foot on the Danube Meadow at sunrise to secure best position – oh, and attempt to persuade Brigitte of the merits of his method.

"You have double odds with the two-numbers," he held forth "because not everybody who gets two numbers up starts running. A lot of people go for the motorbike, even if they get a win before then. And if you're unlucky on the two, there's a chance you come up on the three or four or five numbers. The more there are of us, the bigger the likelihood of winning. Big Xandi is the fastest sprinter, and he'll run with your ticket so he'll get to the checkpoint first, so he'll collect the best prize. I'll be keeping a place for you near the platform close to where they turn the numbers, so you'll see them straight away."

Brigitte remained undeterred.

Aunt Anna consoled herself in advance that in the event Hansl missed the top two number prize, the second in line was a set of cooking pots. Rudi, convalescing from diphtheria, found his funds were ten groschen short of a ticket price. He supported his father in maintaining that winning through exertion of effort, like in sport, chess or in a poetry competition, outweighed relying simply on chance, and scoffed at taking part. But when Pauli offered to purchase a twenty per cent share in a ticket, both boys caught the Tombola fever.

Rudolf would have been interested in observing the mechanics of the parachute jump, but tramway duty on Sundays denied him the opportunity. He said he expected to be transferred back to the 31 Tram route on Tombola Day because of the heavy passenger demand, and he could be travelling over the Floridsdorf Bridge at the moment Seicherl took a deep breath before hurling himself into the atmosphere, and so might witness the big event after all.

Richard Dufft received a commission from the Danube Press to write a humorous story of the day. Somewhere, perhaps on the Northrailway Bridge, coming from the Tombola, he'd locate a winning couple at loggerheads at each other over the choice of prize, interview them and spin a tale around the event.

Milk and Cocoa Block inhabitants, except laundryman Brunner and Brigitte, awaited the Tombola with jubilation. Brunner's stand emanated from Seicherl's huge, crooked nose, even though acquired through years of jovial imbibing rather than bequeathed from non-Aryan ancestry. But Nazi philosophy pronounced heavily against deviation from linearity of the olfactory organ. The anti-Semitic laundry supervisor was happy to be assigned political activity on the day.

Seeing an opportunity to spend an hour or two with Gusti on her own, he brought wood, paper and string for the construction of a kite on which Berti, Manni and Xandi with Poldi's attentive eye, should embark on the eve of the Tombola. The children responded with enthusiasm, hoping that the ascending craft would meet the descending Seicherl half way up by way of greeting. Brunner remained ignorant of the kite-Seicherl connection. He proposed, in order that the kids could get on with the work undisturbed, that they be left alone in the kitchen whilst he and Gusti retired into the bedroom.

The Marriage Certificate

"The empty streets tomorrow will be a bonanza for burglars, Jews and other criminals," Brunner remarked, sat himself on a bed, and invited Gusti to do the same.

"I wish Spagola was here," said Gusti. "It's hard for the children without a father."

"I could be their father, my sweet."

Gusti shook her head.

"Good as." He laid his arm over her shoulders, his fingertips searching for a nipple.

Gusti stood up. He too. Then he ambled to the door: "Can this be locked?"

She walked to the window, looked out at the steady flow of the Danube. As always of late, her mind saw the gushing current with the hapless steamer driven against the Reichsbridge pier, men falling into the river.

"I've got news," said Brunner.

"Spagola's body's been found?"

Brunner produced a paper from his pocket: "What I've got here's as good as a marriage certificate."

Gusti looked at him anxiously. What did he mean? Was this a ploy to get her, now? Had she let him into her flat because she really believed the man's presence would help her children over the absence of Spagola? Was she that naïve? Or was she harbouring a wish ... the woman-eating panther ... Richard ... her bargain with God?

"This is a document, certified by Rosenberg and Rosenberg, notaries, that a wedding took place at the Oberndorf Church, Lower Austria, on the fifth of March, nineteen hundred and eighteen, between Herr Karl Spagola and Fräulein Augustine Schattzburger."

"What?"

"That makes you Karl Spagola's widow. The fire at the Oberndorf Church on the seventh of March nineteen hundred and eighteen destroyed all records. And as Herr Spagola hasn't told anybody where he kept the marriage certificate, and since we can't ask him because he's dead, this document will have to do."

"But I've never been married to Spagola."

"Yes, you have. In Oberndorf on the fifth of March nineteen hundred and eighteen. Peter Speelzeug and Berta Speelzeug acted as witnesses, and their signatures are on this paper. It's all very simple."

"I don't know anybody called Speelzeug."

Brunner joined her at the window: "How do you think we'll get compensation if you're not his widow?"

"Richard said in the absence of a widow, dependants can claim it."

"Leave the Jew out of it, is that clear? You know there's another Frau Spagola, don't you?"

"The one in Tulln?"

"The one in Tulln. Karl Spagola married her also, after he'd married you. The wedding to the woman in Tulln is bigamy. It's null and void. Spagola's dead, so none of this affects him. You are his widow. You'll get compensation. The one in Tulln won't." He placed the paper on a chair. "Keep it safe."

Gusti was appalled. Faced with this obvious trickery, she grasped she had been dreadfully wrong all along. Richard would do everything in an honest way.

"I need to speak to somebody else about this," she said.

"No, you don't. And specially not to Hebrew Richard Dufft. Listen, my sweet, I'm not spending a fortune and running myself into the ground to provide a future for you and your little treasures to watch it come to nothing, whilst Israelite Dufft laughs his head off! Dufft is in league with Danube Coke. I told you he'll collect his share if he saves them money. He's telling everybody your old man wasn't even on the boat."

"Perhaps he wasn't." For the first time Gusti allowed doubt to enter her mind. It reflected the creeping certainty that she had acted hastily in opening the door to this laundry man.

He said, "And his pullover? Did it sprout wings and fly to the wreck?"

"Alexander Anzendrech played a chasing game with Spagola on the Danube Meadow the day before the accident, when the ship steamed up river."

"He didn't. I told you it was another man. He mistook him for Spagola like I did. Look, not everything needs to be explained precisely leading to Spagola's drowning." He walked back to the door. "We are dealing with Jewish machinations here. The Jews wrecked the *Budapest*. They'll have to pay. And if Israelite Dufft interferes in this matter of your marriage in Oberndorf, he's dead meat. Can this door be locked?"

Finding no keyhole, he opened it and surveyed the children's work. "Nearly finished? Splendid. Looks good. Here, ten groschen each. The ice cream shop on the Allerheiligenplatz is open until nine. Get yourself an ice cream each. Don't hurry back."

Gusti ran into the kitchen, shouting, "Wait, I'll come with you."

But the children were already dashing down the stairs. He held her back, closed the door.

The Bread Knife

"At last we're alone, sweetheart." He drew her against his body.

"Don't. I've given a solemn promise not to."

"Who to?"

"To God."

Brunner laughed. "Don't be soft. Come, I'll make you happy."

He pushed her into a corner of the kitchen next to a sideboard. His midriff made contact with her abdomen. His mouth sought hers.

She turned away. "I've promised not to, not until I'm a married woman."

"Your husband's dead, and we shall be married." His fist gripped her chin and he forced her face round. His teeth and tongue laboured to part her lips.

"No."

His craving for her body soared. He tugged at her skirt.

"I haven't... said... I'll marry you," she spluttered when she managed to turn her face away. The pointed bread knife lay on the sideboard.

Filled with sudden fury he hit out at her cheek.

Panting heavily she wriggled to create space between them. At the same time he realised his mistake. Beating her was not on the agenda, yet. "I lost control, sweetheart. I'm asking you now. I want you to become Frau Brunner."

"You want the money."

He saw the compensation slip through his fingers, or end up in the Jew's pocket. He had to do it now, make her pregnant. He flung his arms round her waist, lifted her off the ground. She reached for the knife and pointed it towards his right eye.

He put her down, released her, laughed and took the knife from her hand.

"All right, my pet, if that's how you want it."

He held the knife against her throat and marched her into the bedroom, onto the bed. With the tip of the blade he savaged three buttons on her blouse. Holding the knife in one hand, he tore off as much apparel as he could with the other. Terrified, she gasped, "I am Jewish."

Too late. As he returned with the knife into the kitchen, he mumbled to himself, "By all the blood-boozing bedbugs in Hitler's oratory, I'll marry her even without the compensation!"

When she came out of the bedroom he said, "I know you are no bloody Jewess. You enjoyed it? I did. You have a firm body. Fighting me made it more exciting. I'd have renounced Adolf Hitler rather than missed out."

She simply glared at him, tears running down her cheeks.

"We'll have some more of it. Tomorrow. Without the theatricals." He attempted to embrace her, but she crouched down to avoid him. "Come, I'll say it, I love you. Let it be a boy. He'll have a father. I make this pledge as a National Socialist: we'll be man and wife. We'll be living here together in this flat as man and wife."

Lutschi's Baby

A flushed Frau Spagola called on the Anzendrechs next morning to ask whether Gugi had been lodging with Xandi. She explained Poldi had kept waking up missing her doll. Gugi lay on Rudolf's work table, forgotten there after Poldi and Xandi had tried in vain to play with their matchsticks against the intrusion of a vast typewriting machine that had been deposited on top of the tram network.

"I didn't sleep well either," said Brigitte, "fretting about the green grass on our very-own-wee-little-place. You look tired, Frau Spagola."

Brigitte did not know that her friend had spent a restless night also, worrying over Judgment Day, if a third child by a third man was on its way. Even now she was thinking, praying, 'What will the Milk Block say? At my age? What will Richard think? I'll never be able to turn to him for help, or love. Finished. The end. Marrying Brunner? The woman-eating tiger. Oh God! Lord, please let it not happen. It wasn't my fault. I wanted to keep our bargain. He raped me. Please let my bleeding come.'

As Brigitte let Frau Spagola out, Lutschi Fritzer struggled down the stairs, step by step, holding on to a recently acquired, second-hand perambulator with a recently acquired, first-hand, bawling baby inside it. The carriage looked like breaking free, a calamity that a God-fearing woman like Frau Spagola would do anything to prevent. On the other hand, giving assistance to the rival who had been ravished by her man, though dead, went perhaps beyond the requisites needed to gain passage past St Peter. Brigitte suffered no such qualms. She hurried to support the pram's hooded end to lessen the pull on Lutschi's arms. But the young mother's fingers had slipped on the handlebar, so that perambulator, baby and Brigitte faced imminent danger of hurtling down into the storey below. Gusti stepped forward, and the three women carried the pram down safely. Once on level ground Brigitte straightened out the blanket of the crying infant.

Lutschi said, "I've been to Frau Kristopp. She knows about babies."

"Does she?" Brigitte's query conveyed disbelief. "Frau Kristopp? Where has she learnt about babies?" She examined the infant closely. "Is there anything wrong with her?"

"She's a he," said Lutschi, "he won't stop crying. When he's awake he cries. All the time through. Frau Kristopp says it's the milk. Too much sugar."

Brigitte bent over the tiny, wrinkled face, gently touched the soft cheek with her forefinger and said, "Voogi voogi voogi voogi."

The response: a look of fascination together with a relaxation of the vocal chords, which prompted Brigitte to inquire, in a voice pitched one octave higher than normal, "What's your name then, my *Pupperl*, my dolly?"

Lutschi shot a glance at Gusti, blushed, and said, "Karli."

"He takes after his drowned father in looks," said Gusti between closed teeth.

Lutschi picked up her baby boy and fondled him. "Herr Brunner's up there with the Kristopps," she said, "the way he carries on. Every woman has a duty to bring sons into the world, he says. And, he says, there's no shame on any mother who does so. And, he says, he'd be only too willing to provide the wherewithal. That man. Karl Spagola said he'll marry me."

"Spagola is dead," said Gusti.

"He isn't," contradicted Lutschi, and she prophesied, "There'll be no compensation for you or me, and one day he'll be my husband."

Martha's Kiss

Visitors to the Tombola divided into participants and non-participants. Those with tickets formed a dense knot around the platform by midday, and exerted increasing pressure from outside in. Those without tickets congregated in looser gatherings, amused themselves with playing "It", or were bored until the descent of Seicherl. Xandi, Poldi, Berti, Manni, Martha and Isidor, under the guardianship of Frau Spagola and Frau Kristopp, belonged to the non-participant contingent.

Every ten metres last-minute sellers flourished their ticket blocks at the mass of people making its way to the Northrailway Bridge. Boys let off firework bangers as a tribute to the festivities.

On the Danube Meadow the kite was not a success. Berti clutched the end of the string, Manni threw the frame made from brown paper and thin sticks into the air, the artefact traced the outline of an inverted U, and hit the ground accompanied by the sound of snapping wood. Repairs required spittle and Poldi's weight to weld the ruptured parts together. The second and subsequent launchings fared in like manner, as one inverted U is to another. In the end the innovators were saved from admitting failure by the Skeleton cantering upon them with the edict that the flying of kites on Tombola Day contravened the law. Isidor asked why. His attitude towards policemen fluctuated from total terror to total absence of inhibition. The Skeleton deemed no reply was necessary, so Frau Kristopp volunteered that safeguarding Seicherl from entanglement was worth more than a mill'n shill'n.

The children played "It". Poldi and Isidor squeaked with delight when chased, and Martha kept running at Xandi, touching him saying "It" even when it was not her turn to be "It". Then the cry went up, and all heads turned to the sky, and there flew the aeroplane. A big mushroom hung from the clouds, and people yelled, and the figure at the foot of the artificial fungus hung in the air, and people yelled, and the figure waved his arms and legs, and that was Seicherl. The mushroom disappeared behind the Floridsdorf Bridge.

Frau Kristopp said, "A parachute got to fit to a body like a glove to a hand. If they make the parachute too big, there's the chance it'll go flying upwards instead of downwards, and nobody would never see Seicherl no more."

The serious business of the Tombola began. The clot of people around the platform contracted more tightly. Berti and Manni ran over to see who would walk away with the motorbike. Isidor thought they were playing "It" again. He directed his long, clumsy strides after the departing boys, and in the process fell over. Frau Spagola and Frau Kristopp attended to his bruised knees. Martha gripped Xandi by his shirt and suggested playing Father-Mother-Child. To demonstrate her sincerity of gamesmanship, she pressed her rosy lips against his. Xandi drew back, fearing that Berti and Manni might have witnessed the incident.

"What d'you do that for?" he scolded Martha.

"That's what mothers and fathers do. I'll kiss you again, I will," she threatened.

"If you do, I'll pull your ears."

Martha looked dismally at Xandi. He saw a teardrop grow in a corner of her pale blue eyes, where the honey coloured skin stretched away to form the smooth ridge of her impish nose. Poldi came waddling up and gave Xandi a wet kiss on his cheek, laughed and said, "Are we playing kissing now? Let's play cuddling."

The teardrop in Martha's eye disappeared mysteriously. She turned on Poldi: "You can't play. I'm the mother, Xandi is the father, and Isidor is the child."

"I want to cuddle Xandi, because I love Xandi, I do," said Poldi.

"Well, you can't," said Martha.

Xandi had had enough. He followed Berti and Manni.

Poldi called out, "Don't go, Xandi. It won't be so good playing without you."

The Queen of Spades

Four men clustered around the vacant refreshment hut. The Marschaleks had sold out before noon, and had gone to bring fresh stock. One man sat on the counter, manipulating two cards in his left hand, his right rolling a cigarette. The other men searched the earth nearby for discarded stubs to eke out the tobacco residue. The men composed a three-card gang, taking a rest during the lull in which all of money-carrying humanity concentrated on the motorbike build-up. Xandi stopped and waited to watch when the performance would start again.

A three-card team consisted of a manipulator and several cronies. Although the principle of the trick remained the same, a manipulator drew on many variations. The most widely used deception centred on two cards held in one hand and disposing the uppermost first. Another version, demanding considerable virtuosity, required each hand gripping a card, tossing one away, releasing the second card and nimbly catching the first in mid-air. The accomplices threw ten groschens from a communal fund at winning cards to lure innocent passing people to tarry.

The operator at the refreshment hut worked on an act of his own cunning. Based on double cheating, it set out to catch the no longer *innocent* passing people: those who had already been caught, but eager to find out how it was done to recover their losses. The trick relied on the manipulator's agility unobtrusively to put a dent into, and remove it from, a corner of a card during play. He provided the winning card with a conspicuous kink during the softening-up stages. But at the critical moment, when a client had fingered his ten groschen piece testing the outcome, and was ready to stake it, the dent disappeared from the winning queen of spades to become clearly visible on a losing ace of diamonds.

Children and Gypsies were not welcome. Their keen observation saw a new ruse the moment it was introduced. Street urchins posed the threat of disclosing the trade secrets, and Gypsies represented the menace of sudden bankruptcy. Not long ago a troop from the Mistgstettn, in colourfully patched attire, carrying cloth bags slung over their shoulders, had staked one schilling and sixty groschen on the winning card. The gambling enterprise had been saved from insolvency by the dealer picking up the cards and shuffling them, and from broken bones by the intervention of another three-card gang operating not far away.

The cronies at the refreshment hut scanned the ground in ever-increasing circles. Involuntarily Xandi began to look for discarded cigarette ends in the trodden clay as well. A few centimetres from his bare toe, embedded in the earth and of the same ochre-grey colour, but with a silvery, serrated edge, lay a coin. If he could only transport the fifty groschen into his pocket, it would mean oceans of sugar fish, including ten for Martha because he had made her cry, a dozen for Poldi because she really did care for him, and five for Berti and Manni to keep quiet about Martha's kiss, in case they had witnessed it. The problem was how to pick up the find unnoticed by the men, for they would surely enquire what he had dislodged from the ground, and seeing the money, they would claim it as theirs. The first move in outwitting the cardsharps required placing his foot casually over the coin. His sole felt the hard, cool metal. He began to scratch, first his hips, then his knees, then his shins prior to titillating his toes within capturing distance.

"Been bitten by bedbugs?" the man reclining on the counter called out.

Xandi reddened. "No."

"Buzz off."

"I walked through millions of mosquitoes."

"You got to rub dandelion leaves on gnat bites." The man came over.

Several dandelions grew a little way off. Xandi strained to reach their leaves without moving his feet. The man stopped, watched.

"You nailed to the ground?"

Xandi saw a young woman heading towards the refreshment hut. The men didn't notice her approach.

"Someone's coming," he shouted.

The gang sprang into action, the card shark near Xandi raced back to the counter, and Xandi quickly levered the coin out of its earthy mould.

"Ladies and gentlemen," the card shark addressed his cronies in a painstakingly cultivated voice, "observe carefully: I have here the two red aces and the black Queen of Spades. You, sir, see how easy it is to win. I show the cards to you: two red aces of diamonds, and the black lady, the Queen of Spades. Come a little closer, sir, watch carefully where I place the Queen of Spades, because she's a winner is the black lady, like all black ladies, wouldn't you say so, madam? Now once again, my good ladies and gents, remember the red cards, they lose, the black card wins. I place the black queen here, because this card's a red and this card's a red. Now, madam, watch very carefully, don't take your beautiful black eyes off the beautiful black lady. I move the cards about: here and here and here. Which one is the black beauty, my black beauty?"

And the back of one card displayed a big dent in one corner, and the cronies threw their ten groschens on it, and the card was the Queen of Spades.

Just then Xandi made two monumental discoveries: firstly, the lady was none other than the girl in the shimmering green costume from Prater's Emporium. This time he could not mistake the faint, sad lines from her nose to her downward curving lips, nor the large black eyes, now still, now darting from right to left. Secondly, he just knew she'll stop and lose. Xandi's heart pounded, its rhythmic beat crying out, "Please don't gamble please don't gamble."

"The Queen of Spade is the lucky winner. Twenty groschen paid out to you, sir, and ten groschen for you. And, my good ladies and gentlemen, we go straight into another game."

Xandi made yet a third discovery: the Marschaleks complete with Rolli and handcart laden with fresh provisions, were barely forty metres away, and advancing rapidly. The hammering in his chest screamed, "Please come quickly please come quickly."

"Ladies and gentlemen, the last game before you'll be buying *saure Gurken* with your winnings. Watch carefully, my black beauty. I have here two red aces ..."

The girl opened her handbag. She placed thirty groschen on the dented card, on a red Ace of Diamonds.

She had lost. As she turned, Xandi caught a distinct sob. She walked swiftly towards the stairs of the Northrailway Bridge. He recalled the deserted square in the Prater, the desperate scene on the stage of the Emporium, the hostile noises of the Dragon Train, the loneliness of the entertainers, her forlorn look, the oblivion when the lights were switched off, the abandonment of hope. And now her last thirty groschen gone too.

The Fifty Groschen Coin

Xandi overtook the girl on the pedestrian walk of the bridge. Some distance ahead, he placed the fifty groschen on the asphalt and retraced his steps. She walked on, taking little notice of him, and no notice at all of the small silver disc. He picked it up, overtook the young woman again, and placed the money on the pavement once more. She walked past it without seeing it. So he tried a third and fourth time, without success.

As he passed her yet again she said, "What the devil are you playing at, you little shit? What are you hovering round me for? Shove off, go on."

Xandi's heart stood still. His mouth became an arid desert. A new pain tore at his inside. A pain worse than the agony of the cockchafer grubs' nest, worse than the time when, competing against Uncle

Hans in a race to win a sweet, he had stepped with his bare foot on an upturned drawing pin and continued running to claim the prize, worse than chasing naked after fire engines. The glistening waves of the Danube, the quivering haze over the black girders, how can they go on glistening and quivering?

He did not stir until the girl descended the stairs leading to the quayside. Then he slouched to the coin. He touched it with his big toe, moved it about.

"Xandi! Xandi!" Poldi drew up some way ahead of Martha and Frau Spagola. "We were looking for you. We were afeared you'd fallen into the Danube! Them's fifty groschen!"

Xandi kicked the coin away.

"Xandi!"

He had been a little too quick, the kick a little too fierce. The coin slid away underneath the railings out of sight, into the Danube. Poldi leant over the steel railing. Her eyes scanned the water surface.

"I can't see it nowhere." She turned to the boy, appealing for reassurance that the fifty groschen had not really gone for ever. But Xandi cared little about the loss.

Poldi continued searching the water. Her eyes travelled to the coal barge tied to the quay.

"Xandi!" She spun round. "Look, my dad. On the ship. He's got a beard. He's there on the ship. Hullo!" She waved both arms over her head. "Can you see him? He's gone into the little house on the ship. Xandi," she whispered, "suppose my dad picked up the fifty groschen? Do you think he did? I shall go and tell him it's yours."

Poldi hurried off towards the end of the footway. She met Herr Dufft on the steps, but ran past him in her eagerness. Xandi kept his eyes fixed on the barge. He did not see Herr Spagola, instead he saw the Prater girl stepping swiftly onto the plank bridging the gap between quay and deck. She made her way to the cabin and vanished inside.

A bang ripped through the stillness. The startled Xandi thought a firecracker had been let off by boys. But he could see no boys. Instead an open lorry drew up along the quayside, backfiring as it slowed down.

Martha and Frau Spagola stopped beside Xandi.

"Poldi's in a hurry," said Frau Spagola, "wherever is she going?"

Two men jumped from the lorry. Xandi recognised Herr Brunner. He and his companion raced towards the barge. Poldi placed one foot onto the plank.

"Hey, you!" yelled Brunner.

Poldi turned clumsily. The lorry backfired again. A third man leapt from the driver's seat. Poldi leant forwards, then backwards. Her arms circled like the sails of a windmill.

"Beat it!" yelled Brunner.

The people on the bridge heard the splash. Xandi's eyes flew back to the plank. No one on it. And the waves glistened, and the girders quivered.

And Herr Dufft supported the collapsing Frau Spagola in his arms.

CHAPTER NINETEEN (1933)

The Funeral

Mourners at funerals bury their differences with the dead, if for a short time only.

No one spoke of the resurrected Karl Spagola's arrest on the coal barge. Frau Rosenfinger alerted Frau Kristopp when the slow procession came upon a puddle. Frau Czarnikow inquired of Herr Dufft as to the state of the arthritis in his mother's knees. The children were on their best behaviour, and only a few had to be kept in check. When Martha Bitmann crept up to Xandi, and recalling the chasing game they had played on the Danube Meadow, hit him and said "you're it", her grandmother reprimanded her. And when Manni Czarnikow played the fool and had to be pulled away from the pit next to Poldi's, he had his cheek slapped.

A more elaborate cortege than the Spagola's simple assembly followed behind and gathered round the adjacent grave, which had also been prepared for the burial of a child.

Frau Spagola's cries as the coffin drifted into its cavity hit the mourners' ears like piercing needles. And when it was done, when tears had wetted cheeks and grass, consoling words had been spoken, hands had been shaken, she would not move away. Others dispersed, until only Richard Dufft, Brigitte and her boys remained. Richard's mind, body and soul racked in agonising empathy with Gusti's torment. But he could not quell his burgeoning hope: with her backward child buried, and with Brunner and Karl Spagola in custody exposed in their true lights, there will now be a new beginning.

At the adjacent grave, there too were wails and tears. The grief of the chief female mourner was intense, and Gusti felt drawn to share her sorrow, as only mothers would truly understand.

"She was such an innocent lamb," Gusti sobbed, "never a nasty thought, never a spiteful deed. Never had a proper father. Killed when war was nearly over."

The woman, a widow, briefly told the story of her child, also a girl, of the same age as Poldi, Franziska by name, so bright and lively and having done so well at school, taken away by the diphtheria epidemic. Franziska, just like Poldi, had never known her real father; he too fell in the last weeks of the war.

Herr Dufft looked at the woman: could she be Fanni Hannick, the Jewish vocalist, who sometimes sang anti-Nazi songs? He had seen pictures of her face on hoardings but he had never met her, or had he? The woman looked back at him. Did they know each other? Dufft glanced at the floral tributes lying around Franziska's grave. On one, on two, he read the name: Freiherr. Now he recognised that Frau Hannick had been Fanni, Antonius' sweetheart of long ago.

The full meaning hit him like a bomb. Franziska's father was Poldi's father. The thought raced through his mind: the mothers must not find out, not on this day. He whispered to Brigitte that Gusti was approaching exhaustion. Brigitte responded, took Gusti's arm and, although the weeping mother protested, led her away.

Frau Hannick said, "Forgive me, is your name Richard Dufft?"

"Yes. Lieutenant Freiherr and I were officers in the same regiment. I knew you as Fanni Jannitschek then. Now you are the singer."

"How extraordinary." She placed her trembling hands on Dufft's wrists. "Antonius and I talked about you the last time I was with him. We had quarrelled but he came to see me on the eve of his departure to the front, and we made up. He stayed the night with me, and I never saw him again."

"He stayed the night with us!" Dufft blurted out, already foreboding a dreadful truth.

Fannie Hannick shook her head. "Had he been elsewhere that night I wouldn't be here today burying his daughter." She wiped her cheeks. "He told me you had asked him to stay, but as soon as you had gone to bed, he took your keys, came over to me and we made up. He returned to your house in the morning so not to upset you. We planned to wed as soon as the war was over. But he never came back. Later I married Hannick. He died also. And now Fannie's gone too."

Dufft fumbled for words. Frau Hannick, in her anguish, mistook his agitation as emotion brought on by listening to her tale. And, in a sense, this was true.

She bade him good-bye.

Dufft stood on his own between the two graves. He shivered. So Poldi had not sprung from his dead comrade's loins. If not from

Antonius', from whose? His whole body throbbed. An inner voice whispered, "Let it rest, the child is dead." Whose child? He closed his eyes, concentrated in an effort to remember: the party, wine, beer, schnapps. Gusti singing, Antonius flirting with her, Violetta running off with the colonel. He, asking Antonius to stay.

He stumbled along a gravel track. He turned into a crossing path. He found a bench, sat down, and there called out, though no one heard him, "God, why are You so cruel?"

Then he cried.

He dried his face, his strength spent. He must find Gusti. Say to her, "Antonius didn't father Poldi. I did. I must have done. But I remember nothing."

Then his brain went into reverse. *Perhaps I didn't. There were other men around, at the party. Perhaps she fakes her memory loss. She has not been an advocate of virtue. Why have I been captivated by her all my life?*

He sat quietly, breathing steadily, marshalling his thoughts. *She's had a hard life, and I have missed the joys of loving, of sharing pain and fulfilment, of building respect and trust. Did I say trust?*

His head ached as his thoughts somersaulted. *I have to face the truth. I must confess my guilt. Poldi was conceived during that night whilst Gusti lay in a drunken stupor, and if Antonius was with Fanny, I violated her, in my drunken stupor. She lay senseless. That's why she too remembers nothing. She's not faking. She wouldn't, couldn't live with such a lie, not in a thousand years.*

Then frightening thoughts occurred to him. *Suppose her recollection is restored one day? Suppose she finds out from Fanni Hannick that Antonius didn't stay the night in my house? But Antonius could have been with Gusti before he left, or after he came back. No, not if he had made up with his fiancée. The finger points at me. But I don't remember. Because there is nothing to remember, because I couldn't have done it. Was I not incapacitated? But the doctors said I was okay. So I could have done it and enjoyed it.*

What to do? His racing brain slowed down and he reflected: Freudian therapy, psychoanalysis, hypnosis? No, he didn't hold with such trivia. This was private, between him and Gusti, and no third party must come into it. If a knock on his head would cure his amnesia, he would throw himself against a brick wall.

Would he have loved the backward, tubby child? She would have loved him. He would have dressed her in pretty frocks, showered her with gifts: dollies and Dradiwaberls and marbles, would have listened to her first attempt to gurgle "Daddy", he would have told her stories, made her laugh, helped her with her homework, taken her to the Prater, enjoyed rides with her on the Riesenrad, on the Kalafati Carousel, would have climbed to the top of St Stephens Cathedral with her and looked at all of Vienna, would have trailed with her up to the Kahlenberg, and walked through the Vienna Wood, made a wish at the Agnes Bründl, would have steamed on a Danube boat to Tulln or Krems. And all these years he had done nothing for his child, had seldom bothered to say a kind word to her. Occasionally he had given her a sugar fish or a eucalyptus sweet. Now it was too late.

"Don't be sad, Herr Dufft." Alexander Anzendrech sat on the same bench. He had sneaked up unobserved. "I loved Poldi too," he said.

He moved up close and searched for Herr Dufft's hand. "Mummy says the trams are packed, and we'll wait for an empty one. Frau Spagola is still crying."

Herr Dufft felt the small, warm hand nestle in his palm. The touch calmed him. His fairy godmother, or whoever looked after his luck, turned the gloom into brightness. *I shall speak to Gusti at the earliest opportunity, ask her to forgive me, and once again offer my hand in marriage. I shall heap upon her boy Berti what I had missed showering upon Poldi. I will marry her in a Catholic church if she wishes. And perhaps we could try for children of our own. She's not too old yet. America is a free country, its citizens safe from indoctrination. With understanding, a little give and take, we shall overcome all problems.*

Reibeisen's letter had advised him to become proficient in English, and that New York needed good journalists.

Sitting on the Fence

The fence was rotting away underneath Police Chief Sessl.

Jumping off forward meant splashing into the quagmire of the Heimwehr and the autocratic Dollfuss regime, which stood for Austria's independence and to which he owed allegiance; rolling off backward added up to sinking into the incomprehensible morass of the Schutzbund and the Social Democrats with their strikes; staying put led to being sucked into the Nazi sludge and absorption by Hitler's Germany.

The tensions on the streets heralded a showdown between Government and the Social Democrats, but the Nazis could trigger an avalanche of political ooze by voices shouting "Heil Hitler". The fence would simply disintegrate.

The arms haul from the coal barge *Helena* bore the hallmark of the National Socialists. The arrested laundry man Brunner asserted that he and his men had come to collect a lorry load of coke. On Tombola Sunday when the coal yards were shut? Bader's wallet contained a scrap of paper bearing the address of the Vienna Branch of the German firm Klug und Krapf.

Spagola's statement, though bizarre, was believable. He had overheard, whilst concealed in Madam Fleurie's fortune telling booth, words spoken by a German client, that boxes containing costumes for Prater artistes were hidden away on the barge *Helena* and he had gone onto the vessel to investigate. Madam Fleurie, who had to be visited for questioning in Budapest, had corroborated Spagola's tale. The German client had been identified as Hildebrandt of Klug und Krapf. And he was on the list of suspected subversives.

Gina, the Prater artiste? Her assertion that she had come to the barge because Herr Ottakrink, alias Spagola, had invited her, also seemed credible. For what purpose? To examine the Prater costumes? And at the same time spend a delectable hour in her lover's arms.

And Poldi? The child fell off the plank. It had been a misadventure, nobody had pushed her. Her mother and Herr Richard Dufft had witnessed the accident, and so had the little rascal Alexander Anzendrech who couldn't stop weeping.

Sessl was in a dilemma. Pursuing the case against Hildebrandt would be a messy business, with countless acts of sabotage in reprisals. Should the Nazis gain the upper hand, there would no longer be a need for a Police Chief Sessl. Better to arrange warning noises to alert Hildebrandt and allow him time to pack his bags for his fatherland, where he would no doubt continue his works but be less of a nuisance. Prosecuting Brunner, Bader and the accomplice would be as messy as hunting down Hilderbandt, would be a waste of time, and in the long run, prove of no benefit to Sessl. Better hold them for a week or two, then release them.

Charging Spagola and Gina with trespassing would be feasible, but this would inevitably lead to wider questioning, involving overheard remarks in a fortune teller's booth, and this would lead back to Hildebrandt. Better let them go with a severe ticking off, which would perhaps have little impact on the hardened Karl Spagola, but could infuse fear and respect for the police in the less tough Prater artiste. And this was how things should be.

And what about the confiscated guns and ammunition? The crates were addressed to Reibeisen of Danube Coke. Reibeisen had fled to New York. The Vienna Police had no jurisdiction over persons living in the United States of America.

Shelving the business was the sensible procedure.

Sessl wrote his report.

Apfelstrudel

Brigitte pulled the paper-thin dough over the kitchen table, sprinkled finely chopped apple, raisins and cinnamon as well as ingredients of her own recipe upon it, rolled the whole thing into one long elephant trunk shape, curled it into a flat spiral and pushed it into the oven. She baked the Apfelstrudel to raise the family's spirits after the funeral. Herr Rosenfinger ate a piece on his rounds collecting contributions for Poldi's gravestone.

Brigitte imagined herself in Gusti's shoes. "She saw it all, her child tumble into the Danube, her man rise from the dead, and promptly led away by the policemen. If it wasn't for Berti, she'd jump into the river herself."

"Or throw herself under a train," muttered Herr Rosenfinger.

"Berti has a new railway train," Xandi chirped in, hoping to lift the air out of its gloomy setting, "and Frau Spagola takes biscuits to Poldi."

Richard Dufft rang Gusti's doorbell but met with no response. Next day he came early, just after Berti had set off for school. She was on the point of leaving too.

"Gusti, I'm glad to find you in."

"I'm visiting Poldi. It's a long trek to the Simmering Cemetery, takes you two hours each way. That's why I set off at eight o'clock. Leaves me time to do the library books after I come back."

"Are you managing all right, my Zuckerrüberl?"

"I go every day. I grieve there with Frau Hannick."

Richard wanted to hold her close, wanted to hug her. He resisted the impulse.

"It does me good," she went on, "but Frau Hannick won't be there today nor for the next few weeks. She'll be abroad, on a singing tour. America. She knows people there who don't want our country swallowed up by Germany. It's political, it would interest you. She asked me would I look after little Franziska's grave, that's her poor child's name, in her absence. She's paying me handsomely for it."

He felt a lot easier hearing of Frau Hannick's absence. The urgency to speak up, before Frau Hannick revealed by chance the truth of Poldi's fatherhood, waned. Confess to Gusti he would, but better to postpone the revelation until she had come to terms with the immediate calamities.

"What will Spagola do when he leaves prison?" she asked.

"Let him go to the devil! Look, Zuckerrüberl, you and I, we're no spring chicken, but we are still young enough to have a life together. We'll get wed. I've always loved you. You and I and Berti and Mama, we'll take off to America. Mama wants to go. She'll learn to like you, I promise."

"Spagola is the boy's father."

Her mouth shaped the outlines of her next thought, which remained unspoken. *And Brunner will be... will be another father of another child.*

She laid her head on his chest. She could not tell him, he would find out soon enough. "I have been wicked, so very wicked. I try to be good. But God won't let me be good, so He punishes me." She lifted her head and looked into his eyes. "I'm beginning to think there's no God."

Richard remained silent. Was this the time to venture into profound philosophy?

"Tell me there's no God," she pleaded. "It would make sense."

"You know what I think about religion. I liken the concept of infinity, of endlessness to the concept of God. Who understands endlessness, who understands God?"

"Why does God single me out, Richard?"

He could not be instrumental in destroying her faith. Of all times, she needed to hold on to it now. "I am not a clever man, but I tell you this: a short time ago, sitting on a bench in the cemetery, I discovered a dreadful truth, and the only thing I could do was to call upon God."

"Isn't it strange?" she said. "When misery comes to believing people, they lose God; when it visits non-believers, they find God." She placed a few paper-wrapped things into a basket. "I must go."

"I'll come with you." Now he embraced her.

She let him hold her. *Is the tingle the same I felt eighteen years ago in the Augarten/? Is it love, still? Shall I give myself to him? Do I want this? A fresh beginning, oh yes. I can pretend Brunner's child is his.*

But she said, "No, Richard. I'd like to be with my Poldi alone."

She was glad to have defeated the temptation.

Her Poldi is my Poldi went through his head. He said, "You are not alone when Frau Hannick's there with you."

"With Frau Hannick it's different. She lost a child too."

"And so..." He wanted to say "have I", but murmured, "life goes on."

Brigitte did not think for a moment that Frau Spagola believed any titbits left on Poldi's grave would ever reach the dead child or her spirit. But she understood that such ritual constituted a symbolic gesture in the natural grieving process. She cut the Apfelstrudel into two, and carried half across the Milk Block yard.

Gusti looked crestfallen. "I'm so wretched."

"Come." Brigitte consoled, "you still have Berti."

"Berti's gone."

"Gone? How come he's gone?"

Gusti touched her eyes, took the Apfelstrudel and placed it on the table. "You don't know the whole story."

Brigitte sat down and waited for her friend's words.

"Herr Breitwinkel, he is a policeman, he came to tell me they'd be releasing Spagola. So it wouldn't hit me like an earthquake when he walks in. Berti, with your Xandi, played with the railway Richard Dufft gave him. To take his mind off Poldi. I sent Xandi home as soon as

270

Spagola showed his face."

"Has he come back to you?"

"He said he was sorry for what he'd done. He said he was a reformed man, he said Poldi drowning had shaken the chicanery out of him. He said he'd forgive me for having betrayed him."

"*You* betrayed *him?*"

"Before I could ask him what he meant, he said would we get married, because his real wife had died, and would we move to Tulln into a little house with a little garden and a little dog for Berti."

Brigitte looked at Gusti's freckled face contorted in anguish. "That's what you've always been dreaming of!"

"Brunner marches in, they had let him out as well. The two glare at each other. Brunner asks me have I got the document? Spagola wants to know what document, and Brunner tells him to mind his own business and says I know well enough what document, and so I did. I knew what he wanted, but I can't tell you, Frau Anzendrech, because it's a private matter. I says I've forgotten where I put it, which was a lie because I didn't want him to have it just then, and Brunner struts into the bedroom and pulls open the drawers in the dressing table, and in the process he treads on Berti's railway and squashes it. Spagola sees red and shouts at Brunner would he mind not laying hands on things in his household, and Brunner shouts back he's got every right to certain things in *my* household and Spagola wants to know the significance of that remark, and Brunner says ask the wench, meaning me."

Gusti stopped for breath, and Brigitte sat quite still wondering how to interpret Gusti's words. She guessed.

"I'm sorry to burden you with my problems, but I must tell somebody, otherwise I'll burst. They threw things at each other: the vase, Berti's railway bits, chairs. They wanted to settle old scores as well. I sat in the corner, buried my face in my hands, and Berti comes over and buries his in my lap. I tell you, Frau Anzendrech, it was fearful. They hammered each other. Brunner lies on the floor, not moving, and Spagola looks a sorry mess. He waddles over to us, grabs Berti, says, 'He's coming with me.' Berti's crying like an infant. Spagola drags him away, and that's the last I've seen of my boy."

"Oh my God," exclaimed Brigitte. "Has he taken Berti to Tulln?"

"That's where they are. But what can I do? In the state I'm in, what can I do?"

Brigitte thought: why is it that women, always women, must pay the price for men's misdeeds.

"I haven't told you the end of it. Brunner stirs, wipes the blood off his face and tells me to look for that document, for if *he* finds it - he means Spagola - Brunner says I'm in trouble. I'm not so worried, because I had nothing to do with it; I had no part in it. Then he asks me do I know yet, and I say nothing. Then he asks how long, and I tell him, 'seven weeks.' Frau Anzendrech, It wasn't my fault. It was *not* my fault. The day before they arrested him he forced me, brandishing a knife."

Brigitte gripped and held Gusti's hands whilst rivers ran from those handsome wide-spaced eyes.

"He wants to marry me. That's what he wants to do." Gusti covered her eyes with her palms whilst her face shook so that it was impossible to tell whether the shuddering sprang from crying or laughing. "I have had three proposals from three men. I should be a happy woman."

"If we only knew what brings happiness," said Brigitte.

"Richard Dufft's still hankering after me. He's the one decent man I've ever known, and I should have listened to him. How can I look into his face when the baby comes? How can I go with Spagola, when the baby comes? And I shall never get custody of Berti, if the baby comes. The only route lies with Brunner."

You poor, poor soul, reverberated in Brigitte's head.

"Brunner scribbles something on a bit of paper and says to me, 'See this doctor,' I know what he's after, but I can't go through with that. It's a terrible, terrible sin, even if I don't believe in religion no more. Brunner, he sees me scowling. He swears at me, he curses Spagola, and I get the feeling if I don't do what he wants, he'll pull out, now that there won't be compensation money."

"Men!" Brigitte muttered.

"But then he says, 'You got under my skin. I dreamt of you in the cell. All right, there'll be just the two of us, plus the new one. I won't have his son Bertram. I'll arrange the wedding for December. I'll move in with you as a lodger in the meantime.' He forbids me to speak to Richard Dufft ever again. My fate is sharing the rest of my life with the laundry man, and now that I know what he's like, Frau

Anzendrech, what can I do?"

Brigitte seethed with anger: her neighbour did not deserve blow after blow after blow. Karl Spagola roams around, sleeps around, and in the end gets off scot free, with a little house in Tulln thrown in. And Brunner? She had assessed him from the start. She knew she was lucky: she had married Rudolf, who never gave a thought to another woman.

Gusti picked up the Apfelstrudel. "I'll take it to Poldi, she loves it. I'll put it in a jamjar so the rain and the animals can't get to it."

Leberknödelsuppe

Brunner left police detention without a stain to his character. The municipality had no option but to reinstate him, thereby curtailing Mama Dufft's carefree washdays.

Now, in his new abode on the fourth floor of the Milk Block, he stirred a pot of *Leberknödelsuppe,* liver ball soup. Gusti made good Leberknödelsuppe. Various female hands had rolled sliced onion, crispy bread crumbs, chunky liver pieces and diverse spices into the aromatic golf-style balls for him before, but irrespective of his lady friends' culinary skills, none had ever attained high enough appeal to eclipse his prized freedom to do what he liked, when he liked. Until the early evening before the Tombola.

He diverted his gaze to the collection of grey, black and yellow spotted beetles, long pins driven through their centres, reposing in a glass case. He had brought it with him and placed it on Gusti's kitchen sideboard. The creatures had been hunted and preserved by an uncle, deceased, who had left the assortment to Brunner. He cherished the catch as if he had assembled it himself. He dusted it frequently and showed it off to visitors.

He noticed a brown, oval-shaped insect crawl across the transparent cover. His lips stretched into a grin as he perceived the bizarre connection between the living above and the dead below. He could capture the beast, pierce it and add it to the parade on display. No, he realised the bedbug belonged to a lower grade of beetle species. It was the Jew amongst arthropods. He crushed it.

He attended with equal abandon to his neat, old but not antique, snug armchair. Brunner, when not engaged in political activity, relished cosy comforts. The location of the flat, besides betokening politically strategic advantages, offered superb views, and ousting Karl Spagola kindled satisfying *Schadenfreude*. And when Hitler takes over, having been a political prisoner under the Dollfuss regime will pay handsome dividends. The uncertainty of the whereabouts of the fake marriage certificate had ceased troubling him; he believed Gusti when she said that she had transported it in a torn-up state to the waste bin.

Only one major task remained to be accomplished: Hildebrandt's extinction.

He placed a bottle of Nussdorfer wine next to the afternoon's Apfelstrudel snack.

The doorbell rang. Brunner admitted Herr Halbkrank, otherwise known as the Skeleton. He wore civilian clothes. His host steered him away from the comfortable chair to an ordinary, hard-seated one. He carried over the delicacies.

"Goes well with wine. Home-made for sure," applauded the Skeleton, "Frau Brunner is to be congratulated on her Apfelstrudel."

Brunner shook his head. "Not yet Frau Brunner. But will be soon. I'll invite you to the wedding. The Apfelstrudel comes from across the yard. My Gusti lugs it to the cemetery. She thinks her dead girl eats it. I said spare me the experience, Poldi's dew-fresh choppers popping up from the grave! After all it was the best thing that could have happened."

"Popping up from the grave?"

"The feeble-minded girl copping it. There isn't a place in society for anyone imbued with idiocy, no more than for Jews, Jew-lovers, and Gypsies."

The Skeleton said, "All sorts of objects are popping up from graves. We have been digging up crates full of guns from churchyards. The Schutzbund are running out of ideas where to hide them."

"You'll find plenty stashed away in municipal housing blocks," said Brunner.

"The Milk and Cocoa Blocks?"

"Wouldn't surprise me. Listen, time's ripe for a pact. You kiss my arse, I tickle your balls. In political terms naturally."

"We found grenades in the Engels Block toy store," volunteered

274

the Skeleton.

"You've been running along with us for a long time, but you haven't signed on the dotted line, have you, Officer Halbkrank?"

"I'm police. I enforce the law, I obey orders. That doesn't mean I'm against you. Would I be here talking to you if that's not a fact, Herr *Ortsgruppenleiter*, District Organiser of the National Socialist Party."

"You've got wind of my promotion?"

"The Chief has. I have ways of looking at intelligence as it comes in."

"Since Dollfuss banned the Party I'm an *Illegaler,* an outlawed Nazi Party member."

"We're aware of it."

Brunner nodded, a token gesture meant to show appreciation of police efficiency. He said, "It's unwise to double-cross us, you know that."

"We can work together."

"The police are friends with the nationalistic Heimwehr?" Brunner quizzed.

Now it was the Skeleton's turn to nod. "And foes with the communist Schutzbund."

"Shoot at the Schutzbund, don't shoot at us. There's sand as well as coke in the boiler room of the Milk Block laundry. Sand makes a good hiding place."

The Skeleton meticulously mopped up crumbs of Apfelstrudel and transferred them piecemeal to his open mouth. After swallowing he said, "I'll tell you when the balloon goes up, you give me the names of the ringleaders."

"It's a deal. There's Bergmeister, Rosenfinger, Kranitschek. And Dufft. Herr Richard Dufft, the newspaper man, a Jew of course. Lives with his mother in the Cocoa Block. He's the clever one, the brains behind their operations. Then there are the Anzendrechs, Jew-lovers. Frau Anzendrech baked the Apfelstrudel."

The Skeleton wrote the names in his notebook. "The Chief's terrified of civil war," he said, smacking his lips. "The best Apfelstrudel I've eaten."

"Fancy some Leberknödelsuppe?" Brunner asked. "To celebrate our mutual understanding."

"Suits me."

"I'll make a prediction: Dollfuss with the army and your police with the Heimwehr will smash the Social Democrats. We, the National Socialists, shall then beat Dollfuss. And you'll be Chief of Engerthsrasse Police."

"And you Gauleiter."

Halbkrank, the Danube Meadow equestrian, jumped up, dashed to the window and yelled: "The bastards are playing football."

"Here. Leberknödelsuppe. A bit arse-to-front: soup after dessert." Brunner placed the soup next to the enshrined beetle collection. "Take it easy. Football is an ancient Aryan sport."

"They're streaming down the dam from the Mistgstettn."

"Brettldorf Gypsies. It's a different ball game, when Gypsies contaminate it," ranted Brunner.

"Or Jews," said the Skeleton, although he had no natural inclination to single out any particular breed of humanity for venting his acrimony against a populace of illegal football ball-players. He made the observation for strategic reasons, in case his host should indeed be propelled into high authority in the near future.

"If I was in charge, I'd order you to carry out ethnic purification, right now," said Brunner.

"Like driving spears through them so we can display them in a glass case next to your pinned beetle collection?" remarked the Skeleton exhibiting humour.

"It don't matter how we'll do it as long as it's efficient."

The Skeleton and Brunner watched steam swirl up from their spoons of Leberknödelsuppe.

Scrap Metal

Restlessness, apprehension and disquiet descended into the streets, into the housing blocks, into the dwellings. Herr Rosenfinger responded incoherently to Xandi's "good day". Herr Junge met with remonstration when seeking support on Frau Echenblatt's hips. Herr Dufft showed irritation when losing at chess. Morgenthau's sugarfish tasted stale with Lutschi concentrating on feeding her baby and forgetting to slip in the extra one when Xandi purchased one groschen's worth. Police Officer Sessl received extra ammunition and instructions to practice target shooting with his men. Frau Spagola kept losing weight in spite of her condition.

"She isn't fit to go to any wedding, least of all her own," observed Brigitte.

"What's she want to marry Brunner for?" asked Rudolf.

"I'll tell you when Xandi's not listening."

Frau Bitmann remained the same, sitting in front of her staircase as long as weather permitted, chewing away at nothing; Rudolf likewise resisted the drift into the thickening tension.

He embarked on restoring an ancient typewriter that Walter Nasenroth, tramway colleague, had been on the point of carrying to the Mistgstettn. Herr Dufft had frequently suggested Rudolf's amusing anecdotes should be written down, and here existed an opportunity to do so in style. The mechanism cried out for cleaning and oiling, and this meant taking the whole apparatus apart. In consequence a multitude of components needed to be stored until reassembly. Brigitte designated Rudolf's soft worktable top as the only feasible location to keep the parts in a semblance of order without interfering with normal household chores. Xandi's grooved tramway network became victim to inaccessibility.

Xandi consoled himself that, without Poldi, playing tram games lacked fervour. He and Pauli discovered an alternative pastime on the pedestrian walk of the Northwestrailway Bridge over the Handelskai Marshalling Yards.

Eighteen railway tracks spread out from a single line like a huge fan. Stationary goods waggons, coupled together, stood on them. A locomotive hauled a long goods train up an incline onto the single track. There a workman uncoupled two or three waggons, the engine gave a short spurt in reverse, and sent the freed trucks rolling towards the area where a second workman threw over a number of points, thus directing the trucks to continue on predetermined rails. Pauli and Xandi wagered on which line the waggons would emerge from under the bridge, and ran to the spot directly above. A third workman placed a break iron on a rail; this arrested the speed of the rolling trucks with a screeching noise, and the workman coupled them to the waiting, stationary waggons.

"You see, Xandi," explained Pauli who had worked out what went on below, "a goods train comes from Budapest. The waggons are meant to go to different places: to Linz, to Berlin, to Paris, to Rome. Here they split up the train from Budapest, and make up new ones with all the waggons going to the same places."

Whilst Pauli spoke a bang like an exploding firework made them jump. A cloud of dust rose from an open waggon, which had crashed into the stationery train standing on the track nearest to the Handelskai roadway. The front wheels rested on the wooden sleepers and a stream of small, oddly shaped scrap metal pieces encrusted with rust cascaded through splintered wood. Gesticulating workmen piled onto to the scene.

"This train won't be going anywhere for a day or two," observed one.

"They'll sack him."

"All this rusty iron. Who wants it?"

"They melt it down for cannons."

A man with a clipboard and paper came leaping and shouting over the tracks. He scribbled down notes, and ordered the workmen back to their allotted tasks. The boys left the bridge to inspect the heap of metal pieces: large, small, bent, twisted, like a flow of lava the scrap had spread onto the road. Amongst the uninteresting items Pauli noticed washers of various sizes, some thick, some thin. He selected a fistful of the least rusted ones and pushed them into his pockets.

"Will you make a necklace? asked Xandi, who knew Pauli possessed skilled hands.

"Ah," replied his brother mysteriously, "wait until Christmas."

CHAPTER TWENTY-ONE (1933)

Letter Bombs

Hildebrandt's chaotic reaction, after feasting his eyes once again on Vikki's curves, happened every day until, he told himself, he achieved his heart's desire properly. However, imagining he was master in gauging female emotions, he forced himself to put a little time between the last debacle and follow-on visits.

He returned to the Prater three days later and was dismayed to find her shack locked and curtains drawn. The man operating the Kalafati carousel told him she had gone to Budapest to sort out private affairs, but would be back in a matter of a week or two.

On his desk lay a report from Brunner. It stipulated that the Milk Block tenants had discovered the additional lock on the boiler room door. So? Politics was a cat-and-mouse game. The Schutzbund knew that the National Socialists knew. It mattered little. When the showdown comes, the decision whether to support the Social Democrats against Dollfuss, or Dollfuss against the Social Democrats, or stand aloof, or seize power unaided, will be made by the Führer on the day. In the meantime, he must ensure that the Party is primed. National Socialists use their initiative, even if it means sitting on the fence like the natives.

"I can do this," he said aloud to himself.

He had graduated as an engineer, yet he failed to prevent perspiration soaking his forehead. A cluster of objects, tightly wrapped together with tape from which a short cord protruded, lay on his desk. Two thin wires connected a tiny battery and another pair of wires supported a small capsule. The whole contraption fitted into a cardboard envelope the size of a cigarette box.

Nazi sympathisers in the police had issued a warning that his office would be raided in two days' time. Smaliz, over the telephone, had alluded to the Stohmeyer affair. So it had to be done. Now. The newly appointed *Ortsgruppenleiter* Brunner could not be allowed unfettered freedom of speech.

Contemplation of the laundry man's fate did not produce his

sweating brow, rather awareness of the imminent possibility of his own undergoing a drastic change. This lay embodied in the small capsule. He stared at it. He spoke to it in a low voice so he could hear the words and be reassured:

"The device is stable when disconnected. It is unstable when the circuit is closed, then it will explode at the slightest touch. This cord operates the starter. When pulled the battery is connected to the capsule which is a time switch, and the circuit becomes closed when the timer runs out after thirty minutes. Then it explodes when disturbed, not before. If I connect a wire across the capsule, the timer is bypassed, the thirty-minute delay is inoperative, so it explodes when disturbed *immediately after* I pull the cord. But as long as I do not pull the cord, the device will not explode."

He continued to gawk at the gadget, repeating what he had just said. The operation lay within his skill, but his fingers flinched when connecting the wires. Then, carefully, he nudged battery and capsule into the interior of the pack so the wires could not be seen, but leaving the end of the cord showing.

A brown blob on thin legs emerged, tightrope walked along the cord and continued crawling across the desk. Hildebrandt swore. He covered the bedbug with a piece of paper and squeezed the life out of it.

He marked the envelope with an unobtrusive X, and carried it to a steel cabinet, placed it underneath three similar, but un-primed ones, the first bearing Dufft's address, the second Anzendrech's, the third left blank. He locked the cabinet, sat down, closed his eyes and relished the vision of marching men and white-robed damsels.

Everything had been taken care of. He had sent on his personal effects. He had destroyed incriminating papers. The name in his passport was Franz Glanz. Tomorrow morning he will hand Dufft's and Anzendrech's envelopes to Bader. In the afternoon, he will hand the envelope marked X to Brunner. In this way the two activists will not be together at the same time, and the chance of mixing up the envelopes will be avoided. That done, he himself will pull the cord of the blank envelope and leave it on the desk for the benefit of the police raiders the following day. He will then hasten to the Prater to see whether Vikki has returned; afterwards to the Northrailway Station with a train ticket to Prague.

His exile will be short. Dollfuss' life span will not reach beyond a few months. On his return to a National Socialist Austria he will confer with his compatriots who had organised Frau Spagola's marriage certificate and his temporary passport. Huber was an Aryan name. To procure a document purporting that her mother stemmed from Hungarian nobility will be a piece of cake. And hydrogen oxide is ready available. The blond, white-attired Vikki Huber merged with the white-robed damsels.

It occurred to him that Dufft's mother or Frau Anzendrech could remove the missives. Well, that was a risk he had to take. He ventured that providence would not let him down.

The wonder boy Alexander would be too small to reach for the letterbox.

Hildebrandt's Plan

Bader called in the morning in a heavy Tyrolean overcoat. The December air had covered the rain puddles with ice. Police custody had not subdued his spirits, on the contrary, he glowed with enthusiasm, knowing, like his accomplice Brunner, that the period of incarceration by the anti-Nazi regime would shoot into a fountain of blessings after the *Anschluss,* Austria's incorporation into Germany. He and Brunner had been selected to carry out the bombing missions after their release to demonstrate the futility of the Dollfuss law-enforcement system.

Hildebrandt told his secretary not to interrupt. He secured the door, removed the Dufft and Anzendrech envelopes from the cabinet, handed one to Bader and began to explain how to initiate the bombs.

"What, like this?" asked Bader, acting the fool and pretending to pull the cord.

Hildebrandt was not amused. "Once the device is activated you have thirty minutes before it becomes sensitive to the slightest touch and explodes. It is not a toy."

"Right you are, I shall treat it with the respect it deserves. I'll spray it with rose scent and paint on it a heart pierced by an arrow. I'll send it to Parteigenosse Brunner's wedding. So it starts off with a bang. Ha-ha-ha. He's invited me to the reception. Next Sunday. Can't quite grasp why he's taking the plunge unless it's to breed cannon fodder for our cause, ha-ha-ha."

"Four bombs will go off on the same day. Yours are for Dufft and Anzendrech. They live near each other in the Engerthstrasse. Their addresses are on the envelopes. Visit their abodes in daylight, then place them tonight. Pull the cords so they explode when they touch them tomorrow. Take these keys to the entrances of the housing blocks. Brunner and I are attending to the other two: one for Danube Coke, one for the police when they raid this office."

They parted.

Brunner arrived in the early afternoon. Hildebrandt fetched the envelope marked X. He explained how it functioned, and emphasised that the cord must be pulled immediately before posting the device into Danube Coke's letter box, not before.

"Do it tonight. Bader will take care of Dufft and Anzendrech." Hildebrandt filled two glasses with cognac. "To the Führer. Heil Hitler. And since I won't be around at your wedding to drink to your health, I'll do the honours now. *Prost,* cheers, let all your little ones grow into victorious soldiers."

They downed the liquor. Hildebrandt declared laughingly that the remaining bomb in the cabinet would go off tomorrow in the hand of a policeman. "I myself will pull the cord in about an hour's time and leave it on the desk."

"The police are with us," said Brunner thinking of the Skeleton.

"Yes. They've leaked details of tomorrow's raid," Hildebrandt agreed. "Tough. Such is fate. This is the prelude to conflagration. The police are obeying Dollfuss' orders. We must show them that we are on top of every situation ... Can't the bitch do what I say?" The last outburst was in response to ringing from the telephone.

"I told you not to interrupt," he shouted angrily into the mouthpiece.

"Herr Bader is here," replied a frightened voice, "he won't go away. He says it's urgent."

"Damnation!" The very thing he had striven to avoid: Bader and Brunner in the same room with their respective letter bombs. Bader's unpredictable sense of humour knew no bounds. He'd think it funny examining the envelopes to see which was prettiest.

Hildebrandt said he would not be long, unlocked the office and went out.

"Where is he?" He looked angrily at his secretary, seeing empty space.

"Herr Bader's nipped into the lavatory."

Hildebrandt stepped out into the corridor to join his collaborator.

Left alone, Brunner's ribs throbbed with racing palpitation. Here was the chance to assign Stohmeyer's fate to this other arrogant spoiler of Aryan blood. All he needed to do was to pull the cord on one of the letter bombs and leave it in the cabinet and make sure he's away within thirty minutes. Then, when Hildebrandt later handled the envelope earmarked for the police, bang.

"You certainly won't be around at my wedding," he mouthed to himself, "*heil* my Gypsy whoremonger."

He'll pull the cord of the letter bomb in his hand, then exchange it with the one in the cabinet ...

Hildebrandt's Departure

Hildebrandt heard the blast when halfway to the toilet. For a second he stood still, stunned. He knew what had happened. He raced down the stairs, behind him: Bader.

"No time to discuss anything," Hildebrandt called out on the street.

"The bombs harbour nests of bedbugs," Bader shouted back.

Hildebrandt walked quickly across the road and jumped aboard a tram that was pulling away from its stop. Three hours separated him from his scheduled train departure. He missed his revolver, his overcoat, his hat, but he had his wallet, his passport and Prague ticket. The tram rattled along the Franz-Josephs-Kai, crossed the Danube Canal and headed for the Prater.

"Destiny," he muttered to himself. "This time all the way, if she's back."

Bader guessed that one of the letter bombs had exploded prematurely. No further explanation necessary, he hurried to the bridge over the Danube Canal and released his cardboard envelopes, plus any loitering bloodsucking creatures, into its waters.

On the second day of reopening her business, Madame Fleurie had spent a quiet day by herself, without customers, without Karli. She pursed her lips. To have sauntered off for a fling with that eye-flickering Prater girl Gina, as she had learnt from police questioning whilst abroad, was a little disconcerting. But Vikki understood the world. Her profession had taught her to assess men, and the ways of men. Karli belonged to her past. She could get even with Gina, if she wanted to, any time. Darkness creeping up, she decided to go home and began to tidy up prior to extinguishing the oil lamp.

Hildebrandt entered without knocking. He said, "I am leaving Vienna, but I shall be back. I shall be back soon. You will be my guiding star, now and when I come back." In a whisper he added, "And my mistress."

He paused and looked with screwed-up eyes at her tantalising bulges. He continued in his normal voice, "Although our blood reveals different levels of purity, this can be overlooked in rare circumstances where prominent natural gifts outweigh this imbalance. You are such a special case. You are honoured to be chosen to rank amongst the visionary heroines for whom true Aryan men reach out through falling debris and raging fire. We must keep our association secret until the details of your birth have been rectified. Not everyone fully understands the forces of destiny at work here."

The man is a nutcase, thought Vikki, reaffirming her impression when she had first met him.

He took off his jacket, and continued the process of removing items of clothing.

"I am expecting a client shortly," said Vikki, becoming alarmed.

"We can lock the door and shut off the light." He touched the lamp, moved it.

Vikki shook her head. "I can't do that. My clients know I keep my appointments."

Hildebrandt eyed her quizzically, his gaze finally settled on her breasts. He convinced himself, as fate had propelled him here, and as he had resolved on action, action he would pursue. He noticed a key in the door. He went over and turned it. He came back towards her. She withdrew to the space between a sideboard and a large, cloth-covered box, where she kept an umbrella with a stainless steel rod and a stainless steel knob for a handle.

"I have been waiting long to hold you in my arms. You've been away, now you're back, and now is the time. We shall remember it whilst we're again separated. We'll climax like a bomb. Unfortunately we only have a few minutes."

She angled for the umbrella. She had never found it necessary to use it on a patron before. She did not want to drive the hard knob into his manhood. He was rather cute if unbalanced, good looking and athletic, the scar on his cheek and his accent quite captivating. He had been manageable on previous occasions, and she wondered what had unhinged him. Or had he come to exact restitution because she had upheld Karl's story to the police relating to the *Helena* business. She tightened her fingers over the umbrella.

His palms settled on her bosom, yet still she waited.

"An important client. From the judiciary. He may come any moment," she warned.

The doorknob turned and squeaked, followed by a knock.

"He is here," said Vikki, immensely relieved at the timely intervention, but betraying no surprise in her voice. She held out the jacket for Hildebrandt.

"*Höllenfeuer,*" Hildebrandt swore, "keep quiet, he'll go away."

"He won't. He can see the light." And she called out at the door: "Wait a wee-little-moment, I'll be with you directly."

"I'd better not be seen with you," said Hildebrandt.

She pushed him into the second chamber. "Stay here until I have settled him. I'll leave the door open. Skip away when he's facing the other way."

Vikki unlocked the entrance and her eyes fell on a man in tram conductor's uniform.

"May I speak to you? I have a message for you," said Rudolf Anzendrech.

She ushered him into the interior, into a corner where he could not be seen, her arms spread out so that her gown acted like a curtain shielding the door. From the corners of her eyes she saw Hildebrandt tiptoeing outside.

Rudolf's Errand

Rudolf said, "I haven't come to have my fortune told. I'm here to deliver an errand. You see, I met Karl Spagola on my tram. We talked. He said he was a reformed man. He wants to make amends. He said Poldi ... You know about the accident?"

"She drowned?" replied Vikki as she closed the door. "I don't know the full story."

"Fell off a coal barge. Herr Spagola wasn't involved in the tragedy, but he was on the barge. He said he felt responsible. He said he wanted to change his lifestyle, he begged me to see you on his behalf. He said he was scared to come himself. I didn't want to do this at first. He looked so miserable, so I agreed to do it. So here I am."

"Spagola! He chose to be called Ottakrink after Gusti stabbed him in the back, so he told me. Is he with Gina now, or has Gusti relented?"

Rudolf shook his head. "He's with the girl Lutschi. Gusti Spagola has taken in a lodger, Herr Brunner. The two will be married next week."

"Go on! Even I, Madam Fleurie, wouldn't have foretold that."

"Brunner was also present when the accident happened. Karl Spagola and Herr Brunner were arrested, not because of the accident, but because of a cargo of ammunition on the coal barge. They released both men; they say the real culprit has escaped to Germany. Karl Spagola told me he knew there were hidden boxes on the barge, but he believed they contained costumes for Prater entertainers. He said that's why he brought Gina along because she works with the Emporium people here in the Prater, and he asked me to plead with you not to take revenge on Gina. He said Gina is a mere child and completely innocent. Well, I have delivered my errand."

Vikki had listened attentively. She recalled the previous session with Hildebrandt when she had winkled out the coal barge details, and surmised that the person responsible for the hidden arms was the man who had just sneaked away. Evidently he had not yet managed to escape, but was on the point of doing so.

No longer interested with whom Karli frolicked, she thanked Rudolf and invited him to sit opposite her at the consultation table.

She took his palms into her hands, but she did not look at them, instead she looked straight into his eyes, where she saw an amused twinkle.

She began: "You said you haven't come to have your fortune told. But here goes all the same: Frau Anzendrech is a lucky woman. Because you are a good man. You are a good man, not because you don't have fanciful thoughts, but because you don't act them out. And you are a lucky man, because Frau Anzendrech is a good woman. She will always stand by you, and you will always stand by her, come what may." Abruptly she deposited Rudolf's hands on the table. "I can't fool you. I can't predict the future any more than a bed bug can recite the alphabet. What I am saying stands out a mile."

Rudolf now took her hands, and held them above the table. "Yes, I agreed to carry Herr Spagola's message. Perhaps the opportunity to meet with you had something to do with it also."

"You did the right thing. And you came at the right time. There was a man here, you didn't see him, I was really getting nervous."

"I did see him," said Rudolf. "I know him. He stopped Nazi louts beating me up. But he's a Nazi himself. We had a conversation once. He's fanatical about Jews and ..."

"Gypsies? I am the exception. I have prominent gifts. You know?" She pushed her bosom forward, and Rudolf blushed. "He'll go through raging fire for me, but I shall give him the slip. I shall go to Budapest. My mother's people come from Transylvania. I have uncles in Hungary. Some still move from place to place across the country, right into Yugoslavia. They asked me to go with them, marry one of their sons, my cousins."

"Will you?"

"No. I'm not the marrying kind."

For reasons difficult to analyse Rudolf was relieved to hear that.

"Gina took Karl away from me. Now he's with Lutschi. Karl asks me to forgive. They say Gypsies don't forgive easily."

"It's a strange world," observed Rudolf, "my youngest witnessed the accident. He saw Gina step onto the barge, he was there when Poldi fell into the river. Poldi was his playmate. He was very upset. But he was equally upset when he heard they arrested Gina."

"Your boy Alexander? I remember the day he was born."

"I remember seeing you in the passage with your punctured

bicycle."

"And I remember you giving me the eye."

"I did? You did!"

"Perhaps the attraction was mutual." She looked at him mischievously.

"There is nothing wrong in being attracted," said Rudolf.

Vikki shook her head, but she did so in agreement. "You are a wise man. What would you do if you knew somebody who smuggles guns into this country? Run away to Budapest?"

"Guns," replied Rudolf, "we have learnt nothing from the war. Why do we make guns? The only purpose of guns is to kill people. The Schutzbund threatens to kill the Heimwehr. The Heimwehr threatens to kill the Schutzbund. The National Socialists want to kill Jews and Gypsies. I tell you what I would do if I were in charge of guns. I would give the order to shoot at guns, until no gun is left intact."

"Herr Anzendrech," said Vikki rising from her chair, "would you escort me to the Kuchenstuberl and would you do me the honour of letting me buy you a coffee and an Apfelstrudel. They say the Kuchenstuberl's Apfelstrudel is the best in Vienna."

"They haven't tasted Brigitte's," replied Rudolf.

Pride flushed through his body: to be treated by this young, beautiful woman. He knew Brigitte would not applaud the invitation if she knew of it, but then she would not find out and no harm would be done. If he was a good man, as Vikki had told him, he was not perfect. No man is, he said to himself.

He spent happy minutes at the little table for two. He told her the anecdote of his arrival in New York, the same he had narrated to Hildebrandt. She laughed and laughed again. Towards the end of the story she suddenly shot up from her seat.

"Look!" She pointed at the window.

Through the darkness of the evening they discerned people rushing towards a mass of flames.

"That's Madame Fleurie's," cried Vikki.

She forced her way through the crowd and came face to face with Steffi and Lisl, holding on desperately to their balloons, and at the same time restraining a charred, dark-haired girl, whose pupils danced in wild movements.

"She did it," shouted Lisl, "Gina fired it."

"No, no, I didn't." Gina's eyes settled on Vikki, and their erratic motion ceased. "I wanted to speak to you, to see whether you knew what happened to Herr Ottakrink. I saw flickering behind the window. The door wasn't locked. I went in. The lamp lay on the floor and flames everywhere. I tried to put them out with a rug."

Vikki could not remember whether she had extinguished the oil lamp or had locked the door. She turned to Rudolf who had followed her through the throng. He did not know either; his mind since then had been full with other things.

"Believe me, please. I wouldn't do such a thing," pleaded Gina.

Policemen and firemen arrived and pulled the onlookers back. The balloon ladies released Gina, and the girl kept close to Madam Fleurie.

"Well," muttered Vikki to herself, "saves me the trouble of shifting everything and selling up."

"Are you insured?" asked Rudolf.

"Yes. But I shall need more than insurance in the future. I shall need an assistant." She turned to Gina: "Have you ever done fortune telling?"

"A bit," answered the young girl.

"Do you know Budapest?"

"A bit."

Hildebrandt strode away from Madam Fleurie's, his frustrated sex impulse finding relief in a nearby urinal. That done he walked along dark avenues through the Prater to the Northrailway Station to avoid detection. He was confident that destiny had not deserted him. The very fact that Vikki, having expected a client from the judiciary and Anzendrech turns up, was proof of it. There *was* hanky-panky going on between her and the tram conductor. He couldn't have had a show-down with the man in the fortune teller's booth, as top priority was to escape from Vienna unobserved. His exile wouldn't be for long, he knew that. Smaliz was expecting him, and maybe a climb up the political ladder was on the agenda.

CHAPTER TWENTY-TWO (1934)

The Smell of Gas

"I'm enjoying washday again," remarked Mama Dufft, "and now you want me to get someone in to do our laundry?"

"I am thinking of your knees."

"I can manage. Save yourself the money, Richard. Save it for America."

Richard looked at his mother benignly. "Your knees."

"My knees, my schmees. It is that woman who keeps you here. I don't understand what attracts you to her. She is not our class. She allows herself to be seduced by that friend of yours, *Leutnant* Antonius Freiherr, and ..."

"Mama! It wasn't ..." Richard Dufft checked himself. Six months had passed and he hadn't been able to confess to Gusti, so how could he discuss the matter with his mother.

"What wasn't? Poor child. Drowned in the Danube."

"Mama, leave it."

"And history repeats itself. People say she was carrying another, Herr Brunner's."

Richard flinched. "Brunner is dead."

"And good riddance. The one decent thing he ever did was to blow himself up. What Gusti Spagola saw in him is the biggest mystery since Creation. And what *you* see in her is beyond understanding also."

"Mama, I have finished with her. I did love her once, yes. There are limits in that department too. She carried Brunner's child." He swallowed. He remembered that awful moment after the Tombola on the bridge; together they had witnessed the splash before she had fainted in his arms. And after all that, and their teenage love, and his pleading, she goes and romps with that despicable laundry man. "She chose to be Brunner's mistress. She would have married him had he lived."

Mama Dufft took several sips from the large coffee cup that Richard had placed by her side. "When will they restore the electricity?"

"At least Brunner down in hell can't gloat over me. He'll never know the heartache she heaped on me," said Richard.

"When will we have electricity?"

"I don't know. The gas is still working."

"When that stops we won't be able to cook. So we shall starve. I suppose we must wait until then in darkness."

"It could get a lot darker. The strike is just the beginning. Ssh! I can hear gunfire. Rat-a-tat-tat."

"Richard, America. You have done nothing?"

"I am making enquiries. It takes time."

"Herr Reibeisen was away within three weeks."

"Herr Reibeisen has powerful friends in New York. He was and is a rich man."

"You have influential friends in the newspaper world."

"Mama, I am doing my best. How can we leave now when you are not well?"

"I am well enough. I think it is that woman."

"It is not!" Richard shouted back angrily.

Mama Dufft reached again for the coffee, and nibbled at a Kipferl. "The other day, I was looking at shoes in Gerngross, the popular department store, I saw Violetta. She lives by herself."

Richard strained his ears to discern whether the rat-a-tat-tat had increased in volume.

"Why don't you go and see her. She would like that." Mama Dufft continued.

"Stop match-making. I can look after myself."

"I have been looking after you all my life. Who will be looking after you when I'm gone? That woman?"

"Mother!"

"And I tell you another thing. This morning in the laundry: Herr Kranitschek, the new supervisor. Yes, he is fair with allocating the dryers and the ironing tables. He gives us a lecture. After they cut off the electricity. He said democratic principles are at stake. Maybe he is right, maybe he is wrong. You will say he is right, I know. But the women gathered in groups because we could not carry on without electricity. They want their men to strike. Well. And they were talking about Gusti."

"Can't we leave her be?"

"Frau Posidl said Gusti Spagola had called on her for a library book, and had told her it was the last book she was collecting. A day or two later Frau Posidl realised she had handed over the wrong book. So she went over to Gusti to make good the mistake. She rang the bell, nobody answered. She smelled gas. You can imagine what she thought: Gusti having miscarried on her ill-fated wedding day that wasn't."

"Gusti, dead?" Richard shouted.

"Would I be talking to you about her like this if she was dead? Frau Posidl runs into the laundry and raises the alarm. Luckily Frau Anzendrech has a key. Gusti left one with her."

"Mama, come to the point. What has happened to Gusti?"

"I am coming to the point. Frau Anzendrech, Frau Echenblatt, Frau Czarnikow go in. Of course the poor, innocent lamb has absconded without turning the gas off properly under the potato soup pot. No flame, just gas. So. And there are documents lying around, and they look through them, not idle curiosity mind you, but because they feel responsible for her well-being! So. They see that our Gusti is the wife of Karl Spagola."

"What!" exclaimed Richard. "When did they get married? At Christmas?"

"Well," remarked Mama Dufft, "they see this document, with an official stamp on it, and it says that Karl and Augustine Spagola have been man and wife since the fifth of March nineteen hundred and eighteen."

It took a while for this to register. "Nonsense," he remonstrated.

"Telling you this I am: it is there in black and white. With an official stamp on it."

"Nonsense. Why should she have made a secret of it? All these years. She would have told me. The problems with her compensation claim, when she thought Karl Spagola had drowned. Wives automatically qualify. Her talk about living in sin."

"They were living in sin all right. She kept quiet to shield her husband. Because he married the woman in Tulln as well. He's been married to two women at the same time."

"Mama, do you know what you're saying? You're saying not only Herr Spagola, but Gusti as well. If Brunner had stayed alive she would have married him. She would have committed bigamy."

"Exactly. Spagola, her husband, they say, is doing it again with Lutschi Fritzer. Richard, I am telling you, steer clear of these people."

"No." Richard's features were set in unyielding determination. "There is a mistake somewhere. I'll get to the bottom of this. Because I don't believe it."

He rushed out without his overcoat and in his agitated state he felt neither the cold air hitting his face, nor noticed the sprinkling of snow on the ground. He avoided the main Engerthstrasse because of the sensitive political situation. He entered the Milk Block courtyard from the rear, aiming for the Anzendrech flat.

A few children scraped snow up into their hands but there was too little of it to make snowballs. The youngest Anzendrech boy, a thick woolly hat down to his eyes, amused himself with a game at the Stone. Dufft's path to Staircase 13 led past him.

"Hello, Xandi, is your mummy at home?"

"She's cooking. That's why I can't play marshalling yards in the kitchen. But it's better here because my goods waggon makes railway lines in the snow. It's a bit cold though. Mummy's cooking my birthday schnitzels."

"Ah, it is your birthday today." Herr Dufft glimpsed that Xandi had traced sets of parallel lines merging into one in the thin, white covering on the flat surface of the Stone. "Did you get lots of presents?"

"Coloured crayons and a pencil box. And a steam engine made from chocolate biscuits. But the wheels don't turn round. I've eaten the chimney. But if I eat all of it, I won't have it any more. And Frau Spagola is coming down with squashed passenger coaches, which Berti left behind."

"Frau Spagola is coming down? Now?"

"Yes, she said she won't be long. This is my goods waggon." Xandi held out a home-made toy truck filled with earth. The wheels were constructed from thick and thin washers clamped together with metal screws and nuts, the thin discs slightly larger than the thick. They were mounted through holes of a small, elongated plywood box. It featured buffers made from protruding nails driven partly into the front and rear of the waggon. "Pauli made it. He gave it me for Christmas. He'll know how to fix couplings on it so I can hook Berti's squashed coaches to it. It won't matter that they are squashed, they could have been in a big crash like when the waggon in the Marshalling Yards burst and all its iron bits spilt into the road, and Pauli picked out the washers and made the wheels."

"Xandi, I want to give you a birthday present also. What would you like most for your railway? A tunnel? A signal? Another truck or a coach or an engine?"

"An umbrella."

"An umbrella?"

"It needn't be a new one. A broken one from the Mistgstettn will do."

How weird. Nine years ago exactly to the day, he, Dufft, with the boy's father performed a satirical offering by drowning three broken umbrellas found on the Mistgstettn, and implored the powers running the universe to go easy on Rudolf Anzendrech's offspring. How uncanny. "Why do you want a broken umbrella?"

"Pauli makes railway tracks from the umbrella ribs. The ribs have tiny holes at their ends, and Pauli nails them to wooden strips so I can join them together into a long track. And he makes bends and crossovers and he says he can make points. But he hasn't got enough umbrellas. My truck runs on Pauli's rails ever so good, and don't fall off. Frau Kristopp saw them and said Morgenthau the dirty Jew would sell them for a million shillings."

"Ah, Frau Kristopp," muttered Herr Dufft, "the fountain of priceless gems."

"Pardon?" said Xandi.

"Where would we be without Frau Kristopp' s utterances of philosophical pearls?"

"Pardon?" asked Xandi.

"Whatever Frau Kristopp says is remembered and repeated. I suppose the Jew slant stems from Herr Kristopp."

"Herr Kristopp says playing railways is good for boys because it keeps them on track," said Xandi.

"Well," Herr Dufft replied, "perhaps that depends on who lays the track and where it leads to?"

"Herr Kristopp says keeping on track teaches boys to obey orders when they become soldiers to fight for Hitler."

"Xandi, tell Pauli to make you lots of points, so you can veer off the track whenever you fancy."

"Yes," said Xandi. "Look, Frau Spagola there, she got the waggons."

Gusti was upon them. She carried a small weather-worn suitcase in one hand, and in the other two dented toy railway coaches, which she gave to Xandi who set about testing whether they fitted the lines in the snow on the Stone.

"I've been to collect some odds and ends," she explained." How are you, Richard? There is no electricity. I had to walk from the Danube Canal because the trams stopped running."

Gusti wore an elegantly tailored light brown winter coat, but Dufft was struck by her gaunt features, her eyes set deeper in her face, her freckles larger and more pronounced.

"Everybody is out on strike. Gusti. I ..." He hesitated, not knowing how to broach the subjects weighing on his mind.

"The streets are empty," she continued, "except for policemen with bayonets stuck to the ends of their rifles, and soldiers."

"I must speak to you."

"What is it, Richard? You look terrible."

"I haven't seen you for such a long time."

"I'm staying with Frau Hannick. We go away a lot, on tours."

"What I have to tell you has been preying on my mind. I don't want Mama to hear what I want to say. Shall we go to your flat where we can be alone?"

"No, Richard, no more. I have done with that. I am done with men."

A wave of vibrating pins and needles surged through Dufft's body. *Holy Moses, she thinks I am proposing to re-enact the Augarten experience!* He pointed to a bench underneath an evergreen bush a few paces away and which had remained clear of snow. "You are done with men, I am done with women."

She followed him to the seat. They sat down.

"How could you hurt me so much? You would have married Brunner. They tell me you carried his child. I'm sorry you lost it. I don't want to upset you. That's not what I want to talk to you about. I need to tell you something that will upset you yet again."

"Wait. I need to tell *you* something first. I have given up the library job. I'm looking after Frau Hannick's villa in Döbling. We have become friends. We talk about ourselves, as we are now and when we were young. I've come to the conclusion that Antonius was not Poldi's father."

"That's what I have been wanting to tell you." Richard felt heat gather around his neck in spite of the icy cold of the wooden slats penetrating through his trousers.

"You knew?"

"I have known since Poldi's funeral. I stayed behind with Frau Hannick. She said then Antonius spent that night with her."

After an eternal second of silence, Gusti said, "I don't know what happened during that night. I can't remember."

"I too do not know." Richard buried his head in his hands. The words sounded unconvincing. "If not Antonius, who? Me? I have no memory of stealing into your room."

She said, "Did it never occur to you that it might have been you?"

He tried to recollect whether he had ever entertained that thought. He could not bring such an incident to mind.

"If I took advantage of you during that night ... "

"I didn't think it was you because that's where the bullet hit you."

"It had healed. If I took advantage of you during that night, although I don't remember it, I did so because I loved you." After a long pause he added, "Then."

They sat in silence, feeling cold.

"We believe we know a person, but we don't," Gusti said eventually. "Shall I scorn you for what you did? Perhaps I let you because I, also, loved you. Then."

"Had I known the truth I would have said so, believe me."

"Perhaps we bury the truth, not because we are liars, but because we can't live with the truth. People don't understand that."

A profound statement, one he could have voiced himself.

"Now there's a rift between us. I never imagined there'd be a time when I wouldn't love you," muttered Richard.

"I don't go to church any more. Frau Hannick says she'll help me get Berti back. Berti's with Spagola in Tulln. We are striving to have the matter settled before he marries Lutschi Fritzer."

"Isn't Herr Spagola married already?"

"His wife died. He always said he'd marry me if and when that happened. But I don't want him. I don't want any man. Not after what I've been through."

"Gusti, perhaps you don't know this. There was gas escaping from your room. They thought you had ... Frau Anzendrech and other housewives, Frau Anzendrech has got keys to your flat; they went to investigate. They say they saw this marriage certificate. You and Herr Spagola."

"Oh that. I came back for it. It's in the suitcase. It's a forgery. Brunner's Nazi friends produced it to make sure I get the compensation when we thought Spagola had gone down with the *Budapest*. I had nothing to do with it. I was going to tear it up. I told Frau Hannick about it, and she'd like to see it. She says I should have it certified a forgery in case Brunner had other copies made. If one fell into the hands of the authorities, it might prejudice my case for securing custody of Berti."

Glad he had not believed his mother's gossip Richard took a long look at his companion's eyes. He saw faint lines radiating from their corners, but the subtle creases of maturity and suffering generated the same response as the briefly glimpsed, supple roundnesses some twenty years earlier in the grass under the trees of the Augarten.

Bang!

"Mama at last wants to emigrate to America."

"Yes, you go."

Beyond control, out of the blue, a sob swelled up in her throat, a sob so loud that the two children playing at the Stone looked across.

BANG!

Bang- bang!

The ground shook. Clanging and clanking of shattering glass, and falling snow from branches of shrubs.

Berti's squashed coaches fitted the tracks on the Stone; so they would roll on Pauli's umbrella rails. In the stillness of the courtyard, only broken by the voices of the man and woman on the bench, he pursued his game. He pushed his truck and coaches along the lines he had already made, he branched away to trace out new ones, and he constructed a system just like the marshalling yards underneath the Northwestrailway Bridge.

"Hello, Xandi." Martha Bitmann stood behind him, her hands

hidden in an enormous woollen muff. A string emerged from it and connected to a delicately formed sledge upon which sat a forlorn, unclothed doll. "Come with me to the Danube Meadow."

Xandi examined Martha's accessories somewhat ruefully: "The sledge is too small for both of us."

"It's not. I can sit on your lap. It'll be fun going down the dam."

"I'm not going with a doll."

"You didn't mind going with Poldi's Gugi."

"That was different."

"Why was it different, Xandi?"

Xandi thought, then said, "Poldi was my friend."

"I'll be your friend, Xandi."

"My special friend."

"I'll be your special friend."

"Gugi wasn't so ..." Xandi couldn't find the right word.

"Bare?" said Martha and laughed a silvery laugh.

"Big."

"I'll take her back home. Then we go over the Northrailway Bridge to the dam."

"Mummy said I mustn't leave the yard." Xandi turned his attention to his marshalling yards on the Stone. He placed the two coaches on the make-believe rails, then pushed his truck carefully along another track towards the single line.

"What you doing?"

"This is a train from Budapest, see." He pointed out the squashed coaches. "Now a truck filled with old metal bits is rolling down. It's going to crash into the train because the workman forgot to put a break iron on the rail. Bang. The metal bits are all over the place, and they can't make cannons of them anymore."

"Bang, bang," shouted Martha and laughed her silvery laugh.

"You can see it really happening from the Northwestrailway Bridge. I'll show you. Come on."

"I mustn't. My grannie said I mustn't leave the Milk Block."

"But you were going to the dam on the Danube Meadow."

Martha laughed once again. "I know what. Let's play father, mother, child. My dolly can be the child."

Xandi was not impressed. He pushed the truck up onto the single line again.

"Why are the schools shut?" asked Martha.

"I don't know."

"Let me have a go."

Martha withdrew a rosy hand from her muff, and she guided the truck along the lines in the thin snow. "Did Poldi love you?" she asked.

Xandi shrugged his shoulders. "It's my birthday today."

"I got Sophia for my birthday present. Sophia is my doll."

The sound of a very loud sob made the children look across to where Herr Dufft and Frau Spagola sat facing each other.

BANG.

Bang-bang.

This was no collision of imaginary trucks. The air reverberated, the ground shook, clanging and clanking of shattering glass, and falling snow from branches of shrubs. Martha, in her fright, pressed her head against the boy's shoulder.

"Xandi, I've done some wee-wee." She began to cry.

"It's all right, I won't tell anyone," said Xandi. "People wouldn't understand."

Civil War

Soldiers streamed from vehicles and ran into doorways opposite the Milk and Cocoa Blocks. There they crouched down and pointed their rifles at the attic windows of the municipal buildings. Other infantry sought cover behind the number 11 tram, which stood empty halfway across the points from the single to the double track. Groups of residents, alerted by the cannon fire, emerged from the courtyards. Armed policemen spread out to cluster around the main entrances. Smoke wafted from the mobile artillery piece positioned half way down the Allerheiligengasse, a side street off the Engerthstrasse, its heavy barrel trained at the Milk Block facade.

Richard and Gusti stepped into the street and reacted to the scenario with momentary nonplussed paralysis. Rat-a-tat-tat. Rat-a-tat-tat. Bang. Bang-bang. The racket came from the direction of the Engels Block.

"Halt!" A tall policeman, stranger to the locality, pointed his bayonet horizontally at Richard Dufft's chest. "No one leaves. Open the suitcase."

Richard Dufft placed the suitcase on the pavement and unclasped the fastenings. So this was it: the Dollfuss Government forces against the Schutzbund and the Social Democrats. Guns versus a general strike. The policeman poked his bayonetted rifle end into the contents, stirred them about, and strewed personal clothing, a crucifix, and documents into the scanty snow. He picked up the papers and fingered through them.

A short distance away more soldiers, headed by the commanding captain and Chief Police Officer Sessl, stood opposite several Milk Block men. The captain and Sessl held clipboards in their hands.

Sessl called out, "Bergmeister."

Herr Bergmeister stepped forward, believing he was summoned for parley. Sessl hailed two constables. They threw themselves upon the bewildered man. He struggled. Men leapt to his assistance. The captain nodded and soldiers lowered their bayonets to belly height and drove the men against the Milk Block facade, whilst Herr Bergmeister was marched towards the parked vehicles.

Sessl shouted, "Rosenfinger!"

Sullen silence.

The police chief recognised the wanted man amongst the angry faces pinned against the Milk Block. He moved forward to detain Herr Rosenfinger personally. Just then a bunch of people surged from the passage. Soldiers and policemen diverted to hold them back. A scuffle. People shouted, pushed in every direction. Herr Trapfen fell over. A policeman slipped on an icy patch, performed a ballet-like dance routine to regain his balance, failed. He and his rifle parted company. The firearm slid along the pavement and ended up with its sharp blade between Isidor's gigantic footwear. The retarded teenager picked it up, nearly castrating himself in the process. Voices shrieked at him not to touch it. He let go of it at the same time as the butt end of the Skeleton's rifle crashed against his temple. The clumsy boy collapsed and the snow turned crimson where his head came to rest. Women screamed and Frau Echenblatt knelt down by the side of the fallen youth. The captain fired three shots from his pistol into the air. A large body of people turned back to regain the protection of the Milk Block courtyard. Several policemen followed.

Out in the street the captain looked at the remaining people, then at his clipboard. He raised his voice: "Richard Dufft."

Silence. Gusti's hand grasped Richard's. Her fingernails dug into his palm.

"Surrender your weapons," the captain commanded.

No one moved, no one spoke.

"Next time we shall not fire blanks. We are not firing blanks at the Engels Block."

"We have no weapons," Frau Bergmeister said nervously. "Why have you seized my husband? Where are you taking him?"

Heavy snow began to fall. The captain beckoned his soldiers. "Search the buildings. The Kindergarten, the attics. The laundry, look under the sand." He turned to Frau Bergmeister: "If we are fired on we shall retaliate with full force."

Sessl collected four policemen. He handed two over to Breitwinkel, gave him some papers and said, "Locate the dwellings of the ringleaders. Look for incriminating material: letters, scribbles, pamphlets, books."

Richard Dufft, shaken by the proceedings and the attack on Isidor, strode up to the commanding officer and said, "Sir, I have been a captain myself in the Imperial Army. I fought in Italy. I understand military discipline; I understand that orders must be obeyed. But I am concerned with innocent people living in these housing blocks. I seek permission to evacuate women and children to the Danube Meadow until the operation is over."

The captain looked long and hard at Dufft, then he turned to the tall policeman who had prodded Gusti's belongings and asked, "Who is this man?"

The policeman handed over a document taken from Gusti's suitcase. The captain studied it, and consulted the list of names on his clipboard. Subsequently he said to Dufft, "We are not ogres. We are here to maintain law and order. You have ten minutes to assemble women and children in the courtyard of this housing block. Keep them to the left. They will be escorted to the Danube Meadow. The men are to assemble on the right. You will then identify for us the men on this list."

Dufft replied slowly, "Sir, we are indebted to you for your humanity towards women and children. But I cannot identify anybody, as this sort of thing does not lie within the brief of civilians in relationship to the military."

"You will do as you are told," barked the tall policeman.

Dufft shook his head.

"You are obstructing the police in the execution of their duty."

The next events happened quickly. The policeman advanced menacingly, Dufft held out his arms to check his approach. The policeman gripped the barrel of his rifle with both hands, and encouraged by the Skeleton's conduct a few minutes earlier, swung the butt end at Dufft's head. Dufft joined Isidor in the snow. Now it was Gusti who screamed and knelt down beside the prostrate body.

The captain had witnessed the proceedings with detached indifference. He summoned a soldier and spoke to him in a loud voice so that people could hear. "We are not ogres. We use humanitarian judgment when dealing with civilians. There is a telephone box there on the corner of the Donau Eschingenstrasse. Call an ambulance so that Herr..." he glanced at the document in his hand "...Herr Spagola here and the boy get hospital treatment. They were foolish to use threatening behaviour towards police officers, and in consequence they were incapacitated by the police officers acting in self-defence."

Snowflakes settled on Richard's closed eyes. He wearily raised his lids and perceived white flecks whirling in a sea of grey. Round and round they whirled. Then Gusti's nose, first far away, came near, very near, until the bluish-ochre freckles appeared as large as the dancing-white snowflakes. Words reached his ears. A throbbing ache in his face. He remembered where he was: the white snow. He felt something being laid over his body. Did they think he was a corpse? Was this the end? White sheets. Gusti's nose coming nearer. Gusti, naked, settling over his body. "What are you doing, Gusti?" Her bare breasts pressing on his chest. "Sssh! you'll wake Antonius" she says. "He wouldn't say no to this, but I prefer you." Richard wriggles to move away from underneath her, but she holds on. "Gusti, we mustn't. Go to your bed." Her fingers glide down his side and hips. "Not much of an injury there'" she says with a giggle. He says, "This isn't right. We are full of drink. Gusti, you are drunk." It happens.

Was he dreaming? Was this real? He opened his eyes. The white snow. Where are the white sheets? *She had seduced him.* She had crept into his bed, she had forced her body upon his. He remembered as clearly as if it had happened yesterday. How could he have not remembered for sixteen years?

No wonder her mind had shut out the harsh facts. The throbbing pain returned. Yet he let out a laugh. Would she ever discover the truth? Perhaps, if she ran head first against a police rifle butt. He laughed again. He searched for her face. He found it. Her eyes were grey-green.

No Ball Games on the Danube Meadow

The Skeleton, shunted away from continuing in the anti-Schutzbund action, which could yet divert into an insurgence for Hitler, disgruntledly climbed the steps to the Northrailway Bridge at the head of the procession. Another policeman made up the rear, both carried rifles with bayonets. Between them a line of people, young mothers with babies, middle-aged women and their children, old grannies, trod the loose snow into a hard crust. They wore winter coats, shawls and headgear covering their ears.

Bang. Bang, bang. Rata-tat-tat. The racket came from the direction of the Engels Block. A distant rumble of bangs and rat-a-tat-tats drifted over from the Göthe Hof, a municipal housing estate beyond the Reichsbridge on the Floridsdorf side of the river. Women's lips quivered when alluding to the likelihood of a Milk and Cocoa Block bombardment.

Eyewitness accounts of the events in the Engerthstrasse passed from mouth to mouth. Frau Echenblatt said to Richard's mother: "Herr Dufft wasn't badly hurt. He sat up when they carried him into the ambulance. He even managed a laugh."

"Why did they go for Richard?" Frau Dufft asked.

"Herr Dufft was on their list," explained Frau Rosenfinger. "They arrested Herr Bergmeister, and they wanted my man as well. But he and Herr Kranitschek gave them the slip in the confusion when everybody was running and shouting."

"And why did they call him Herr Spagola?" Mama Dufft wanted to know. "Did they mistake him for Karl Spagola? Richard doesn't look like Herr Spagola. Why did he not say who he was?"

"He's better off in hospital as Herr Spagola than in an interrogation centre as Herr Dufft," replied Frau Echenblatt. "He's the lucky one. God knows what will happen to our men."

"They will be gunned down." Frau Posidl, like Herr Posidl, habitually gave voice to the worst scenarios.

Frau Czarnikow said, "If we don't shoot at them, they won't shoot at us."

"Yes?" Retorted Frau Rosenfinger. "Who started it? We haven't started it. The Schutzbund hasn't started it. The strike is for lifting the ban on our Social Democrat Party and for restoring democracy."

"Soldiers have been trained to shoot up Municipal housing," said Frau Posidl.

"And folk the likes of us will be paying for rebuilding the ruins," said Frau Kranitschek.

"A bullet from the big gun costs a milli'n schilli'n'," said Frau Kristopp.

"This wouldn't have happened if we had Hitler instead of Dollfuss," said a woman from the Cocoa Block.

"We all speak German. Why don't we get together and hit our real enemies?"

"Foreigners stealing our jobs and our housing. Jews."

"Herr Dufft is Jewish," shouted Frau Rosenfinger, "thanks to him we are allowed escape to the Danube Meadow!"

"But why, of all names, Spagola?" questioned Frau Dufft.

"They took him for Frau Spagola's husband," explained Frau Echenblatt. "That must be the reason why he laughed. They had this scrap of paper. You know. Spagola's marriage certificate document, or whatever it is."

"A forgery," Xandi butted in.

"They wouldn't let me go in the ambulance with Richard, but Frau Spagola went along. I saw the policeman hand the paper to her," observed Mama Dufft.

"What's a forgery, Mummy?" Xandi asked.

"Where did you hear that word? Your half-cooked birthday schnitzels may look like forgeries by the time we see them again. A forgery is a deception."

"Of course it's Xandi's birthday," said Frau Dufft, relieved that the conversation had drifted from the anti-Semitic motif. "I can see the day you were born. I cooked your brothers' dinner. It wasn't schnitzels though. What a birthday. You'll remember it for the rest of your life, like we all will."

"What's a deception?"

The boy's quest for knowledge diverted the women's minds from their ordeal. They listened to Brigitte's explanation: "A lie is a deception. If you make out you are ill when you are not, that is deception. If you paint a picture and say it's by somebody famous, that's a deception, that's a forgery. And if you know something important and you keep quiet, that also is deception."

Frau Dufft suddenly became smaller. Frau Echenblatt saw her kneeling on the snow, but Brigitte realised that her knees had given way.

BANG.

"That came from the Milk Block gun!" shrieked Frau Posidl.

"Holy Mother of God!"

"The bastards!" hissed Frau Kranitschek.

Frau Echenblatt and Brigitte raised Richard's mother, and dragged her forward. The procession contracted in width as children pressed closer into the coats of their mothers, and it contracted in length as people at the rear pushed hurriedly ahead. Xandi, who walked behind Martha, saw her clutching Sophia.

Frau Bitmann's chewing motions with her toothless gums speeded up.

Brigitte worried about Rudolf. He had not come home, and the trams stood still.

Tramway men were stranded on their units when the electricity went dead. Foot messengers arrived and ordered them to walk to their tram depots. Eventually managements sent all men home. At the Wexstrasse Depot Rudolf heard that the streets leading to the municipal housing blocks swarmed with police and infantry. He trudged through the snow along a detour up along the Danube Canal, and over the allotments behind the gas works to the Northwestrailway Bridge. He crossed the Danube, trekked on top of the Hubertus Dam to approach the Milk Block from the rear via the Northrailway Bridge. The meadow lay under snow. From a distance he saw dark specks streaming onto it, like a foray of bedbugs on freshly laundered, white sheets.

BANG!

Brigitte realised she had been right. There was nature and human nature. And human nature was rotten. To the core. People had scorned her dark prophecies, but here it was, the cataclysm.

BANG.

Rudi, having attained esteem with his Bread poem, found ready listeners when he railed that this shooting business was utterly irrational, totally unscientific, against all human aspiration in nature, morality, art and literature, the result of feeble-minded police and dim-witted, autocratic government.

Brigitte thought she or Herr Dufft couldn't have put it better. Rudi reassured his mother and brothers that the big gun in the Allerheiligengasse presented no real threat to their dwelling, as the barrel could only reach a small end portion of the Milk Block, and that any bullets fired from the Engerthstrasse at windows could only hit ceilings, and everybody here would be safe on the Danube Meadow.

Martha said, "I didn't bring my sledge."

Xandi consoled her, "We'll make a giant snowman."

"We'll have a gigantic snowball fight," said Pauli.

And a gargantuan spectacle it turned out to be, the antidote to their trepidations. Boys hurled massive snowballs at girls. Girls retaliated. Mothers joined in. When the scrimmage was in full swing, when the rat-a-tat-tats and bangs were drowned out by shrieks and laughter and a few wails, their plight momentarily forgotten, Xandi aimed a loose lump of snow at Martha, but the Skeleton stepped into the line of its flight and received a direct hit on his neck, his dignity violated. He turned to face the culprit.

"You lousy scumbag!" he screamed. He fired a shot into the air, and thundered into the stunned, suddenly motionless silence:

"No ball games on the Danube Meadow!"

CHAPTER TWENTY-THREE (1934)

Dufft's Prediction

The Army found no weapons hidden in the Milk and Cocoa Blocks. They fired several blank artillery shells, then withdrew from the Engerthstrasse to reinforce the beleaguered Engels Block.

Gusti and Dufft didn't converse a lot in the ambulance. The bizarre situation, he journeying to hospital in the guise of her husband, the turmoil in their souls and the turmoil on the streets did not encourage idle chatter, and the presence of medics hampered any attempt to deal with their personal problems and the rift between them.

After Dufft had been seen by a doctor, Gusti with her small suitcase walked back to Döbling. He, with six stitches in his temple, returned the same day to an ailing Mama. Her knees had weakened, her legs had swelled up. She could hardly stand. There was neither milk nor coffee in the pantry. He called on the Anzendrechs to borrow some.

He said to Xandi, handing him a long, heavy, round parcel wrapped in newspaper, "Your birthday present."

"Umbrellas!" shouted the little boy expectantly before unravelling the package.

The shredded newspaper revealed brass tubing.

"Papa's telescope," apologised Dufft. "The shops are shut, I couldn't buy you anything, not even an umbrella."

"We can search the sky and become famous when we discover another planet," cried Rudi.

"We can look at people changing after a swim in the Danube," came from Pauli.

Xandi said, "I'll use it to look out for old umbrellas on the Mistgstettn." He flung his arms round Herr Dufft's neck: "Herr Dufft, I love you so."

Thinking of his own child, moisture dampened the man's eyes.

The guns turned silent after four days.

Dufft brought back the borrowed coffee. Sitting down and drinking some, he said, "What has Dollfuss achieved? Lorry loads of dead. Now he wants to hang the ringleaders. The Social Democrats will clamour for revenge. They'll rally to join the Nazis. Dollfuss has dug his own grave."

He saw the telescope leaning in a corner. Putting it to his eye, he continued, "Looking into the future I see Hitler in the Chancellery before the year is out, I can see the extinction of Austria."

Brigitte sighed, "If only I could believe we've seen the last of the shooting, that what's behind us wasn't like playing 'to the soup to the soup the dumplings are starting to simmer, to boil and now they're farting' compared to what lies ahead."

Rudolf said he had heard enough pessimism. He invited Dufft into his room and pointed to the ancient typewriter reposing on the soft table top. "I've cleaned and oiled everything," he said.

The journalist picked up a few identical typewriter parts, held them next to one another, and soon the two men were engrossed in rebuilding the ancient machine. Rudi and Xandi aimed the telescope towards the windows of the building opposite to capture bedbugs crawling on the walls. Pauli's fingers blackened as he worked on his charcoal picture of the Gross Glockner. Brigitte's needle set the finishing touches to Xandi's shirt, a conversion from one of her obsolete white blouses.

A voice on the street rang out: "Heil Hitler!"

Brigitte closed her eyes. 'Lord Almighty, do not let that man spoil it all.'

Before the Year is out

Before the year is out:

Vikki and Gina reside in their fortune-teller booth in the Angol Amusement Park, Budapest.

Karl Spagola and Lutschi Spagola wheel their baby through the streets of Tulln.

Berti's little dog is called Spitzl. He lives with his mother in Frau Hannick's villa in Döbling on the edge of a wood.

Rudolf types three stories in English using one finger per hand and making many mistakes: *Americans on a Vienna Tram*, and *A Day with the Bread Delivery Cart*, and *How I Arrived in New York*. Dufft says he'll get them printed in New York if he ever gets there.

The very-own-wee-place near the refreshment hut continues to provide recreation to the Anzendrech-Jarabek contingent. On one occasion Herr Marschalek examines admiringly his cousin's motorbike. At the same time Xandi, training his telescope on the marshalling yards across the river and not looking where he is stepping, treads on a wasps' nest and is stung four times on his heel. Within minutes his entire body erupts in closely spaced, angry coloured blisters. Uncle Hans sprints for the ambulance station on the road to Floridsdorf. Frau Marschalek, at the sight of Xandi's octopus exterior, mutters, "Werewolf. Caught him changing his skin."

Herr Marschalek picks up the bubble-skinned boy, sits him on the pillion seat of the motor bike, shouts "hold on tight," starts up the engine, roars past Uncle Hans.

After this Uncle Hans purchases again the odd pickled gherkin from the Refreshment Hut. Brigitte regales anyone who cares to listen to the story with the question at its end: "If we can settle our differences, why can't governments?"

The Skeleton continues harassing ball players.

Chief of Police Sessl dreams on about police forces in other countries.

His deputy Breitwinkel reads *Das Kapital* by Karl Marx, a book confiscated from Bergmeister's abode.

Richard Dufft advises everybody he knows, Jew or non-Jew, to leave the country. He and Mama Dufft, however, stay on, his mother's physical health showing no improvement. He frequently visits Döbling, strolls along the tree-lined avenues and rests on a bench in the Beethoven Walk. He does not catch sight of Gusti.

Franz Glanz, alias Hildebrandt, meets a sober Smaliz accompanied by Vivian complete with bubikopf in Prague.

The senior man says, "Franz Glanz rhymes, but the name and providence don't coalesce in my ears."

"I and my real name shall be back in Vienna before long."

"They don't coagulate in the *Ostmark,* our name for Austria, where a description of your facial insignia is pinned up in every Dollfuss-loyal police station referring to a persona non grata wanted for suspected murder. The Brunner incident was unfortunate. He seemed to have been an ardent fighter for our cause. We shall incorporate him in our list of martyrs."

"My destiny lies in Vienna," insists Hildebrandt/Glanz, "Dollfuss is still Chancellor. I've been planning the reception when the Führer's troops march into Vienna."

"Until such time when a National Socialist regime governs Austria your work is in Düsseldorf, helping to steer it towards a *judenfreie* city. You can shed the name Glanz there."

"This goes counter to my destiny!" storms Hildebrandt, convulsed about his absent Vikki, and Schmalz's present Vivian. He makes aggressive eye contact with his mentor's escort, who returns his stare with a spellbinding smile.

Smaliz enters Austrian territory in April 1934 to set up a ship repair workshop at the Kuchelauer Hafen, the Danube docks at the foot of the Leopoldsberg near Klosterneuburg, which enables him to supervise arms shipments by river, and to participate in the scheming of Dollfuss' assassination.

Dollfuss is assassinated.

A rumour spreads in Nazi circles that another Stohmeyer type, a *schmaltzy,* a lardy, high-ranking SA officer operating in the Ostmark, is carrying on with a Jewish pansy. The bodies of Smaliz and Vivian are found with bullet holes in their backs during the Night of the Long Knives, when Nazi SS purged Nazi SA on September 30th 1934. They killed many SA officers, allegedly to thwart a plot against Hitler, and to demonstrate opposition to homosexuality in the SA.

Hildebrandt replaces his brown SA shirts with a wardrobe of black SS ones and fits out his visionary marching men in like colour. At the same time he rises to the rank of *Sturmbannführer* in the Nazi SS, the Storm Squadron, originally Hitler's personal bodyguard. Rivalry exists between the SA and the SS, the SS emerging more elitist and dominant.

He puts into hibernation Rules 1 and 2 of the Smaliz doctrine.

The Brigittenau School Summer Excursion to Greifenstein, a ruin on the Danube some twenty kilometres upstream from Vienna, postponed due to the Chancellor's assassination, takes place in the autumn. It is the first time Xandi and Martha travel on a railway train. The lower grade children occupy the rear coaches. With heads hanging out of windows they chirp away at the new song that the school has drilled into them, and which when freely translated, goes like this:

> Ye young ones step in line with pride,
> A dead man is our guide.
> He shed his truly German blood
> Only for Austria's good.
>
> The murder bullet hit him deep;
> It roused the people from feud and sleep.
> We young ones stand nearer
> To Dollfuss in the New Era.

The front coaches, brim with older pupils, chant the following words:

> Ye young ones step in line with pride
> A great man is our guide.
> We'll shed our truly German blood
> For him and Germany's good.
>
> Past murder bullets hit us deep;
> They roused the people from feud and sleep.
> We young ones stand nearer
> To Hitler in the New Era.

The young ones "stand nearer" to Dollfuss or to Hitler for another four years before Richard Dufft's prediction of map revision comes true.

Ye young ones - German version:

> *Ihr Jungen schliesst die Reihen gut*
> *Ein Toter führt uns an.*
> *Er gab für Österreich sein Blut*
> *Ein wahrer deutscher Mann.*
>
> *Die Mörderkugel, die ihn traf,*
> *Die riess das Volk aus Zank und Schlaf.*
> *Wir Jungen stehn bereit*
> *Mit Dollfuss in die neue Zeit.*

CHAPTER TWENTY-FOUR (1935)

His All-seeing Eyes

Mama Dufft said, "Richard, hear me. I have written to Gusti Spagola. She is coming over for coffee on Sunday. I have something to say to you both."

"Her name is Schattzburger," corrected Richard. "You have addressed the letter properly?"

"Yes, I have. I know. You told me. She was not married to that man."

"What do you want to tell us?"

"You will hear."

Richard speculated what had persuaded his mother to call this conference. He considered various possibilities, foremost that she had experienced a change of heart and wished to make amends for her inimical attitude towards Gusti. When the woman he had loved arrived he dismissed her enquiring look with a slight shake of his head, but expressed great joy at seeing her so comely and radiantly well.

They shook hands all round, and Gusti said, "How have you been keeping? It's been a year since I travelled with you, Richard, in that ambulance."

"I'm all right, and Mama's knees are getting better, aren't they? You're able to walk a little," Richard replied looking briefly at his mother. "Yes, a whole year we haven't seen each other. We've been free agents and it's through Mama that we meet again."

"Now then," said Mama Dufft. "The coffee is ready and there are *Kipferl*. Sit yourselves down and listen to what I have to say."

Near to each other on the sofa, not touching, Richard and Gusti were aware of the unresolved tension. It would need a catalyst to melt the barrier that had grown between them, like Richard saying to Gusti, *"The blow on my head twelve months ago restored my memory. Yes, I fathered Poldi. Listen though: it wasn't me who seduced you, it was you who seduced me."* Even in complete privacy he would not bring himself to let the truth pass his lips. The secret would have to remain his, and the rift would linger.

They watched Mama Dufft struggle with the crockery. Richard wanted to assist, but his mother waved him away with her crutch.

At last she seated herself, "I am an old woman, I don't know how long I shall be here. What I shall say to you, I have known for many years. But I hesitated whether it would be right to tell you, or right not to tell you. I am a Jewish woman, and I wanted Richard to marry a Jewish girl. I thought Violetta would have suited. Well now, a year ago, to be precise exactly one year ago, because we were on the march to the Danube Meadow and I remember it was young Alexander Anzendrech's birthday."

"Holy Zechariah," the words escaped Richard, "I've forgotten his present. I promised him a special present because he's a special boy. I told him to come round to collect it."

"Well, there is still time. The day is not over yet," said his mother.

"Morgenthau's shut on Sunday afternoon."

"Last year when likewise you had forgotten, you gave him Papa's telescope, of all things."

"I hope he's found some use for it."

"Perhaps you thought being a special boy, he's got special powers and can focus it on the future?"

"I thought I could do that," replied Richard, "but it's no good. Foretelling the future means saying good-bye to hope." He hurried into another room, rummaged about, came back with a long black object tucked under his arm.

"You want to give him Papa's umbrella?" exclaimed Mama Dufft. "It won't keep him dry. It's got a tear in the cloth."

"Xandi wants old umbrellas because his brother makes rails from the metal ribs. For his train set. He's crazy about railways and trams."

"Well. But let me finish what I was saying: when we were on that walk to the Danube Meadow, a year ago, Frau Anzendrech explained to her son Alexander the meaning of deception. She said to know something of importance and keep quiet about it, is deception. Hearing this I fell into the snow. As if God had struck me down. Ever since then walking has been difficult. I have been troubled more and more; should I divulge what I know or should I not. So I have decided to tell you. Will you be wishing for another *Kipferl,* Fräulein Schattzburger?"

Gusti's mouth had not quite cleared the remnants of the previous bite. She swallowed, gulped, spluttered. "It's a delicious *Kipferl*."

Richard recognised that his mother needed a diversion to gather strength for delivering the final pronouncement.

"So. Richard. Do you remember your fellow officer, Antonius Freiherr?"

"Yes, yes."

"Do you remember the night Herr Antonius stayed with us after your party?"

Gusti answered, "I remember the party. I don't remember the night, nor does Richard. You know that, Frau Dufft."

And Richard added, "There's no need to resurrect what happened so long ago, or to speculate why and how. The episode ended tragically."

"Yes, I know. I do know. I know this is painful for Gusti. But I cannot keep silent any longer. It will be painful for you too, Richard."

"Mother," said Richard, "Gusti and I have spoken to Frau Hannick, and she has spoken to us. Frau Hannick was Antonius's fiancée. We know."

"Know what? This has nothing to do with Frau Hannick, whatever the lady has to say. Listen to my words: Matilda, the kitchen maid we had then, no doubt spoke the truth when she said she saw Herr Freiherr on the stairs in the early hours of the morning. And I spoke truthfully when I said I passed his bedroom during the night, saw the door open and an empty bed in his room. Now Gusti and you, Richard, have no recollection of anything that took place during that night because you were so brim-full of alcohol that it drowned all your mental faculties. This also is true. No?"

"Mother, I..."

"No?"

Richard remained silent. To admit to the restoration of his memory meant he would have to recount the whole truth, and he had just resolved not to inflict it on his ex-love sitting next to him.

"Now it is clear that Gusti's child - I am sorry I cause you anguish, Miss Schattzburger - was conceived during the hours of mental oblivion, as at any other time, the event would have been remembered." Mama Dufft astonished herself in speaking so plainly. "Everyone drew the conclusion that Antonius Freiherr was the man responsible, and the circumstances left no room for doubt."

Frau Dufft had difficulty coming to the point. It exasperated Richard, so he blurted out: "Mama, we know. Gusti and I know that I am Poldi's father. We have known for a year, and we have been struggling to come to terms with it."

"You knew?"

Richard stared ahead, Gusti pressed her lips together.

"You can't give him a shredded umbrella," Mama Dufft admonished her son. "What will his mother and father think? We are tramps?" and turning to Gusti: "You were seen, only with my eyes. And with His all-seeing eyes above."

"I don't know what you mean," said Gusti.

"What I haven't told anybody," Mama Dufft said vehemently, and Richard detected the slur of trembling lips, "what I have kept to myself all these years, is that I saw you - you were a mere child, Gusti - it was around two o'clock in the morning, in the night after that party which robbed you of your memory, I saw you, come out of Richard's room, just as..." She paused.

"Yes...?"

"Just as our dear Lord had made you."

"You mean you saw me wearing no clothes, no nightgown, no nothing?" Gusti looked over her *Kipferl* at Richard's mother. "Coming out of his room?"

Mama Dufft moved her head up and down. "Just as our dear Lord had made you." Then whispering, "Doctor Willberger told me Richard could function again normally."

Gusti leant forward, buried her face in her hands. She sat like this for a while. She slowly raised her head. On the wall opposite a brown speck meandered from left to right. *They've got bedbugs too*, went through her mind. She felt a touch on her arm, a gentle pull, her hand coming to rest between two strong palms. Her eyes found Richard's.

He opened his mouth once, twice. The third time he said quietly: "What I had started in the Augarten, we finished then. And we lived on in ignorance of it. For years."

Mama sat erect in her chair, her wrists crossed over her lap, her fingertips pressing the aching spots on her knees. She had aged.

But there was still coffee left, and Richard refilled the cups. Gusti placed her hands on his arm and said, "Come and see us. Frau Hannick, Fanni, would like that, and so would I."

"I shall."

"It's better indoors than sitting on that bench in the Beethoven Walk," she said mischievously.

"That remark," he replied, "deserves a kiss."

They embraced. The warmth of his body mingling with the warmth of hers. At last. Was this the happy ending?

"Come before we leave," said Gusti.

"Leave? Where are you going? When?"

"Fanni's been asked over again. Another tour through America. We are going with her, Berti and I."

"I'm losing you, just when I found you?"

"Everything's arranged. The boat sails in four weeks."

"Returning, when?"

"Fanni is Jewish. She doesn't get so many engagements here." After a short while, she added, "You will be coming too? You always wanted to go to America."

Richard glanced at his ailing mother. She had fallen asleep in her chair.

"What choice is there for Mama?" he whispered. "Should she wait for the arrival of the Nazi jackboots? I've seen them perform in Berlin. No, not that. Will she get through the upheaval of crossing an ocean? Has to be done, no other way. One snag: hard cash."

He spied the bedbug, which had begun an ascent towards the ceiling. He placed the tip of the umbrella onto the wall a centimetre above the insect and watched it crawl onto the spindly end. He strolled over to the window, opened it and flicked the bug into the cold air.

"Give him Papa's chessmen." Mama Dufft spoke with her eyes shut.

"You're awake?"

"He'll do well to master chess; it's not a game of chance, nor is it a game of live-and-let-live. Its rules call for strategic scheming and tactical bluff, no?"

"The real world is a different ball game altogether," said Richard. "It's got no rules."

"The different ball game says I'm tired. I'll go and lie down. Don't forget Alexander Anzendrech's present." She struggled with her crutches through the door.

Richard clasped Gusti's hands. "I shall come. As soon as I can, I shall come. Mama too."

"I'll wait."

The End

Before The Cock Crows

Look out for the remarkable sequel to *And God Created Bedbugs Too.* Coming soon...

Printed in Great Britain
by Amazon.co.uk, Ltd.,
Marston Gate.